Erotica Vampirica

Thirty-One Tales of Supernatural Desire

Edited by Cecilia Tan

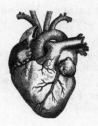

QUALITY PAPERBACK BOOK CLUB
NEW YORK

Contents

Blood Kiss

Erotica Vampirica

Cherished Blood

The Beast Within

Blood Kiss
Vampire Erotica

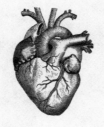

Editor's Note

I believe that the vampire is a perfect subject for erotic fantasy. First, the vampire has always been viewed as a sensual creature. In past eras of human history this was seen as evil, like all "sins of the flesh." But I would like to think that in America in the 1990s some of us have a finer appreciation of the wonders of sensuality, the primal attractions of flesh and blood, the magic of erotic surrender. We think of vampires as hunters and as seducers of their prey, the hunt as primal and animal as sex itself. Second, the vampire has always been outside of the strictures of "common" propriety, the chastity of marriage broken, the purity of the virgin defiled, and vampires hunt both men and women, so it is no surprise to find gay and lesbian, bisexual, transgendered and kinky vamps herein.

Third, sex and death are as deeply intertwined as sex and life are, the "little death" we call orgasm, and the intense power of life that is erotic power... and congress with a vampire could mean death, everlasting life, or both at once. The vampire embodies both extremes.

You may find that the vampires you will meet in these pages, are not quite the same as the blood-suckers commonly found in many horror novels. These stories concern themselves with something more than gore and serial killers. These stories celebrate the eroticism inherent in the vampire mythos, and elucidate it, drag it out into the open rather than sublimating it. Fear becomes excitement, predation becomes seduction, and death becomes eros. I invite you to explore and enjoy the sensual side of the night.

Cecilia Tan
October 1994

The Perfect Form

Pat Salah

10:15 on a Saturday night. Pandemonium is already packed. Arriving ten minutes from now and I'd be cueing in the rain for half the night. I pay my cover and spot Reg and Suzy shooting some stick. Kiss. Kiss. Hi. Hi. Throw my leather down and cruise up to the bar, scoping the action. Used to be the Olympia Theatre before Eckhart bought it up. Mighty pretty place: Victorian parlor decor all in red and black and gold; rococo frescoes on the walls and huge fuck'n stained glass skylights, and girls dancing in the opera boxes, except the top two where Eckhart holds court and toasts his most honored guests. I love it. Too bad Eckhart owns it. Guy's a pig.

Notice Dré working the floor, looking sweet as usual in green velvet and fuck'n thigh-high docs, black braids slap'n against her tits. Don't know how the prick does it but he's got the rockingest chicks in the city working for him: all his barmaids take a turn in the boxes, and, when they're on the floor,

it shows. Like when I spot Colette my eyes are
nailed to the place where the back of her shift rides
down around the curve of her ass. So I nearly knock
some pubescent punker chick over. Don't see many
of those around here these days.

Essen pours me a Kier, eyebrows arched, painted
mouth making a moue that's supposed to be questioning, provocative. Guy's such a poseur. Used to
think he was so styl'n, when he played with Univer-
sal Rejection. His punk days. My punk days. Now
the Elders of the Kin—goddamned Vampires is
what they are—openly walk the earth and anybody
who knows shit hangs at Pandemonium and em-
braces the Gothik lifestyle. I read it in *Interview*
magazine: Montreal, the Canadian New Orleans.
But fuck, *Propaganda* said the exact same thing. I
swear. Life has gotten weirder, its not just me.

Trade-offs. Like when I was a punk I hung with
a regular crew of pretty cool guys. When the Vampires came out of hiding I turned Goth. Most of
those guys became warm fascists—shaved their
heads and started jacking off to the idea of staking
members of the Kin. Fat fucking chance. Nothing
can kill the already Dead. I moved into a cooler
crowd. Cooler, as in, Dead-loving, and also, as in
chillier. Lars didn't need to pull attitude to be cool
though. A good guy. When the Vampires came to
town we both knew what we wanted. He got it, sort

of. They moved on to some new scene, taking him with them. But they'll be back—Lucrezia, Lars' maker, said so in the last *Engarde Quarterly*. These days I'm casual with lots a folks. Keep to myself. Which suits. It's how Lars got taken.

Man! Didn't even recognize him the only time I saw him after the Kin Elder sunk her teeth into his neck. At least that's the rumor, that she's an Elder, which makes sense, she is their spokesperson. Besides the young ones aren't supposed to be able to make new ones: otherwise he would have taken me, I'm sure of it. We both swore we would. The other thing they say is that the young ones are slaves of the Elders that make them. But that's gotta be bullshit, a system like that would never work, because they're all immortal: that would mean they're all slaves of one or two really ancient Kin which is obviously ridiculous. Of course with immortals, you've got to wonder what would count as elder anyway. Over one hundred years, for sure. One thousand? And how could you tell?; Thom says they're shapeshifters besides. Lars Changed. Fuck, he was beautiful...

Remember how he appeared before you out of the darkness of the club, his black hair in curls, with waif eyes and rose petal lips, an ingenue, and yet so pale and tawdry in a red satin dress and too much

*blush—like a prostitute dead and risen under a lu-
rid sun. Or, as the Vampire thought, like a boy too
pretty to be left alone with his sex, too in love with
his cock to be made a girl: only after the Change
was worked upon him, to become as pale as the
bones of the moon. The Vampire left him neither
living nor dead no longer wholly male nor quite female. That one shaped his body to suit his deepest
desires, during the bloodletting when its will was
strongest. It walked his dreams and saw his wishes
and answered them. It imagined Lars as voluptuous
as any Vargas girl, a body fitted to his gutter angel
face and his slut's soul. The dreams of the Vampire
possess such force. What a shock for dear Lars
when he woke. His is the perfect form aspired to by
those tormented men who hound surgeons and psy-
chiatrists, pointing to their men's magazines,
begging: "Make me like her. Make me Marilyn,
Bardot, Madonna. Inside I'm more woman than any
woman." Though Lars is not complete in that respect. He still has his beloved cock, and of course,
he is Dead. All this, and more, you knew in that
first moment of matched gaze. You knew the stories
of the Vampire's preternatural strength, both of will
and of form, to be true. You knew it could have you
as it pleased—you would give your blood or flesh up
willingly. Lars would not have to take you forcibly,
though it thrilled you to think the thing he had become could. That was, after all, your pact.*

*And moments after Lars left, you were drown-
ing in the absence of its perfume, drowning in your
memory of its beauty. Until then you had caught
mere glimpses of the Kin, in the dark, in your
dreams: you had never seen one revealed. Now you
know. The supple white length of neck, delicate
curve of ankle beneath silk, arch of red rhinestone
stiletto... Then you noticed you had come, your legs
were weak, and you mouthed: "Come back to me,"
pleading.*

Slight pressure against the lace cuff of my
blouse has me nearly jump out my skin. It was like
I was tripping out; I guess the Yin is starting to hit;
Thom said it comes on stronger every trip, but fuck,
I went from thinking about something to reliving it,
except that last bit, I want to be a Vampire, sure,
who doesn't, but not like that, like Lars. Fuck!
"Your memory, a guided tour with commentary by
Vincent Price." Jeezus! Actually, that voice was
more honeyed than slimy, like Christopher Walken,
or...

"Mr. Eckhart!"

"Hello Brett. You looked faint for a moment. Are
you not feeling well?"

"I, ah, no. I was just feeling dizzy there for a
minute. Uh, were you talking to me, I could swear I..."

The owner of Pandemonium just smiled at me.
"You seek the Vampire, as we all do. They infect us

with a love of too lush flowers, overripe fruit, the
pungency of decay. To smear ourselves in the earth
of gravesites, to open our wrists and quaff one
anothers' blood to clotting: this is our self-immo-
lating desire, this is what they have done to us with
their luscious death. We are all sodomites now, and
vain primping things, compulsive in our person-
ation of those other dead, goddesses of the screen.
The world has seen terrible changes these last few
years. And we yearn for more.

"Still They come but rarely. Their ways are mysterious to most of us—"

"Not to you Mr. Eckhart. They obey—" It was
Essen, draped over the bar, one hand twirling a
strand of auburn locks, while the other toyed with
his Kier. Momentarily, I wondered if anyone drank
beer anymore.

Eckhart turned and softly hissed, "Enough,
bitch. Don't you have work to do?", so quickly, I
nearly missed it. Essen was fleeing down the length
of the bar, his heels clicking, as Eckhart returned
his attention to me.

"You've grown so pretty these last few months,
almost as pretty as Lars was, before he was taken.
It is almost as if your body is yearning for the
Change it sensed in him, striving beyond its natural inclination for that fatal delicacy.

"Have you been sampling Thom's chemicals?"

I pause before answering, partly to cool my heels: "Pretty," my ass. The guy's a slimy s.o.b. but obviously I can't say jackshit to him if I don't want to be banned. Which I don't. Pandemonium is the only place north of New York the Vampires frequent. Anyway, Thom couldn't work the club without him knowing, so I just mumble, stupidlike, "Yin. Gets you pretty fucked up."

"Ah. It is a popular intoxicant. But surely you know that in sufficient doses it has other effects."

"They say it attracts the Kin, if that's what you mean."

"Attracts the Kin. As like to like. It brings out a certain luster in the skin, softening and slowing the growth of body hair. Some say it slows the aging process. It makes one more sensitive, sensuous, and too, almost empathic. Certainly it incites desire. But Yin can only take you so far. You should come to one of my gatherings in the upper chambers."

This is getting to be too much. "I'll think about it. Thanks man."

Eckhart continues to smile in that superior way of his. "Only with our help, will you stand a chance of winning their favor, when they return."

"What do you know about that?"

"As your friend Essen noted, I have some knowledge of their ways."

"Essen ain't my friend and... and I'll think about it. Excuse me, I think I see someone I need to talk to."

I can almost sense the cold set of his face as I turn and cut through the crowd towards the dance pit. Sound system's booming retro Sonic Youth: *Cool thing play'n with the kitty, now ya know ya sure look'n pretty.* I know it's a risk pissing Eckhart off like that but I need to get away from him, think about what he said. I know what goes on at those gatherings of his. One hundred days of Sodom style orgies is what I heard. Sometimes you can see them in the opera boxes, fucking and sucking, whipping one another. I should jump at the chance, because he's right, they're why the Kin come here. Everybody knows that. Suddenly, I'm not sure. In my head I see Lars the Vampire again, his lush tits spilling out of that gown, his eyes all green fire and alien. What if joining the Kin makes me like that. Maybe I should just get pissed and skank some warm chick. God knows there are lots of tasty ones on the floor.

It is foolish of you to deny him.

I look up at the chick stepping out of the pit towards me, go suddenly dizzy. She's totally delish and its only after a second I recognize her. Upswept mass of jet ringlets, smoky eyes with long shadowy lashes; lips puffy and bloody red; still it seems a child's face, scared by those lips, by the rings through her eyebrows, ears, nose. She's teetering on spike heels, as if drunk, and her breasts shake in her jewel encrusted black bustier. One of the dancers. Felicia, I think's her name. Then it comes to me. She's Dead. Kin. The only Kin I've met. I don't know I could have missed it before. *Lars.*

Dance with me pretty boy?

It's not a request: without noticing myself do it, I step towards her, begin moving with the low beat of *Bela Lugosi's Dead*. It occurs to me that she hasn't opened her mouth to speak to me.

What's happened to you?

She's looking at me askew, plucking with crimson nails at the netting of her black petticoats, distractedly. She's trembling slightly—it's only been a few months, she's still newly Dead. My god, how could Lars look so choice. Behind her the crowd has turned to watch us. They've recognized her for what she is, the way I have. The closest appear paralyzed: hands snaking towards Her, frozen midway.

Don't you realize Eckhart represents your best, maybe your only, chance of joining the Dead?

Stealing myself, I ask: "What about you? We had a deal. A pact."

God, Brett—I could just have you for a snack. I'm so hungry. Besides I'm weak, Brett, forty-ninth generation, Lucrezia says. My blood's thin. What kind of Vampire would I make?

She's looking at me straight on now, sizing me up, for dinner maybe. She must be delirious. What she's saying makes no sense. I've got so many questions. Lars. Suddenly, I'm hard, hot for her. Not Lars. Felicia. I reach out and stroke her cheek.

Brett, don't. Go to Eckhart. Flatter him. He likes you. He'll get you a strong maker. Thirtieth, maybe even twentieth generation. You don't have to be like this.

Ignoring her, "Don't fuck'n mock me, Lars. You know Eckhart doesn't know shit. You're here. I want you to do me. Come on." I'm feeling foolishly bold, grab her hips and pull her to me. Surprisingly she comes. I smell roses.

Brett! Don't! I haven't been fed in a long time. Don't you recognize me?

Her body is so light, like a bird's. I lift her to me. Kiss her. It's easy, she's not Lars any more, she's my Vampire lover. "Of course I do, Lars. If you won't keep your promise, then feed on me. Better that than to end up one of Eckhart's pets."

Still suspended in my arms she grins, loopily. One of Eckhart's pets. *Okay Brett, if that's what you want. I bet you'll make a pretty one.*

Then she's on me and I don't know how I ever could've doubted her strength: her talons, her teeth are inside me. The first claw, tears through denim and inner thigh, paralyzes. Canines rip in and out of throat, breast, belly, as other nails rake down expanse of back. Blood's leaving my body through a dozen excruciating wounds: simultaneously rushing to erect penis. A fierce heat, the trajectory of her teeth, closed around groin. The world explodes.

Darkness tracing a cool breeze across naked body. Icy all over. Feel—muscle, skin stretched. Where? Trying to move, feel satin rustle beneath me, but don't have the strength to raise the head from the pillow it rests on. I am in a bed, somewhere. Eyes adjust to the dark and I can see tree shadows dancing through the room, the tops of French doors thrown open, a corner of night sky holding a sickle moon. From outside comes clearly the sound of loons, crickets, wind and ocean. I think: I'm in another country. Blood's chill moving in my veins. Then abruptly, what must have wakened me: an exquisitely fine tracing of pain across my chest. Nails, like razor blades, moving delicately, slowly, almost slyly in what I imagine as the most elaborate of patterns rising upon skin, like tattoo, like scars. Something sharp and hard pressing against, in and out my ass. I hear a slow moan, long and low, and then after a time her response, moist exhalation of breath all over my body; her tongue scraping like a cat's along my inner thigh and a wash of hair breaking over my belly, then the puff of lips tender and yet taut around my cock, her tongue scraping along it, flaying with little barbs. This goes on and on, my body engorged with blood and sweat, and swimming in it—I'm suspended, almost dreaming. I see Eckhart hovering around the bed, watching, smiling. The pressure is unbearable. Until she begins the draining. For a moment, I'm burning water. Then, gone.

When I wake again, it's morning. I know without opening my eyes. I feel the shimmer of the world around me. Everything is crystal. That clear. I'm no longer warm. I see through my closed eyelids. I'm alone, for the moment. The room has the look of one of Eckhart's bordello affairs done in rose satin and velvet, excessively feminine: the canopied bed I'm in, a huge skirted white wardrobe, a pink and white vanity table, the diaphanous pink drapes on French doors leading to a balcony, a white shag rug.

Memory washing back, lays over my vision. Sex with Felicia. Lars. On top of me, sculpting me with tongue, claws, dreams, blood. I can feel her somehow, inside me, in blood, semen.

I'm lying in bed. But I can see myself. As if watching from above. *My how you've changed—*

Eckhart's voice echoes in my head. What was Lars trying to tell me, before...

I'm a little girl—a naked porcelain doll with dabs of rose at the lips, nipples. Golden blonde ringlets, frame delicate features. Eyes turquoise blue. Lovely small breasts. Silky smooth little cunt. I look maybe thirteen. But what a perfect thirteen. More like a pixie or a sylph than a vampire, even the incisors behind the pursed bow of my lips are tiny, delicate.

Eyes open, I sit up and shrug away too blonde hair. Little fingers cup my breasts—my skin is so pale and baby soft! I don't know why I'm so calm. It's like I'm waiting for something. I get up and walk over to the huge vanity mirror on the doors of the wardrobe. I can see myself in it, my new self. It's not just my body, she's done something to my mind, because I can see from my reflection that my every move is totally sensuous, sexy, provocative. I'm standing on tippy toes as if I were in heels, my breathing makes my breasts jiggle, and I can't help but flutter my lashes, purse my lips as if I were gonna blow some guy— This is crazy. I wanted to be made a Vampire, not some fucking sex kitten! Why would she do this to me? Just looking at my reflection makes feel funny, wet in my pussy.... My hands caress, trembling, the curve of my now pillowlike ass, insert a finger between virginal lips.

I can't believe I'm thinking like this, doing this. The feel of my fingers brushing between those two soft lips, catches my breath and my nipples tighten up. I settle back down onto my ass, my back, immersed in the sea of white carpet. I wince in slight pain as one too sharp nail flicks against my pussy lips, another swirling round my clit, it's hard, swelling, but not like my dick used to. One hand massaging my hardened tits and my cunt, so soft; wet with blood pulsing through it. I wonder if I'm still dreaming—getting hotter, my fingers stroking a steadier rhythm inside me, my pussy stretching to fit more in, moving faster. I can't believe what they've done to me. I want to fuck them both, Eckhart and Lars, I mean kill them. I....

I don't hear them until they are practically right on top of me. Eckhart. Lars. I'm buried in the shag, taut skin burning all over, on my back and ass, my pussy thrusting up, humping my hand, my tits and pussy bleeding—the knowing smiles on their faces don't matter, I'm coming blood, sweating blood, crying it under their feral gaze.

Until at the last, he must know I'm on the verge, Eckhart nods to Lars, and her hand dives down into my hair and whips me to my feet.

"No fair," I huff, surprised hearing for the first time, the breathless purr of my voice. My pussy and tits are throbbing, and it's humiliating but Lars and Eckhart are just turning me on more.

Eckhart is wearing his usual tux and tails, and is looking smug. Lars—she, I can't help but thinking of her as she, despite the huge erection she is sporting—is naked except for her heels and stockings. *Are you happy now Brett? I've made you a Vampire, just like we promised.*

Eckhart grins, speaks in my head. *So sorry to interrupt, but we thought it time to proceed with your education. Under the circumstances you have turned out quite nicely, Brett, I must say. A good thing considering you probably lack the strength to Change. You are something of a weakling among the Kin. I do look forward to using you later. For the moment though I merely intend to claim you from the stupid slut who was so eager to make her own child.*

I don't feel myself moving, it's as if his will has taken over my limbs. Suddenly I'm in his arms, rubbing my pussy against the hump of his cock. I hear myself moan "Please. Fuck me! Please."

His hands slip about my waist, lift me, and gently he begins kissing my breasts, his tongue lapping the blood off them. The heat in me gathers. I scream as teeth pierce the flesh around the nipple, my vision narrows to a thin band of red.

As other colors return me to the room, I realize I'm sitting at the vanity. Lars is fussing with my hair. She looks sad. I hear her voice in my mind. *You must call me Felicia now. That is the name my maker gave me. Perhaps you can keep your name though. After a moment she adds, I tried to tell you. Eckhart liked you. Perhaps he still does, but now it's too late.*

I must look puzzled because she continues. *Look at me. I'm a Vampire. You've felt how powerful I am. But among them I'm nothing, nearly human. I belong to the youngest generation of Vampires ever. Until now. My maker, Lucrezia is almost two hundred years old, Brett. She can Change her form, send her mind on the wind. Things I might never be able to do. She's so much beyond me that I can't imagine it—but she's still got to bow and scrape to most of our race. We're slaves Brett. Creatures who exist to serve the whims of our elders.*

"Can't we run away. Escape." My little girl voice doesn't even convince me. Lars just laughs gently.

Don't get excited, it won't do any good and I've just finished your make up. You don't want to muss it before you go down to work. You don't get it at all, do you, Brett? You know who Eckhart is? Of course not. It's not his oldest name. Lucrezia once told me what his first name was: Arpad, that's old Arabic or Aramaic, or something. It meant great warrior, literally, "he who tastes first blood". He's the one, Brett, the Necromancer, the self-created Vampire who started all this. There is no running away from him. He owns us, all of us.

"Oh", I hear myself murmur, feeling suddenly very strange, both sleepy and giddy. Lars— Felicia, is finished with the comb and is standing back to survey her work.

Very pretty. The clients will be pleased to see a new girl. Now don't get all glum. You're immortal, beautiful, powerful and you live for pleasure. Its not all that bad. Now get up and take a look at yourself. The old Brett would cream his jeans watching you dance in one of the opera boxes. So would the old Lars.

Swaying to the mirror—wondering how I manage the lift of the heels, at least four inches—I know she's right. Part of me is already starting to like this. As I stare at the fresh faced darling posing in the mirror, bust out, hips cocked, I see the beginning of a smile pulling at her rose colored lips. Felicia has done me all nouveau hippie: kohl makes my eyes deep, dark and sexy and my platinum mane is piled atop my head, with long curly tendrils down each side. The dress is a pink chiffon babydoll that positively depends from the tips of my breasts, short enough to glimpse the tops of my white net stockings. The heels are pink patent leather with ankle straps. I squeeze my thighs together and blow my-self a kiss. A girl couldn't be more feminine if naked. My tongue plays over concealed incisors that have just started to throb. I send for the first time: *Oh, Felicia, I'm a good girl, aren't I?*

Cinnamon Roses

Renée M. Charles

I don't know if it's because people buy so heavily into the mythos of vampirism (y'know, the gal/guy-in-a-sweeping-cape-swooping-down-on-her/his-prey's lily-white, blue-veined throat batcrap), or if it's because they have this idea that we vampires just need a suck of blood every day or so to keep body and soul in one just slightly undead package, but being a twentieth-century working vampire is *not* just a matter of staking out a little patch of earth under an abandoned warehouse somewhere out in the hinterlands of the city—c'mon, get real.

Spending twelve or more hours a night biting and swooping and not much else is fucking *boring*. And it doesn't contribute squat towards the rent or utilities on my basement apartment in Greenwich Village, either.

Besides, just because a gal gets a little more than she bargained for during an admittedly dumb unsafest sex of all fling with some guy she met in some club she can't even remember the name of (oh, I made him wear a condom, but that didn't protect my neck...) it doesn't mean that she suddenly becomes the reincarnation of Dracula's Brides. I still needed to make a living, and since I'd been a barber/hairstylist before...well, you've got to admit, scissors and razors do have a way of occasionally drawing blood.

And from personal experience, I know that vampire bites feel a heck of a lot like the touch of a styptic pencil...down to the not-quite-needle-sharp tip pressing down on warm flesh.

Getting my boss to let me change my hours from mid-afternoon to evening to evening to pre-dawn wasn't difficult; the place where I work, the Heads-or-Tails, is one of those places that specializes in punk/SM/adventuresome types—full body waxes, razor and lather shaves, even a little extra stuff on the side (regular customers only—cop shops can't afford to send in decoys week after week) so it isn't unusual to see just about every type of person coming in for that special cut or shave at any hour of the night.

And at $100 bucks a pop and up per session, the Heads-or-Tails never closes. So when one of the stylists demands a *right now* change in working hours, the management is more than happy to oblige, especially when she (as in me) keeps drawing repeat nocturnal customers....

Another misconception about us vampires is that if
we keep on doing what we do best—a.k.a. neck-
biting and blood-sucking—eventually we'll infect
the entire fucking world, because our victims will
infect victims of their own, and so on until you're
looking at one of those Andy Warhol's *Dracula* situations (the whiny vampire strapping his coffin on
top of the touring car and motoring off in search of
fresh "wurgin" blood). Get off it, do you think that
one sip from a person is enough to make them go
mirror   invisible   (which   is   another   load   of
bullsheet—sorry, but the laws of physics don't work
that way, though it makes for a nice special effect
in the movies, I'll admit!) and start draining the
family dog for a pre-bedtime snack? I had to spend
a week with my nightclub Nosferatu before sunlight
began to make my skin itch, but I can still put on my
lipstick in the mirror, thank you!

So, a slip of the disposable razor here, or a nick
with the scissors there, and it's good-bye hunger,
but not necessarily hello fellow nightwalker. Not
unless *I'm* interested in some continuing companionship over the course of a month or so. And even
then, I make sure I know the potential victim well
enough to be sure that she or he will be in a position to tap into a private food supply without
attracting attention. C'mon, do you think that some
of those E.R. nurses on the graveyard shift keep

missing your veins by accident? Or those dental technicians who can't seem to clean your teeth without drawing blood?

But sometimes, no matter how much a gal exercises caution, and forethought, not to mention common-sense, there will come the day when that certain customer walks in—and every vein in my body, every blood-seeks-blood-filled throbbing vein, cries out to my brain, my lips, my cunt: *Take this one ... don't ask any questions, don't think about the night after ... just take this one.*

(Doesn't even matter if this one is a gal or a guy; skin touching skin is gratification enough, and fingers and tongues more than equal a prick ... there's nerve endings enough to go around all over the body).

For me, the first signal of a customer being a *taker* is their smell. The smell of clean, healthy blood surging under their veins just a few millimeters under the unbroken flesh—for each of us, the name, the associative taste, we give to that good blood-odor differs. For me, it's cinnamon; cinnamon that's been freshly scraped from the stick, that raw, so sharp-it tweaks-your nostrils tang, so fresh and unseasoned the smell soon becomes a palatable taste even before the first drop caress my tongue.

(How else do you think vampires avoid HIV and AIDS? Once you've had a whiff of that moldy-grapes and stale-bread odor—naturally, this perception differs from vampire to vampire—you can smell a victim coming at you from two blocks away. Three if the wind is blowing past them.)

Oh, all non-infected normals smell somewhat like cinnamon to me now; as long as you're reasonably healthy, the cinnamon-tang is there, but in some people ... well, it's more like a cautious sprinkle of the spice over toast, or across the top of an unsealed apple pie. Maybe it's all the stuff people take; additives, drugs, you name it. But in a taker, that fragrance is a living part of them, like an extra finger or breast. Richer and more lingering than the smell of sex, more piquant than ejaculation seeping out of your crevices.

But the blood isn't the whole reason for that desire to own, to make a normal into a new-blood kin; even though it is the most tangible reason; for me (at least), there has to be a certain look in their eyes, a vulnerability that goes deeper than mere submission. The look which says What I am now is not all I could be. Doesn't matter if the look comes from eyes in a straight or gay or female or male body, either. Like I said before, there's nerve ends a plenty all over the body. Age isn't a biggie either, although most of the clientele of the H. or T. is youngish, adventuresome.

Color, background, whatever—none of those things matter either. Maybe because we vampires live so much in ourselves, and are ruled by what runs through our bodies and not over our bodies, that which is within others speaks to us so eloquently, so desperately.

Even if they themselves do not realize that inner need ....

Despite the air conditioning in my private cubicle (set on 72° instead of something cooler—newly shorn flesh, especially large areas of it, does tend to chill easily) the muggy heat of the late July night managed to seep into my workspace that particular evening, and I was just about to slip off my panties and position myself directly in front of the unit for a few moments when that smell hit my nostrils. Taker coming. I quickly lowered my suede skirt and smoothed down the short-cropped hair which covered my head like a sleek skullcap, before glancing about my workspace to make sure everything was in perfect, customer-ready order. Unopened bags of flexible-blade razors—check. Cleaned and oiled clippers, trimmers, edgers—check. Shave creams, mug soaps, depilatories—check. Thin rubber gloves—not that I really needed them, but Health Department regulations are regulations—check. Hot wax—check.

By this time, I could hear footsteps coming closer down the narrow tile hallway between work-stations. This one's a woman, my brain told my body. My labia began to do a jerking, twitching dance against the already damp fabric of my pant-ies, but I made my other set of lips form themselves into that slightly vacant, blandly professional smile all of my customers got when they parted the thick curtains separating my cubicle from all the others in the H. or T. salon.

In deference to the heat without, she was wear-ing a halter top, shorts, and slip-on cotton-topped shoes, the kind the Chinese make by the thousands in an hour or so. Can't rightly say I remember what color any of her clothes were; but her colors ... well, you know how it is when you see your first really brilliant sunrise, don't you? (Even though those are forbidden to my kind, the memories—the skills, and the like to need to go on surviving—remain.)

Within, she was a molten cinnamon, and with-out, she was a sunrise, or a sunset ...whichever is the most vivid, the most heart-aching. Russet hair flecked with streaks of natural gold and near-or-ange fell across her forehead and shoulders like lava arrested by a sudden chill, while her eyebrows were twin arcing bird wings above green like gumdrops and suck-it-'till-your-mouth-puckers hard candies, or new leaves in the sunlight I could no longer see green, green eyes. And she had the type of skin that let that cinnamon-scraped-from-the-stick lifeblood of hers shine through in delicate vine-looping trails of palest filtered blue and labia pink. Real redhead skin. And I don't know why it is, but so many true redheads like her are so naturally thin, not to the point of bones sticking out, but covered with just enough flesh. Breasts small enough to cup in a woman's palm, but the nipples would be big and hard enough to make an imprint on that same smallish palm.

It was painful not to be able to drink her in for as long as I wished; but staring at the customers, especially new ones (and most especially takers) can sometimes send them turning on their heels and diving through those heavy curtains, never to be seen or smelled again. Fortunately for me, she was nervous enough not to notice that I was staring at, no, devouring her, for her green-beyond-green eyes were timidly lowered, darting to a picture she held in her left hand, then back at a point right around my waistline. She probably didn't even realize I was doing the looking.

Which suited me just fine.

I could see the picture she was holding; a newspaper clipping of that one model, the French-Canadian one with the dragon tattooed on her shorn scalp. Well, at least it wasn't Susan Powter; I'd have been loathe to try and bleach that exquisite liquid cinnamon hair of hers.

"Uhm, the woman up front said you do...what'd she call it? 'Full head shaves?'"

Customer or not, taker or not, I felt a sharp pang not at all unlike the first time my lounge-lizard Lothario sank his incisors into my neck when she said that. Even if it meant being so close to her exposed neck, shearing off that mane wouldn't give me the usual pleasure I felt as my labia quivered in time with the buzzing hum of the heavy-duty clippers which would send my hand and arm to quivering as I'd take off the longest layer of hair. Usually, shearing off hair could be a sensual, aesthetic experience above and beyond the sight of those subcutaneous veins resting in the flesh of the newly exposed neck; the way it rippled as it fell away from the scalp, drifting down in feathery piles to the floor, sometimes thick swaths of it touching my bare legs on the way down, tickling like a man's hairy leg brushing against my own, or the way light picked up the sheen of untanned, milky skin under the quarter-inch stubble, and as the lather was swept away by each pull of the blade, the play of diffuse light on naked flesh and the silky feel of it through the thin rubber gloves were usually enough to give me an orgasm on the spot.

Then again, most of my customers had average, unremarkable hair. Being obvious about my potential pleasure would've driven her away before I'd come even within tasting distance of her exposed flesh and spice-laden veins, so I smiled more naturally and replied, "That's my speciality... I can do either lather shaves, or just clipper—"

Somewhat reluctantly, the taker replied, "No, not just clippered ... my boyfriend, he has this thing about skin, y'know... all over."

The words "my boyfriend" were an explanation—and a challenge. Most of my female customers went for the Powter or O'Conner look because their lovers were spending too much time ogling those chrome-pated, unattainable TV visions, and judging by how few of them returned for touch-ups, either their boyfriend took over the daily shaving chore, or they realized that wearing a wig on the job was a consummate drag (the salon also sold wigs on the side), and went back to doing the hair-spread-over-the-pillow thing, and to hell with what Boyfriend thought. But there was always the possibility that Boyfriend might like an entirely naked girl, too, so as casually as possible, I assured her, "I'll do a close job, so your boyfriend should be pleased ... you said 'all over,' didn't you? As in—"

At that she blushed; the rush of blood coming to her cheeks made my mouth water and my labia jerk so hard I had to (albeit casually) cross my legs as I leaned back against the counter top behind me. Reaching up to toy with a thick curl of hair for what might be the last time in a long time—depending on how pleased Boyfriend was with my efforts—she licked her lips and said softly, "I was embarrassed to ask out front, but I figured since there's the word 'Tails' in the name of the shop ... he'd like it ... y'know, down there, too. He said he'd like to be able to—" at this she blushed deeper, until the reddish glow seeped into her make-up free eyelids "'see the rose as he's plucking it.' I know it sounds weird, but ... well, he's given me a lot of flowers, on my birthday and on our anniversary of when we met and all, all of them these pink bud roses ... and what he has the florists write on the cards can be a little, y'know, embarrassing, especially when they deliver the flowers to the bank where I work, but ... you know. It's not like it's real cool to send a guy a rose in a bud vase ...."

Her words took me back to my first few nights with the one who took *me* into this world, the same world I was aching to bring her into with a few styptic-stinging kisses. I'd been spread open before him on his bed, a pillow placed beneath my behind, and he'd been tracing the contours of my glistening pinkness with a lazy forefinger, telling me, "Do you ever look at yourself, opened like this, in a mirror? I thought so ... have you noticed, how each lip curls just so, like the petals of a bluish rose, until they meet in a tight cluster right ... here?" With that, he rubbed my clitoris in a feathery, semi-circular motion with one finger, while using the other nail-down to trace a thin jagged line from my navel to my slit, which became a reddish inkless tattoo for a few seconds against my growing-ever-paler skin. "See how you'd look if you were a rose? 'Rose is a rose is a rose is a rose?'" he asked, indicating the carmine "stem" he'd drawn upon my flesh.

I'd had to arc my neck at a slightly painful angle (mainly it made those tiny incisions there hurt) to see his handiwork, and even then all I had the power to do was moan a soft assent before the full force of the orgasm swept me away into a crimson, eye-lids-closed private world...

One slightly deeper whiff of this woman's scent told em that Boyfriend couldn't be my old sanguinary sweetheart—all vampires have a special, very undefinable sweetness, like old chocolate, in their blood—but I felt a certain kinship to him anyhow ... even though he would soon be my rival.

Poor man ... I can understand why you want to see all of her, touch and taste and caress it all... even if you're willing to forgo the ripple of hair under you hands, or the moistening mat of curls surrounding that soon-to-be-plucked rose....

A little too much time had gone by while I was bathing in the sweet come-like stickiness of my memories; the girl's face became slightly anxious, and she asked timidly, "I know it *does* sound silly ... I mean about the rose—but could you do it?"

Not letting the sigh I felt escape my lips (although I couldn't resist the urge to lick them), I replied, "Of course, Would you mind slipping out of your shorts and panties? It'll just take me a couple of minutes to get ready."

While the young woman slowly unzipped her shorts, her face wearing the expression of a thirteen year old reluctantly disrobing for the first time in gym class, I prepared the small rolling table with the clippers, five-pack of razors, shaving foam, and scissors. Then, as she wiggled out of the shorts to expose her pale green, lace-trimmed cotton briefs (I could make out the plastered-down arabesques of russet curls over her mons), I placed the long fresh towel over the seat of the barber's chair in readiness for her. As she watched me pat the white towel down on the leather seat she gulped, but stuck her thumbs down into the lacy waistband and—with her her heart pounding so hard it made her left breast quiver infinitesimally—pulled down her panties, then gracefully stepped out of them. With a schoolgirl-like neatness, she bent down, knees together, and picked up the briefs and shorts, and placed them on the stool where I usually sit between customers.

You must really care about your boyfriend to put yourself through this...I only wonder if he'll be so grateful once I get through with her, I asked myself as she sat down primly on the barber's chair, legs tight together, and arms gingerly placed on the padded armrests. Barely able to suppress a smile, I picked up a drape, put it around her neck (the sensation of her hair sliding over the tops of my hands as I secured the Velcro tab behind her long, thin neck was like silk rubbing against my most sensitive parts), then said, "You'll have to open up ... I can't do a full job otherwise."

For a second she just sat there, looking at her draped body and exposed, tousled head for a moment in the numerous mirrors surrounding the chair, a shocked expression on her face... until she caught on, and obediently parted her legs, so that the drape tented over them above her spread thighs. The funny part was that she had the drape hanging over her snatch....

Before I picked up the clippers, I gently gathered the hem of the drape in my hand and pulled it upward, until the extra fabric was bunched in her lap. Across the room, she was reflected in all of her waving, curling, sunset-varied hues, with the deep pink rosebud center of her right in her line of vision; from the sharp intake of breath she took, I realized that she'd never seen herself so open ... or so vulnerable.

"It won't ...y'know, pull, when you cut it... will it? Going against the grain—"

"You'll be surprised how good it can feel," I assured her, before asking the standard question at the Heads or Tails salon. "Which do you want done first, heads or—"

"Uhm... I never thought about... Maybe my bottom ... no, wait, better do the head," she finished reluctantly; most women go that route, even though it seems illogical. I suppose it has to do with the thought of someone touching the private parts ... especially when no woman has done so in such intimate circumstances before.

And like most first-timers, she kept her eyes closed once I switched on the clippers. Usually, shearing takes about ten or fifteen minutes, if you're careful, and feel for any unexpected bumps or irregularities on the skull. But doing this one, this taker, took a full twenty minutes. With each slow, cautious movement of the clippers, another drift of sun-kissed hair filtered down, caressing my shins before it rested on the floor at my feet. The reddish stubble still caught the light well; from certain angles it resembled the nap on velvet, with a pearl-like white base.

And this close to her scalp, her bare neck, the odor of fresh spicy cinnamon was overpowering, achingly intense ... but I knew I'd have to wait for my chance to savor her. Clippers seldom cause nicks serious enough for a stinging kiss ....

Once the last of that rippling, gorgeous hair was liberated from her scalp, I tilted the chair backwards, so that her head rested on the sink drain, and—after warning her what I was going to do—ran warm water over her scalp, prior to lathering her up. By now she was beginning to relax; a thin smile even played on her lips. But she still wouldn't open her eyes, not until I'd massaged her wet scalp for a few seconds, and she fluttered her eyes open before asking "Is the cream heated? My boyfriend, he does that before he shaves—"

"Naturally." By now, I was shaking so much inside I was afraid I might cut her for real, but once I picked up the can of heated cream and sprayed a dollop of it onto my left palm before smoothing it onto her scalp in a thin layer (too much lather and you can't see the grain of the hair —and shaving against it can be painful—but too little, and the razor pulls), my pre-vampire days hairstylists' auto-pilot took over. Once she'd been fully lathered, the foam barely covering the velvety bristles of her remaining hair, I washed off my hands, then pulled on the fresh pair of rubber gloves necessary before I could pick up one of the new razors from my little table. Even before I'd gone permanently nocturnal, I'd been the smoothest shaver at the salon; the trick is applying just the barest amount of pressure against the gently rounded surface.

And this time, when she closed her eyes, it was purely in ecstasy; the heightened rhythm of her breathing was unmistakable, even under the clinging drape. Whether or not a female customer I was shaving was an intended meal or not, I loved to see that blissful look on their eyes-closed faces as the gently bending steel caressed and cleaned their scalps; I suppose it's the look men strive for on the faces of women they're fucking—that away-from-it-all gratified expression.

I was so taken with stealing glances at her face in the surrounding mirrors as I worked, in fact, that her head was smooth and pearl-like before I'd had a chance to inflict a deliberate, although albeit minor dripping wound. Her eyes were still closed, so I debated whether or not to run the razor across her delicately veined white flesh once again, as if seeking stray hairs, but it would've spoiled the moment, somehow. It was my fault I'd missed my first chance at her; going back to correct my omission would be too cruel—

She's just a taker, not anything that special to you, I sternly reminded myself as I lowered the chair for a second time, to wash off the last bits of cream from her head, prior to lathering it up with an aloe-based shampoo. That she'd moan when I worked the foamy lather around her smooth, moist skin was a given ... but what wasn't so much of a given was the way that low, purring moan made me reflexively arch my pelvis, the muscles in my inner thighs twitching in time to her barely voiced cries.

That was when I realized that her heretofore unnamed boyfriend was definitely going to get more than he'd bargained for when he sent her here. After all, roses and pearls are equally beautiful to more than one beholder....

Once I'd toweled her off, and then slathered a fine coating of the most delicately-scented oil I could find on my counter onto her shorn pate (I didn't want to risk obscuring that heady cinnamon bouquet which all but radiated from her newly bare skin, like shimmers of heat coming off a smooth road in the summer sun), she timidly reached up to run a smooth hand over her satin-fine skin ... then gave me an unexpectedly wicked grin, her eyes twinkling.

"I didn't think it'd feel like this," she whispered throatily, her breasts rising and sinking deliciously beneath the drape, "I'm glad I left the best for last....."

That a customer got into the whole bareness thing wasn't unusual, but the transformation from schoolgirl shy and demure to completely relaxed and ready for more in this particular customer-cum-taker was enough to make my heart lop so crazily I was afraid that it would stop from the extraordinary effort. It was only then that I glanced down at her waiting quim; the image of roses after the rain, when the sunlight (a still poignant, missed memory for me) hits the petals, revealing the subtle blend of colors on each petal came to mind ... and this time, the scent of that brown, powdery spice, mixed with her own rose oils, was all but intoxicating. I had to steel myself against simply going down on her then and there, and tearing into that delicate wrinkled flesh with incisors bared openly.

Now my problem would be restraining myself; it would never do to drink too deeply, especially from such a nest of tender folds and hidden creases, lest her boyfriend (*and my enemy,* I decided) notice my handiwork too quickly before she left him.

That she would eventually leave him would now be a given; for a brief moment I wondered if my vampire master, he of the no-name nightspot so many years ago, had known that I'd end up leaving my previous boyfriend, as he looked and spelled and wanted me so very deeply, with a yearning beyond reason, even beyond basic desire. (Once, he'd

told me that my "scent of dark coffee" was like a
syrup cascading down his throat....)

But still, he'd been so intuitive to her potential
shorn beauty, and so eager to witness that naked
splendor, that this act of taking would haunt me ...
even as it fulfilled me in a way no palm pumping
mere *man* could fully understand.

Putting on my best, most professional face (at
least for the moment), I switched on the smaller set
of clippers and let my hand be guided by the individual mounds and deep valleys of her flesh; once
I asked her to spread her legs out wider (I'd already
lowered her chair to a reclining position, the better to see her curl-hidden petals), but apart from
that, neither of us spoke—or had need to. Clipping
the mound of Venus is trickier than clipping the
scalp; the area is tighter, and more springy under
the clippers, but this time around, gathering up my
concentration was an almost super non-human effort.

Freed of the damp ringlets and tufts of russet
hair, her mound was a mottled pink-white (from
the pressure of my fingers as I spread the flesh to
accommodate the clippers), but when I applied a
small disposable make-up sponge (sea sponge; it
has a rougher, more French-tickler-like texture)
dripping with warm water to her stubbled flesh, it
soon turned an even, conch-shell pink. I couldn't
resist pulling aside her inner labia, to expose the

glistening slick skin within to the light, and was rewarded with a subtle upward thrust of her pelvis. That she was enjoying this gratified me, almost as much as taking a sip of her blood ... *almost.*

The lathering was dream-like in its slowness; up, down, and around the tender, sweet-scented flesh (by now, her own unique scent formed a heady counterpoint to her blood-bouquet), until the patch of foamy white was fully covered up to the tips of the stubble. Taking up the first of two fresh razors (sharpness is essential... and not just for my own vampiric purposes), I freed her flesh from the coating of foam stubble and drying foam, until she was almost entirely naked, more naked than she'd been at birth, in all likelihood... save for a last tuft of hair I'd left untouched, close to the gently rounded spot where the tip of the mount meets the tuck of the flesh hiding her clitoris.

True, that tight curve was the most difficult place to shave, but that wasn't why I left it for last. Unless I became as animal-like as the bat most non-vampires erroneously think we can turn into at will, I'd have to be cautious now ... lest my actions become too obvious, too potentially frightening...

"Could you be very still now? This is the trickiest part... otherwise I might nick you." Getting the words out without bending down and biting and sucking and drinking her in was difficult, but she didn't seem to notice that anything was out of the ordinary.

As she spread herself even wider (could she be into gymnastics? I wondered), so that the last daub of nearly dried foam covering that dime-sized patch of remaining hair was almost perfectly level before me, I had to release some of the pent-up desire in me ... if not my thirsting desire, then my sexual wanting.

Using both hands, I gently fanned my fingers over her taut lower belly, her tight thighs, not letting myself touch her exposed petal-softness, her intricate folds and crevices of glistening flesh, until I was sure that my hands wouldn't shake too much. I only needed a tiny nick, not a bloodbath... even though I would have loved to have felt her cinnamon warmth coursing over me in hot, spurting runnels ....

Taking up the second of two razors I'd used on her, I let the sharp steel bite ever so superficially into her pale skin on the downstroke. I don't even think she felt the nick, it was so slight, but my mouth flooded with burning saliva when I saw the tiny dark pearl of blood rise up in all its spicy-warm splendor.

"Uh, oh, I drew a bit of ... lemme get the pencil," I mumbled, before grabbing the styptic wand off the little table ... and then clutching it so tightly in my fingers that it bent out of shape as I knelt down and ran my tongue over the welling beads of ruby sustenance, before my incisors bore down on the pliant, perfumed flesh of her outer labia, her mons, her inner thigh....

For a moment, a deeply shamed, yet animalistically exalted moment, I felt a stab of fear-pleasure—here I was, being so obvious, so greedy, and with an uninitiated taker. But in the next moment, as I stopped my inhalation-like feeding, I realized that she was moving her pelvis and hips in time with my movements, my feasting on her very inner essence.

Sated enough to stop what I was doing, I guiltily wiped my bloody lips clean with the back of one hand (then licked said hand with a fly-flick of my tongue), before standing up between her still-splayed out legs, and letting my gaze meet her own. Reaching down with her right hand, she gently touched the place where I'd been sucking out her blood, gave me a smile, one that did reach up to those memory-of-sunlit-leaves green eyes of hers, and then said softly, "I suppose I can tell my boyfriend that even my rose had some thorns ..." before beckoning me back to sup once more on her glistening feast between her outspread legs.

But the best part of what she said was the way she made "boyfriend" sound so casual, like something ultimately fungible after all....

*   *   *

Later, without needing to ask, she simply agreed to come to the salon on a thrice-weekly schedule, for "more of what you did tonight." I didn't ask her her name; eventually, she became Rose for me, and that was all either of us needed. But that first night, as she dressed and covered her pearlescent scalp with a scarf she'd brought along in her shorts pocket, I busied myself with a little gift—a token of future losses, actually—for her soon to be ex-boyfriend.

It's funny, but if you take those pink and red colored specialty condoms (like I said, the Heads and Tails offered occasional "extras") and—after opening the packages—twist and bunch them just so, then attach them with plastic-covered twist ties (green ones, naturally—we keep them on hand for securing garbage bags full of clippings) to those wooden sticks we use to stir hair dye, they'll look an awful lot like rosebuds.

Maybe her boyfriend did find my gesture touching (Rose never felt the need to say, later), but from my point of view—not knowing just how faithful he might be—I was only protecting my investment against blood that stank of moldy grapes and bread long gone stale.

The Hunger

Warren Lapine

Hunger consumes me, pain beyond comprehension. To think, I entered the ranks of the Nosferatu willingly, nay, eagerly. Immortality at any cost. I could not have known the price that I would pay.

How could a man reborn in 1890 even imagine the horror of today; the first hint of disaster was still more than fifty years away. Had I known had I even suspected, I would have stayed among the breathing.

To live forever, it was too strong a dream, too much a temptation. I followed you, Janette, eagerly to the grave. And who wouldn't have? You were a beauty beyond compare, a lover with unlimited passion, a companion to spend eternity with.

Do you remember the first time we made love? I didn't know than that you were Nosferatu. You seemed so warm, so alive. I couldn't have known that you were straight from the kill; that you had killed because you desired me. When fresh blood pumped through your veins, no mortal could have resisted you. I can still remember the way you smiled as you told me you loved me. Yes, I remember, I remember everything. You said, "I love you," and then you reached out for me. I took you to my bed and we undressed, ever so slowly, in the candle light. You were exquisite, long brown hair, beautiful blue eyes, delicately structured face, and such inviting lips. I could not resist you naked there before me. Looking back on it, it seems to me that I held you for hours, enthralled by your beauty and the feel of your skin. And when I mounted you and felt your moist warmth surround me, it was more than words can describe. At that moment, somehow, I knew that we would spend a lifetime and more together.

I remember how your moans of pleasure became louder, the way you began to thrash beneath me; and I will never forget looking into your eyes as you opened your mouth and revealed to me your fangs. I should have been frightened, I should have run away, but the look of love in your eyes held me, it told me that all was well, I could trust you. And when you said "Come give me your neck," I didn't hesitate. Certainly there was fear, but that was part of the allure. The thought of eternal damnation seemed insignificant in comparison to your beauty. It seemed that the fangs that would be my death would also be my salvation. I didn't know that you planned to make me Nosferatu, but I would have surrendered up my soul to you even if you had not. The burst of perception that I gained when your fangs penetrated my neck will always live in my memory. Suddenly, we were truly one, not just pathetically striving to be one as mortals are when they make love, but truly one. All the veils were ripped aside and we were granted a view into one another's souls. What I saw shook me to my core; as much as it terrified me, it aroused me, making me wish to share eternity with you. I wanted you to take every drop of blood I had, leaving me nothing. I'll never know how long it lasted. It was such ecstasy, and you knew then that I was yours for eternity.

Afterwards, you helped me find my first kill. I was almost helpless, overcome as I was by my heightened senses. Everything seemed so beautiful and so alien all at once. You brought her to me. Truthfully, I cannot remember what she looked like, but I will never forget when my fangs parted mortal flesh for the first time. I felt the beauty of her vulnerability, and yes, I felt her desire for death at my hand. And then you joined us. I felt your presence as your fangs entered her flesh. Our victim seemed insignificant, serving only as a medium to intertwine our souls. With each beat of her heart, the ecstasy of our union grew stronger. Until finally, her heart beat no more. With her death,

we were bonded more closely than mortals could
ever hope for. A bond that would hold us together
until the end of the world.

My love, where are you now? Have you found
rest, or do you suffer, as I do, somewhere amongst
the ruins? If only we hadn't parted. No, I could not
wish that on you. It is better to think that in the
end, you found the peace that I was denied, that
you did not escape the holocaust that devastated the
planet.

If I believed in the power of Heaven, or Hell for
that matter, I would pray for you. It seems to be too
late for me. I am here and all else is gone. For a
brief moment I thought that the world could escape
this fate, that mankind would unite as brothers and
vanquish all ours fears. Alas, that moment faded.

It faded with the hunger that spread across
Eastern Europe, after Bolshevism died. Freedom was
no match for hunger, I understand that now. The
hungry seized power, and tried to make the rich
feed them. When that failed, they destroyed everything. Almost everything.

Why did you have to spend that day away from
me? In over a hundred years we did not spend more
than a handful of days apart. How could this have
happened to us?

After the world ended, I searched for you. I went to all of your favorite places. If you live, then you know that I did not find you. But I tried, my love, I tried. I can not bear to think of you trapped somewhere, being consumed by a hunger that you can never feed. No, I prefer to believe that you were spared my fate.

If only I could think of a way to end this existence, I would follow you. If this were Hollywood, I could impale myself upon a wooden stake. But alas, I must accept reality, wood has never been sufficient to kill a Nosferatu. No, it was only used to pin us in our coffins, so we could not wander about the mortal world by night.

My only hope of escaping this hunger, lies with the Sun. If I could expose myself to it, then I could die. But even that is denied to me. Will this nuclear winter never end? Will the Sun, that I lived in fear of for so long, once again caress me and send me to oblivion?

I don't know. Rummaging through what is left of the world's libraries, I have found that man knew little about nuclear disaster. Some accounts said that the winter would last for a year, others that it would not happen. It has been two years, and still the winter has not broken. The Sun refuses to shine.

Two years without sustenance. Agony beyond mortal comprehension. And so, as it must be, I think of you, as I await a dawn that may never come.

Wanting

Amelia G

I was surprised when the DJ said that last rockin' number was off the new Motley Crüe album. Gotta love that nouveau underground sound. Well maybe. Then the DJ added that Madison is in the video for "Hooligan's Holiday", the song we had just heard. Like anyone in this part of the country knows who Madison is. Made me wish we got cable around here though.

I was guiding my monstrous old Caddie along the route to the grocery store, when the DJ turned on The Cult's "Fire Woman." I blame that—maybe credit that—for everything that came after. I gave a passing guy in a pickup the one-finger salute just in case he was thinking my car was too big for a woman. Never look down on anyone in a vehicle big enough to take you out without slowing down.

I'm old enough to remember seeing Southern Death Cult live. I was spending three years abroad. Pissing my parents off. They'd pissed me off with their reaction to 'Cilla. "It's not your fault, honey.

It's a sickness." Please. I'd charged the plane tickets on my mother's platinum AmEx and made my
dramatic gesture. Such a rebel. Ha. At 32 now, I can
see that if I had really loved 'Cilla, I would have
stuck around. But hindsight is always 20/20. Besides, true drama would have been a one-way
ticket.

As I got off the country highway and turned
onto the street that led into town, fucking Pearl Jam
came on the radio. So I turned it off. The money
had just about run out so I knew I was going to
have to return to the world soon. Contract out with
Oribé. Do fashion or something. I had made the
transition from Goth to glam without pain. I may
be the only person on the planet who enjoyed "Fire
Woman" as much as "God's Zoo". But the thought
of doing makeup in a grunge world made me ill.

A comfortably warm, clean springtime evening,
the sort that can only be found in upstate New
York, was just beginning to settle in around the
town. I parked outside the market.

I noticed her immediately after stepping across
the threshold of the store. Maybe it was her coat.
I'm not sure. I was only slightly chilly in my tank
top and cutoffs, but she had her shoulders hunched
under a dirty leather trenchcoat. She was pale.
Sickly-looking really. But the shock of recognition
was sharp and fast. There was no mistaking the

perfect arch of those thin eyebrows, those unnaturally angular cheekbones, the thin upper lip contrasting with her pouting lower one. Begging for deep red lipstick. Begging for something. She was small and thin and ludicrously out of context next to the fresh strawberry display.

"Danielle?" I asked incredulously, although I knew it was her.

"How do you know my name?" the waif asked.

My heart sank. I'd only done her makeup a few times, but she had been more a part of the whole glam thing, while I'd hung out mostly on the Gothic scene. There really was no reason she should remember me more than a decade later. "You are Danielle Hazzard, aren't you?"

She smiled thinly, but with humor. "Danielle Jones now really. Did I know you then?"

I held my hand out to shake. "Rachael Bloom. Pleased to remake your acquaintance. I, uhm, did your makeup for you a couple of times. When you warmed up for Hanoi Rocks."

When she shook my hand, her hand was cool to the touch and she left it in mine a beat longer than appropriate. "I do remember you now. It must have been your longing. Opening for that band was so terrific. So terrifying. They were so good. Omnisexual and androgynous. Michael was so beautiful. Is so beautiful. Almost enough to make you change your mind." Her voice was low and not quite accented, but not very American either. I wondered if the Michael comment was a test.

I took my hand back and I was about to hold forth on my opinion about standards for beauty being the same, regardless of gender. Then I caught sight of the shopkeeper watching us. I pretty much kept to myself, but the last thing I needed was to arouse any more comment than my reclusive lifestyle already did. "Would you like to go have a drink or something?" I asked Danielle.

"I don't really like to eat anyway." Danielle gestured around the little market disdainfully.

I couldn't remember what I'd needed to pick up for myself. So I led her back out to my car.

"The black Cadillac. Is that one yours?" she asked.

"I'm a sucker for nice tail fins," I said, mentally raising my estimation of this woman who seemed somehow conjured from my past.

I opened the passenger door for her and maybe it was my imagination, but it seemed that she wiggled for my benefit when she replied, "Nice tail fins are important." Not that I could really tell what her ass was like under that long muddy leather. It looked like she'd been slopping pigs in it. "Aesthetics in general are important," Danielle added after we were both seated in the womb of my big black Cadillac. Funny words, given how she was dressed. I was actually concerned about the mud she was tracking into my car. I swear it was even in her hair and everything.

I started up the powerful engine of my car and felt it come to life, rumbling reassuringly beneath our seats. The thin delicate creature sitting beside me turned and said, "You didn't go by Rachael Bloom ten years ago, did you?"

I blushed. "No."

"What name did you use?"

I guided the car back onto the main street of town. Drove past the antique store and the sole sad little bar. There were four dusty pickups and a beat-up Pontiac sitting outside and we could hear male laughter, even over the purr of my Caddie's motor. A teenage boy was climbing out of the least dust-covered of the pickups. "This is the only real place to get a drink in town." I pointed.

"Looks charming," she said sarcastically.

I stopped the car but did not turn it off. "They water down all the good stuff," I told her. "I've probably got a better bar at home and I never even entertain."

"Let's go to your home, then." I looked at her, but her expression was unreadable.

I put my metal monster back in motion. "Are you sure?" I said. I pointed at where the teenage boy was going into the bar. "He's kind of cute." I waited for her response. Testing. Not even breathing.

She watched the boy's faded blue jeans and red plaid shirt with the sleeves ripped off, watched them disappear into the bar. "Don't they have a drinking age in America any more?"

I exhaled. Still unreadable. "It is a small town. The barkeep pretty much overlooks everything. It's hard enough for him to stay in business as is. Besides, the sheriff is his brother-in-law."

Danielle said nothing. Just hunched her shoulders and held herself.

"What do you want to do, Danielle?"

"Let's go to your home and sample some of your fine bar. I could really do with a shower too. Then maybe you could do my makeup again."

Images from the last time I did her makeup flashed through my head. I could barely see the road as the Caddie took us up the winding dirt road to my house on the hill. Danielle had been in this band which played music too bouncy to totally appeal to the Gothic audience. But she was a Gothic wet dream to look at. She never stopped moving during a show, never ran out of energy so long as the crowd wanted more. She still looked cool, but it was odd to think of this sickly-looking woman as that hyperactive girl who had seemed to feed off her audience's excitement, strutting across the stage in nothing but black netting and bat wings.

I had hoped I'd get to do her wings, but she did her own costuming. Just liked getting a hand with the painting part. I had loved accenting the planes of her angular face, but I had almost died of embarrassment when she had me rouge her nipples. My housemate who had gotten me backstage—she knew the guitarist—had almost died laughing. Danielle's perfect high round breasts did show in that outfit though. And the rouge had made her nipples stand out through the black netting.

"So what name did you go by in England?" Danielle interrupted my reverie and I blushed at what I'd been thinking about.

Then I blushed at what I was about to tell her. "Uhm, Razor. Razor Flower."

"That's pretty."

"Yeah, pretty pretentious."

I stopped the car and Danielle gasped. "Is this your house?"

"No, I live in the servants' quarters." She looked at me, searched my face. "Yes, this is my house. Real estate is pretty cheap around here. Joys of living in the middle of fucking nowhere."

The gravel crunched under our feet as we walked across the driveway to the front steps. I let us in and showed Danielle the bath. It was a beautiful old thing with claw feet, but I'd had the plumbing modernized so the water could be wonderfully hot. And I had an eighty gallon tank so I never ran out of hot water. Different luxuries are important to different people.

I had hoped she would be naked when she got out of the tub and I waited for her in my bedroom. The country sun was setting outside my windows as I laid my zillions of little jars of makeup out on the little dressing table with the antique three-part mirror. I had just brought out two glasses of ice and a couple of bottles of my favorites, when Danielle entered the bedroom. She looked a thousand times healthier even though she was technically paler without all the dirt on her. Her hair was blacker and longer than I had realized.

I wished she was not wearing my huge fluffy white terrycloth robe, but I forced myself to take a couple of scarves out of the dressing table drawer so I could pick one to tie her incredible hair out of the way. Forced myself to act like playing with makeup a little was all I wanted. At least she left her awful muddy clothing in the bathroom.

Her skin was warm from the bath as I ran my fingers over her face, using a combo of Bob Kelly purples and greys on her eyes. They were already big, but the makeup gave them a knowing look. I rimmed her eyes in blackest black. All makeup artists have their own little biases. Mine happens to be that I believe black eyeliner is the only one that counts, the only one that is ever genuinely in fashion.

As I worked, Danielle made casual conversation. We talked about how much we had loved the dark bondage-inspired fashions of the early eighties, about how much we hoped that look was coming back in style. She asked me how I could afford such a mansion. Even in upstate New York. I surprised myself by telling her the truth. About my trust fund. About the lawsuit with my parents. How they'd said I wasn't competent and how they just hadn't thought about what ten percent means when they'd offered the judge their proof.

"That's great," Danielle said, "the judge even awarded you punitive damages."

I used my index finger to stroke the Chanel red lipstick onto her smiling lips. It might have been my imagination, but I thought she licked my finger when I added the X-Rated lip gloss as a top coat.

I guessed it wasn't my imagination, though, when those shiny red lips moved to ask me, "You should put some blusher on my nipples. Nobody does that like you do." She let my robe fall open just enough to reveal two coral circles tipping two breasts that were far too high and too firm for the age she had to be. Maybe she'd had surgery. She didn't seem like an exercise freak.

I wanted her to admit she wanted me before I risked anything so I just started to rouge her nipples with a nonchalance I had been unable to muster at 21. "I thought you said you didn't remember me."

She moaned softly as first her left nipple and then her right grew stiff and hard between my blush-slick fingers. "I remember you. I guess I just wasn't thinking clearly." I decided that counted as enough of an admission of desire and I leaned forward and buried my face between her breasts. She smelled like gardenias, like my soap, and she moaned again when I kissed her there. "I'm usually fuzzy when I've just woken up," she added, "I like to sleep until there's really a need. Really a need to do otherwise."

There was almost an electric shock when our lips met. I'd wanted to kiss her for so long. I'd wanted to kiss her so badly. Her tongue explored my mouth like a wild intruder, forcing my tongue back out from between her lips with her strength. She held me with a fierce urgency, tearing my tank top up over my head and dragging my shorts down to the floor, following them with my little black silk panties.

"You've smeared your lipstick," I said when we finally came up for air. I reached a finger up to fix it.

"I don't want you distracted from your pleasure. Can I tie you up?" she whispered. Danielle's breathing was already heavy. It must have been even longer for her than it had been for me. "Please," she moaned, "if you like bondage, I know you'll like what I want to do."

"Okay." I nodded and picked the scarves up off the dressing table. Some part of me knew that this was what I had brought them out for. That this was what I wanted. I felt incredibly self-conscious and aware of every part of my body as I walked naked over to the double bed. Danielle, still in my terrycloth bathrobe, followed me and I handed her the scarves. I lay down across the country-style quilt and held my wrists up to the red wood bedposts.

The bonds she tied around my wrists were quick but gentle. I tested them lightly and realized that the knots were perfect. I was firmly secured, but my blood would have no problem circulating.

"Do you want to be mine?" she whispered huskily. I nodded.

"Do you want to be mine?' Her tone was sharper this time.

"Yes. Yes, I want you. I want to be yours."

"Give me your leg," she said, gripping my ankle. I felt so vulnerable once she had me tied spread-eagled on the bed. The setting was so wholesome, so countrified. And there we were, two fair-skinned, dark-haired creatures of the night. How had I ended up in the country.

She stroked her hand up my thigh.

"Oh. Take the robe off."

"Later." She took an ice cube out of one of the pair of glasses I had intended to put drinks in. She ran the ice up the thigh she had just stroked. "Do you like this?"

I moaned.

She ran the ice cube up my thigh, over my hip, along my tummy, up my rib cage, and circled my left nipple. It was instantly hard and aching. She ran the ice cube across my cleavage to the other nipple where it melted.

Danielle pulled another ice cube out of her glass and, with no warning, plunged it into the place of secret need between my thighs. "Oh." I was so hot, it started melting fast. She took another piece of ice and ran it teasingly over my clit. I almost screamed, it was so intense. She ran the corner of the ice up over my body, then back down teasingly across my aroused clitoris, down across my lips, then lower. A cold damp puddle was forming on the quilt beneath my ass. I shivered with both chill and arousal.

She put a new ice cube into me. "Do you like that?" she breathed.

"So cold, so cold."

"Do you want me to stop?"

"No, no, don't stop." I thrashed around on the bed, my pelvis reaching for her. Her eyes were alight with a mischievous glint. Her closemouthed smile driving me mad with lust. "Don't stop," I begged her, "I want you to go on. Take off the robe."

"Later." Danielle stuffed another ice cube into me. I was so so hot and they were so so cold. She was running another piece of ice from side to side, thigh to thigh, when she suddenly dropped her head, hiding my pelvis beneath her ebony hair. Her

tongue burned on my clit and this time I did
scream. Her name. Incoherent sounds. Then I think
her name again. The top of her rough tongue
scraped a sweet circle of intense sensation and I was
coming so hard, I nearly blacked out.

Danielle lay down next to me on the crazy
patchwork of the flowered quilt. She held me, but
she made no move to untie me. "Do you always
come like that?" she murmured. She sounded sort
of sated herself.

"Only when I'm as turned on as you make me."
We lay together for a moment. Then I asked, "did
you come too?"

"Mmm-hmm," she replied, smiling lazily.
"You're so responsive. It's really beautiful. It's really exciting."

"You'd like it better with your skin on mine," I
said. "I want to taste you."

"You promise it will be okay," she said. The last
remnants of sunshine streaked through the lace
curtains, highlighting her glossy tresses. She looked
pretty healthy now too. Still pale, but not in a bad
way. And I wanted so badly to see her naked. So
badly.

"I'm sure it will be okay," I told her as firmly as
I could manage while tied to the bed.

She put her feet down on the wood floor and
stood. Then, with a shy look, she shrugged off my
white terrycloth robe to expose the black leathery

wings I had known she was hiding. "Are you sure it is okay?" she asked me.

"Let me prove to you how okay it is," I told her. "Let me please you."

"You please me already," Danielle answered, but she crawled up over me anyway and placed one white white thigh on either side of my head.

I lifted my head up off the pillow and tasted her. I've been with a lot of women and I'd heard honey metaphors before. Always thought they were stupid. But Danielle, Danielle tasted like candy apples. "You're so sweet," I spoke into her mound.

"It really is okay with you." She laughed a small giggle of freedom and then moaned.

"It's okay," I groaned between licks, "you're so beautiful, so sweet, so, so, so, I couldn't want you more if I tried." And I settled into pleasing her in earnest. All too quickly her little moans turned into a violent body-wracking shaking. She slid back down my body, her wetness affirming my power over her.

She enfolded us both in her dark wings and the leather was soft and smooth and supple and alive, not like her coat at all. I thought maybe I should be freaked out or something, but the surprise never came. Motley Crüe doing an industrial-influenced album was more surprising to me than her wings being real. "I'm all turned on all over again," I told her. "Maybe not again. Maybe just still. I want you."

"What I want is your wanting. Do you want me?"
I opened my eyes and looked at her, her thin frame somehow managing to loom over me. "Yes, I want you. More than I've ever wanted anyone else."

She smiled. Open-mouthed. Showing her fangs for the first time. The fangs I had known were there. "Are you going to drink my blood?" I asked.

"No, silly." She threw her head back and her long heavy dark hair flew up into the air behind her and cascaded back down over her shoulders like a black waterfall ending on my breasts. She laughed and it was the most beautiful music I had ever heard. "What I need is your wanting. Just your wanting."

For a moment, I was almost disappointed, but my body always knows what I really want. And my body throbbed for her touch. "I want you. I want you so much. Please touch me. I'm almost there."

And, smiling, she reached down between my trembling thighs and stroked me in that last gentle circle I needed to put me over the edge.

My orgasm broke through me. The release was incredible, but the wanting didn't go away. And neither did Danielle.

Predator

Raven Kaldera

It was raining hard, and the poor visibility interfered with Val's driving. Reyna watched her struggle with a sharp turn and felt the jolt as the brakes slammed them back in their seats. A car much faster and sleeker than theirs cut them off and slewed by, its jets churning up the water. Val cursed and glanced at Reyna, who was still sitting like a statue, unable to move, and the smaller woman's glance flinched away as if the sight hurt her. "Um, love," she began, and Reyna could hear the weariness and trepidation in her voice. "I haven't eaten since early this morning. Do you mind if I pick up some takeout? It won't take more than five minutes, I promise—"

"Yeah, sure." Reyna cut her off with a wave of her hand. Gods, what an effort it was to move. "Go ahead. I'll wait in the car."

"I could pick up some for you, I know you like Thai—"

She snorted. "The doctor said it wouldn't do me any good."

"I know, but you can still taste—"

"It's not worth wasting the money on." Her voice sounded dry and cracked to her ears. "Go on. You need it."

Val hesitated, reached over and gave her hand a squeeze, and then parked the car, slipping out into the wet night. Reyna was left alone with her shock and fear and the bundle of papers clutched in her lap. Her skin flashed back and forth from numbness to near-irritating sensitivity to her clothing, even though the leather jacket and boots were well broken in from years of wear. The shirt and kata pants weren't clean; Val had grabbed the first things she could find when the hospital had called to tell her that her lover and mistress was awake from the three-day coma. Reyna's short fingernails dug into her knees. Eighteen hours a day Val sat next to that prone and wired form, or so the nursing staff told Reyna on her way out. *Only went home when she dropped from exhaustion, and was back the next morning. People I don't respect might say it was only what one would expect from a good slave; people who didn't have the trust and love for each other to pass the exhaustive psychological testing necessary before becoming licensed as official consensual slaves and slaveowners. People who didn't understand how love and power could sleep in the same bed.*

"Of course, your marital status will be automatically dropped back to standard domestic partnership," the psychiatrist had informed her. "The government regulators feel that allowing someone to choose to be owned by an individual in your condition might be opening the situation to ....abuse." He obviously didn't wish to elaborate, but seeing the look of horror on Reyna's face, he'd rushed to reassure her. "I'm sure you can reapply in a year or two as long as you can prove you're following the no-harm guidelines. Now, we'll contact the local support groups listed in your information packet, and they'll send someone around within 48 hours to check on you and answer any further questions you might have about your condition. It's completely possible to live a long and nonharmful life with this virus. You just have to take your medication and stick to the rules. Do you have any idea where you got it, by the way? We have to ask that question because knowing transmission of the HCARVV virus is a felony, and the CDC will want to follow the disease vector."

Reyna had shaken her head no. Where she had picked it up? Who knows? As an experienced sexual sadist, you did occasionally see blood from the whip welts of the dangling submissives you were flogging into ecstasy. What could be more natural than to lick it off? Had it been that woman

Natalie, or Kern Haining, or that pretty boy lent her for the evening by his master whose name she had never been told? God knows. The psychiatrist had continued, pursing his lips fussily between sentences. "Contrary to popular belief, you can contract the virus from someone who still has it dormant in his system, who hasn't had it triggered yet by brain death. The CDC ought to be pushing safer sex guidelines."

Brain death. The truck careening out of control, the painful thud as her hoverbike connected with its fender, the crunch as her precious Falchion was sucked under its jets—these were faint in her memory, vague, as if seen through smoke and felt through padding. There had been a flying sensation, and lightning-shot blackness as she hit the pavement, and then nothing until she awoke in the hospital ripping out tubes and wires.

The nurse who had walked in and screamed to find her curled up in the bed nursing on the spare bag of plasma hanging above her, its rivulets running down her chin and breasts in delicate tattoos, that memory was clear. Within fifteen minutes her room was sealed and the specialists were called. She had never seen the SWAT team that must have surrounded the wing while the shrink tested her with careful questions, but she knew that they had prevented Val, poor Val, tiny and dark and tough as shoe leather, from entering until it had been determined that Reyna was not suffering from one of the rare strains that caused dementia. She'd been let go, finally, with a list of support groups and another of the Federal HCARVV Non-Harm Guidelines, a scrip for powdered plasma and another for the new drug, Vrykozine, that was supposed to dull the hunger. "Now this drug is legal only for you," the shrink had told her. "When used on non-HCSARVV sufferers, it's very addictive and causes illness. Don't give it to anyone else." As he left the room, it occurred to Reyna that he'd managed to talk to her for an hour without once using the word vampire.

The door opened and Val climbed back in, struggling with packages. "All set. I'll get you home in a jiffy, OK? Here, could you take this?" She held out a bag of what smelled like Thai food; Reyna's senses were suddenly incredibly sharp and she cradled the bag lovingly in her hands, turning it this way and that and discovering the wafts that meant fried rice with peanut sauce, or curried chicken. It didn't make her hungry, exactly; the scents were just a euphoric symphony that sang to her nose alone since her stomach was now deaf.

She was distracted by the scuttling sound in the other bag Val set down between them. "What's that?" she asked, reluctantly setting down the grease-stained bag of food.

"Well, I went into the pet shop, and..." Val closed the car door, glanced around guiltily, and opened the bag. There was a small plastic cage inside, and in it was a good-sized rat, sniffing the corners if its tiny prison. "I thought you might get hungry later. They sell them to feed to pythons. Don't name it."

Reyna turned her head and made a sound that was half sigh and half growl. "Val, damn it! I can't! The guidelines say I can't feed on living things, just the plasma. I'll start to crave it, and pretty soon I'll be attacking human beings." Squirming rats and dogs would lead to squirming human victims; it was against the no-harm guidelines, as was not responsibly taking the medications.

The dark-haired woman started the car. "How do you know?"

"It says so here, I guess...I can't afford to take the chance that they're wrong."

Val sighed. "Let's go to Canada," she said.

"What?"

"They won't let me be your slave here. So fuck them. We can go to Toronto, I know people in the leather world there—"

"Val, please, stop it." Reyna covered her eyes with her hand. "I can't just up and move. Besides, I can't be your mistress any more anyway. It would be too hard to resist...the kind of sex we have...I mean, I might not be able to stop..." She didn't say that she could smell Val's luscious iron-rich blood from here, that the delicate vein at her temple was far more tempting than that damn rat.

Her slave sniffed and wiped one eye. The streetlights glinted off the ring of her metal collar. "Don't say any more till we get home, love. You're making me cry and I can't drive while I'm crying." They passed the rest of the drive in silence, pulling into their apartment garage without noticing the rain had stopped. The light was becoming too bright for Reyna's eyes as the clouds parted, so once in the house she pulled all the curtains and then shut herself in the bathroom.

Val got out a pan and threw some oil and chow mein noodles into it to eat with her food, and began to chop an onion. Fortunately that thing about garlic was a myth, she thought to herself, and then realized that no food she could ever make would nourish her lover now. It would go through her undigested. A waste of money, Reyna had said. Val was proud of her gourmet cooking; had been proud to serve it to her mistress. After such a meal, she would be rewarded by tight elaborate bondage of silk cord or industrial chain, whipped by Reyna's loving tortures into paroxysms of pain and pleasure. Tears from more than the onion's pungency burned her eyes.

Her mistress came out of the bathroom and moved to the refrigerator, opening it reflexively. Then her shoulders stiffened under the leather jacket and she slammed it shut. Her depression rolled off her in waves. Val took a deep breath, nerved herself, and carefully moved the kitchen knife from the onion to her finger, slicing into the skin near the tip.

The pain caught her by surprise and she gasped aloud. Reyna turned from her funk to look at her. "You OK?"

Swallowing, the collared woman turned and held up her hand. "Oops," she said as the blood ran down her palm.

The taller woman took a step back. "Oh gods, Val, don't—"

Her slave advanced on her, holding out the bleeding finger. "Please, lover. Take it. It'll just go to waste." *And I want so much to make you happy,* her eyes pleaded. One scarlet drop hit the floor. The next moment, Reyna grabbed the injured hand in an iron grip and began to suck off the blood. Val gasped again and deliberately moved against her, pressing her crotch into Reyna's thigh. The taller woman smelled blood and sweat and the redolence of Val's cunt, and it was like magic, like humming, like climax, almost. Golden sparks danced behind her eyelids, and her mouth, finding no more blood on the cut finger, moved to Val's lips and chin and then to her throat.

"Yesss..." Her slave's voice was throaty in her ear. "Take me, Mistress. Take me, lover. Do it." Reyna was holding her up now, almost off her feet, with a strength she had never felt before. Upper lip curled back spasmodically. Aching in the jaw like singing, or eating lemon juice, the soft skin of Val's neck, her lover, her slave, her precious treasure—and then the phone rang.

The spell was broken and Reyna pulled away, slamming her leather-covered wrist into her upper lip with a muffled cry. Val stumbled and caught herself against the table. Keening faintly in anguish, the taller woman flung into the other room, the door slamming behind her.

Val shook her head to clear it and lifted her hand. Where the cut had been was a tiny white half-healed line. She stared at the door that had closed behind her mistress, and then took her bowl of Thai food and went up to their bedroom, determination in every line of her body.

Reyna slumped to the floor in her workroom on the pile of cushions beside the easel and grabbed the phone. "Hello?" she growled. Her upper jaw still ached and her lip hurt where she had slammed it into her teeth.

"Hey there," came a tenor voice on the other end. Male. New Yorkish accent. "Taken that Vrykozine yet?"

The breath let out of her in a hiss. "Oh. You're the one they said would call, from the support group or whatever? No, I haven't filled the scrip yet." Feeling embarrassed, she hastened on, "I'm tired, and they gave me a lot of plasma at the hospital. I figured I'd do it tomorrow."

"Don't do it. Throw the scrip away. Better yet, sell it to a dealer. You can make a few bucks that way."

Her face froze in shock. "What! Who are—"

"Look." The voice cut her protest off. "Tomorrow, somebody'll come check on you. They'll be from the local support group, but they'll probably also be a government toad. You'll be able to tell them easy, because they'll stink to high heaven."

"Stink?"

"Like rot. Listen, that virus in you body is all that's keeping you alive, and it regenerates your cell tissues. Vrykozine retards it. It makes you weak, no stronger than anybody else, makes you look like the living dead, and smell that way, too. And don't let them tell you it's not addictive. They made it that way. You'll be easily controlled, and very, very visible."

"But—" Reyna stammered. "The hunger...I'm afraid."

"You want me to keep talking, or hang up? Say which. I'm calling from outside the country, and it's my dime, and my risk if you tell anyone." The man was sharp, hurried, edgy.

She took a deep breath and let it out slowly. "Yeah, go on. I'm listening." Running her tongue over her teeth, she suddenly realized that she had been absently licking two sharpish lumps that had partially broken through her gums. She turned her face away from the phone and retched, covering her mouth, and almost missed the man's next words.

"—sure, it stops the hunger, and that means you don't eat, and you're weak. Don't you see? They want you that way."

"How did you find out about me?" she whispered.

He ignored that. "Have you tasted live blood yet?"

Long silence. "I—yes. But I didn't mean—"

"Good. Then you've already broken the guidelines. You're a predator now. Look, this virus of ours is what lets us feed and then close the wounds so the feeder is OK, right? It's in our saliva. But if you decide to grab someone after you're on the drugs, you'll have a gushing fountain and a corpse real fast. Bad for you, good publicity for the anti-vampire lobby in Congress. 'Course, if they find out about you, you'll lose your job, get put under watch, maybe they'll get a court order to hook you to an IV in a very, very strong cell."

The stumps were slightly loose; she could push them in and out of their sheaths with her tongue. "So what would you suggest I do, then?"

"Get out. Soon. Now. I'll email you an address, but only if you're sure. I mean it. You're now a member of a minority that barely has a right to exist. You'd better start acting like it."

Reyna's thoughts whirled and her belly grumbled. So soon? Shit. Go to Canada, Val said. Val...Three days by my bedside. She was crying, and I threw away her gift. "Send it," she said abruptly. "But not to me. To Valerian Sayres, here in Boston. My girlfriend."

"Lucky woman," said the voice, and hung up.

Reyna sat against the wall for a long time, running her tongue over the sheaths of her fangs, trying to get herself accustomed to them. Predator. The grey daylight had faded and she felt better, not so dragged-out. Finally, sighing, she pulled herself to her feet and went up to the bedroom. Better face Val with this tonight, while it was still fresh in her mind. Before she had a chance to get scared again.

The door was closed, but opened at a touch. Val lay on the bed, naked, hands secured behind the small of her back. Her knees were drawn up slightly and her dark hair was carefully brushed back, exposing her throat.

The rat, in its cage, scuttled noisily on the night table.

Reyna closed the door slowly and took off her jacket. Val's dark eyes flickered open and blinked in the light. "Mistress?" she said huskily. "I fell asleep waiting for you. Are you feeling any better?" Her hips moved suggestively.

Her mistress shed her T-shirt and boots and paused, unknotting her kata pants. "Val, I'm not sure we can do this. I mean, it sounds romantic and all that, but I'm really afraid I might hurt you." She dropped her pants and sat on the bed, stroking the soft dark hair. Val moved into her touch, rubbing her face against her mistress' hand. "No, let's be honest. I'm afraid of killing you. And it would kill me if that happened."

Val sighed. "Kilogram." It was her safeword. She struggled to sit upright with her hands bound. "Love, haven't we been through this before, years ago? I've been your slave for four years and you've never even sent me to the hospital, although there were probably a million times when you could have lost it and killed me. You didn't. I trust you." She rubbed her face against Reyna's bare shoulder. "There's no one more qualified to hold someone's life in their hands than you. I can testify to that."

The collared woman's pulse seemed to thunder in Reyna's ears. "What if I can't stop?" she whispered.

"That's why I bought the rat. I figured it might take the...uh...edge off." A giggle, and Val lay back down on the bed, wiggling her hips again.

Reyna blinked and then suddenly found herself laughing. "Got it all planned, huh?"

Val kissed the stroking fingers. "Love, considering our activities of the last four years, I've probably got this virus dormant in my own system. Some day you may have to do this for me." Her teeth nibbled gently on Reyna's knuckle.

"Oh." Her breath came out of her in a whoosh. It was a full minute before she realized that she had no physical need to inhale, except to speak. And there seemed to be no more need for words. Her hand went for the rat's cage, flipped open the lid, and dived for its wriggling body. It seemed to move far slower to her than a rat ought to. Should I kill it first, she wondered, or just... Her nostrils flared, and she could just barely hear the tiny heartbeat, the pumping of the veins, the quick whoosh of breath as it fought for its life in her grip. The sharp teeth slid out of their sheaths as easily as a cock from its foreskin, and then she had a faceful of furry squirming rat as they sank into its tiny beating heart. It bit her ear, which distracted her but didn't seem to hurt much, and she broke its neck with one squeeze and emptied its little body.

Gasping, she flung the corpse across the room and sat, breathing heavily. Her ear was starting to hurt now. "I don't want to be the one to clean it up," she croaked. "Not this time. And now I know to kill them first."

Val, still bound, got up to her knees and nuzzled her mistress. "I'll slit their throats and serve it to you warm in brandy snifters," she whispered.

Reyna smiled and kissed her forehead. "Yes," she said. "You do that. Slave."

The collared woman lowered her head. "Yes, Mistress," she whispered. "Would my mistress like to take her nourishment from me now?" She rubbed her crotch in circular motions on the bed. "Val has missed you so."

Her body was deliberately inviting, pale and vulnerable with the delicate blue tracings of veins. Val had always known how to inflame her; it was the great power of the submissive. Heat flooded upwards from Reyna's crotch, and she realized that she was wet, very wet. Mine, screamed the overpoweringly irrational urge of the predator, and she grabbed her lover and hauled her face down over her lap. Val moaned and thrust her ass upward. "Hurt me, Mistress," she gasped.

I could break her bones, Reyna realized. *I'm that strong. But I won't.* She slapped the upturned ass a dozen times, not very hard, but the red marks were coming up and Val was crying out and thrusting upward even more. Her legs were open, and the redolent scent of her cunt was almost like mist in the air. Reyna tumbled her off the edge of the bed, holding her by her dark hair so that her head wouldn't meet the ground. "Lick me, girl," she commanded, lisping around those damned fangs, thrusting her slave's face into her own crotch. Then her hand went to the wall, to the whips hanging in a fan-shaped array. A split-second decision —not the horsehair tail, not the braided whip, I know Val, she needs it hard!—yes, the broad-tailed indigo cat—and then the chosen implement slammed down on her slave's shoulders as she nuzzled her way between Reyna's nether lips to her clitoris. She whimpered, but kept her tongue flicking, circling, rubbing as another lash followed, and another.

Reyna felt as if her mouth was a second erogenous zone, aching and swollen like her cunt. Val whimpered and flinched as the cat fell on her back, getting up on her knees and thrusting her reddened ass out to take more of the blows, but her mouth never left its work. "Enough," her mistress growled. Hunger filled her to the point where she couldn't finish the whipping, or even make it to orgasm.

Hauling Val up by her hair, she lifted her off the floor with one arm and flung her onto the bed. The dark-haired woman had one second of astonishment at the ripple of strength in that move before Reyna was on her, straddling her thigh, one hand going for her cunt and the other scrabbling desperately at the hair tangled around her neck. She twisted to help the effort, baring her neck above the collar, and spread her legs as wide as possible. The first thrust was three fingers, and the second found her wet enough to jam four fingers inside her, fucking hard.

At her throat, Reyna froze. She could smell the iron-rich river in that blue vein, could hear Val's pulse like thunder in her ears. Her hand on Val's cunt, her own cunt pressed against her lover's thigh, she paused and forced herself to take five deep breaths. *To prove I can stop,* she thought to herself. *Even here, even now, yes, I can stop. I am in control Oh, gods, but it hurts, it hurts!*

Val thrust her hips up, moaning, taking in more of Reyna's hand. She arched her neck back even further, wanting, wanting..."Do it, love," She whispered. And the next thrust was five fingers below and two fangs above, and she orgasmed.

Then it was like floating, like pain and ecstasy, like drowning. Reyna climaxed, but it was almost an afterthought to the relief in her jaw as her lover's blood slid down her throat in gulps. It was all tied together now, she realized dreamily, sex and feeding inextricably linked.

Val came again and again, three times, four, cunt contracting around Reyna's hand over and over, sweet pain in Val's throat mixed with the faint feeling of strangulation, and then she was thrust up out of the watery crimson depths like a fish thrust out of water, gasping.

Reyna had collapsed next to her, also gasping. Then she closed her eyes and stopped breathing for a minute, seeming to draw into herself. Val waited, turning her own head from side to side, trying to feel the holes in her neck. There was nothing but a faint tingling. Finally Reyna uncurled from her trance and opened her eyes, smiling at her lover. "Roll over," she said huskily, "and I'll get you out of those cuffs."

"Are, are you all right? Was it...enough?" There was both love and trepidation in Val's tone.

A chuckle from her mistress as she struggled with the cuffs. "I should be asking you that. I'm fine. Completely fine. Are you?"

Hands free, Val touched her throat. Two small indentations were fading fast. "Tired, but no more than I usually would be. Kiss me?"

Their lips touched. Reyna's fangs were still out; Val ran her tongue over and around them, playing, tasting her own blood on them as they slid back into their sheaths. "I like them," she mumbled around the kiss.

Reyna pulled away. "Can we make it to Canada in forty-eight hours?" she asked hoarsely.

Val was silent no more than ten seconds. "Yes," she said. "Tomorrow we close out our accounts, quit our jobs, sell the car and buy a camper. We can do it."

"I love you," said Reyna. Then she didn't feel that it sounded like enough, so she said it again. "I love you."

"Love y'too. Wanna sleep." Val buried her head in Reyna's shoulder.

"I'm awake. I should stay up and pack."

"Hold me. Till I fall asleep..." her voice trailed off. Reyna pulled the blankets up to her lover's collar and snuggled in next to her. *I wonder, she thought idly, are there deer in Canada, still? And could I run fast enough....*

The Brass Ring

Gary Bowen

When I returned from the shower the evening sun was shining directly on the front of my house. Thick hazy sunbeams forced their way through the shutters of my room, and dust motes danced like a cloud of tiny pixies. The pale birch furniture glowed in the light, and the thick gold and cream rug looked like a magic carpet ready to fly. It was like crossing the threshold into another, better world.

I piled up the pillows and lay down against them, sinking down, damp ringlets of black hair sticking to my white bathrobe and clinging to my neck. The soft pillows and clean sheets felt good. I was all those things a man is when he has just awakened: a little sleepy, a little hungry, and little horny. I burrowed into the pillows, reluctant to get up and face the day.

Michael's car rumbled to a stop in front of the house, and I bestirred myself. I rolled to the edge of the bed, opened the top drawer of the nightstand, and deactivated the burglar alarm. His key scraped in the lock as he let himself in, and I turned the alarm back on once he closed the door behind him. A few moments later he called, "Rafael?"

"Upstairs!" I shouted back. I settled back against the pillows while he trotted up the stairs.

He took a jaunty step into the room, and I smiled to see him home again. He was clad in a red sleeveless muscle shirt whose large armholes emphasized the bulging roundness of his shoulder muscles, while his jeans were worn to white threads at knees and crotch. Enough skin showed through the holes that I wondered if he were wearing underwear or not. The possible lack of lingerie made my blood simmer, and I grinned up at him with keen appreciation. He was my denim Adonis, and I adored everything about him, right down to the battered brown cowboy boots.

"I saw Ponch today," he said cheerfully.

"Ponch?"

"Ponchartrain. But he's so fat, I call him 'Paunch'. Don't tell him I said that." His twinkling eyes said he meant no harm.

"George Ponchartrain?" I asked in bewilderment. "Fat?"

He leaned against the bedpost. "Well, I guess it depends on how you define 'fat'. Not so bad for an old guy."

I cringed. The George I remembered was young and burly, with muscles like a Greek hero.

"How did it go?" I tried to sound enthusiastic, but it was hard. I was distressed about George.

The sparkle in his eyes grew even brighter. "He bought one. And he took three on commission."

"Great! Which one did he buy?"

He grinned easily. "Your picture, of course. The one I just finished. His eyes bugged out of his head and he pulled out his checkbook and wrote. No argument."

George had photographed me plenty of times; I could well imagine his appreciation of Michael's painting. "I wonder what Damon thinks of it."

"He asked George if he was keeping a tart on the side. I told him not to worry, you were already taken."

"I've been called a lot of things, but that's the first time anybody ever called me a 'tart'!"

He leaned forward and kissed me. "Good to eat," he murmured.

"Glad to oblige you," I replied.

He straightened. "I cashed George's check on the way home so I have two thousand dollars burning a hole in my pocket. We're going out to eat."

At that moment I would have agreed to anything, but the thought of dining (and throwing up) in public gave me pause. I sat on the edge of the bed, looking up at him. "Wouldn't you rather have dinner at home? We could have a lovely candlelight dinner, a little wine, a little music, just the two of us..."

"You're very tempting, but I know if I stay home alone with you, I'll never get my dinner. You have an irresistible way of distracting me. You have to keep my strength up if you want me to satisfy your appetites."

My eyes dropped to his silver belt buckle. "I'd be happy to keep you up."

He shook his finger at me. "That's exactly what I'm talking about! But tonight I'm holding out for steak and champagne before you get yours."

Barbarian, to mix white wine with red meat. But if that was what he wanted, I was willing to go along. "All right. Toss me my suit."

"I'm going as is, and I forbid you to wear a coat or tie." He tried to give me a stern look, but his eyes twinkled and he grinned when I laughed.

"Your wish is my command, O Mighty Sultan," I said reclining upon the bed and pretending to smoke a hookah. "Your slave will wear whatever you desire." With emphasis on 'desire'.

"Do I get three wishes, like Aladdin?"

I grinned. "Of course. And until the three wishes are granted, you are my lord and master." Lying on my side hampered me a bit, but I made an flamboyant bow by touching my fingertips to forehead and chest, then flourishing them in a circle. That might not have been exactly how the Arabs did it, but it was good enough for our little game.

"My first wish is that you go a whole week without wearing black."

I laughed. "Done. And your other wishes?" I asked lewdly.

"I'll let you know as soon as I decide on them."

I could imagine all manner of things worth wishing a lover to do, and the erotic images made me fidget. For example, mutual kissing starting at the toes and working in to the middle. Unfortunately, I had neglected to stipulate that he had to rub my lamp to get his wishes.

Michael was rifling through my closet in search of something not-black when he suddenly seized on a sliver of yellow at the end of the rod, mostly obscured by the other clothes.

"Not that," I said in alarm, sitting up straight.

His hand clamped onto the hanger and pulled.

"No," I said, "I won't wear that in public."

He held the dress against himself. "And you told me you weren't a queen."

It was a yellow frock, covered with coral cab-
bage roses and olive green leaves, with short
sleeves, a wide white collar, and full skirt. It buttoned up the front with yellow cloth buttons. I had
it so that when hunting was lean in the gay clubs,
I could take female form and hunt the straight
clubs. The dress was not a fetish; it was a hunter's
camouflage. But I could not tell him that.

"I'm not a queen," I protested lamely, not wanting to explain my promiscuous feeding habits. We
could burn that bridge when we came to it.

He was grinning as he peeled the dress off the
hanger and tossed it at me. "Get dressed. I want you
to wear it when we go out. That's my second wish."

With my eyes I pleaded for mercy.

"Go on, I want to see you in it."

I let my robe fall, exposing my mostly hairless
pale body, then blushing furiously, stepped into the
dress. It was tight across the chest as I buttoned it
up. I tugged it uneasily, trying to find a more comfortable position.

He pulled a second hanger from the closet,
unclipped the white lace garter belt and sheer silk
stockings, then passed them to me. My face was burning with fiery color as I pulled up the skirt and
fastened the garterbelt around my waist. Then I sat on
the side of the bed and pulled up one sheer stocking
and hooked it to the garter belt, then the other.

When I was in female form, getting 'dressed' did not embarrass me, but with him leering down at me, it was definitely kinky. It dawned on me then that he liked this particular form of deviancy. I glanced coyly up at him and said, "O Mighty Sultan, do you wish your slave to go barefoot, or will you provide her with shoes?"

He tore his eyes away from my legs, and knelt to rummage among the shoe boxes in the bottom of the closet. After opening and closing several, he found the black leather pumps with the four inch heels and ankle straps. He knelt before me, and ignoring his own prohibition on black, slipped the shoe on my left foot buckling the strap with trembling fingers. I offered him the other foot, and he kissed it softly before slipping it into the shoe. He fastened the buckle, then slid his hand around my ankle and up my sleek calf to the hem of the dress.

"It's a muscular leg," he said with a low voice. "But with all the women who work out, it's perfectly believable." The baritone tremor of his voice sent shivers up my spine.

I crossed my knees, letting the skirt ride up to my stocking tops, but still preserving my modesty. "You like me like this?"

He nodded. "You look like a beautiful lady, but underneath you're all man. It's amazing; it's like you're twins, one male, and one female." He grinned crookedly. "Twins are a fantasy of mine."

I could readily imagine him in the middle of a three way with a man and a woman, and I wondered if my shapechanging ability could manage to produce two of me at once to oblige him. "I'm a shapechanger," I said huskily. "I could be a woman if you want."

His eyes popped. "You could?"

I nodded. "Want to see?"

He nodded mutely.

I closed my eyes and concentrated, my body softening and reforming, the dress still in place, but fitting properly now. I unbuttoned the four cloth buttons and showed him two perfect breasts.

"Those are great tits," he said in honest admiration.

I uncrossed my legs, and spreading my knees wide, lifted my skirt to my waist. His eyes dropped to my black haired pussy, then bugged out of his head.

"Is it real?" he asked. "I mean, if I touch, will it feel like it looks?"

"Yes."

He put his hand between my legs, laying his palm over the mound of soft flesh and hair, leaning his body between my knees, face thrust close to mine, lips seeking mine. The pressure of his hand against my pussy sent startling waves of heat through my body, and I lifted my mouth to his. He kissed me strongly.

"I've never done it as a woman," I murmured against his lips.

"I'm good with virgins," he replied.

His mouth ravished my neck, soft lips caressing my skin while I lifted my chin to allow him full access to my vulnerable throat. He nipped it, and I let out a sharp gasp of air. His tongue trailed down my neck, then paused as he nestled his lips against the cleft in my collarbone, kissing it devotedly, sucking it, and running his tongue along the bone.

He pulled the front of my dress open to reveal a narrow triangle of flesh which his lips followed, walking softly down the cleavage between my breasts while my nipples strained against the fabric, eager for his touch. He peeled the fabric back, exposing my right breast, his hand cupping it gently, then firmly as his mouth came down upon it. I arched, forcing more of my flesh into his mouth, a line of fire burning through my body straight to my cunt. Fluids began to ooze and drip between my legs.

"Oh, stop!" I whispered, overcome by the sensations that were at once familiar and alien. I felt as if reality had taken a half twist to the left, so that everything looked the same, but nothing fit.

Michael lifted his head and looked at me, then pulled himself up so that he could embrace my shoulders and kiss me. His hard groin pushed against my crotch, and rockets of desire shot through me, obliterating minor technical differences between who I was, and who I had been. I wrapped my legs tight around his body, thrusting up against him, groaning in passion, wanting the union of our bodies, totally engrossed in the unfamiliar (yet similar) female sensations.

Michael slid down my body again, using his strength to force my legs and arms to loosen. He slid lower and lower until suddenly he was kissing my nether parts. His lips planted soft, firm kisses on the hairy mound of flesh at the bottom of my belly, and I collapsed onto the bed limp with astonishment, feeling like I was drowning in wet velvet. I could smell myself, the ripe, voluptuous female smell like fruit that would rupture on the vine if it were not picked.

I moaned long and low, my hips writhing, when suddenly his tongue flicked a small bump of intense pleasure. He nursed it with his mouth, electricity shooting down my legs, making my feet tingle, limbs twitching helplessly as he alternately sucked and licked it. My hands clawed the bedspread, and I groaned and tried to drag myself away from him, but he held me fast.

At last he took pity on me, and releasing my clitoris he slid his tongue up and down my dripping wet slit. He sucked on one labia, then the other, then held me open with his fingers while he licked me from hole to point. I buried my fingers in his hair, pulling unmercifully at his head. He deposited kisses all over the softly swollen flesh of my sex while I jerked and twisted.

"Fuck me!" I cried.

He caught my clit in his mouth again, pinning me to the mattress, while one hand slid down my slit, fingers gently probing for my opening. My back arched and I trembled, because Michael was taking me where I had never been before, and I was desperately afraid I was going to like it.

Two fingers sank into the soft, wet, warm opening of my body, and I squirmed, pushing myself onto his hand while my brain ran screaming in the opposite direction.

"No!"

He lifted his face and watched my reactions while his fingers found something inside me and tweaked it. A bolt of white heat shot through my body.

"Do you really want me to stop?" he asked mischievously. "I will, if that's what you want."

For answer I groaned wildly, hands beating the coverlet, then spread my legs wider. "Take me!" I cried, too far gone with lust to make any other answer.

He squeezed me gently with his thumb on my clit and his fingers inside my cunt, then rubbed them simultaneously. The internal pressure made me feel like I was going to pee, and I clenched my muscles, trying hard not to wet myself with excitement. But in spite of my efforts, pearly white fluids oozed around his hand, and the aroma of bitch in heat wafted through the air. The coverlet under my ass was getting very wet, and I squirmed, desperately fucking his hand, yearning for the intimate congress of his lust and mine.

Michael removed his dripping hand, then sat up and unzipped his pants. The prick which had given my male self such pleasure now seemed huge and impossible when it was pointed at my newly deflowered flesh.

I scrambled to a sitting position. "Oh no you don't! Not with that!" I cried in sudden panic. This fantasy was going much further than I was prepared to handle.

He caught me in his arms and bore me down, his hard flesh poking against my sopping wet hair. "I want to," he whispered hotly in my ear, "It's my third wish."

I wanted to change shape and run far away. But at the same time, I would curse myself for a coward if I quit now.

"Please?" he asked.

"Do I have a choice?"

"Yes, of course." He tried not to look disappointed as he sat up. Putting his hand on his cock he began to stroke himself. I watched him enviously because it was a gorgeous cock, and I did want it, even if it scared me.

"I didn't say no," I told him.

He leaned forward so that his breath was brushing my lips. "Will you let me make love to you?"

"Yes," I whispered. The panicked rats started to run wild through my brain, but I ignored them because I wanted to please him.

He stripped off his shirt and pushed his pants further down his legs, then lay down between my legs.

"Be gentle. I've never done this before," I begged.

He nodded, then sheathed himself in my body. I screamed.

It was a perfect fit, my hot, wet flesh taking him easily as he buried himself to the hilt. He held still, waiting for me to calm down, but I did not. The sensations were indescribable, and I kicked violently, then locked my legs around his waist and thrust my hips against him, nails biting into his shoulders, wild animal noises coming from my throat. I wanted to fuck him senseless, wanted to engulf the entirety of his hard body with my soft wetness, wanted to suffocate him with my thighs, to reduce him to nothing but the hot seeds of sex that grew inside me, swelling my belly from the inside, the ultimate invasion of my flesh.

He began to pump me, his hardness sliding easily through my slippery flesh, his eyes closed, his
expression blissful. His arms wrapped under my
back and neck, supporting my head so that he could
kiss my face. He was a well-practiced and skillful
lover, pacing himself and not letting the primal
thrashing of my body overwhelm his consideration
for my pleasure and my comfort. I hated him for it.
I wanted to come, I wanted him to come, to crash
into the mind-stopping double climax—no, I did
not want him to come! How stupid of me, I was
female, and we were not using a condom, I could
get pregnant!

I don't want to be a woman!

His body heated up, the expression on his face
becoming more intense. Perspiration gleamed on his
brow, and his strokes became harder, deeper, more
demanding. My back arched, my heels drummed on
his ass, and my fingers clawed his back as I fought
him, trying to tear him away from me with my hands
while my legs locked him tight against my belly. A
great pressure built in my body, and I shrieked,
having no other way to release the intensity.

Suddenly he slammed me with short sudden
strokes, driving the sensations of my body to a
higher, intolerable level. A floodtide of sensation
rushed through me, drowning me in a maelstrom of
velvety wet softness. Suddenly my body went rigid

and my breath stopped, my pelvis jerked and shuddered, then my back went limp, and I sprawled in sudden relief, stars circling inside my closed eyelids. Slowly I realized that this was orgasm, female style.

Michael lay languidly against me and I wondered if he had come. He was so relaxed he must have; I had been so busy with my own climax I had missed his.

"Don't you ever do that to me again," I hissed at him as soon as I caught my breath.

"Did I hurt you?" he asked in surprise.

"No."

"What did I do wrong?"

"I'm a man, and you fucked me like a woman!"

"Well, you are a woman, at least for the moment," he replied in bewilderment. "What was I supposed to do?"

I pressed my hands to my head as if to crush my skull. "You like me better this way, don't you?"

"I like you every way I can get you. Yes, this was a lot of fun, but you're also a lot of fun when you're male."

"Which do you prefer?"

"Both."

I glared at him.

"Really, Rafael. I do. I like you both ways, and I like doing it both ways, and I would hate to be stuck with only one, whichever one it was."

"Life would be easier if I was female."

He laughed then. "Who cares? I would rather have an interesting life than an easy one."

"You don't understand how I'm feeling!"

He sobered. "I've fucked you before. Is it really so different?"

"Yes!"

He cocked his head curiously at me. "Wanna tell me?"

"All my life I've been a kinky gay man. It affects everything I do, everyone I meet, everything I feel. That's a very intense and very different kind of life. Now suddenly, here I am, flat on my back, female, vanilla, and normal! It isn't fair! For years I've been persecuted because of who I am and who I love; now suddenly I'm socially acceptable, just because my plumbing has been rearranged. It's the rankest kind of sexism!"

"I see your point, but it doesn't matter to me. I think you're wonderful, and anybody who doesn't agree with me is an idiot."

"Thank you very much. Now get off of me; I want my body back and you're in the way."

He obligingly lifted himself off me, and I sat up, yanked the dress off, shed the garterbelt, shoes, and stockings. Then I squeezed my eyes shut, and gratefully reclaimed my natural masculine form.

Michael pulled up his pants. "Still want to go out with me?"

"Do I have to wear a dress?"

He grinned wickedly. "Are you gonna welsh on my second wish?"

"I never welsh on a deal," I said hotly, then squirmed. "Of course, if you've changed your mind—"

"I haven't."

"You're not going to let me off easy, are you?"

"Do you want me to?"

This was discipline of a different kind, more subtle and more psychological than the discipline James had administered with whips and chains. That was pure physical sensation, like skydiving or other daredevil sports. Michael was playing with my head, illuminating the dark places in my mind where I had never cared to look too closely before. Did I have the courage to play his version of the game? And yet, what courage did it require to play a game I could quit any time? Michael would never force me, never threaten me, never hurt me. Michael was safe.

I smiled, and pulled the dress over my head. "All right, but if anyone gets too close, you have to deck him for me."

He grinned easily. "I have a brown belt in judo. I'd be happy to protect your virtue."

"Hmph. If I had any virtue you wouldn't have talked me into this." I was stronger, faster, meaner, and tougher than him; if there was any fighting to be done I was the one to do it. Yet even though logic told me it was silly, his gallantry made me feel safe. It was nice to have someone looking out for me instead of always having to look out for myself.

He rose and offered me his hand. "Shall we go to dinner?"

I accepted his hand and rose gracefully. "With pleasure."

I stepped out on the front porch while Michael locked the door behind us. The warm breeze blew my skirt around my legs, and the fabric fluttering across my groin tickled and teased. I had often gone nude under my pants, but a skirt without underwear felt distinctly lewd, dangerous, and most of all, accessible.

We crossed the avenue without incident. Nobody was looking twice at me; the passing motorists and occasional pedestrians were paying no attention to us. There were no dropped jaws, no crude leers, and no shouted insults. I was passing as a woman. As long as I could keep it up, we could enjoy the same privilege straight couples enjoyed: to walk hand in hand without fear of ridicule or assault.

I hooked my hand in the crook of Michael's arm and smiled at him. He grinned back at me, white teeth gleaming while his other hand came to rest possessively upon mine. Like Siamese twins joined at the elbow we cut through High Hill Park towards the respectable, touristy heart of the city.

We came onto the red brick quay between the pentagonal tower of the World Trade Center and the green glass of the Pratt Street Shopping Pavilion. The mingled smells of popcorn and dead fish wafted through the air, giving a unique scent to the breeze, which apparently did not bother anybody but me. Men and women in business suits lingered after leaving their offices, mixing in with the crowd dressed in shorts and sports shirts. A mime walked along an invisible wall, and a clown was selling helium balloons. Moored around the edges of the basin was a collection of ships: skipjacks, Baltimore clippers, a lightship, a submarine, water taxis, paddleboats, and many kinds of pleasure boats all of which scudded blithely beneath the cannon of a great black frigate.

Faintly the sound of a steam calliope drifted across the water.

"Look! A merry-go-round!" Michael pointed towards the glimmer of lights further along the shore.

"An old one too. It's missing some animals."

"If we hurry, we can catch it!" His long strides thoughtlessly ate up the distance while I tottered desperately on high heels trying to keep up with him.

"Don't you think we're a little old for carousels?" I protested breathlessly as we arrived at the ticket booth.

He grinned and said, "Two please." He accepted the chits and handed one to me. "Maybe you are, but I'm not. Besides, I guarantee a ride on a merry-go-round will take ten years off your age!"

I balked. "I don't want to take ten years off my age."

He stopped short of the white metal gate, puzzling over the problem for a moment, then his face brightened. "You said I was your lord and master until the three wishes were granted."

"You've used up your three wishes, Aladdin," I countered.

"Ah, but it will be a week until the first one is granted, and you said that until the wishes were granted I was your lord and master."

My mouth quirked in a suppressed smile. "I said that, didn't I."

"You did indeed."

I smiled at him, bad humor evaporating before his twinkling hazel eyes.

"Very well, what is your command, O Mighty Sultan?"

"To ride the merry-go-round. And more than that, to have a good time while you're doing it."

I curtsied grandly. "It shall be as you command, O Puissant Prince. The sun shall halt in the firmament, and the stars shall shine during the day. Ten thousand nubile maidens shall feed you pomegranates and honey while forty thousand naked youths rub your flesh with oil and a hundred thousand slaves strew your path with willow leaves."

"One is enough for me. I wouldn't know what to do with a hundred thousand slaves."

"Your Majesty's faith in this humble servant will not prove unfounded." I swished through the gate, glancing coyly over my shoulder at him.

"I'm sure you will live up to my expectations," he murmured in my ear, then seized me by the waist and lifted me lightly to the deck of the machine. He jumped up beside me as quietly as a cat in spite of his boots. My heart did flip flops but he was oblivious to my emotional vertigo.

"Look! Pigs!" he exclaimed starting towards them.

"It's undignified for the Great Sultan to ride a pig," I objected, taking refuge in the game. I stopped beside a prancing white horse.

"Horses are boring. Every merry-go-round has them. The pigs are cute."

I glanced around for an alternative. Grandparents were picking up small children and seating them on zebras and lions; our choice of animals was dwindling. "How about the roosters?"

He bit back words, then succumbed to temptation. With a wicked grin he retorted, "I really don't think gay men should ride cocks in public."

My jaw dropped. Then I tried to answer him, but could not. I resorted to non-verbal communication: I hit him.

"Ow!" He darted to the other side of the pony. "That smarted!" He rubbed his arm.

Looking around quickly to make sure nobody was near enough to hear me, I retaliated, "If you're going to think such dirty thoughts, then let me remind you that the Latin word for 'pig' is 'cunt'! I don't think you ought to be riding pigs in public either!"

"Touché!" He laughed delightedly. "Well, how about the goats?"

"Horny as a goat, are you?"

He grinned. "You win. We'll ride the horses."

"Mmm. Studs. The perfect choice."

He hit me back. "That's enough!"

"You started it!"

"Okay, truce?" He held out his hand.

I shook it. "Truce," I agreed.

We self-consciously mounted two white ponies, our puns having made us all too aware of the ribald interpretations of the act. I settled myself side saddle, legs twined together and my skirt tucked around them to preserve my modesty. The wooden animal was frustratingly hard against sensitive portions of my anatomy.

"And I thought merry-go-rounds were such wholesome family entertainment," he lamented.

"Blame it on the Victorians," I said. "They developed the carousel as we know it, and they sublimated sex into everything."

The carousel cranked up with a jerk and a rattle, cutting off any answer he might have made. A worn recording of a steam calliope began to play John Philip Sousa's Washington Post March at a deafening volume.

"There are times when being a musician is a definite drawback," I shouted over the noise.

"It's fun!" he yelled back.

The carousel picked up speed, the brass poles lifting our horses in a relaxing rocking motion, like waves rocking a boat. Michael grinned at me. His knees stuck out akimbo because his legs were too long, but he had put his feet in the stirrups anyhow.

"I haven't done this since I was a kid!" he called to me. "I forgot how much fun it was!"

In a flash of sudden nostalgia I remembered what it was like to be young. "When we were kids, they had a machine with an arm that dispensed metal rings. As you went past it you tried to grab the rings. All of them were grey, except for one, which was brass. The girls would always beg the boys to grab the rings for them because they were in skirts and had to sit sidesaddle. But sometimes a girl would try for the rings too, and then she'd topple off headfirst, her skirts flying."

"What happened if you got the brass ring?"

"You got a free ride on the carousel. But some girl would beg it from you, and you'd have to buy yourself another ticket to ride along with her. And the boys would compete to see who could get the brass ring the most times. Oh yes, we spent a lot of money for the privilege of going around in circles!"

"If I caught the brass ring, I'd give it to you. You wouldn't even have to ask!"

"I was going to give it to you!"

He grinned wickedly. "Considering what you're not wearing, I'd love to see you try—and fail!"

I blushed badly. He sat grinning at me as we went round and round, and I sat smiling back at him, the two of us gazing at each other in mutual adoration. I was a cynic, I knew we were acting like a couple of pudding-headed teenagers, but oh! It had been such a long time since anybody had ignored my dignity and made me enjoy myself!

I was sorry when the carousel began to turn slower and more slowly. At last, with a clanking of machinery, it came to a stop. Michael swung off his steed, cowboy boots thumping on the deck. He held up his arms to me, and I leaned into them. He gathered me to his chest and kissed me tenderly, slowly, and thoroughly, my toes trying vainly to find the floor. Then I forgot about the floor, for I was floating on cloud nine, kissing my boyfriend in public for the first time.

"Look Grandma, that man is kissing that woman!"

"Yes, dear. They're in love. Don't bother them."

Michael lowered me to the floor, our lips parting reluctantly. His pupils were huge, completely obscuring the hazel irises, their darkness sucking me in, my legs unsteady beneath me. I closed my eyes, feeling like the two of us were at the center of a hurricane; the world whirling past, but leaving us untouched at the center.

The female dress had given me an evening of freedom I had never known and could not bear to give up. How could I go back to censoring myself, to pretending that I was indifferent to the one I loved, to acting straight to avoid offending people, to making up excuses to appease my family, to letting other people control my life?

"Michael, I can't go back in the closet. You've brought me out of it, and I like it. But I'm worried too, because I don't want anything unpleasant to happen to you because of me."

He clasped me gently in his arms. "Nothing is going to happen. And if it does, it won't be because of you, but because of some redneck who butted in where he didn't belong."

"But—"

He put his finger against my lips. "No buts. Other people don't arrange their lives to suit you, and you don't have to change your life to please them. Just be yourself." He grinned. "Whichever self you feel like being at the moment."

I laughed. "Whatever you say."

"No. It's your life, whatever you say."

Emotion shot through me, emotion I had not dared to feel for the thirty-five years of my unlife. In less than a week Michael had breached my armor and found a soul I thought I had lost.

"I love you," I whispered.

"I love you too," he replied.

Our kiss went on forever.

Loved to Death

Dave Smeds

Tom leaned back against the pillows, chewing the complimentary mints he'd found on the bed. The flavor of the candy blended pleasingly with the traces of alcohol lingering on his tongue. One more thing gone right.

The woman ran her eyes over his naked body with an appraising intensity. To judge by her hungry smile, he must have met her standards. Draping her gown across the back of a chair, she began languorously removing her lingerie.

Tom gasped as the bra dropped away. Once he'd seen the padded cups, he'd expected to be disappointed. But this was better than anticipated. Her breasts, still ample though not as full as they had seemed while clothed, hung as if gravity didn't apply to them, as symmetrical as a model's, capped with sharply defined, cloud-pink nipples and areolae.

Already nearly hard, his cock stiffened to hammer-handle rigidity as she glided out of her slip

111

and panties and casually tossed the articles over her shoulder. Tall, slim, not a mole or chicken pox scar out of place—Tom couldn't believe he'd found such a classy, and classic, dame just by cruising a hotel bar.

It puzzled him that she would bother with the padding. Or with the wig. The hair looked good, but he suspected her natural curls would win in a comparison. Didn't she realize what a prize she was?

"I'm going to give you the fuck of your life," she said. The confidence in her tone certainly didn't fit the picture of someone with a low self-image.

She climbed on hands and knees up the length of the bed, stalking along his body like a lioness claiming her meat. She took firm hold of the headboard and lowered her crotch to within two inches of his mouth.

Her fresh, delicate aroma settled on him, summoning his tongue. He parted her lips by plowing gently from perineum to clit. She sighed as he completed a circuit around the outside of her labia, working her over with soft strokes until every part of her cunt gleamed with slickness.

"Yes," she murmured.

Tom opened his mouth wide, pressed his lips just inside the halo of her pubic hair, and drew her labia inside, sucking and rolling her flesh back and forth with his tongue. She squirmed with delight, tensing and rocking so much that she accidentally lifted herself out of his mouth.

"Oh, oh," she said urgently, and lowered herself down. "Again."

Tom's cock throbbed. His hips lifted off the mattress and came down again, humping the air. It was a turn-on to see how hot he was making her. It would make the moment when she finally touched him all the better.

He locked his mouth in place and stroked across her clit with the flat of his tongue with slow, broad, clockwise strokes. She arched up, breathing in short, barely audible gasps.

Suddenly her thighs shuddered. Her breath exploded from her in deep, heaving gusts.

Damn, he thought, what a great comer. She put every single one of his previous lovers to shame. He kept licking, making sure not to cut her off early.

She puffed less intensely, in quick, shallow bursts. Tom kept working her, just to be sure.

Good thing. As his hands caressed her butt and the backs of her thighs, he felt the tension rebuild.

She came, even more thunderously than the first time. Tom grinned inwardly and kept up the rhythm.

She came again. And a fourth time, barely pausing in between. Full, shattering climaxes, the kind that knocked most women down for the count.

But she seemed ready for more. This was getting ridiculous, Tom thought. His cock was seeping, begging for attention. He pulled his mouth away.

"My turn," he said.

She smiled wickedly, but to his relief, she immediately did what he was hoping she would. She slid down his body, running sweat-slick boobs along his chest and abdomen, and scooped his hard-on into her mouth.

Tom moaned gratefully. Damn. She was good. She kept one hand against her lips, extending the sensation beyond what her mouth could do alone. She took him all the way in, right to the root, without the slightest hint of gagging. In, out, coordinating with his throbs.

She never *sucked.* Tom's girlfriend back home always did that, and the vigorous suction always numbed him, taking a lot of the pleasure away. But this woman did it just the way he liked, keeping constant but soft pressure on every side of his cock, never clenching, letting his shaft tunnel into her like a piston in a brand-new, well-oiled cylinder.

She quivered. Though she never stopped milking him, never lost the rhythm, Tom was certain she was coming again. Jesus! Just from sucking him?

She ground her slick pussy against his knee and did it again. He could feel the convulsing of her pelvis through the bones of his leg.

Tom couldn't believe this was happening. This wasn't a real woman. This was some kind of dream chick. He was afraid he might wake up.

And if she were real, how the hell could he keep up with her? He could feel his load—thick, heavy, and massive—building up in his tubes. He was going to gush like he hadn't done since high school. Hell—like never before. Like everything he had in him was going to blast out.

She really was giving him the fuck of his life.

His balls rose up tight against the base of his prick, brushing against the palm of her wet hand. She suddenly quit sucking. She sighed deeply, straddled him, and lowered her cunt around his glistening handle.

She pumped him vigorously, pelvic bone riding on his, and his load gathered like a torpedo settling into its berth. To his awe, she shuddered again, the most intense orgasm yet. She laughed, tears popping, and then she looked at him.

His come surged. Their glances locked as he exploded. He pumped three tremendous wads into her, then a fourth, a fifth, a sixth, until he was sure white rivers would flow out of her cunt and down over his balls.

More than ever, it felt like something more than just semen was pouring out of him. The pupils of her eyes seemed to grow larger and larger and larger, until a huge field of glittering black covered him.

He surged up into that blackness and was gone.

Phil, night bartender at the Sheraton lounge, strolled nervously down the corridor beside the hotel security officer who'd come to fetch him.

They knocked at the door to Room 511. A lean, clean-cut man in a business suit issued them curtly inside.

Half a dozen similar types filled the room, writing notes, taking pictures, talking on the phone. A tall, lanky man in a trenchcoat was gazing at a motionless, sheet-draped figure on the bed. He turned and held out his hand.

"Alexis Ward, FBI," he said, shaking Phil's hand with a no-nonsense grip. "Glad you could come."

Ward turned back to the bed and gripped the edge of the sheet. He paused, checking Phil's expression. Phil knew from the chill on his bald head how pale he must look.

"It's not that bad. No blood. You'd almost think he was still alive."

Phil swallowed. The walls of his throat clung together as if he'd tried to eat a handful of lint. "Go ahead," he said, screwing up his courage.

As soon as Ward had pulled down the sheet, hair rose on the nape of the bartender's neck. The body lay arched upward in a pose of erotic intensity, ecstatic grin frozen on its lips.

"This the man you saw last night?"

"Yeah," Phil replied.

"You're sure?"

"Yeah. He had a gin and tonic." The bartender, though worried he might throw up right on the detective's shoes, stared unblinkingly at the body. "He looks so happy."

"Like he was fucked to death?" Ward suggested.

Phil let loose a sudden, alarmed bark of laughter, and instantly reddened, realizing the seriousness of the circumstances. "Yeah. Now that you mention it. What a way to go..."

"This is the ninth case like this I've seen in the past five years," Ward said. "Dreamy smile, not a mark on him. I'm sure there've been others, but those probably got chalked up to heart attacks."

"No shit?"

"They've happened all across the country. They're called the Love Attacks."

"I've heard about them."

Ward flipped the sheet up and stored his hands in his pockets. "Now you know how important this is. I'm told you saw this man leave the bar with a woman last night."

"Yes. I did."

"Did you get a good look at her?"

"Sort of. Bar's pretty dim. She was white, not too tall, dark hair. She had a Kahlua."

"Anything out of the ordinary about her?"

"Well, yeah. There was. I can't explain it—she was just different. Hard to say why, except..."

"Go on."

"When she reached for her drink, I could've sworn that her forefinger was the same length as her middle finger. But I never got another look."

Ward shrugged. "Probably just the way she held the glass." He gestured at a chair. "Thanks. If you'll wait here a sec, I'll schedule a visit for you with our composite artist."

"Sure. Glad to help," Phil said, relieved to be able to leave the death scene. "Say, Detective Ward. Am I in any danger?"

"No," the man answered firmly. "She never strikes in the same city twice."

The new stud fucked Marta like an athlete. She looped her ankles behind his neck and met him thrust for thrust. Her cunt ached delightedly, barely able to contain his thick probe. She came for the seventh time.

Sweat beaded his forehead. As her orgasm peaked and another began to sprout, she knew he couldn't hold off any longer. She captured his glance and held it as he erupted. Intense joy flooded his face as he drenched her snatch, replaced at the last instant by a mild pucker of surprise. Then out "he" came, every last bit of his vitality, funneled into her.

Marta cried out, fulfillment spreading to fingertips, nipples, scalp, and heels. Like a junkie getting a fix, she sagged against the sheet and let the wave break carry her away.

Her lover's body, sapped of both semen and life essence, collapsed across her, though her cunt remained rigidly impaled.

Marta sighed. Already her sense of satisfaction, so incredibly deep a moment earlier, fumed away like steam from a tea cup.

She groaned and rolled over, laboriously hefting her ex-lover onto his back, and peeled herself off his cock. Damn. He'd been a solid catch—healthy, young, enthusiastic, and even skilled. He'd given the kind of performance that would make most women cream just to remember.

For her, it had momentarily salved an itch, lasting scarcely longer than the spark she'd burned out of the one at the Sheraton—was it Tim or Tom?—only a week before.

She'd taken everything they could offer, and it hadn't been enough.

She cleaned herself up and threw on her clothes. The sooner she left, the better. She glanced moodily at the corpse. How many had she left like that?

Marta dreamed of a day when she wouldn't have to murder anyone again. Would that be when she was caught and sent to prison, or when she was too old to maintain the urge?

She doubted it would be the latter. The desire ruled her now. One week. In times past she'd controlled herself for many weeks, sometimes six months. But she'd forgotten how she ever managed to bear it. At this rate, she was sure to be caught.

As she reached for the door handle, she took one last look at the bed. The dead man's smile chipped a flake off the marble block of her guilt. Nothing that sent a man to his grave with an expression like that could be entirely unwelcome.

She didn't *want* to kill. All she wanted was what any normal human woman wanted—someone to love her and fuck her as much as she needed to be loved and fucked. A male version of herself. Barring that improbability, she would take what she could get, as seldom as her willpower allowed.

At an airport rest room, she stripped off her make-up, removed the padded bra, and tucked her wig into her purse. An hour later she walked up to the boarding gate bearing little resemblance to the hotel barfly she'd posed as.

She canted her index fingers so that their extraordinary length didn't seem obvious—second nature to her while on these excursions. The newspaper accounts of the Love Attacks had never described a murderess with such an distinctive physical attribute, and she meant to keep it that way.

The airline attendant checked her boarding pass. The name it contained was not Marta's real one, but as usual, no I.D. was requested. She had false documents just in case. As she passed through onto the jet that would take her back to her apartment, nine hundred miles away, she wondered if she had covered her tracks well enough, and how long she would stay lucky.

Two weeks later, a knock resounded sharply on her front door. Judging by the time of day, she thought it might be a parcel delivery of the exercise equipment she'd ordered, but with inbred caution, she kept the chain attached as she opened the door.

"Marta Kendrick?" asked a tall, lanky man in a trenchcoat. She knew she'd never seen him before, but something about him seemed familiar. "I'm Alexis Ward, FBI."

She gulped and shut the door. What now? She looked toward the sliding glass door leading to her patio. She lived on the second floor, but in her shape it was an easy jump.

"We've got the place surrounded," Ward called through the door panels.

Marta's head filled with images of disguises, false trails, avoidance of hotel personnel, and all the other measures she'd taken over the previous five years to feed her hunger. The tactics had worked only because she had a mundane existence to return to and hide within. If her true identity had been discovered, the game was over.

She relaxed as if she'd just shed barbells from her shoulders, and actually laughed. All day she'd laid about the place in a bathrobe, masturbating every fifteen minutes, knowing that she'd have to take another plane trip that weekend, and would come back with one more grinning cadaver in her memory's hoard.

She tied her robe more modestly about her waist, slid the safety chain out of its slot, and swung the door wide. "How...do you do?" she asked, stepping aside so that Ward could enter.

He strode forward, turned, and faced her.

"I've been looking for you for five years," he said.

"You could say I've been waiting for you," she replied, sighing. Then, cocking her eyebrow, she glanced into the hall.

"Where are the rest of your people?" she inquired.

"I lied. I'm alone."

"But..." The furrow in her forehead grew so deep it felt like a canyon. She'd never heard of an FBI operative confronting a suspected murderess without plenty of back-up.

"The agency doesn't know I'm here. In fact, there's a lot about your case I never put in the file."

She'd so thoroughly conceded defeat, she had to struggle to realize that maybe there'd been no reason to give up.

"If you're not here to arrest me, why are you here?"

"Arresting you would be one way to retire the Love Attacker, but I didn't get myself assigned to your case to let that happen." He lifted his hands out of his pockets. "Like I said, I've been looking for you for five years. I've looked for a woman like you for a lot longer than that."

Her eyes widened. "Your hands," she whispered. His forefingers extended to the same length as his middle fingers. She knew now why he'd seemed familiar. She'd recognized him the way a pair of lions recognize their kinship amidst a serengeti full of antelope. A smile ignited on her face; she fanned it to a roaring grin.

No more guilt, no more victims, just a man who could match her stroke for stroke. Her bathrobe suddenly seemed like far too much clothing.

"Wanna fuck?" he asked.

"For about five days," she answered.

And they did.

Erotica Vampirica
Sensual Vampire Stories

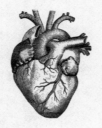

Introduction

Once upon a time, the secrets of the night were well kept, whispered in hushed voices behind curtains of brocade, unseen under cover of darkness. There were things that everyone knew, but that could not be spoken of in polite company. Two of these things come to mind in particular: sex being the foremost one, and evil being the other, as in "evil in your midst." Indeed, to the Victorian mind, sexual lust and evil were close to synonymous, and nowhere is that more evident than in the potent mythic figure of the vampire.

But we are approaching a different millenium now, one full of the bright lights of television talk show studios, the cinemagraphic silver screen, and the glow of the computer connected to the Internet/World Wide Web/BBSs. In twentieth-century America, sex and evil are dragged into the spotlight: on confessional talk shows, in movies about serial killer cum heroes, in valuable fora where the most intimate details of sexuality are discussed among peers on the Internet, and with the scientific study of sex. Now, when sex, evil, and even death, seem so commonplace, what place is there for the dark bearer of secrets we call vampire?

I say it matters not that the bright lights of celebrity, science, and tabloid inquiry have come upon these subjects—indeed, have come upon the subject of vampires themselves. The vampires in these stories play many roles, some to be feared even as the most trusted partner in S/M play can be feared, some to be adored even as the most fleeting of one-night lovers is fondly remembered, some to be desired as the wildness of sexual ecstasy often discussed in the tabloids but rarely acheived in reality, some to be worshipped as dark redeemers whose mercy is as compelling as heaven's in this seemingly godless age. There is plenty about vampires to remind us of the sex we have in the dark, the sex we have perhaps only in our own minds, the sex which touches our deep, primal places which no amount of psychobabble or chic can dull.

To say more would reveal the secrets these authors have so carefully crafted. So from here, I will let their voices speak. It has been a sublime pleasure to assemble these stories and bring them into your hands. Drink deep.

Cecilia Tan
August 1996

Mist Kisses

Renée M. Charles

Every time someone well-meaning tells me, "But male vampires can't have erections"—I just shake my head and whisper "Bullshit," before going on my albeit lonely way.

And not a one of those kindly souls ever has the nerve to contradict me lest they get sucked into an argument none of them really wants to win—or actually learn more about. After all, the notion that the handsome young man they've been talking to really was conceived by a vampire (and not just one of those Gothic-punk bloodletters who hang around eyeliner-required coffee houses, either!) is just a bit . . . *much* for most eligible ladies out there.

Especially the younger ones, the ones you'd really think would be turned on by the whole concept. After all, doesn't the term *dhampir* sound just the tiniest bit romantic, exotic . . . sexy?

I used to think so, back when Mother was still alive, back when her memory of my Father was much clearer, much more detailed—

I first saw him as a shadow, my son; a profile etched in solidified mist against my bedroom wall, each feature sharply defined, even as no one detail was totally clear in my later memories . . . but I knew he was beautiful. And when he came to me, smelling faintly of cinnamon and shaved iron, and pulled me into his arms, I myself was like mist—open to him in all ways, in all places, ready to absorb his essence even as he filtered into my very being.

And when the pain first came, by my throat, and my other places, I knew it for what it truly was, yet felt no fear. . . .

I like to think that Mother passed on still remembering, still reliving each mist-fine touch of his eldritch flesh upon hers. After Father's final kiss of mist, and his penultimate blood-gift, Mother had seen him no more.

Just as I like to think that Father found other bedrooms, other willing occupants, to quell his thirst for blood which came from regions other than the neck. In life, he had to have been one hell of a lover, for in non-life, he was prolific enough to have spawned *me*—

—and Mother swore until her last that I was conceived in the Missionary position, with no need for erotic aids like cock rings or those disgusting vibrating shafts sold in the back of men's magazines.

And, if somewhere down the line another *dhampir* such as myself, a natural born vampire-killer, if you prefer, ever managed to track down my father, let's say that the *dhampir*'s wooden stake wouldn't be the only instrument capable of doing some serious impaling in sight during that particular confrontation.

Mother claimed that my father never needed much prompting from her.

Considering that Father was the original up-and-comer, I still can't quite come to terms with my own lack of success when it comes to the ladies (or the gents— *dhampirs* may be thought to have no real bones, due to yet another misconception about vampires, but that doesn't mean that I'm immune to the sight of a well-veined, proudly erect boner). Oh, I suppose I should be dishonest, lie about my origins, but my mother's people have already been branded liars (and tramps, and even thieves, if you believe that old song Cher used to sing!) for so many centuries, I wouldn't be able to live with myself if I based any sort of lasting relationship on an implicit lie—not to mention a means of perpetuating yet another myth about Gypsies.

After all, should a casual liaison happen to turn into something more lasting, perhaps permanent, and things reach the let's-meet-each-other's-folks stage, the question of paternity can become stickier than a pool of you-know-what dripping from a neatly incised jugular.

So, I choose to be truthful.

And, as a result, I end up being lonely. Most of the time. Oh, occasionally I meet someone who claims to be turned on by my origins, a person who initially treats me like an exotic erotic toy, but once they find out that 1) I'm *not* jelly-boned, or slippery, or all *that* pliant anywhere on my body, and 2) I'm not about to pretend that they are a vampire, just to satisfy whatever little Me-Vampira-You-Van Helsing fantasy that's been playing in their minds since they first saw Tom Cruise put the bite on Brad Pitt in mid-air, I get dumped.

That hurts so much I end up doing what I seem to have been born to do, as ironic as it seems considering the great thing Mother and Father had going and all—I go out looking for the real thing.

Genuine bloodsuckers, Fangers, daughters (or sons) of the night, what-have-you. *Upir lichy, nelapsi, eretiks*—all those aconite-hating folk. All I have to do is be in their vicinity, literally close enough to smell them out, and for me, they're *marked*. Outed, in the most intimate sense. Like being able to smell a woman who is in heat.

Too bad they can't bottle it; the smell of a vampire is perhaps the most sensual fragrance on earth. Start with a base scent of old, dust-dappled lace and linens, that soft almost cloying fragrance, like old crochet-trimmed lawn handkies in a top trunk drawer in your greataunt's attic. Add a pinch of ground iron filings, still warm from the grinding file. Overlay with cinnamon, raw broken sticks of it as well as the talcum-fine powdering straight from the jar. Then, just a touch of milk—yes, for I don't know how else to signify the calcium tang that is subtle, but *there*.

And that odor just wafts off them like sweat would from a human. Most of them are smart enough not to try and mask it; after all, vampires like to seek out their own kind once in a while too. But even if they try and lay on the Chanel or the Brut, it's still there, tweaking my nostrils, as if pulling me along by the nose like a brass-ringed bull.

When it comes to some of them, that odor *does* act as sweat would, seeping into things like clothing, or pieces of paper—

—Especially bits of paper they write upon by hand. . . .

There must have been a good fifty or more small hand-written, typed, and computer-printed notices up on that open-air bulletin board near the bus stop, but as I began to walk past the graffiti-scarred board, I had to stop in mid-stride, booted foot hovering over the pavement, while that invisible ring of scent began tugging the tip of my nose. Over there, among all those irregular bits of paper ("help wanted—" "—room to let" "—non-smokers only") fluttering like impaled butterflies on a killing board in the evening breeze, was an unknowing invitation from a vampire to his or her potential killer . . . all I had to do was get closer to that board, and begin surreptitiously sniffing out the right message.

But as the last New York smog-hazed rays of the sun filtered through the upraised-fingers of the surrounding office buildings and apartment houses, I only had to inhale while standing in place to realize that this was no ordinary vampire I'd located. . . . This one's scent was subtly different, warmer somehow, with a quick-running undercurrent of flowery/tangy grace-notes in the perfumed air.

As I slowly lowered my foot to the pavement, I felt as if I'd become unhinged in time; the lurching cars and taxis around me first went slow, then so fast they merged in a blur of mingled colors, while the street-noises first became hushed, then sped up to a flutter of sound, like the wind-displacing rush of some massive bird above me.

Once I was standing still against this heady mingling of strange sound and sight, I closed my eyes and let that invisible tether lead me to the right message, least the surrounding verbal and visual clutter further distract me from my birth-mission.

Walking slowly, eyes closed, I felt the insides of my nostrils grow warm, fluttery, as I approached the board. A step to the right, and a bird-quick movement of my head to a spot on my left, and I was able to open my eyes. To read:

WANTED: *Model (male) for experimental folklore photographic fantasy series. No experience necessary,* *but must be sensual, open to experimentation, of age, and willing to shed clothes, inhibitions and some body hair during duration of shoot. Race, size, etc. unimportant. Pay neg., starting at $500 for first session, must be available for 1 week shoot or longer. Hours flexible. Call 555-1047 for more info; ask for Tia, or leave message.*

Reaching out a tentative fingertip to caress the smooth surface of Tia's note, I immediately knew that she'd so carefully penned her advertisement not with ink, but with blood of some sort—the tingling buzz from that purely organic colorant was electric under my forefinger.

But whose blood did you use, Tia? I'd felt the dried remains of human blood before, and never had it felt so vital, so . . . ferocious.

If she'd dipped her pen in the neck of one of her conquests, he or she couldn't have been human. . . .

"—please leave your name, number, age and a brief description of yourself after the tone. You have thirty seconds, starting . . . now."

Tia's voice (liquid, fluttery, but with an undercurrent of something much darker, throatier) stopped just as a shrill, parrotlike screech cut through the slight crackle of her answering machine tape, then it was time for me to begin casting my net:

"Johannes Plogojowitz, 555-1847, twenty-two, darkly good-looking, five-eleven, trim build, spiked hair, and I'm a dhampir—if you have to ask about the last part, it doesn't concern you. Bye."

Heart lopping hard and fast against my ribcage, I slammed the pay-phone receiver down hard on the waiting silvery fangs of the upright metal and plastic phone. Even if Mistress Tia had Caller-ID, all she'd get would be a pay phone number. . . . So, even if she wanted to, she couldn't locate *me* (the number I'd given was that of my phone service). I wasn't quite sure why I'd let her know what I was right away, before I'd had a chance to check her out first, see if she was a purely predator type, or one of the more sedate vampiric folk (the kind who preyed selectively, surreptitiously, not aiming to enslave or kill but just survive . . . something like my usual barber over at the Head and Tails salon, who only took what blood she needed from the inevitable—if occasional— nicks and scrapes from her deftly welded razor or clippers; she wasn't a danger to anyone, so I'd never even bothered to reveal myself to her, even if she had taken a few sips from my own neck); perhaps it was the seductive oscillation of her voice, perhaps it was a form of boldness heretofore unknown to me.

A way of daring her to take the bait, rather than simply dangling it in front of her. . . . Or, perhaps, a way of keeping myself safe, should she be too powerful for even a vampire's son to subdue.

Whether she was, indeed, out that afternoon, or whether she'd been sitting there screening her calls, Tia played her own game on me: Let the kid sweat it out.

Not wanting to miss the forwarding call from my answering service, I stayed in my apartment, body tense and selectively rigid with anticipation, wondering about Tia . . . and about my own father, that vampiric *pater* who'd chosen my mother (a shy, timid woman, who still slept in lace-trimmed nightgowns when in her thirties . . . gowns seen nor touched nor lifted up with a muted rustle of fine soft fabric by any live man) for his series of nocturnal trysts.

After that first time, my son, I would lie awake in bed, covers thrown back, gown down and smoothed against my body . . . and he'd come to me, his hair and clothes so dark against the waxy-smooth paleness of his face, his hands, I'd shiver slightly as he gently lifted the hem of my gown, then snaked it up along my legs, my waiting mound of Venus, exposing me an inch at a time to the cool night air, until my bared nipples would contract from the chill and from the light touch of his fingertips lingering there. . . .

And always, he was ready for me, stiff and slippery-cool like a thick icicle, but burning-hot, too, the way ice can also burn against unprotected flesh. His clothes were rough, almost scratchy against my flesh, but each movement became ecstasy, each bit of rubbing fabric yet another pair of caressing rough hands. As if the hands he had weren't well enough used. . . .

Once he was finished, my father would inevitably leave in a swirl of mist, which would rise up and then drift out of her window. . . . But once I was conceived, he no longer came to her, as if already knowing that he'd sown the seeds of his own potential destruction with the last of his mist kisses and caresses.

Mother missed the vampire's kisses, and everything else about him, but to her credit remained stoical, even as her relatives spurned her for bringing forth the spawn of the undead, her illegitimate *dhampir*-son.

What was your father like in life, Johannes? That I don't know, but he must have been a man among men. Whether he was born with the caul or born with two teeth, either a viesci or a upier, or whether he'd merely been a suicide, I never learned. He never spoke. . . . There was no such need. Nor did I think to question him, my beautiful child.

So Mother had raised me proud, yet humble; I was unique, and my natural talent was a useful one in the right circles. But yet, she never instilled the necessary hatred of vampires in me, the hunger to hunt them down at will. Her most lasting legacy—her honesty—was the one which caused me the most trouble.

Nothing about me betrayed my unholy origins, at least outwardly: Just as I'd described myself to the unknown Tia, I was swarthily handsome, with a good body, and a mane of spiked hair that was more tactile than socially terrifying to women, or men. Plus I'd inherited Father's main attribute, his endowment, if you will, so from the outside, I was appealing in both the conventional and unconventional sense. . . . But yet, the circumstances of my origin continued to haunt me, and give me a slightly unclean feeling. Perhaps that was why I continually showered myself, and kept my chest and nether regions shaved smooth, to better *feel* clean . . . even though I'd been with enough people who would've preferred me less sanitary, less sleek.

The kind of people who would've appreciated my father's undead state, purely for the sake of him *being* undead.

Resting diagonally across my daybed, listening to the muffled gurgle of the water in my apartment's radiator, I began massaging my own lower chest and thighs with my right hand (my left was crooked up and under my neck), as I wondered if Tia preferred her victims innocent, or adventurous. *Oh, true,* I reflected, as my hand found and began cupping my manhood, the thumb gently rubbing lazy circles above the uppermost part of my shaft as my fingers kneaded the flesh under my balls, *she* asks *for the openminded ones, but does she turn away the greenhorn who's strapped for cash and willing to do anything to earn some fast?*

If she was the latter sort of vampire, I'd deal with her in the traditional way of my kind. Not out of spite, but out of compassion for my Mother's kind, the unknowing victims. I was still half human.

But if someone were to approach her with a willing, open mind, not truly caring about the consequences . . . does the term live and let live apply to the undead?

The echoing jangle of the phone made me jerk and almost slide off the bed, and my jewelbox ached where I'd inadvertently squeezed myself too hard with surprise. Flipping over onto my belly, I reached across the bed to the handset on the brick-and-scrap wood nightstand, and picked up the receiver, barely able to blurt out a choked "'Lo?"

"Johannes?" Tia's cool liquid voice slid into my ear.

"Tia?" I sat up, cross-legged, and continued to lightly caress myself as she spoke:

"Your service didn't want to give me your number, but I told them it was an emergency. . . . From now on, I'm your Great-Aunt Tia, ok?"

The surpressed mirth in her voice was infectious, yet coolly sexy. I wanted then and there to know what she looked like, if she could possibly be as beautiful as she sounded. . . .

"Johannes, are you still there?"

"Uhm, yes, sorry . . . bad connection, Great-Aunt Tia."

"Oh, good, you're not ticked at me . . . so, I'm speaking to a 'darkly good-looking' twenty-two year old, am I? You sound so young—"

"Not young enough for Calvin Klein's people to be interested. . . . People say I look twenty-five," I countered, as my member grew rigid and warm within the encircling cave of my palm.

"Just as long as you *are* legal . . . I have the same

problem myself, only in reverse—I look much much younger than I am."

Never met a vampire who didn't, Auntie.

"But I'm old enough to be 'willing to shed clothes,' and whatever else you wrote," I replied, as my pelvis began to arch up slightly, with each shuddering wave of impending orgasm. As Tia spoke to me, I began looking around for something to ejaculate into—I may only have a small walk-up student's apartment, in a crappy neighborhood, but it's not a flop-house, and I never leave wads of sticky tissue underfoot (I may be half-undead, but that's no excuse to live in filth).

"Hair too? You mentioned spikes—"

"They grow back."

"On your chest, too?"

"Already gone there . . . and a foot or so below that, too."

"Good, good . . . I love the feel of exposed hot skin under the spotlights . . . and the way it shines."

"Those lights hot enough to make a guy sweat?" I'd only been able to find my peeled-off tee shirt, but it needed to be washed anyhow. Tia's words came to me through an orgasmic fog, sweet soft chirping sounds:

"Until you're dripping . . . but I have plenty of towels on hand. And the camera just adores wet flesh—"

That Tia would live in a loft didn't surprise me, but the swanky neighborhood she lived in was unexpected, in a good way, though. I felt both out of place and proudly intrusive as I stepped from the cab in front of her building: There was a doorman, marble floors and brass fittings beyond the glass doors, and that scent of $200 a bottle colognes and perfumes which, although mingled, still indicated that People of Importance have Trod these

Floors. Not the sort of place where a guy with spiked, stiffened hair, a worn bomber jacket (with personalized adornments like embroidered monkshood patches and little silver and brass crosses and metal-dipped knotted configurations—the latter a reference to the old, old practice of securing vampires with many-knotted ropes) and personally-torn jeans might be known to frequent. Yet all the doorman did was ask me whose apartment I wished to visit, and, once I gave him Tia's name (her surname was something virtually unpronounceable, something that sounded like an island-type word, even worse than my own Plogojowitz), he simply replied, "Last floor, only one apartment there, sir. Have a good evening."

The building was twenty stories high, which gave me plenty of time to think as the elevator chugged upwards. The interior of the cubicle was mirrored, heavy-veined smoked glass that gave my already dark complexion a smoky, hazy cast. Vaguely wondering if I resembled my father, I was more concerned with a connection my mind had finally made while I'd sputtered through the pronunciation of Tia's last name.

During my undergraduate days in college, before I'd earned my BFA, I'd had to take some history courses, one of which dealt with the island nations in and around the Indian Ocean. Many of the words from that course were similar-sounding to Tia's name. I'd not been terribly interested in the class per se, but some footnote in one of the textbooks *had* mentioned Malaysian vampires, so I'd done some digging on my own in the library—

And had come across the *langsuyar* and the *pontianak*, the flying banshee demons of the Malaysian and Java cultures. The same type of female vampire, called the former name in Malaysia, the latter in Java (I dimly recalled that there were infant demon/vampires called by similar names in those countries, but I wasn't dealing with any vampiric infant, not considering how sensual Tia's voice was), but by either name, a creature to give even a seasoned *dhampir* reasonable pause: A nightflying birdlike being, of unearthly beauty when in human form, who had either died in childbirth or died a virgin, whose long, flowing hair masked a hole in her back. There was more to the legends, something about babies that had repulsed me, but Tia *did* stress that her "subjects" be of age, so I had no need to try and dredge up that part of the mythos. However, as the elevator neared the sixteenth floor, I could see the fine worry lines crease my forehead and the skin above my nose—I just couldn't recall what else a *langsuyar* or a *pontianak* actually did to a man. Something other than merely suck the blood from him, that much I remembered, but there was something else, about the hair besides it covering that hole in her back. Something to *do*, that (as the elevator glided up another floor) I-just-couldn't-*think*-of.

But an important something, easily as crucial as the use of the cross, the stake, and the vial of holy water . . . a task that a man had to complete—or die.

That much did come back to mind as the elevator reached the top floor of the building, and the doors slid open to reveal a lengthwise slide of hallway punctuated by a single door. Tia's apartment . . . and her studio beyond.

The doors were just beginning to slide closed again when I finally decided to go for it, to get out of that mirrored box, and step out into that long, narrow hallway. Once the elevator doors whooshed shut behind me and I heard it descend, I regretted my decision, but before I could turn around to press that button, I heard movements behind Tia's door—accompanied by her chirping, lilting voice.

"Is that you, Johannes? The door's open. . . ."

Do or die time, buddy, I chided myself, as I strode up to the door and took the ornate brass knob in hand. It felt coolish in my palm, slightly greasy, yet the deeply etched design seemed to bite into my flesh as I turned it.

The lock gave way easily, silently, and before I had time to think about what I was stepping into, the door swung open, revealing a vista of color and pattern so intense, so vivid, I could almost feel my irises contracting.

Fragments of vegetation, foliage and wide-splayed blossoms were captured in O'Keeffe-like angular slices, their colors and two-dimensional forms trapped on pillows, draperies, woven throws and fabric-covered privacy screens, their hues all the more potent and refulgent because of the contrast between their patterns and the stark, depthless mahogany of the oiled panel walls, and the muted raffia floor mats below my booted feet.

And, beyond those hovering spots and splotches of primary colors, and the surrounding dark walls, were huge, shadeless windows, mere rectangles of city-light-spackled blackness. From the lack of reflection in at least two of those windows, I realized that they were devoid of glass . . . perfect for an owner whose need for flight was literal, not psychological.

It was only when she moved that I noticed Tia herself. Her long, satin-fine black hair hung down like a sheaf of ebony arrows, while her walnut-toned flesh all but blended into the surrounding dark walls, leaving her wraplike draped garment to hover in floral brilliance in the surrounding clash and contrast of florid textiles.

True to those Indonesian legends I half-remembered, Tia was perhaps the most incredibly beautiful woman I'd ever beheld, would *ever* behold. So gorgeous, it was easy to understand why any man would risk his doom to so much as touch her. Every feature was perfectly balanced, with no one aspect of her face dominating the others, and her eyes . . . no jeweler could ever so cunningly fashion ebony into such shining, spherical orbs, let alone fringe them with the most delicate filigree of thick-curling lashes.

"You must be Johannes," she finally said, and her lips parted in a smile that was all rounded plump curves and softly shining ivory teeth . . . none of them the least bit pointed about the incisors.

"In the flesh," I replied, before taking a more careful look at her loft, which I now could see was bisected to form two areas by an extended row of privacy screens. Beyond the fabric-swathed screens, I could make out the glow of banks of photographer's spotlights.

"May I see a bit more of it?" Her voice was simultaneously coy and professional; obviously, she did more than explore her fantasies for a living. For a second, I wondered, *Could I have been wrong about her note, her smell? Might the note have been touched by another vampire?*

"Here?" I pointedly glanced around at the fully-exposed windows which surrounded us.

"Only if you want to give the people in the neighboring buildings the thrill of their urban monster lives," she chortled, in that same birdlike thrill which had so stirred me back in my apartment, before leading me past the row of unfolded screens, and into a roughly twenty-five foot by thirty foot room within the loft which was totally ringed (save for a narrow opening between two screens) by the wood and fabric shields. No profusion of pillows, throws or rattan furniture here; instead all I could see were lit spots, snaking coils of power cords plugged into power strips, and about a dozen or so 35mm cameras, some mounted, some resting on tables or the floor. In the center of this was a raised wooden platform, painted beige, and a nearby box of props like robes, feathers, and what seemed to be some chains of faux pearls and gold links . . . mostly feminine things. Noticing my interest in the box, she languidly brushed her waist-length hair off one bared shoulder, and said, "My day job is doing insert shots for those men's magazine 'letters from our readers' special issues . . . illuminating the unimaginative daydreams of truck-drivers and horny frat boys. Women seem to like posing for another woman . . . and the money is good, quite good. But the work is very numbing . . . always the lacy panties pulled to one side of the crotch, or the rope of pearls dangling between jutting breasts. Hard-core extensions of that lingerie catalog for the man of the house, if you will."

"I've probably seen your work," I said, "but the letters around them tend to be even more numbing . . . so little variety, when you think about it."

Nodding her head so quickly I couldn't help but be reminded of a bird pecking seed, she said, "Just the way I feel about the fantasy images I wish to photograph. Ever notice how the vampire mythos tends to be so similar? Pale guy, vapid girl with the arched neck, and always the flowing cape and the tuxedo? Or the long-haired languid fellow in the foppish day coat and top hat? Out of all the vampires and vampire variants in this world, why must everyone imagine a clone of Lugosi? Or one of those *People* sexiest man alive types? Yet there are so many rich images waiting to be captured. Where are the *Yara-ma-yha-who*? Or the Mexican *Camazotz*?"

Taken somewhat aback, I echoed, "The '*Yara-ma-what*?'"

Tia came closer to me, and, as she slowly began to unzip the front of my butter-smooth leather jacket, explained in that softly chirping, deliciously lilting voice:

"A vampire known only to the Aboriginals. . . . A red fellow, much smaller than you are, with a large head and mouth, toothless, but still able to devour a victim whole . . . no nails, either, just little sucking pads at the end of each digit, so it could climb the fig trees where it lived. The original version wasn't much to look at, but the *concept*— think of a smooth, red-fleshed blood-eater, only half-seen through surrounding foliage . . . hummm, you weren't exaggerating about being smooth-shaven," she concluded, as she continued to lift up my tee-shirt past my already hardening nipples, and then hooked a strong, long-nailed finger around my metal jeans button, until it pulled free of the opposing buttonhole.

Her crooked finger continued its downward arc, as my zipper made a slightly oily *zuuuppping* sound, until the metal made contact with the French-seam of rolled and stitched fabric at the crotch of my jeans. Since I wore no underwear that evening, she could immediately see that I was both smooth-skinned and aroused—both by her, and by the uncertainty of the situation.

Even though she was close to me, close enough for me to feel the radiant heat of her cotton-draped body, I couldn't smell that telltale vampire odor about her. . . . I could smell her deeper essence, that piquant spicy musk, but the perfume she wore (an almost harshly chemical creation with hints of sharp lemon and the undertone of acetone) masked her own natural sweat. But then again, the *langsuyar* and/or *pontianak* wasn't anything like the vampires I'd encountered before, those variants of the Slavic/Romanian/Italian/Polish cultures . . . perhaps she could mask her natural odor? What I'd smelled on her note wasn't typical—

Her fingertips and palms were slightly moist, yet firm as she shucked off my jacket, and then hooked one fingertip into the torn neckline of my tee-shirt, prior to ripping it free of my torso; by the time she'd worked her way down to my jeans, I helped her roll them down my thighs and knees (I could stand the loss of the shirt, but there wasn't any way I could wander home bare-assed should I make it out of this loft alive), then kicked free of my boots and the rumpled jeans.

I was about an inch or so shorter sans boots, but Tia was still a good half a head shorter than me, as she stood there, rather coolly appraising my nakedness, with those same bird-quick jerking motions of her eyes and head.

"You must work out a lot—no? Then you inherited good genes. . . . Your father must've been quite a man before he became a vampire—"

So she'd known what a *dhampir* was all along . . . and for some reason Tia wasn't bothered by the fact.

Trying not to let the dryness of my throat become obvious, I demurred, "My mother said the same thing. . . . Apparently I resemble him. Whether or not he was a Gypsy like she was, I don't know, though."

"Does it matter what nationality the undead are? If they're of the common ilk?" The flatness of that last bit was enough to make more than my ego a *tad* limp and humbled. I actually began to half-cover myself with one dangling hand as she went on, now circling me with a series of short, precise steps, "Did he come to your mother in a haze of swirling mist? While she learned to wait in shuddering, obedient patience for his cool embrace and icy impalement? I'm not even surprised to learn that he was dark-haired. . . . How I would love to see an albino vampire, just for the starkness of it against the night-sky. . . ."

"Like that German guy in *Nosferatu*? Count Orlock was fairly colorless—" I wanted her to get back to discussing known vampires, in the hope that she'd once again begin to speak of those ethnic variations . . . like the Indonesian bird-creatures I still yearned to remember more about, but she instead backtracked to one of her earlier subjects:

"The shiny-pated Count? We'll get to him, in time. . . . First, I want to take advantage of those thorn-like spikes of hair, before I shear them off. . . . He's been captured on film, but I'd still like to continue with the Schreck silhoutte— the Kinski version was so ugly, so inhuman. Perhaps simulated moonlight on a shining domed head. . . ."

She was behind me now, taking in the relative tightness of my behind and the firmness of my calves, as she went on, "We can begin tonight. . . . Your hair is perfect for the pelt of the Yara-ma-yha-who as it is, all I'll have to do is slick it down a bit—"

Rising up on tip-toe, Tia reached up and began flattening my hair with her palms, standing close enough to me that her breasts began to rub sensuously against my lower back, and her hips brushed warmly close to my buttocks. Keeping one hand on the nape of my neck, she moved back in front of me, to get a look at her hairdressing efforts.

I could feel the gel-stiffened spikes rise up slowly once free of her pressing palms, but apparently she liked what she saw, for Tia made a thrilling, throaty noise behind her closed lips, before saying,

"All I have to do is get your makeup on, and bring out the tree props, and we can begin. Stay here, I'll be back in a moment." With that she turned around, and for the first time, I saw her unshielded back-side; her hair formed a thick, undulating curtain across her shoulderblades and upper back, while right under the terminator of that hair-drape her behind swelled out like the twin curves of a fine vase, or a succulent pear. Her draped-gown dusted the bottoms of her firm calves, while her feet were thrust into woven sandal like shoes.

The Indonesian legends always referred to a hole in the back of the bird-vampire, but Tia (*must be a* pontianak, *the name she's using is just too similar, too obvious*—) appeared to be whole—her hair was resting so flat against her shoulders and upper back any indentation there would've been obvious. . . .

Her loft wasn't entirely composed of one open space; I heard a door open and shut before she came back through the narrow aperture between the screens, a bottle of some reddish-orange liquid in hand.

Uncapping the clear glass bottle, she poured some of the viscid fluid onto one palm, then began smearing it onto my upper chest and arms.

"I was expecting an airbrush," I managed to say before she began rubbing the fluid onto my bare skin; immediately I was enveloped in a flush of tingling warmth, the kind of physical rush I only felt when blood touched my flesh. And the odor was unmistakable—it was the same as what I'd smelled back at that bus stop bulletin board.

Using both hands now, Tia coated my chest, my waist, then began working down lower, her smooth-fleshed fingers and palms smoothing the reddish-ochre tint into my skin, so that I was covered with a thin but opaque film of color . . . even my manhood, which she deftly coated, but stopped short of actually massaging to the point of pleasure. Once she'd finished with my legs and buttocks, she worked her way up my back, to my neck and arms, then, finally, smeared the last of the liquid pigment over and around my features, keeping clear of my eyes and lips.

Never before had I ever felt such a kinship to my unknown father; I was all but intoxicated with bloodlust, blood-sated and satisfied beyond any sort of inebriation of the human kind I'd ever experienced. Empowered doesn't quite describe the sensation, but I'd say it was close.

As she smoothed the last of the colorant onto my neck, her fingers lightly circling my Adam's apple, I managed to ask, "Whose blood is this? And what have you mixed in it?"

"To answer your latter question, plain old dry pigment, the kind you can buy in any art supply store . . . as for the former question, let me assure you, I suffer from no disease, so you need not fear contamination through a cut or scrape—"

"It *is* yours?" As the substance dried, it didn't grow cakey or flake off my skin, nor did it make me feel as if my pores were suffocating. . . . The elasticity of it was amazing.

"Oh, not menstrual blood, if that is what you're afraid of. . . . I do selective bloodletting, actually a beneficial process for one with high blood pressure if done correctly. And judiciously." Holding the empty bottle before me, she smiled and said, "All gone . . . and I can't mix more for months. And even then, it takes months to accumulate this much. . . ."

Running my red-tinged palms over my torso, my thighs, I mumbled, "But I'm a painter, and dry pigments never blend this smooth, or dry so well on the skin. . . . How you did it, I have no idea—"

"You're a painter too? Does that interfere with or augment your duties as a *dhampir*?" Not waiting for a reply, she teased with a voice too serious for true levity, "How does one hold a paint-brush in hands with bones of jelly?"

So she'd heard that myth, too. And knew it wasn't true . . . even if *dhampirs* themselves were real. If she could be so forthright, perhaps I could give it a try, too—

"Once we take these Yara-what-have-you pictures, might we take advantage of your loft's decor and try out some of the Indonesian vampires? I've heard they're mainly female, but I've taken some photography courses myself . . . part of the BFA program and all."

"My cameras have timers," was all she said in reply, and her dark eyes were unreadable in the cross-wise glare of the surrounding lights, before she darted between the open doorway between the screens, and came back pulling an artifical stylized tree on a wheeled stand, which she pointed at as she ordered me to crouch down behind the branches, and begin to peer out at her. . . .

Tia took half a roll or so of me affecting various poses behind those lushly covered branches, after placing several filters fitted with theatrical gels over some key spotlights—the greenish ones turned my dyed flesh a brackish brownish-black, while the reddish ones turned my body oddly colorless. All she said by way of instruction was for me to keep my lips over my teeth . . . and once Tia had snapped enough poses to satisfy whatever whim had set this project in motion, she switched off the colored lights, and said, "There's a shower stall in the back of the loft . . . but don't shower off all the color, just your legs and lower abdomen. The next series I want to try involves the Chinese belief that salt has a corrosive effect on the skin of a vampire—the remaining red tint will be enough to suggest flesh scoured raw." As the streams of pulsing hot water cut through the soap I'd smeared on my legs and lower belly (regular pump shower soap, oddly enough), I wondered when Tia would make her real move . . . her inevitable one.

She'd held back on rubbing my father's inheritance, and aside from that brief time when she'd pressed against my back while slicking back my hair, she'd been rather chaste when it came to enticing me any further . . . yet, as I rinsed away the last of the vermillion pigment from my lower body, I distinctly recalled that the *pontianak* always made the first move on the male victim, embracing him, then—

That's where my memory shut down. She'd embrace, perhaps kiss him, and then—total blank. For a *dhampir* who'd been in contact (sometimes close, dangerous contact) with more vampires than years I'd been alive, I kept voiding out when it came to recalling exactly what it was a *pontianak* did—or what I could do to prevent her from doing it. Crosses, garlic and knotted ropes were no good in *her* culture.

"Remember, Johannes, not your whole body, just the bottom—"

Reluctantly shutting off the water, I gently toweled myself off, being careful not to smear the remaining color (*funny, even the steam in the stall didn't make it run*) along the terminus of red flesh/ bare flesh. She'd be smearing me with whatever it was she was going to use to simulate salt, getting close enough to embrace me, perhaps kiss me while I was unaware, and I still had no idea how to stop her from killing me (the latter destiny was usually inevitable with vampires . . . or else I'd become one, which was anathema for a *dhampir*).

"Come, I've arranged the scene—"

Cupping my swinging, drooping manhood with one hand as I walked, I reentered the shooting area, and saw that Tia had been quite busy in my absence: Several Chinese-style screens and pillows surrounded the raised wooden platform, which was now covered with a silken black drape. And she'd dredged out something for me to wear, black satin loose pants, and a dragon-patterned jacket which she said had to remain tossed on the platform floor just under the spot where I'd be reclining. And she had a box filled with a fluffy, yet glittering substance which she began sprinkling inside the jacket on the floor, and then rubbed on my chest and arms; it felt like bath crystals, or some-such feminine thing. As Tia crouched down next to me, she frowned, then said, "Oh, I forgot, your face shouldn't be red . . . just a moment—"

Tia was back within a minute or so, soapy washcloth in hand; once she'd cleaned my face and neck, she leaned back on her heels, surveyed the effect, and said, "I'm not going to try and put on makeup. . . . Against the red, your face seems pale enough. All you need is your hair slicked down more. . . . Here, I have a tube of gel—"

I could feel her breath on my damp flesh as she squirted a glob of gel into one palm, then massaged it over my scalp, slicking down my hair in a glistening mass. As Tia worked, she mused more to herself than to me, "Should've shaved it . . . or left a tail in the back. But this should do. . . ."

Remembering the connection between hair and the *pontianak*, I tried again to trick her into revealing her true nature.

"Shouldn't I keep the hair until after we've done the bird-vampire series? After all, don't the men of your culture have hair? Shiny black hair, like yours?"

Tia smiled, a slightly sad uplifting of her lips. "Oh yes, the men of my land are quite beautiful, with glossy hair somewhat like yours . . . they don't need gel to keep it lying flat, though. But yours looks okay now. Time to begin the shoot." And with that she was up, and positioning herself behind the cameras. . . .

For another half roll, I writhed in mock agony as the salt someone had supposedly sprinkled inside my jacket burned away my skin; it seemed like Tia was more interested in my gyrations than in their faux cause, though, for she began asking me to thrust out my pelvis a bit more, or to rub my hands harder against my chest. . . .

And as I squirmed for her unreadable stare, more of my mother's words drifted into my mind:

Always I knew your father was taking me in with his eyes, as well as with his mouth, his hands. . . . When he was with me, I was the only woman on earth, just as he was the lone man in my universe. And even when he'd dissipate into the mists of morning, while my lips missed his kisses, and my loins immediately yearned for the weight of his body upon them, I knew that in the eye of his memory, he, too, was carrying a part of me with him. Into the pre-dawn air. . . .

When I no longer heard the *whirrr*-click! of her camera, I relaxed against the silky sloe-black draped platform, waiting for her to give me my next set of instructions, or comment on my "performance," what-have-you. But Tia remained silent behind her cameras, simply watching me with those burning-coal eyes. Was she capturing her own mental picture of me, one which was too special for her cameras? *Will a part of me fly with you in the night air, during your feathery banshee journey?*

Not knowing how long she might be content to merely stare at me, while continuing to do nothing overt, I again decided to coax her into some sort of action; rolling over onto one side, I propped myself up on one elbow and began dusting the gritty, micalike "salt" off my torso and onto the platform drape.

"Oh no, I'd rather you didn't do that. . . . It's a form of

soap, and you might as well use it to shower off the rest of the pigment. If you want, I can help scrub it off your back, since it might be hard to reach—"

Finally. Tia's shower stall was barely big enough for one person, so two in there would necessitate at least a little body to body contact . . . and what better way for me to see if she did, indeed have that legendary hole in her back—for wet hair tends to cling much closer to damp skin than dry hair does. . . .

I didn't even wait to shuck off the silken trousers she'd had me wear during the second scenario until I reached her small bathroom, but instead doffed them while still on the platform, and walked naked past her unshaded windows, not caring at all if some bored telescope-wielding yuppie got an unexpected show. Let them wonder why I was half-red and smeared with glittering white granules . . . I couldn't let the opportunity to arouse Tia get away from me. I suspected that the thought of unseen, unknown others enjoying the sight of my body would at least make her jealous, or kindle her heretofore discreetly tamed desire.

Not waiting for her to follow me, I stepped into the stall and turned on a mixture of hot and cold until it was just warm enough to caress the skin without scalding it, and began lathering my arms and chest, letting my thumbs encircle each nipple in lazy, teasing half-circles. I barely heard her open the stall door over the drumming, pounding gush of the water, but I did feel the immediate warmth of an additional body in that tight space—even though she didn't make any actual contact with me. Turning around so that my back was tight against the ceramic corner of the shower, I had to force myself not to reach out to caress and rub her smooth, slightly oily dark flesh, with the taut, gently rounding curves and mounds and valleys of waiting skin; she was just out of the direct reach of the shower spray, but close enough that the most distant droplets covered her in a fine mist which began to run down her body in ever-twisting and crisscrossing rivulets. A mist finer and more transparent than even that of my own father. . . .

Tia merely stood before me, hands half-fanned over the barely tufted cleft roundness of her mound of Venus, breasts jutting out unfettered and darkly nippled under the delicate wings of her collarbone; she said nothing, as if by keeping silent, she'd somehow avoid my inevitable interest in her human form. This sort of behavior was so unlike that of the Indonesian bird-vampires I'd read about. . . . Those women were so eager to capture and—

—emasculate their prey. The memory of what I'd read came back to me even as my own manhood began to reach out blindly toward that fleshy solace half-hidden by her splayed-out hands, but my thoughts weren't enough to cool my ever-building ardor this time; while I'd been bared before her, letting her take in all of my being, I'd been imagining what treasures must be hiding beneath her flowing drape of a gown, even as the worry about her true nature, her true agenda, had kept me from taking her there and then, under the spotlight glare.

Now that she was before me, equally bared save for that glossy curtain of hair, my earlier fears were washed away like the runnels of vermillion pigment which swirled down my thighs and calves, before vanishing in the silvery orifice of the drain at my feet. For too long, I'd let my birth obligation, and my mother's burden of truth and honesty at all costs, beyond all reason, to form a barrier between me and any hope of lasting happiness. Legend said (along with the foolishness about the jelly bones, and vampires not being able to get much of anything up) that *dhampirs* seldom lived long . . . and while I'd been grudgingly buying into the need to hunt those vampires I deemed a danger to others, I'd been ignoring the fact that by doing so, I had no real life, no real purpose, of my *own*. Even my art was little more than busy work, a means of obtaining work-study, and some odd gallery jobs. . . .

Then, something occurred to me . . . something which explained an element of Tia's vampirism that should've been plain to me from the start—

—she was too shy to do much more than look and touch but fleetingly. Which probably explained why she was a *pontianak* in the first place. . . . They *were* said to have originally been women who either died in childbirth—

Tia had no stretchmarks on her taut, slightly concave belly

—or died a virgin. Could she always have been reluctant to do much more than tease, touch glancingly, and engage in mere banter?

"It's too bad we *dhampirs* don't have bones of jelly—it would make washing my back a lot easier," I ventured, holding the bar of soap I'd found in her soap tray toward her. As I suspected, Tia actually backed up a bit, to the opposite diagonal corner of the stall, until I added, "If my being a *dhampir* didn't scare you, will you at least do what you offered to do for me back in the studio? I meant it when I said I couldn't reach back there—"

"Turn around," she said, the softness of her voice belying the brusqueness of her command; once I did so, I almost immediately felt the circular motion of the bar of soap rubbing against my shoulder blades, then the bar moved lower, toward the place where my waist met the beginnings of my hips. Once I was covered with that soapy residue, Tia began using her hands—barely making contact with me at first, then easing the bottoms of her palms into my pliant wet flesh—to massage off the remaining reddish residue As she worked, she began to speak, her lilting voice mingling with the drumming water like the distant chirps of a bird blending with the droning pound of a waterfall:

"I've heard of *dhampirs*, but I had to see one. . . . I'd heard the jelly-bone legends, too. It is a Slavic word, no? A hunter of the traditional vampire of the swirling cape and dangling pendant over a crisp white shirtfront . . . a hunter whose tracks might sometimes be made in the snow, in places where birds flee the coming cold, and the vampires might more easily flee disguised as a scudding mist or dustcloud, rather than a screeching, flapring bat or a fragile-winged moth.

"Not a hunter of things bright-colored and winged, of creatures whose cries rend the night air with an echoing banshee wail. . . . My people know nothing of your kind, perhaps because we *pontianaks* do not give birth. Our Malaysian sisters the *langsuyars* can be captured, and bear the fruit of human seed, but their young do not stalk them or their kind. Why do you do so . . . was your father so unkind to your mother that ridding the world of his kind is so essential to your being?" With her last words, Tia slid one lathered hand around my hip-bone and down toward my pelvis, stopping just shy of my waiting aching penis. Letting her fingertips dig lightly into the flesh of my lower belly, she came closer to me, so that I could again feel the twin pressure of her breasts (this time bared to the puckered nipple) against my back; her breath was a round warm spot on my upper back as she whispered close to my body:

"Or was your father so wonderful, so unapproachable,

that you hunt his kind out of covetousness? Because no
man of flesh can best a man of mist and pure passion?"

Taking one steadying hand off the slippery tiles and
covering hers with it, I leaned back gently against her, and
said, "I never knew him . . . but until the day she died, my
mother couldn't forget him, or stop speaking of him. . . .
Does that qualify as jealousy? Envy?" I tried to guide her
hand lower, but her flesh and submerged bones were
seemingly rooted in that spot. "I never thought of him in
that way . . . and I don't dispatch every vampire I meet. I
don't need to . . . only the greedy selfish ones. The ones
who hurt instead of bring pleasure and life after life for
those who seek it out. What kind are you, Tia? One who
feeds for the sake of filling herself or one who simply
takes? I've heard of your kind emasculating a man—
literally, or figuratively? Will your fingers dig deeper, or
open to form a clawing rake?"

They did neither; instead, she slipped her hand out from
under mine, and then pulled it toward her hidden spot . . .
which, when touched, revealed far more plumpness under
the labia than might be expected—as well as the
unmistakable jutting hardness of a tiny, half-hidden penis
surmounting the well of deeper warmth within. Turning
around, I saw her standing there, head bowed under the
pulsing stream of water, so that her hair hung down in a
glistening straight sheet of purest black . . . where it
formed a natural part, baring her back, and the small,
deeply indented hole which rested parallel to her breasts
on the opposite side of her torso . . . her so overtly female
torso—

From under that drape of hair, she whispered in a voice
so liquid, so softly feminine, I could barely hear it through
the pummel and splash of the waters, "Did your mother
miss your father's kisses? Not merely his manhood, but the

softer mouth-to-mouth contact? The sharing of the teeth and lips? All of my other life, I missed kisses, did not receive them, because I feared their reaction to me, to my male/femaleness. . . . Might they seek me for my beauty, for what was hidden between my cleft soft places . . . or be repulsed by the sight and feel of what they themselves already had? And so I died unkissed, unparted by the body of a man . . . and as a form of eternal castigation, I was reborn as a flighty, feathered thing by night, and a beautiful-beyond-beauty being by day—save when being confronted with a man, any man, of any kind. . . .

"Then my beauty would overcome any reservations he might have about me, my . . . kind, strip away his veneer of civility. My animal nature would speak to the beast within all men, until we culminated that bloodlust with a single, unchaste kiss and embrace—but nothing more could follow. Save for the man's doom—"

"But there's more to it, isn't there?" I asked, stepping close to her, my arms and manhood outstretched, ready to take that glistening brown softness which was her human form into my final embrace. "I've read of your kind, just as I've heard that not all men are doomed by your touch. . . . It's not something instinctive to this *dhampir*, but it's something you can share with me—"

She shuddered slightly at my touch, as we pressed tightly body to body, my erection resting parallel to her not-so-common mons, so that my hardness was cushioned by the springy flesh of her labia/scrotum (a sensation both sensual and unique to any man, *dhampir* or not), but she still would not raise her head to offer me that deadly kiss—so I lifted her head by cupping my fingers under her chin, and stroked the hollow of her throat while bringing my own lips down to meet hers, while running my hand across her exposed back.

Tia tried to rear her head away, but suddenly, she rushed toward me, moving so quickly that once our pursed lips met in a pillowed caress, I began to lose my balance on that soap-slippery tiled stall floor, and instinctively grabbed her hair for purchase before crashing down hard on the unyielding porcelain.

The pain in my buttocks and thighs was agonizing, but the humiliation of landing splayed, limbs akimbo, in front of perhaps the most perfect woman I'd yet managed to meet (regardless of the . . . extras) was far more painful. It was only when I got awkwardly to my feet that I noticed the dark winding ribbon of shining black on one arm, and, even though there was no pain, I told myself ruefully, *Too damn bad my bones* aren't *jelly—must be a compound fracture, to show black blood like that.*

Then as the water continued to pound my body, I saw the streamer of ebony writhe and dance across my skin, like a snake sliding across a shallow puddle, and knew the thread of darkness on my flesh for what it was . . . a small bunch of Tia's hair, pulled out by the roots as I'd slipped and fallen before her.

From above me, Tia's voice was a joyous chirp, echoing with crystalline purity in the small stall:

"Does that bring back your book-reading to you, my lovely *dhampir*? Is that what you'd forgotten in all your fear?"

Holding that thin sheaf of thick black hair in my still-clenched fist, I began to nod dumbly, as the words which had eluded me came back with all the stark clarity of strobe-lights blinking against the night sky:

. . . If a man can grab hold of a single strand of hair while in the embrace of a Pontianak, *and pull it clean from her head, he will avoid the curse of emasculated vampirism and death, and instead live a long life. . . .*

Was it that last bit, about the "long life," that had kept this information away from my consciousness? Was I that jaded with my life as a *dhampir* that I would've willingly risked almost certain death? Or was I seeking a means of becoming the sort of man my father was?

"I yanked out more than one strand," I mumbled, even as Tia bent down to help me get back to my feet, "Won't that negate things?"

"No . . . it just means you have an extra long life in store," she replied sweetly, before reaching for my now flaccid organ and gently caressing it back to a semblance of its former state, "and that I have found myself a workmate . . . someone to fly home to each night. But first—" she reached up and ran the fingers of one hand through my wet but still sticky hair "—I'd love to finish that set of photos, starting with the *Nosferatu* series."

"So you won't be spending the depth of the night flying the skies above the city?" I asked, before grabbing her by the buttocks, and guiding her waiting softness closer to my upright penis; as she wiggled herself onto me (her own small member rubbing against me exquisitely) she whispered, "Even birds stay out of the rain . . . and I intend to stay wet for a long time tonight, and into the morning . . . time enough for the photos tomorrow—"

"As long as we do take a series of *pontianak* ones, before my appearance is transformed—I must see you in bright plumage. . . .

"After tonight, *after* this night. . . ."

And while I thrust myself into her, over and over until we both leaned, shuddering and spent, against the resilient white tiles, I imagined not a man-being of mist and rough pressing garments, but a creature as slippery-smooth and taut as a snake, or a water-being, one which found intense pleasure in the pressing and commingling of the live flesh against like/unlike flesh, and for the first time since the coming of my own manhood, my own time of fleshly experimentation, the voice of my mother, of her singular remembered passions, did not echo in my mind with each movement of our synchronized, slippery bodies, as it had during every other meeting of the flesh my body had experienced. . . . I'd finally bested my father, by moving past my fear of his kind and actually seeking out that object of dreaded desire.

That I'd won my life was a matter of happenstance, a bit of luck aided by elemental water and some soap suds. If I'd never fallen, I'd have never remembered my only means of defeating Tia's curse.

But, as Tia's blood essence warmed against my thrusting flesh, and I now was able to take in the deep, spicy essence of her inner being, her *blood*-being, I decided that even if I hadn't fallen, hadn't been able to save myself, even that one kiss would've made up for all the mist-kisses I'd passed by during my life.

And later, after I'd seen her in her feathered banshee state (a magnificent flutter and bursting-forth of color and fleeting form which quickly vanished out one of the loft's opened windows, only to return at dawn in a momentary blur of brilliant green-fuschia-yellow before Tia once again became Tia), and that shrill night-cry echoed in my ears, I realized that even though I'd won my life, she had indeed captured my former freedom, despite my being kept in a cage with no doors or bars. . . .

Oh, I still carry the dark gift of the *dhampir*. Tia could not sap me of that ability, and on rare occasion (after unforeseen encounters with the blacker members of my father's kind, those night-beings of the dank soul and base desires) it is put to brief, necessary use. . . . But now, my visage is more reminiscent of a comely Orlock than an angry punk Adonis, and, since Tia's showing of her vampire fantasies (along with examples of my own artwork in the same gallery) was so well received, she and I have done continued variations on those themes, so my visits to my own vampire barber have become more frequent. She still sparingly partakes of my own blood essence, just as I keep my own inheritance from her fellow vampire a continued secret.

I've even considered asking Tia to accompany me to the Heads-or-Tails . . . lately, she's been spending more time in front of the camera with me, and has asked me, during our own lovemaking, whether or not the touch of her hands, her breasts, against my bare scalp is truly as sensuous as it seems to be. Before, she had need of that clinging drape of hair, but lately, I haven't been able to get enough of *her* smooth flesh, either . . . and she swears (without my asking her to) that she has no need to seek out other models, other men to embrace and kiss, claiming she does not miss them, or their offered masculinity.

Besides, maybe *she* could ask my barber about what it is to dissolve in a vampiric mist, just so that I might get to the memory of my father without needing to consult my Mother's recitation of kisses mist and missed.

I wouldn't dream of asking my barber myself . . . if I did, I'd just *have* to tell her about being a *dhampir*. Being with Tia hasn't cured me of that little remainder of Mother's influence. . . .

Anyhow, I'm sure Tia will tell me all about it once she does get around to asking her.

With thanks to Willum H. Pugmire

A Most Nonsensical Night

Cypress Quinn

Aristide glared across the nightclub at Tessa, sickened by the way the young one teased and flirted with the mortals who so eagerly surrounded her. The elder vampire drummed his fingers on the polished hardwood of the bar and closed his eyes, trying and failing to drown out Tessa's revelry and the blatant adoration of the mortal crowd. Their thoughts and feelings ricocheted through his mind like firecrackers in a cave:

"I'll do anything to be with you. Fuck me. Make me what you are."

Their sinewy bodies and beautiful pale faces and eerily empty eyes were always the same. Night after night they stalked him; male or female, they all wanted the same thing: him—or more accurately, what he was and what he could offer them. Aristide endured them this night only because he knew his sons lingered among them, and because he hungered for Maya.

He sighed and burrowed deeper into his wool overcoat, realizing he could not hold Tessa responsible for playing to the fawning mortals. Tessa was too young to have experienced the centuries of secrecy and blissful anonymity; all the fledgling had ever known was the desperate attention of public life. Aristide couldn't loathe Tessa just because he longed to be invisible among mortals once again, but he could loathe her maker for creating a fledgling as flawed as she. Simon was wrong to have created her. She had no respect for the dignity and solemnity of eternity.

Aristide drained his goblet and gracefully rose from his seat at the bar. The throng of mortals surrounding him ebbed away, allowing him just enough space to move freely. To his relief, most people still did not dare to touch a vampire without permission. He glided toward the door, suppressing the urge to run, to blur through the bar patrons and the denizens in the streets until he could disappear once again into the isolated safety of his penthouse high above the sparkle of the city.

The door swung softly shut behind him, releasing him from the stifling horde within La Maison Noire, and he deeply inhaled the crisp air of the November night. He turned on his heel to face the breeze, luxuriating in the sensation of the wind ruffling his thick hair, rustling his loose clothing, brushing the soft silk of his garments against his cool, hard flesh. The people on the sidewalk were less intense than those in the clubs. Many of them wanted to join the ranks of the immortal, but outside the clubs, their desire was quieter, less imposing. Aristide hated being the fountain of youth for the vain, so he let the allure and temptation of the city pull him in and carry him down the boulevard, lost in his own memories.

A delicious swell of passion arose in Aristide as he remembered his maker, Constantin, and his eight centuries of furtive undeath: more peaceful places, more comprehensible times, and unsuspecting but no less enthusiastic lovers. Aristide had never known such wanton ecstasy until Constantin brought him over to vampirism—but now the noise and bustle of modern humanity shattered his reverie, and Aristide stopped in his tracks, consumed with carnal cravings and the stirring in his blood. He cast his haunting glance to the club across the street, a flashy place called The Web, knowing he would find Maya there.

Aristide brushed past the layers of flimsy gossamer fabric which curtained the doorway of the club. The heavy smell of mortal blood washed over him, serving only to intensify his hunger. The familiar hush flowed like quicksilver through the room as its occupants acknowledged the arrival of a vampire; the only sound to reach Aristide's ears over the quietly throbbing techno music was Maya's sultry whisper: "Aristide." The nightcrawler focused his pale amber eyes on Maya as she stiffened and rose from her seat to greet him.

Aristide smiled and unbuttoned his overcoat, closing his eyes to enjoy the wash of emotions he sensed from Maya. The usual excitement, attraction, and arousal were there, but her fear had escalated to terror on this night. Aristide could tell she had felt the difference in him, understanding that perhaps the time—her time—had finally come, and her instinctive fear of death was almost too much for her to bear. She was obviously struggling to approach him, but even more than she feared him, she wanted him.

Maya crept slowly toward the vampire. A fine sheen of

sweat broke out on her upper lip, and her nipples hardened
through the tight sheath of her emerald-green velvet dress.
She drew in close enough to glance up at the delicate blue
tracery of veins on the porcelain skin of his neck and face
before she demurely lowered her gaze and fixed her eyes
on the floor between them. Maya remained silent and
motionless before Aristide.

Aristide studied Maya. Her glossy black hair was cut in
a chin-length bob near her face, tapering back to the nape
of her neck where her hair was shaved close to the scalp.
The exposed almond-colored skin on her shoulders and
the back of her neck was smooth over her elegant bones.
A delicate tattoo of a black widow, emblazoned with a
crimson hourglass, perched on the bony protrusion of her
top vertebrae. Aristide sucked in his breath sharply while
he watched Maya's almost-exposed breasts heave. His
desire was cresting, but he relished her tormented silence.
Maya never spoke to her vampire until he indicated his
wishes to her.

Aristide's balls tightened as he slid the icy fingers of his
left hand around her fragile neck, resting his thumb
against her frantically pumping jugular vein. His pulse fell
into dizzying rhythm with the escalating beat of Maya's
heart. Every instinct, his very nature, demanded that he
claim her tonight. The swirling dark dance must begin.

A mocking tinge of gentle laughter invaded his swoon.
Aristide scanned the tide of faces in the pulsing strobe lights
of the club until his glance landed on the source of the
familiar vampiric voice: Giovanni lounged at a table in the
back of the club, nestled among a flock of hopeful victims
like a smiling jungle cat ready to spring at the nearest
helpless animal. The steady, knowing gaze of his deathless
son held Aristide bewitched and awakened memories of
another time and place: Giovanni's piercing green eyes, his

muscular build, the passion of the long-ago night of his vampiric rebirth—all tinged with glimpses of barely-controlled feral rage. While Aristide continued to hold Giovanni's gaze across the crowded club, he pushed his fears about vampiric insanity aside, and their shared memories inspired a new wave of desire to rush through his body.

At Aristide's psychic bidding, Giovanni stood and moved swiftly to his master's side. Aristide's fingers dug slightly into Maya's flesh as Giovanni kissed him deeply, allowing Aristide to pierce his tongue and savor a few drops of his immortal blood.

"Am I to assume that I will soon have a new sister?" Giovanni whispered the question so softly that only another vampire could hear his query. Aristide's blood lust had proven contagious; Giovanni was ready to introduce Maya to the dark embrace of vampirism.

"Yes, Maya has been obedient and patient, and tonight, she will find her reward for such devotion. And I invite you, and Diego if we can find him, to assist me," Aristide purred the words very close to Maya's ear while lowering his hand to the mound of her right breast, massaging the flesh and twisting her nipple between his thumb and forefinger. She gasped and wrung her hands behind her back, a spasm of heat and moisture exploding between her legs. She gyrated her hips gently as Giovanni slid his hand under her dress, pulling aside the lace of her panties to part her moist labial lips and slap her pubis.

A tangible ripple of anxiety and envy spread through the mortal occupants of The Web. Every eye in the room focused on Maya and the pair of vampires, beguiled by their blatant fondling and intensely jealous of Maya's good fortune. The vampires ignored the attention, dismissing the mortal herd and focusing on their fragile plaything, but Maya flushed under the voyeuristic attention.

"You will find my brother in Persephone's Den. Diego finds the harpsichord music there more pleasing than electronic songs," Giovanni paused to drive a finger deep into Maya's slick pussy. "What shall I do to occupy and amuse the lovely Maya while you retrieve our Diego?"

"I trust you not to do anything too dramatic. Escort my beauty to the penthouse and have her ready for our arrival," Aristide breathed the words as much as he spoke them. He delighted in the shudder his statement inspired in Maya. He raised her chin until their eyes met and bent to kiss his anxious victim. Her face showed a mixture of trepidation and wonder. She was proving to be a worthy consort.

"As you wish, Aristide. Don't keep us waiting." The blood lust quickly rose in Giovanni. He inched his finger out of Maya, scraped her clit with his fingernail, and pulled his moistened finger back between her legs, pressing the tight ring of flesh around her anus. Slight smiles inched across the vampires' faces as they watched Maya's blush intensify and spread down her throat to her decolletage.

She gasped again and folded her arms more tightly against the small of her back as Giovanni continued his exploration. He pressed against her back, raising his body and the clingy fabric of her dress simultaneously. Content that the shimmering lace of her thong was exposed to the club, Giovanni pushed his thumb into Maya's anus and slid his ring finger back into her pussy, flicking her clit with the long nail of his little finger. Maya moaned, and Aristide moved both of his hands to her breasts, squeezing and clasping them as his mouth roved over her face and throat, pausing occasionally to kiss Giovanni over Maya's left shoulder. The bar patrons built to a silent frenzy of lust while watching the show, drinks and cigarettes forgotten. Several of the mortals brazenly masturbated themselves or their companions.

Maya pitched her head back, locking her neck over Giovanni's shoulder, when he moved his left hand over her hip and past her garments to more fully massage her clit. This final stimulation plunged Maya into orgasm, and Aristide seized the moment to prick his fangs into her full lower lip. Giovanni curled his lip back, exposing his deadly teeth, poised to tear into Maya's flesh, but Aristide raised his head and hissed a warning to his son. The two vampires locked gazes, Aristide helping Giovanni regain control over his blood lust, before lowering his mouth over Giovanni's snarl and letting Maya's blood trickle out of his mouth and into his son's.

Giovanni savored the warmth of the girl's blood as it flowed down his throat. He removed his hands from her genitals, spanking her before he smoothed her short dress down to cover her again. The Web was utterly still; even the pulsing dance music had ceased during the exhibition. All eyes remained trained on the trio, watching Maya's chest heave as she struggled to regain her composure while the vampires discussed her fate in their inaudible whispers. Aristide and Giovanni reached an agreement and kissed one more time before Aristide dismissed them and they all prepared to leave.

Maya looped her arm through Giovanni's waiting elbow and clung to his side as they passed under the gauzy curtains and disappeared down the street. Aristide also turned to leave, noting the shift in mood within the club. Both of the vampires were abandoning The Web with only one privileged victim. The crowd of mortals despaired, left again with only their fantasies. They would return to the nightclubs the following sunset with new strategies and schemes to attract and seduce an immortal master; their perverse ritual would continue.

Aristide quickened his step and lengthened his stride, until he was rushing past the small groups of people still wandering the boulevard. His thinly-veiled excitement only made him more desirable to the mortals surrounding him. In their eyes, his slender limbs were more serpentine, his eyes more luminous, his veins more spidery than ever before. He was nearly monochromatic, from his finely tailored, neutral-colored clothes to his virtually transparent skin, glowing amber eyes, and the thick crown of auburn-hued hair which swung just past his shoulders. If Death was fabled to be a dark rider on a black steed, traditional mythology had miserably failed to warn mortals about this beautiful pale angel who haunted their sleeping streets. He was charged with the knowledge that he could gorge himself at the throats of any and all of them, but he was focused on the promise of Maya. He would have his fill of her before dawn.

He spotted the classical threshold of Persephone's Den, styled after a Greek temple facade, to his left. A line of supple, mortal flesh snaked toward the door, a cherub chorus of gaunt-faced boys in crisp black jackets and girls with whitened faces, dark hair, and brilliant jewel-toned dresses. They silently pleaded with him: "Take me." All Aristide could smell was their blood.

Persephone's Den was a labyrinth of small sitting rooms and private alcoves tucked away in subtle half-light. Wafts of incense, mingled with the smoke of clove cigarettes, clung to the halos of candle flame on every table. Aristide darted from room to room, finding a handful of vampires, impatiently scanning for a glimpse of Diego. When he heard the strains of harpsichord music drifting down from the second story, he knew Giovanni had directed him to the right place.

Aristide wound his way up the club's somewhat out-of-place spiral staircase and continued his systematic sweep of the Den, following the sound of the harpsichord. He rounded a final corner and found the antique instrument nestled in a large dormer window where Diego sat, playing the masterpieces of the European composers of the 1700s for a trio of transfixed mortals. The humans haltingly fled the loft at Aristide's psychic compulsion, leaving him alone with his son.

Aristide's heart leapt with recognition as Diego launched into one of his earliest original compositions. It was a song he had debuted for Aristide and Giovanni the night Diego joined their vampiric family, but the music halted mid-phrase as Aristide's presence broke Diego's concentration. The younger vampire extinguished the candles on the harpsichord, finished the concoction of blood and wine in his glass, and smiled at his maker. The excitement and hunger in Diego's expression assured that he would participate in Maya's rebirth and made him perhaps the most beautiful creature Aristide had ever seen.

Diego swept his long black hair away from his steeply angled face as he pressed Aristide to his body in a crushing embrace. Aristide inhaled the earthy smells of Diego's hair and clothing before releasing him to run the fingers of one hand across Diego's full lips, down to his smooth chest. Diego had remained closer to Aristide, emotionally and sexually, than most fledglings did their masters—even Giovanni—and Aristide suddenly felt compelled to fuck him before they even left the club, right here in the harpsichord-filled niche, because it reminded him so much of their chamber in Seville. But they had a more pressing, and equally pleasurable, engagement elsewhere.

After a lingering kiss, the pair descended back through the maze of Persephone's Den and walked briskly through the night toward the penthouse where Giovanni and Maya awaited them. Aristide doubled their pace, both in

renewed anticipation and with nagging concern about
Giovanni's blood lust.

Aristide's thoughts seeped into Diego, who scanned
Aristide's tightened face with his spicy brown eyes,
finding a disturbing mix of elation and fear. He grasped his
maker's hand, clenching and releasing his trained fingers
in a comforting attempt to soothe the elder vampire and
speed their journey.

Aristide welcomed his lover's concern, returning a
reassuring smile and tightly clasping Diego's hand. They
strode through the night in uneasy silence until Diego
could no longer bear the tension. Gathering his strength,
he pulled Aristide to a halt and ushered him into the
mouth of a quiet alley.

"You know I share your concerns, but I have to ask one
thing: why did you send Maya off alone with him?" Diego
asked. Aristide momentarily bristled in anger at the
impudence of his beloved son, but hastily realized Diego
was frightened and upset. Aristide sighed, only wishing he
could calm them both.

"I don't know. I can't remember what was going
through my mind. My thoughts were so garbled. The
blood lust. . . ." Aristide hung his head in helpless defeat,
the weight of his words shocking Diego. Diego swept
Aristide into his arms, letting his maker nestle his head
against Diego's neck, burying himself in his son's hair.

Diego held Aristide in silence for several moments
before he spoke again. "Giovanni has been doing a better
job of controlling himself in the decade since our
discovery," he offered.

"Only because he has had to. The humans have been
watching us so closely. The instability is still in him, the
violence, the base ferocity," Aristide said, sounding as
hopeless as he felt.

"We must go. I've heard that the Wrath of God is here," Diego whispered as though afraid the walls might hear him.

"Where did you hear this?" Aristide demanded with alarm, pulling away from his son.

"At the Den. Claire told me the Wrath took her maker two nights ago for violating the Code. Their business here should be finished—maybe they've left town," Diego added.

Aristide could see in Diego's eyes that his son understood what the savage clan known as the Wrath of God could truly do. Aristide smiled and renewed their embrace; Diego had refused to kill a human being since his first night as a vampire so long ago, so he had nothing to fear from the Wrath, and Aristide hoped to shelter Diego from encountering them for as long as he could.

The pair held their embrace for several more precious moments, trying to lose their worries in their mutual love, before separating. They had to reach Giovanni and Maya. Diego turned to reenter the street when Aristide stopped him, wrapping around him from behind, brushing his hair over his right shoulder, and extending his son's left arm. Exposing Diego's wrist, Aristide pressed his fangs into the veins while offering Diego the chance to drink from his free hand. Diego bit into Aristide, sucking gently at the wound before it too rapidly closed under his lips. The rush of vampiric blood, far more potent than the human variety, steeled their nerves in preparation for the remainder of the night. Aristide pulled Diego tighter in his embrace, kissing his neck before releasing him; both vampires hurried back into the street, resuming both their journey and their concerns.

Upon arriving home, Aristide and Diego flew through the building to the penthouse, spurred by their worries over Giovanni and their blood lust. Once over the threshold of their lair, Aristide was shocked and impressed by the sense of control and restraint emanating from Giovanni and relieved to smell Maya, very much alive and so incredibly aroused. The elder vampire grasped Diego's hips from behind and ground his pelvis into his son's buttocks while ordering him to disrobe. Diego obediently complied; his cock hardened as Aristide chewed gently on his neck, moving one hand to press Diego's erection up against his lower belly while teasing his nipples with the other.

Turning his son to face him, Aristide kissed Diego's mouth and stripped off his own garments, leaving the two vampires naked, hungrily kissing each other, and rubbing the lengths of their cocks together. Aristide abruptly broke the embrace and commanded Diego to take his place alongside Giovanni and Maya in the other room. Aristide admired Diego's nude androgyny as he walked away, waiting to move toward the windows until Diego had disappeared down the hallway. Aristide walked into the sitting room where the tattered remnants of Maya's clothing conjured an exciting image of the mortal girl's ordeal. He stared out the windows, gazing at the hypnotic lights of the city, and asked himself one final time if Maya was truly worthy of being his immortal consort. The city offered him no answers, but the smell of Maya's blood and pussy permeating the penthouse did—Aristide ran his fingers down his deadly fangs before slinking toward his waiting slaves.

Aristide hesitated when he reached the sliding pocket doors which separated him from the rest of his coven, bathing in the sexual tension which radiated between him and the three inside the room. He silently opened the doors, closing his eyes as he did so, stepped onto the thick carpet, and closed the doors behind him. The elder vampire breathed deeply of the smells of the room:

burning candles, richly polished leather, and everywhere the essences of sex and blood. A renewed lust ignited in his groin before he finally raised his eyes to survey the room.

Aristide was tantalized by Giovanni's handiwork in preparing Maya for his arrival. His future daughter was fastened into an elaborate harnessing device, and she had obviously been teased and tormented to the brink of sexual excitement. Her legs were spread impossibly far apart, her knees slightly bent, and her ankles were strapped firmly into place in a pair of widely spaced stirrups. Her pelvis was elevated to a height even with Aristide's chest and cradled into a smooth metal seat, anchored there by a tapered latex plug inserted just inside the rim of her anus. The metal platform sloped down from her hips, underneath her spine, allowing her a firm foundation upon which to balance her body at the unusual declination; a roll of leather padding on the plank underneath her shoulder blades arched her spine, forcing her breasts farther up and away from her body. Another leather cushion supported her head and neck at an even steeper downward angle, almost 90 degrees with her back. The buckle of her wide leather blindfold was secured to the headrest so she couldn't move her head in any direction. Her arms hung straight down toward the floor from her shoulders, placing what looked to be almost excruciating tension on the pair of nipple clamps which linked her straining breasts, and her wrists were fastened into leather cuffs at the base of one of the device's steel support posts.

Diego knelt to Aristide's left, bowing his head and letting his flowing hair swirl around his naked body, enticingly veiling everything but his hands wrapped around the base of his genitals, offering his cock and balls to his master. Directly in front of Aristide, Maya's beautifully displayed pussy, wet and gorged with her precious blood, gaped from its nest of black pubic hair, stretched open by a spider's web of dainty gilded chains attached to chain garters high on her thighs which reflected the room's candlelight as brightly as the moisture seeping from her interior. Giovanni completed the right portion of the scene, mirroring his brother's kneeling posture; gently swaying to acknowledge Aristide's presence, the dark son tightened his grip on his deeply colored organ, eager for the ritual to commence.

Aristide's blood lust climaxed—he could no longer resist the current of carnality which electrified his normally serene lair. He approached Maya, choosing to stand between her straining thighs, and motioned for his deathless sons to join him. The girl's harnessed body had become their altar in this primal ceremony, and her willing sacrifice began.

Aristide dug his nails into the flesh of her thighs and clamped his mouth on her pussy, lapping her juices, exploring her folds, plunging his tongue into her aching orifice, closing his lesser teeth around her prominent clit. Lacing his fangs through the fragile links of the chains surrounding her pubis, he used their tension and bite to enhance her pleasure. Diego tugged on Maya's tethered nipples, releasing the clamps with agonizingly pleasurable deliberateness, working her tits with his strong fingers and gentle mouth while his hair brushed tantalizingly across her entire torso. Giovanni simultaneously opened Maya's inverted mouth with his thumbs and plunged his thick cock deep into her throat, letting his balls slap her leather blindfold with every thrust.

Within moments, Maya convulsed with the most intense orgasm of her mortal life, struggling against her restraints and moaning with abandon into Giovanni's crotch as he spent himself into her eager mouth. Maya's head was spinning—from the sudden flourish of release, the attention of her vampiric masters, the intoxication of immortal seed—as the six cold hands released her from bondage, even removing the blindfold, and nestled her down onto the silken cushions of the floor. The trio of vampires kissed and fondled one another just out of her reach, giving Maya time to relax before the next stage of her rebirth.

Aristide leaned away from his sons, allowing Diego's soft mouth to move over his master's chest, before returning his full attention to Maya. Aristide held her gaze as he licked his way up her entire body, pausing to suckle her breast before covering her mouth, raising her face to meet his. Aristide knelt to the right of her head, leaning back on his heels and guiding Maya firmly down his torso before pressing his cock between her warm lips. She eagerly sucked him in long strokes and stretched her body out to meet the touch of the other two vampires. Diego slid into her pussy, thrusting slowly as he faced her on his left side, nestling his head onto Aristide's thigh and nuzzling Maya's throat. The girl rolled completely onto her right side, ·securely planting her right elbow on the floor to support herself, while running the fingers of her left hand through Diego's hair, around to Aristide's ass, and finally past the muscular ring into his anus. Giovanni lay on his right side directly behind her, driving into her tight backside and moving his hand around to her tits. Maya was filled in every way, lost in the rapture of the frantic triple penetration.

The vampires came in rapid succession, feverishly spurting into her and gradually easing out of her pulsing body, watching her spasm in renewed orgasmic bliss.

Maya sank back into the cushions, her eyes closing, when Aristide's teeth broke through the flesh of her throat. She sighed her last mortal breath as Giovanni drank from her left wrist, and Diego pierced her right breast around the nipple. Maya settled into oblivion, and the vampires felt the pounding of her heart slow and then fall chillingly silent. Giovanni and Diego crept away from the girl, heavy with her blood, their hungers temporarily sated, as Maya's life ended. They reclined in each other's arms against the room's opposite wall in a rare moment of intimacy, to watch their master reincarnate Maya to eternal darkness.

Aristide lifted the lifeless girl to his chest and slit the flesh above his heart with the razor's edge of his thumbnail, letting his undead life's blood pour into her mouth. As the gash supernaturally closed, Maya gasped one shuddering breath. The room fell utterly still as her newly immortal heartbeat gained strength. Aristide scooped her up and carried her silently out of the room to his bed.

Behind the closed door of the windowless master bedroom, Aristide drifted back into consciousness after an all-too-short respite, groggily aware of Maya's weight curled on his chest and entwined around the right side of his body. Her flesh was no longer warm against his, and he knew she would awaken soon, full of wonder and awe and questions about her new life. And she would feel the unearthly hunger for living blood for the first time, compelling her to leave his bed in search of prey. He needed to feed as badly as she did. His limbs were heavy, and he felt graceless and cumbersome—almost mortal. But he had expected to feel this way, as he had after making both Giovanni and Diego. In the moments before Maya returned to the waking world, he wondered what she was dreaming in her first taste of vampiric awakening.

Suddenly, she gasped and shoved away from him in shock, sitting straight up and peering around the room with her new, preternatural eyes. Every detail of the room beckoned for her attention, even in the complete darkness. Her head filled with a cacophony of noises: heartbeats, voices from other apartments, cars on the streets below, rats in the underground sewers. Her skin screamed under Aristide's gentle touch as he sought to steady her in the onslaught of her awakening, laughing softly at her wide-eyed disorientation and confusion. She marveled at how loud his laughter seemed, remembering its inaudibility to her mortal ears earlier that evening. She placed her hand over his heart, amazed at the vast textural difference between his hard porcelain skin and the slight, rough scar which marked where she had fed. His heart thundered under her palm, and she watched the scar heal, regenerating and blending gradually back into his smooth chest. A brief inspection proved that her own wounds from the multiple feedings were closed and smoothing into the new quality of her skin.

"Will it always be like this?" Maya asked, jumping at the clarity and resonance of her own voice. Aristide knew that her vague question referred to her senses, her appearance, the unique acuity of knowing that she would live forever beyond death—every aspect of her vampirism.

"Yes, my child. Welcome to our eternity," Aristide paused as Maya's attention drifted away from him to some unknown distraction.

"I have much to explain to you, my darling child. This was all so much easier before our kind was debuted to our human counterparts. . . ." Aristide let his voice trail off as he searched for his next words. He gathered Maya back into his arms, and the couple curled together in a tight embrace while he continued the vital first lessons of her new life.

"You understand the Vampire Laws, do you not, particularly the statute which forbids us from killing?"

"Of course. I read all about it. I work in a bookstore. Or at least I used to, but now my job doesn't seem so important . . . " Maya responded, falling back into silence to let her maker continue.

"Your first hunt must yield a great deal of blood to replenish your strength. In the past, you would have simply drained a human or two, but since we can no longer kill, you will have to take smaller amounts from several mortals before dawn. It will be difficult, but you must stop feeding before your victim's heart falls out of rhythm with your own. You will know when to stop when the time comes, and we will be with you to help you. We all need to feed, but your hunger far exceeds our own, so we will be at your side to ensure that nothing unexpected happens. Do you understand?"

"Yes, I think so."

"The feeling we share, the hunger, will show you what to do, but you must not give yourself entirely over to it because *you must not kill*. Your immortal life depends upon your control. If you kill, not even I will be able to protect you from the Wrath of God."

"The Wrath of God? I thought you didn't believe in God," Maya seemed genuinely confused, and Aristide laughed at the puzzled human expression on her increasingly vampiric facade.

"The Wrath is a coven, like ours—but theirs is a story which will take far too long to tell. I'm hungry, and so is the rest of my coven. We must feed."

Maya hissed in response, and Aristide sensed her recognition of the undefinable stirring in their vampiric blood: blood lust. Aristide thrived on the primal urge emanating from his fledgling. Her need was reckless, uncontrolled, and wild; the master vampire embraced her passion and let the flood of savage emotion overwhelm his own refined and carefully-managed blood lust.

But another, even more familiar sensation radiated between maker and fledgling, and Maya seized the moment to roll Aristide onto his back and mount him, amazing him with her strength and physical prowess as she straddled him. He stared up into her glittering black eyes and remained still beneath her, anticipating her thrill when her newly heightened senses were exposed to the ultimate test: sex. Maya moaned when she felt the tip of her master's growing erection nudge her already pulsing pubis. She let her knees slide further apart on the satin sheets, opening and lowering her wet pussy halfway down his shaft. She stopped there, clenching and releasing her vaginal muscles around his cock, causing Aristide's breath to catch in his throat every time she flexed. He closed his eyes and arched his hips up to her while she held his cock, still only partially penetrating her, and swung her pelvis in slow circles, dragging his stiff organ around with her, slowly lowering herself down to meet his groin, then rising above him again. Maya continued the gradual, rotating grinding until Aristide's eyes rolled open again, and his mouth darted forward, catching one of Maya's hanging, swaying tits.

He sucked eagerly on her nipple, gripping it between his lesser teeth and shaking his head rapidly, feeling her excitement increase as she tightened her inhuman grip on his wrists and rode his cock faster and harder until Aristide began to twitch with orgasm. She growled and drove her pussy down the full length of his shaft, finding his mouth with hers and darting her tongue between his teeth while they thrust together to a shuddering, unearthly climax.

Maya collapsed on top of him, Aristide softening within
her. He knew she was feeling the rapture of her first
vampiric orgasm, so he held her and let her enjoy the bliss
until she broke the silence: "I am now what you have
made me, your daughter and your lover in your own
image. Teach me to hunt."

Her eagerness stirred the hunger in Aristide's veins; he
moved out from under her, and the two rose from the
tousled bedsheets. He took her hand and led her over to
the closet, opening the door to reveal a burgundy satin slip
dress he had purchased for her earlier in the week. He
raised her arms above her head and slid the dress onto her
body; Maya twirled, both to show herself to Aristide and
to feel the material flutter against her thighs. He laughed
at her again as he dressed, then drew her body toward his
and kissed her, remembering that the totality of his
vampiric awakening had become clear to him shortly after
the first time Constantin had fucked him after his rebirth.

As Aristide's mouth continued to cover hers, Maya's
canine teeth throbbed, then elongated into the strong,
curving fangs of a vampire. Her master teased the tip of
his tongue down her new teeth before he pulled away
from her and motioned for her to follow him.

Aristide led Maya through the hall, and Giovanni
emerged from his room behind them, falling in step
behind his newly made sister. Aristide was bombarded by
their thoughts: Giovanni was in turmoil, encased in
mayhem and brutality, and Maya was afraid of Giovanni's
madness. Aristide's own hunger had quieted to a slow
burn, so he used his psychic influence to help balance the
chaos of Maya's fledgling mind, knowing her fears were
warranted. Giovanni's mind quieted as well, allowing
Aristide to lower his guard and relax to enjoy the scant
remainder of the night. The trio filed into the warmth of

the sitting room, Diego rising from his seat by the fire to join them, and without a word, the hungry coven left their lair to hunt among the waiting victims who populated the streets.

The quartet of vampires was a vision to every mortal they passed, hurrying toward Club Vampirica in the last waning hours before the deadly dawn. Aristide laughed again at Maya; she was seeing mortals for the first time in what he knew seemed a sensory riot. He could tell by the dismayed look on her face that she was finding humans to be dull and flat, and the master vampire understood that Maya's disappointment was grounded in her inexperience and lack of mastery over her newfound abilities. To accentuate her first hunt, Aristide continued her lessons by explaining how to properly view the masses of humanity.

"My dear Maya, you must begin by forgetting the means and limits of mortal sight," he said as they turned a corner and drew within blocks of their destination. "In time, you will learn to see beyond mere flesh and bone. You will see the inner features of humans through their unrefined outer husks; their every quality and desire will be laid bare for you—lust, innocence, attraction, curiosity, terror, passion, rage, devotion, love. And perhaps most important, you will recognize in them what our kind may never again possess: a hunger for every breath of life in the face of each mortal's impending death. There is still superficial beauty to be found, but the spirit of living without knowing when that life will end holds the true attraction for me. All three of my children are lovely to behold, but I came to love all of you for your passion and love of life." He paused to let his sentiment sink into Maya's unfolding consciousness before concluding his thought: "And above all, you will see their blood, everywhere and forever."

Aristide smiled at her again as the group stopped in front of the looming Club Vampirica facade. This nightclub was smaller than the rest, and somewhat garish to the eye with all of its overwrought gothic intricacies, but only the best potential victims spent their nights here, and the coven's seductions would be swift, effortless, and strangely fulfilling. Maya would feel the full force of her glamorous sway over mortals here; she could adjust to their adoration and find a truly memorable premier victim. The towering walls of the club's single interior space echoed with the tremor of excitement and awe which greeted the hungry coven; all other vampires had already abandoned mortal company in preparation for the day, so Maya would have her first choice this night.

The vampires scanned the elite throng of men and women in the club, scattering as each of them approached a chosen victim. They were all receiving waves of desire and trepidation from the bar's patrons, and Aristide was pleased when Maya found her first chosen victim: a petite woman with flaming red hair. Maya's quest was over and it was time to seduce and feed.

Diego had already enthralled his selection, a solidly-built man with sharply detailed features and remarkable ebony skin. The vampire leaned against the bar and kissed the man before silently guiding him to his knees. The mortal gazed up at him and opened the vampire's trousers, taking Diego's cock deep in his warm, pink mouth. Diego cradled the back of the man's neck with one hand while stroking the back of the fleshy hand which rested on his cold chest, watching the mortal bob eagerly on his erection.

Far to Diego's left, Giovanni slid his hands up the creamy thighs of a voluptuous blonde, raising her skirt and pressing her naked pussy down on his waiting cock.

She wrapped her knees around his waist as her back reached the wall; Giovanni roughly pinned her, thrusting deeply into her and digging his fingers into her round ass. The girl moaned and breathed heavily into Giovanni's ear while obeying his command to describe to him how the other mortals were reacting to their passion behind his back.

In truth, Club Vampirica regulars were accustomed to displays of this kind; many of them fondly recalled the nights they had been so publicly subjugated and fucked by any number of immortals while eagerly absorbing every aspect of the coven's activities. Diego's expression was serene and tender as his consort continued to fellate him; Giovanni's muscles tensed as his hips pounded vigorously against the young girl. Aristide, clearly the coven's master, was unusually relaxed among all this mortal attention, allowing one man to suck his cock while a woman feverishly kissed and caressed his face in a futile attempt to draw his attention away from the actions of his children. But most eyes, including Aristide's, were trained on Maya, the humans jealously recognizing her as a fledgling experiencing her first vampiric encounter from her newly immortal perspective.

Aristide was glad that Maya herself was oblivious to all the scrutiny. The woman was about the same age as Maya, but she was much shorter and smaller than the vampire, which lent her body the charming innocence of a child half her age. Aristide watched as Maya held her still at arm's length, admiring the copper and crimson lights in her hair, the subtle outline of her fragile skeleton, the rising heat of her arousal, and the intoxicating rush of the blood through every vein in her body. Maya pulled the human into a tight embrace, and the women began kissing and fondling each other.

They kissed deeply, caressing one another's breasts and grinding their still-clothed pubic mounds together, until Maya demanded more, exploiting both her vampiric glamour and the natural tendency of every mortal clubgoer to submit to a vampire's wishes. Maya plunged her fingers past the girl's hemline, probing her wet depths with practiced efficiency. The mortal gasped in delicious response, pitching her head away from Maya and panting; the vampire stared spellbound at the hot blood throbbing through the tautly exposed jugular, enraptured with the knowledge that the vein was meant for her alone.

Aristide in turn watched Maya. Her features and actions were growing more entirely vampiric in the wake of her rising blood lust, and he ignored both the mortal man who was sucking his cock and the annoying woman at his side who insisted on talking to him while she licked his neck and clawed at his upper torso. Aristide caught Maya's attention and held her gaze when she sent the redhead down on her, supporting herself on the edge of a table while the woman parted her legs and raised her dress, burying her face and tongue in Maya's pussy. Maker and fledgling reached orgasm together, their eyes locked on one another.

Diego watched Aristide and Maya come, holding his man gently, resting the mortal head against his shoulder while the man swooned under the vampire's spell. Giovanni had also finished with his victim, spending himself into her and finishing her with his fingers and tongue. The couple was wrapped in each other's arms against the wall, and Aristide felt the intensity of Giovanni's hunger radiate from his dark son.

Aristide acknowledged Giovanni's need, and felt his own hunger peaking. Maya needed to feed as well, so he brushed the woman away from him, claiming the man at his feet as his only victim. Rising from his seat, Aristide silently commanded his coven to follow him, and the quartet escorted their mortal consorts out of Club Vampirica, choosing to sweep them into the dark alley adjacent to the club instead of taking the time to guide them back to the penthouse.

The alley offered them some privacy for this most intimate act, and the coven wasted no time indulging their unearthly thirsts. All four bit deeply into their victims' throats, cleaving the flesh open and sucking eagerly at the escaping rush of blood. Aristide finally focused his full attention on his victim, letting his children fend for themselves and enjoy their meals without his scrutiny, feeling his own strength replenished with the man's life blood, until Giovanni ripped into his reverie. Aristide finished quickly with the man and let his weakened body drop to the ground, wheeling to face Giovanni with an equally alarmed Diego at his side.

Giovanni had fallen victim to his own blood lust, and he was draining the blonde girl to the point of death, opening her throat farther with each draught, oblivious to her screams and struggles. He was no longer thinking in any recognizable way, his mind adrift in a feral tide of blood and death. Aristide moved to physically separate him from the girl, knowing that there would be nothing he could do to protect his son if he killed her in this rage of passion. He hurled her body to Diego and wrestled his son to the ground.

He hovered above Giovanni, waiting for his eyes to clear, and exerting all the psychic assistance he could to calm his son. Giovanni struggled against the elder vampire, but he was no match, physically or emotionally, for the strength Aristide's ancient blood afforded him. After several seemingly eternal moments, Giovanni began to quiet, the haze leaving his consciousness, cringing like a defeated cur underneath his master. Aristide relaxed a bit as well, settling back onto his heels, watching Giovanni transform from a savage creature back into the son that he knew and loved. He helped Giovanni to his feet, both of them trembling from the brief interlude, when a new wave of alarm swept over the coven.

Maya had been in the midst of her first victim when Giovanni's splintered urges had overtaken him and seeped to the other three vampires. Aristide and Diego had reacted the only way they could: Aristide working to calm Giovanni, and Diego ushering the used and imperiled mortals out of harm's way and back into the Club Vampirica in one imperceptible blur of motion. But they had momentarily forgotten Maya, and in that moment, it was too late.

Maya had killed.

She stood in the darkness, holding the dessicated body of the dead girl. When she realized that the rest of her vampiric family was staring at her in shock, she looked down at the girl, clearly seeing what she had done for the first time. And she panicked.

Aristide reeled in shock and dismay. Diego turned away from the pathetic sight of Maya and her lifeless victim and reached out to hold his maker. But Giovanni snapped into clarity with the strength and purity of the vampiric emotions and the lingering cloud of death in the alley and sprang into action. Aristide knew Giovanni had covered up this inconvenient problem before, so he let his son take control.

Giovanni grabbed the corpse from Maya and threw the body over his shoulder. He turned and stared at his coven, urging them to follow him, and they all ran with Giovanni, moving too quickly for anyone on the streets to see them, heading for the waterfront.

They ran for miles along the coast, stealing three tanks of propane from suburban grills along the way, until they reached a desolate cliff, hearing the crash of the waves on the rocky shore far below. Giovanni ripped the valves off the tanks and doused the clothing and flesh of the corpse in the volatile liquid. Without hesitation, he pulled his lighter out of his overcoat and crushed it, letting the splinters of silver fall to the ground. He snapped the flint between his fingers and ignited the girl, backing away from the flames as her dead body burned rapidly to a pile of ashes and charred bones. He heaved the smoking remains over the cliff, watching them fall into the surf so the ocean would clean and scatter the only remaining evidence of his sister's crime.

Aristide, Diego, and Maya stood silently by, watching Giovanni with a mix of horror, admiration, and gratitude until the task was complete. Giovanni turned to them and smiled, drawing closer in preparation for the coven to leave this place and return to the sanctity of their lair. As Giovanni approached, Aristide stiffened, his amber eyes fixed in terror on something behind his dark son. And then, out of the corner of his eye, Giovanni saw the descending Wrath of God.

They were clad entirely in simple black, elegant and evil in their tailored clothes and capes and cowls, and at first appeared as a swirl of pale, disembodied faces and hands, a dance of sharp angles, teeth, and talons. The air sang between the two rival covens, pulsing with the Wrath's ancient power, sinister serenity, and strength of purpose.

"We have come for the fledgling. She must die for her transgression," Isaac said simply in an authoritative but emotionless tone. And on his command, the eight other vampires of the Wrath of God—Gabriel, Isaiah, Michael,

Sarah, Jacob, Rachel, Rebekah, and Elijah—swarmed like the mythical harpies, using a divide-and-conquer plan of attack.

Maya screamed, snapping out of her blood swoon as three of the Wrath herded her toward the cliff, but she was helpless. The Wrath easily overwhelmed her and drained her to the point of death. Michael drove a stake through her heart while Rachel and Rebekah chained her to the ground to await the dawn and final death.

Aristide watched her flail and suffer, but Isaac and three of the strongest members of the Wrath pinned him to the ground before he could move to her aid.

"This does not involve you," Isaac said, placing his hands on either side of Aristide's face, holding him still so their eyes met. Sanguine tears slid down Aristide's face as he continued to weakly struggle against the ancient vampires, even though he knew Isaac's word was law.

Diego edged toward Aristide, shrinking away from Maya and her tormenters, when he came face-to-face with Isaiah. Diego sank to the ground in front of the ancient vampire, sobbing. Diego prayed that once Maya's death sentence was served, the nightmare would be over and the Wrath would disappear as quickly as they had emerged from the night, but then he heard Giovanni howl in rage, and he knew the worst was yet to come.

The Wrath brutally hemmed Giovanni in, surrounding and outnumbering him. When Giovanni saw Maya being fastened to the rocks, bucking on the stake that impaled her heart, he knew she would only suffer briefly before the sun incinerated her body, but that knowledge did nothing to ease his guilt. He tried to look at Aristide, but his maker was trapped by part of the coven, and Aristide's thoughts were too painful to fathom. And Diego, poor useless Diego, was no consolation to Aristide; Giovanni hated his brother's feeble weakness in that moment—that was his last cognizant thought as he plummeted headlong into the final, jagged spiral of insanity.

Giovanni raged against his captors, slashing and tearing at random, lashing out at every target he could reach. His rampage was brief; every vampire on the cliff knew of Giovanni's decline, and they were all prepared for this moment. The Wrath moved in tandem, brushing past their injured comrades and overwhelming Giovanni with the power of age, numbers, and experience. He struggled to the end, even as they drove a stake through his chest and anchored him alongside Maya to face the sun's inferno.

His howls and anguished screams echoed off the cliff as Isaac's followers allowed Diego and Aristide to rise and flee from the threat of the impending dawn, from the horrors of blood justice, from the barbaric clan known as the Wrath of God.

Aristide and Diego dashed through the streets with the first hints of dawn scorching their backs. Diego sobbed and tried to comfort Aristide with shaking hands and a tremulous voice as they reached the sanctuary of the penthouse with scant moments to spare; Aristide hadn't taunted the sunrise like that in centuries.

Diego continued to babble to him—all panic and nonsense—as he undressed Aristide and himself, and the pair curled together in Aristide's bed to sleep through the day. The cool, silken touch of his beloved son eased the slices of ragged agony which still ripped through Aristide's body, heart, and soul as the two sank uneasily into the rejuvenating sleep of the undead.

Aristide and Diego awoke an hour after sunset with hollow, gnawing feelings in the pits of their stomachs. The couple lay in bed together, and Aristide was chillingly aware that his dreams that day had been memories, not flights of imagination—Maya and Giovanni had both fallen cruelly to the true death—when he sensed Isaac somewhere in the penthouse. Aristide and Diego rose and dressed, silently steeling their nerves to meet the angel of death.

Isaac sat alone in the sitting room, majestically perching in the shadows cast by the fire, drinking wine and blood from a crystal flute. Aristide felt like a humiliated child being punished by a disciplinarian parent, a feeling he equated with the foolishness of his long-forgotten mortal life and his first, somewhat awkward decades as a fledgling, when he had struggled at times with immortality under the careful tutelage of his maker. And with somber clarity, the full, crushing reality of his failure where his own children were concerned settled squarely onto Aristide's narrow shoulders. He choked on coppery tears and braced himself again for the impending encounter. Aristide could sense Diego's fear as well, even as Isaac relaxed his posture to greet them. The three sat in deafening silence, staring at each other, until Isaac spoke in his cold, firm voice.

"You know it had to be done. We can ill afford renegades putting all our kind in danger. Do not blame yourselves for what had to happen; we all must be accountable for our own actions. Maya and Giovanni did not blame you, even in their final moments. We bear no animosity toward the two of you, but do not seek retribution against our righteous justice, or you too will feel our wrath." Isaac spoke in a clear voice, his tone both gentle and firm. Isaac's words were neither mocking nor hateful; he simply spoke the truth.

"Our rule is the traditional rule of the immortals, and all vampires agree to live, or to die, by our code of conduct," Isaac continued. "Upon the discovery of our race, I assured mortal officers of the law that my clan would continue to govern the immortal populace; it was the only way to convince humanity to leave matters of blood justice in my hands. We are efficient and fair, and we are inescapable. Aristide, your children had to die so the rest of us may continue to live."

Isaac stood, smoothed his black clothing, and walked toward the mourning vampires. He fondly stroked Diego's hair and kissed Aristide's forehead before he backed away from them and glided to the door to disappear again into the night.

As the door latched, closing Isaac out of their world, Diego took Aristide into his arms and held him. Aristide nestled into Diego, so lost and so sad. He felt guilty about Maya and Giovanni, knowing that despite Isaac's words to the contrary, there surely was *something* he could have done to save his innocent fledgling and savage firstborn son. Aristide eased into silent tears, shaken from his daze by his lover's understanding, and clung tightly to Diego.

"Please know that I will stand by you through anything. I will always be with you, always be a part of you," Diego whispered into Aristide's ear, delicately brushing his lips against the tense muscles of his maker's neck.

"And I am with you forever," Aristide responded, pulling Diego down, deeper into the couch with him. Aristide took refuge in Diego, and decided not to go out this night, perhaps never to go out in this city again. So they huddled together in front of the fire, not speaking, each trying not to think about the previous night, but each heartsick, confused, and more desperately alone together than ever before.

When Michael Comes

Whitt Pond

Night has fallen and Michael is here. I feel him waiting, outside in the storm, confused and frightened like a lost child in a strange place. It has been ten nights since he last left. Setting my book aside, I hurry to find him.

Tonight he's on the roof, tapping frantically on the skylight glass, a pale figure peering in through the rain, his long dark hair wind-plastered across wet skin. He doesn't know what place this is nor what instinct has brought him here, yet in his face I see the anxiety, the fear that perhaps no one will bid him enter, or worse, that no one will be here at all.

Then he sees me. He frowns in puzzlement, staring through rain-streaked glass at a face familiar yet grown strange. And in the faint reflection between us, I see the face too. I smile sadly at another bit of legend gotten wrong. It is not Michael who fears the mirror.

"Michael." I say his name softly, as I unlatch the window, opening the house to the night. It is all the invitation he needs.

He enters, naked and dripping across the layered rugs, eyes childlike yet darkly dangerous as he scans the room. I close the window, wondering what happens to the clothes I give him. And resign myself to not knowing, or really even wanting to know. I do not care. He is here.

I watch him in silence as he moves about the room, graceful in his uncertainty. He pauses at the familiar, wariness slowly giving way to fragments of memory as he touches a polished brass bedpost. An easel. Drawing charcoals and sketch pads half filled. A framed photo.

His pale slender fingers, artist's fingers, linger on the last. The photo is old, but the faces are young and of an age with each other. He looks back at me, trying again to see the face within, and I nod. A name half-forms on his lips and I nod again.

"Yes, Michael. It's me. You . . . you're home again."

I ache at the sight of him standing before me, tall and slender and naked in his bone-white need. He absently brushes his hair out of his face as his eyes, so exotic even in life, flicker with echoes of things remembered. It comes quicker now, the remembering. Or at least it seems to.

The clock on the mantel chimes slowly in odd accompaniment to Michael's steps as he draws nearer. He pays it no notice. Cocking his head left, then right, he tries to puzzle me out. Finally he touches my face, his cool fingers once again seeking the familiar. As always, he is surprised by my warmth.

Slowly, carefully, I take his hand in mine. His eyes narrow with uncertainty, but he does not pull away. Even cold as his flesh is, I have to fight the urge to draw his body to mine.

"Come," I say softly, nodding toward the doorway.
"You need . . . food . . . something warm. . . . Come."
He hesitates a moment, glancing back at the window
and the night. Then he follows. His feet make no sound as
we walk down the stairs. I think of Orpheus and do not
look back.

In the kitchen, I set the warming bowl for body level. In
a different life, we used it to heat the sake. I take one of
the special bottles from the back of the fridge and
immerse it in the rapidly heating water. A memory
touches my lips, of hot sake dripping from his mouth to
mine.

As the bottle warms, Michael wanders through the
house in ghostlike silence, trying to remember. I manage
to slip a bathrobe on him as he stares in puzzlement at
unfamiliar rooms filled with two decades of post-Michael
accumulations. He turns to me, the question on his face.

"It's a different place, hon." I pull the robe closed,
lingering on the sight of his smooth chest, longing to kiss
and lick him there. "You were never here. Not . . . before,
anyways."

He listens, as always. I am never sure if he understands.
Later he does. But at this point, I'm never sure. I lead him
to the living room where bottle and bowl are waiting on
the coffee table, along with a single porcelain cup.

Outside, the storm has settled into a slow, even rain.
Michael stares out into the darkness, thinking what I
cannot know. I open the bottle, careful not to spill a drop
of what comes so precious.

The barest scent is enough. Michael turns, his dark eyes
gleaming as the hunger comes suddenly to the fore, and
quicker than the eye can follow he's at my side. I fill the
cup not quite to the brim and then offer it to him. In spite
of his need, he hesitates.

"Go on, Michael." I push the warm cup into his hands. "It's okay. It's mine. Go on."

He takes the cup, cautiously sniffing it. The aroma is heady, even for me, yet his fangs do not emerge. Not yet. He sniffs again, this time in indulgence, closing his eyes as he savors the moment. Then he drinks and is lost in ecstasy.

I watch, almost in envy, as he feels the warm life flowing down his throat. The redness lingers a moment on his lips before his tongue licks it away ever so slowly with sensual thoroughness.

He drinks again, and I am drawn into his moment by the thought of my blood flowing into his body, filling him with life. My cock begins to swell with another thought, another kind of filling with another kind of life. I refill his cup and savor my own desires.

Even in the dim light I can see the change occurring. His skin is no longer the bone white of delicate china but the slight tan of summer remembered. And in his eyes, the light of memory begins to burn with awareness. And recognition.

He pounces, suddenly, into my arms, his mouth locking onto mine. His lips and tongue are cool as they wrestle with mine, but they warm quickly along with the rest of him as one need gives way to another. Only when I begin to struggle does he remember that I, at least, still need to breathe. He smiles, unabashed, as he reluctantly breaks the kiss.

Miss me? he asks, breathless. His lips do not move, but his eyes speak and somehow I hear him.

"Yes," I sigh, reaching up to pluck a bit of leaf from his hair, smoothing it back into place. "Oh, yes."

My hand lingers, tracing the contours of his ear and we both laugh, remembering when I'd checked to see if they were pointed. He presses against me and again we kiss.

How long this time! He pulls impatiently at my shirt, ripping some of the buttons before finally tearing it away.

I shrug and shake my head, not wanting to release him either. He moans softly into my mouth as he runs his fingers through my chest hair and I run mine around his sensitive nipples.

"Ten," I murmur. "Ten long, pointless days and even longer nights."

His face clouds and I regret my words.

"It doesn't matter." I smile gently into his dark uncertain eyes, then kiss his chest. "You're here now. That's all that matters."

It is what he needs to hear. His face lights up and we begin again, touching and pulling as we fall to the floor. The clothes go quickly and are forgotten as skin presses against skin.

The sound of rain is mixed with the bumping and shoving of furniture unfortunate enough to be in our way as we make love on the floor. We wrestle and roll, chest against chest, thighs grappling, hips grinding for maximal groinal advantage as hands and mouths caress and devour. We are full-body lovers, Michael and I, using everything given us to pleasure and be pleasured. In that, at least, neither of us have changed.

God, you feel good! Michael rises up above me, his eyes aglow as he pins my wrists to the floor. His fangs are quite visible now, sharp and shining with desire. He pushes himself up with his toes, his hips undulating in a way that rubs our urgent genitals together.

"So do you," I moan. His grip is supernaturally strong, and I can do nothing as his cock duels with mine, his hardness rubbing the length of mine between our writhing bodies as our scrotal sacks nestle and bounce, driving our heat ever higher.

Suddenly he relents and it is I pinning him to the ground. I bend to lick the sweet smoothness of his chest, teasing his dark brown nipples with my teeth, and now he struggles in delightful agony beneath me.

The dance of flesh continues in ever shifting turns, each flowing smoothly into the next, the lead being the desire of the moment, the where and how we wish to touch and be touched.

Yesss Michael sighs in silent, close-eyed bliss as we lay hips to face, his hot hard cock pressing past my lips as mine presses past his. Our hands explore each other, touching and guiding as we settle into the familiar ease of the sixty-nine.

I close my eyes, enjoying the trembling in Michael's body as my tongue swirls about his glans, driving him to near frenzy. It is my secret pleasure, the feeling of control, of mastery, that having his cock in my mouth brings. I concentrate on the moment and take my pleasure while it lasts, knowing he will not permit what I miss so much.

Michael responds in kind, teasing and licking me in return as his fingers seek out the secret places in my ass that he knows so well. He is hungry this night for more than blood. I fuck his mouth with mounting need as my balls pull up tight in their sack, excited to bursting by the danger-thrill feel of coaxing fangs along urgent shaft.

Gripping his smooth hips, I take him deeper into my mouth, fanning the flames higher with lips and tongue. Feeling other yearnings. Secretly hoping that maybe, this time, he'll give in.

Please, Michael begs, his need echoed in fevered mouth and urgent hands. *Feed me . . . shoot it down my throat . . . I . . . I need it bad. . . .*

The image triggers it. I cry out, muffled, pressing my hips forward as my cock swells and pumps within him, feeding him at last. The pleasure waves run through me like a hammer as pulse after pulse of hot white life is spurted and swallowed. It is love and life in the most intimate form, and I lose myself in the inexpressible timelessness of the moment.

That was . . . wonderful!

Michael is kissing me, and I realize that we are lying face to face again and that his cock left my mouth unspent. I kiss him back and smile, not intending to bring it up, but he senses my disappointment. He props himself up on an elbow, raising an eyebrow.

Okay, what's the matter?

I laugh. Even without his speaking, I hear the words with all the inflections I remember.

"Why won't you ever let me finish you? I miss it too, you know."

His face grows serious, and he runs his finger along my chest, tracing little patterns in the hair.

It's not the same thing. Your cum is like blood, for me. But my cum is blood, and it could turn you into what I am. Are you ready for that?

I start to answer but hesitate, unable to say yes but unwilling to say no. "Maybe."

Well, I'm not.

Michael stands up and goes to the window, staring out into the darkness, and suddenly the floor is a cold and lonely place to be. I rise, slower, and stand behind him.

You don't know what it's like, he insists, his reflected eyes avoiding mine. *Not knowing who you are, where you are. Not*—he shudders—*not remembering the things you do half the time.*

"Sorry." I put my arms around him and hold him, and he leans back, folding his arms around mine. We do not speak for a long time. When I lead him away from the window, he does not resist.

Upstairs, we lay together in the brass bed—his bed, before—and listen to the rain. I put on some music, songs he remembers, and he listens quietly in my arms. He needs the familiar, and I try to give it to him.

Another song begins and Michael wants to dance. It is our song, the first one we ever slow-danced to. We move to the center of the room and come together again in the moonlight, our naked skin warm between us. Laying our heads on each other's shoulders, we circle slowly in the night, playing that one song over and over again.

Finally the music stops and we do not start it again. We begin to explore each other anew with small kisses and caresses, our yearnings rising insistently between us. I slip my hand lower between his buttocks, looking into his eyes as I probe him gently in opening gambit. He nods, then brings my hand up to his mouth, looking back into my eyes as he teases my fingers with his fangs. I smile, then kiss him deeply as we head back to the bed.

We prolong the anticipation with a bit of mutual voyeurism, Michael laying down on his belly, looking back over his shoulder at me as I oil up my cock. I gazing down at his lean smooth body, his legs spread and ass up in open invitation. Then slowly, we begin.

Michael moans soundlessly as I enter him, arching his back against my chest, a shudder of pleasure/pain running through him. I lay myself across his back as I push in further, entwining my arms and legs with his, taking him, possessing him. It is what he wants. It is what I need.

My cock grows harder and thicker inside his incredible tightness, his sheath rippling the length of my shaft with each stroke. A side benefit of his change.

Having fun? Michael asks playfully, sensing my thought.

"Yeah." I shove deeper and he gasps in silent close-eyed pleasure. "You?"

Our lovemaking grows intense. Driven. Michael claws the sheets in ecstatic abandon as I buck and pump into him, his fangs nipping and teasing my fingers and hand. He has not drawn blood yet, but he will.

"Michael, I . . . "

so good . . .

"I'm . . . "

feels so good . . .

"I'm gonna . . . "

tastes so good . . .

"I'm gonna cum . . . "

inside me . . .

My balls contract in warning. I cry out, ramming my cock in deep just as his fangs sink into my wrist, and suddenly I am filling him, feeding him, from both ends, a double helping of everything. Waves of pleasure shudder back and forth between us, fading away at last and leaving us as one.

Afterward, we talk softly in the remaining night about little things, lover things, things from before. I have learned not to ask about other things, things he either does not know or will not tell. It does not matter. He is here.

Still, in the quiet moments between us when we speak through touch alone, I cannot help but wonder. Why did twenty years go by before he came back? How did he find me without memory to guide him? And above all, why me? I was not his first lover, though he was mine. Neither was I his last. And the time we were together was brief, however large a place it holds in my heart.

It does not matter. I do not care. I am the one he chose to return to. And now he is here. It is enough.

Dawn has come and Michael has gone. The first light of morning falls softly on the empty place beside me in the bed, and I feel the pang of loss and longing once again. I did not see him leave. I never do. The morning comes and he is gone.

I sit up, slowly. There is no hurry to rise. The day has little to offer since Michael's return to my life. Only the night holds promise of something better.

As I dress, one of the sketch pads catches my eye. The cover has been folded back, left open to a new page. I pick it up and turn it to catch the light.

It is Michael's gift, the thing worth a thousand words. He has sketched us together, asleep, my arm wrapped protectively around his chest, his hand clinging to mine. Strength and innocence. Trust and love. And, somehow, a promise of something eternal.

Doing Time

R. Boyczuk

My cell is small, Robin, seven paces from end to end, three from side to side, and sometimes I think it is too small for sanity, too narrow for any sort of clear understanding. You of all people should know what I mean, trapped in your own prison, your own desires. Not like this one, no. But a prison all the same.

Sometimes I imagine us walking together, pacing off the minutes of our sentences, in tandem, you with your small strides stretching to keep up with mine, ten seconds for each circuit, front to back, your soft voice in my ear, patient, more patient than you ever were in our time together, rhyming off the steps with me one by one. I know you are satisfied for now, and with each passing moment I can feel your smile growing inside me like a tumor. For I have done what you wanted,

Robin, spoken in your place: I killed her, I killed her for you.

I hungered for you Robin.

I remember when you first came to St James Town, small and ginger skinned, angry dreadlocks spilling from beneath a loose knit beret of green and gold and black. Looking for *kicks*, you said, in mock high school seriousness (though you were older, far older, in your nakedness), meaning drugs and sex and colorful memories, you wandering among the run down tenements and swirling garbage like a goofy eighteen year old kid, another of Mick's disposable uptown friends, another clean face slumming for a thrill, stepping delicately around the dog turds in your scuffed Docs and meticulously torn jeans. He introduced us, knowing I liked your type, but not for the reasons he ever believed. He thought I was tired of Janine, poor worn out Janine, greasy blonde hair always obscuring half her tired face, shivering and shaking most of the time now when she wasn't high, wobbling down the shabby corridors of crack houses like a top about to fall over. No, I wasn't tired of her, nor she of me, but I knew she might dry up at any moment, and I didn't want to take that chance.

But you. You were young with a whole life ahead of you. A clean-cut kid. I imagined comfortable, middle-class parents for you, a lace-filled room populated with stuffed animals, and your own pink princess phone, me wanting to revel in your freshness, your naive, soap-scrubbed smell, to use you, to taste you, to consume you whole.

You said you wanted kicks.

You were shy at first, as I expected, trembling as you slipped out of your clothes though it was warm and humid, covering yourself with crossed arms, timorously, as if this were your first time. You were beautiful, untouched, a pristine sculpture, and I remember my heart, my blood singing out, my desire rising.

Gently, hesitantly, you placed your hands on me, and I let you roam, drinking in your pleasure, the edge of your excitement, as if all this were new to you, all this unexplored, you touching me, first here, then there, cool fingers around my cock, happy to prolong your pleasure, to revel in my ache one minute more. I directed your hands, your mouth, your legs, and after a time I kissed you, long and deep and slow, rolling you onto your side then on top of you, lightly, lightly, one hand cupping your ass, the other guiding myself into you. For a moment you looked astonished, a sudden exhalation, eyes wide, shocked. Then you saw me again, lifted your legs and bent your knees, locking ankles behind my back, rocking your hips forward until our pelvises ground, bone on bone.

I began to move in a slow rhythm, knowing you were almost ready for me, for both my hungers, slipping more deeply into you, feeling the rush of your blood now, the rhythm of your heart, moving in and out of your lungs with your ragged breaths, touching the edges of your mind, spinning round your memories, ready at last for the final plunge. . . .

But I held myself. I stayed there, lingering at the boundary of your consciousness, mind jangling, catching at one of your thoughts, startled to see this wasn't your first time, that the gentle fumbling was an act only for my pleasure. I hesitated then, surprised.

And before I could begin stealing time from you, your body surged violently under mine, your mind flaring out like a lick of fire, you turning and twisting wildly beneath, a shock of energy desperate for pleasure, every nerve vibrating like a plucked string, shivering with a desire so strong I fell into your rush, your cadence, humming with your faster pace, my other need forgotten, your eyes open and fixed on mine, your small heels beating my back with the rhythm of my strokes, your lips drawn to show the too white tips of teeth, back arched above the sheets, shuddering with the rush, cause you knew, you knew somehow I was experiencing it too, searing across my arms, my chest, a shuddering warmth in my loins, pouring out in staggered waves of you.

I came, I remember thinking in the shattered silence. Dear God, I came.

And then I collapsed on top of you.

Oh, you said after a polite interval, *you're heavy*, pushing at my shoulder till you levered me over, spooning yourself into my side. Then you laughed, face flushed, sweat-slicked breasts against my arm.

Well, you said. *That didn't take long.*

What? I said, numbed, uncertain, my body trembling restlessly at this old sensation, confused, one hunger sated, the other still clamoring in anger and frustration, wanting your moments, your breath, your time. How long? I wondered. How long since I last came?

You were done, weren't you? you said, sliding your fingers lightly over the damp of my shrinking dick.

I said nothing.

You smiled sweetly, sat up, and gave my cock a peck. *Don't worry*, you whispered to it, pretending like you were keeping what you told it from me: *There's always later*, you said. *Plenty of time.*

Did you know, I wondered then. Did you know that I was going to steal a little piece of your life, adding it to mine? You'd have liked it Robin, the best orgasm you'd ever had, all your synapses firing, rocketing you into a state you'd never be able to equal, one that would have left you rubbery-legged and drained and bragging to your friends for months. A good exchange, a kick well worth a few weeks of your life.

I watched you sleep later, small, sharp breasts rising and falling in a steady rhythm, the trace of hip bone beneath skin, a shiny tuft of black hair. Wrapped in the smell of you and me. The smell of soap. Thinking about those moments I could have stolen from you. Might yet steal from you.

Just before midnight I grabbed my stash and slipped out. My hunger became too intense to bear. I didn't like doing it this way, so public and violent, stealing moments from an anonymous body in the street with an offer of drugs or money. But time was creeping up on me, and I knew it was somehow too late for you, had been too late the moment I met you.

Have I ever told you, Robin, it was that night, after my second feeding, in a dark, roach-infested room off Forty-Eight, I shivered, frightened you might be gone when I returned, frightened you might be there.

I have stolen lifetimes from men and women, a few weeks at a time. At the moment of orgasm, when the mind is an incoherent fiery ball, I dash in like a thief and slip out with a week, perhaps two, to add to mine.

But I never thought to ask myself what you were stealing from me.

It wasn't long before you moved in.

For me it is an indistinct time of recollection, a swirl I remember only vaguely. Comings and goings. You showing up and dragging me out to a play or movie, something new, something experimental that momentarily excited you, a different restaurant, sharp new spices, another cheap thrill, anything to try to eradicate the memory of what you insisted was a mundane life. You stayed at my place some nights, left others, until you stopped going back to your parents' place altogether.

How you loved my friends and their vials and foil packets. I lied, told you I didn't have any money, not enough to buy that shit, but you still managed to cadge a pill here, a joint there. Sitting cross-legged on my worn little couch with your prize, puffing seriously, face falling when the effect wasn't what you craved. You falling asleep to dream of what new kicks tomorrow might bring. And I'd carry you to bed, again and again.

Robin, you needed me, I'd convinced myself, even though it was the other way around.

Do you remember how our lovemaking became more intense? Growing progressively longer, draining and exhilarating at the same time, you always wanting to push it further and higher, happy in the pool of the exhaustion afterwards, but never for long. For me it was as I had never imagined it could be. Yet painful all the same. Only part of my completion; a death half felt. Satisfaction and frustration spun together. You see, that hunger only served to fuel my other, the one I could never tell you about. A longing deferred. A desire to steal time from you, from your perfect future. My need was a burning stone lodged in my chest, so intense that after we uncoiled, always afterwards, my yearning would drive me to slip out and wander the streets, careful to make sure you did not follow.

To swallow other less appetizing futures.

I knew often you lay awake as I drifted out, feeling your eyes trailing me to the door. Where did you think I was going? To see other women? It was always an understanding we had, a convenient part of our relationship. After all, you saw other men. And you never asked. Maybe you thought it wasn't cool to speak of it. Or perhaps, I reasoned, you were fearful of losing me, your latest kick.

Me your latest kick.

Did I ever tell you that you were mine?

Once a week a bus comes from the county lock-ups. I stare at the faces as they drift past, appraising them, their expressions calculating and cagey, some desperate, some stupid. First-timers look tired, harried, dark rings beneath their eyes, while the pros are cool and uncaring, flashing smiles at half-remembered faces. Then there are those trailing at the end, slack-jawed, eyes dark and withdrawn, nervous or too stupid to be nervous, unaware that time has already begun to slow with each step.

Once in a while, there is an innocent face. Fresh meat, I think, and later, after they've settled, I offer them a cigarette.

We smoke in silence, leaning against a wall, and I remember you, Robin, your lip caught between your teeth, staring at a magazine, or your tongue twisted with mine, your body tense and waiting, and I think, my God, my God, I'm caught, I'm a captive and I'll never be free.

It was a foolish pang of hunger.

You were supposed to be at work, breakfast shift. A job in the diner around the corner for pocket money. Perhaps it was that moment of weakness for which you never forgave me. Not the act itself, which I think you understood for what it was. Three months together, and I had been careful, to rent rooms, to haunt neighborhoods far away.

You were supposed to be at work.

I shouldn't have brought Janine back to our place. Should never have talked her into our bed, hiding our circle of dampness beneath the sheets from her. A promise of twenty dollars. Me on top, brushing her greasy blonde locks from dispassionate, empty eyes. But I was desperate, so desperate, for her time. . . .

Had you waited for this, Robin, biding your time?

I saw you first in her mind, me sliding into her without thinking, a reflex wrapping myself around her memories, her moments yet to come. She must have seen you over my shoulder, leaning over us, for there you were, Janine's idea of you, a naked woman-child with an odd expression, seeing you in a way, as an image, I no longer could.

Then I felt you pressing against my back, distantly, for my mind was already submerged in hers, your arms and legs covering mine like a sheath, your wetness moist on my leg, urging me on, your mind, your thoughts there too, the three of us now connected by our urgency, our need.

I knew this was what you wanted, more than anything else. The ultimate kick.

I pulled too hard, pulled too fast, and she bucked beneath me with a frenzy you had never matched, could never match, eyes white and rolling in her head, her mind wild with longing and death, spittle at the corners of her mouth, me drinking her in, taking her in monstrous gulps and passing it all to you, a conduit, not careful, not caring, but doing only what you demanded, draining her future away, in her mind until there was nothing but us, together, howling as our hunger became a single roaring beast, dragging her life out, not thinking to stop as we raged through her, only the hunger important, consuming us as it consumed her, ripping from her a deep scream that tailed away.

She passed out, her body quivering, spasming, losing control, the stink of her coiling up around as she soiled the bed. I tried to withdraw, to pull out, but it was too late, for it was you, Robin, you who were in control, compelling us forward, drinking her lives through me as if I were a thin wire, overheating, mind blinding white and burning without remorse, until the feeling was everything, everything, and I remembered nothing more . . . .

When I woke you were gone.

A pounding on the door.

I shivered, sat up, drained and weak, in a pool of congealing blood and vomit. Could any of it have been yours? Janine was propped on the floor next to the mattress, hands arranged neatly in her lap, half my stash tucked between her legs, needle hanging from the bruised flesh of her arm, a trickle of blood dripping from her earlobe onto the crumpled baggie. *Police*, a voice shouted. And you weren't there. I pressed my thumb against Janine's neck, felt nothing. Dead. Sucked dry. A husk. What had you done, Robin? How many lives did you steal from us that day?

Yet I don't grudge you any of it. Not a single minute.

Here in the prison yard I watch men measuring out their lives in small steps, grudging the moments stolen from them bit by bit. They are filled with bitter and unrepentant spirits that I swallow only reluctantly. Sitting on the edge of the bleachers, watching with a detached air the ebb and flow, the comings and goings, trying to imagine it through your eyes, seeing if I can feel the thrill for you, drawing on the parts of you left in me, as you would have wanted to, letting it wash around me, through me, without touching anything inside but you.

Why, Robin? Why didn't you take everything? Why'd you let me live?

I watch them standing in clutches, cigarettes burning down with their lives, and try to let your hunger direct me, perhaps to this one, perhaps to that one, helping me pick the life you'd have wanted.

I have every right to hate you. But I don't. Life is too long for that, and I won't be here forever. I know now that I've only been marking time, stealing bits and pieces of other lives like a petty thief, waiting for you. But when I get out, will you be waiting for me, Robin?

Will you?

Prey

Raven Kaldera

It was early morning when they caught her; earlier than any but the kids ever got up. Val had woken to the sound of Saturday morning cartoons and dragged herself out of bed. The kids, all five of them, were eating dry cereal out of the boxes and throwing some of it at the TV screen. Sherri, their mother, was as sound asleep as Reyna, just like the other nine vampires in the compound. The sleep of the undead. It generally fell to the mortals like Val to deal with Sherri's brood before the afternoon sun began to fade, so Val sighed and fixed them all scrambled eggs and then went out with an axe to collect some firewood.

As she emerged into the morning sunlight, the air was crisp and cold with the impending Canadian winter. None of them were looking forward to the change of seasons, especially Joachim and Rosalinda, who had never been

further north than East LA until three months ago. A bit
of frost shone on the edges of the huge concrete slab
topped with the satellite dish that was all that showed of
their bunker. Val thought about getting a warmer coat and
then shrugged. The sweat from chopping would do her
good, foolish as it was for her to waste her energy on it.
Any one of the vampires, including her lover, could have
done a better job with their superhuman strength. Hell,
Reyna could break the damn logs with a blow of her fist.
Why bother?

Because, she told herself fiercely, *someone has to look
after these babes in the bloody woods. Gotta check those
mines daily, make sure no damn deer run into the
tripwires.* When she'd left the military six years ago to be
Reyna's legal consensual slave ("more appreciation, better
food, and at least you get to sleep with the CO," she'd
joked), Val assumed she'd probably never have to look
over a defensive hardware layout again. Settle down to a
nice life with her mistress, kinky sex, regular whippings,
the gourmet food place just a block away, she thought
sarcastically to herself. And here she was in a compound
in the Northwest Territory worrying about the tripwires
and the fertilizer mines.

It could be worse, she told herself as she rolled over a
frost-covered log and started to hack at it. *At least we're
together.* She paused briefly to touch the collar around her
neck, its steel ring nestled against the hollow of her
throat, and then her fingers slid inexorably to the tiny
marks in the skin just above and to the side where Reyna
had fed last night. It still burned, just a little, pleasantly.
So did her wrists, where she'd been tied to the bedposts.
*Oh my love, I'd do anything to make the world safe for
you, my reluctant predator, my bewildered sadist. Even
live in this godforsaken hole in the ground with five brats*

and a lot of sensitive artists who aren't good for any decent conversation until past three in the afternoon.

They'd made the border just before it was closed to Reyna's kind. Now there were SWAT teams with flamethrowers, and dogs to sniff out the lungs that no longer needed to breathe. News from the States was still sketchy; there were rumors of camps, prisons as solid and impenetrable as the bunker they lived in courtesy of Lance's rich dead lover. Rumors of ovens. They'd heard that the Canadian government was talking about extraditing any noncitizen vampires they might run across; Val hoped against hope that it wasn't true. When they'd come to this compound, no one knew anything about defending themselves. They were all just a bunch of ordinary people who'd died and come back again to find themselves members of the single most discriminated against minority. Not one of them had ever handled a firearm except for Shango, Sherri's ten-year-old son. He'd been in a gang for a year before his mother got beaten to death-and-rebirth by her boyfriend. Val had seen a need, a desperate need for defense, and she was getting to work on it.

That collar around Val's throat had gotten in the way at first. Not many were willing to listen to her opinions on weaponry and protection. ("But she's just a slave, for godssakes!") Joachim and Agba were especially dismissive. Eventually, though, they caught on, and now her nickname among the kids was "General Val." Huh.

She lifted her axe for an especially high chop and someone behind her grabbed it, wrenching it out of her hands. She squawked and spun, and her hand went to the bowie knife at her hip, but it was too late. She was looking down the muzzle of an M-28A2 tribarrel torch gun. Six of them, to be exact. The men wielding them were wearing chameleon suits, designed to blend with the foliage, and were clearly not local rednecks. "Don't move, lady," said the one who was holding her axe.

"Shit," she said softly. *Oh, damn. Here I am, the weapons expert, out here without a fucking gun. How the hell did they get past my tripwires without disturbing a thing?* "Who the hell are you?" she demanded, trying to keep her voice steady.

One of the men came forward, and she held her ground, glaring at him. He completely ignored her question; just pointed something at her and turned a dial. A loud sound came from it, like an uneven drumbeat. She realized suddenly that it was a microphone. "This one's got a heartbeat," the man said in surprise. Then he looked straight at her for the first time, and the mirrored shades focused just under her defiantly lifted chin. Val knew exactly what he was looking at, and watched his expression change. He stepped forward and reached out, as if to touch the glinting steel ring. Val made a harsh sound in her throat and he dropped his hand.

"Are you a slave, darlin'?" he asked. Before she could answer, he went on in a coaxing voice, "It's all right. We're here to rescue you. You won't have to be hurt by those monsters any more. We promise."

Hysterical laughter echoed silently through Val's head. *Bloody hell. Do I dare use this?* She let her lip quiver just a little, let her shoulders droop, looked imploringly up at him as if begging him to tell her it was really true. "Are you . . . the rangers?" she whispered. "I didn't dare to hope . . . "

"Yeah, darlin', we're the rangers," the man said. *Lie,* screamed his body language to Val. "Can you show us where they are? Then we can get you out of here."

She playacted terror—easy for a bottom. "Oh god, don't make me go back there, please," she cried. "Please. I can't—"

"Just in sight of the place," he promised. "Then we'll get escort you out of here. C'mon, darlin'. Help us out."

Yeah. Sure. So I can be a good little hostage. She bit her lip and pointed northeast, the wrong direction. The man gestured with his gun and the others followed as she led them clumsily up the hill to the place she knew was the trap door and the old mine tunnel. And then, at the top of the hill, she pointed west—and when they had all taken their eyes off of her, she slammed a foot into the solar plexus of the leader, yanked his gun out of his hands, and dropped to her belly firing.

They were fast, but not fast enough. *Oh, for vampire reflexes,* Val thought briefly as she mowed them down. Two shots went past her, making a sound like tearing silk, then they were down. Never even got around to firing the grenade launchers mounted on the barrels. *Certainly not regular military,* she thought as she grabbed two more torch guns up off the ground. *Not even well-trained for mercs. Bounty hunters, probably.* A chill ran up her spine. *That must mean we're officially outlaws.*

A whirring sound came from behind her, about four miles back and up the hillside. She rolled over to see and drew in her breath; it was an armored hovercraft coming down the road. The thick trees didn't allow for a direct descent except right over the bunker, where Solly flew in their supplies. She glanced up at the sky and her heart sank. A chopper glinted silver through the trees. With a cry of anguish, she rolled off the hilltop and started running for the bunker with all her might.

Reyna tied her black bandanna around her head with trembling fingers, scrubbing her reddened eyes with the back of her hand. Val was in the main room yelling at Lance and Ellis and Joachim to wake the fuck up. "One hovercraft, coming down the main road. APC with plenum skirts, basically," she yelled. "Get me those damn mine detonators, Dave. I want to see how many tripwires we've got left. Have they reached the maple tree yet? No? Well, set the detonation for that one. Maybe we can head it off at the pass. Don't know how we're gonna take down a chopper, though."

Easy for you to speculate, babe, Reyna said to herself. *You're used to this stuff. I'm an artist, dammit. I never signed up for this. Never. I never intended to get hit by a truck and end up undead. . . . Oh, god, I'm so hungry. If only I'd had a chance to hunt a rabbit or something yesterday.* She ran her tongue over the fangs that had half slid out of their sheaths.

"They're coming?" That was Sherri's voice, high and wavery; Sherri the welfare mother, emotionally brittle and always scared. "They're not gonna fucking take my kids!" she shrilled. "They tried once before, but it's over my dead body!"

"Calm down, Sherri." Lizard's voice cut her off coolly. "We're all in this together. Val, what have you got there?"

"M-28A2's. Splinter guns loaded with two-millimeter caseless rounds," came Val's voice. Reyna heard the weariness in it and her heart moved for her lover, in spite of her own fear and feelings of uselessness. "Looks like one hundred twenty-five," Val continued. "Variable laser focus. Coaxial grenade launchers, forty millimeter, loaded with explosive, or it might be Willy Peter. White phosphorus, I mean. That means we'll burn. But they're stupid. Gear-heavy, but stupid."

Reyna sighed in irritation and shame. *You're the damn top,* she said to herself, *and the damn vampire, and it's your fault we're here. So go out there and do something useful before it's too late.*

She squared her shoulders and went out into the main area. Sherri was trying to quiet her two littlest kids. Lance and Ellis were loading the hunting rifles; Lizard stood by the door waiting silently in her platinum punk haircut. Val stood in the center, slumped wearily under a huge tribarrel gun slung over her shoulder. She seemed very small in her oversized fatigue jacket. Reyna moved to her and put one hand on her shoulder, uncertain. "What can I do?" she asked.

Val focused in on her and the relief in her expression was visible. "I taught you to fire that hunting rifle, right?" she said, and unslung the gun. "You'll do better with this than I will. The weight won't bother you. Just aim and fire; this model doesn't have much of a recoil. Here's the mechanism for the grenade launcher—" She paused for a moment. "Wait a minute. I had two more. Where's the third?"

There was the sound of an explosion outside, and then another. "What the hell!" Dave screamed, tearing off his headset. "I haven't detonated any of the mines yet! That must be the chopper coming down!" He yelled it to a room emptied of half its occupants; Val, Reyna, Lance, Joachim, Ellis and Lizard were all out the door.

Then Sherri counted her kids mentally and shrieked, "Shango! Where's Shango, damn it!"

Shango was standing on top of the bunker, jumping up and down and yelling in triumph like a small brown banshee. His jumps were hindered by the weight of the huge torch gun he had lugged out. Thirty yards away, the chopper lay, burning, on its side. "Jesus!" Lizard yelled. "Get back here, Shango, damn it! Get down or you'll get killed!"

"I done it!" he sang out. "I done it, just like Captain Mario, man! I got 'em, man!"

Ellis shook his head in wonder. "Eleven vampires and they got done in by a ten-year-old. Figures."

Reyna noticed a man running through the woods, away from the burning wreck of the chopper. Willing herself to hold steady, wanting desperately not to fail in front of her lover, she hefted the torch gun and fired. The swift flutter of rounds startled her, and she missed, and would have flushed in embarrassment had the vampirism virus not taken that reaction from her a year ago. Lizard had the second gun and took him down. Reyna cursed under her breath and felt her arm squeezed. Val's touch steadied her.

"Shango!" It was Sherri, come out of the bunker. "Shango, you little brat, get back in here!" Her high voice cracked with fear.

He grinned and waved at his infuriated mother, saluting her with the gun. "I am the greatest, Mom!" he yelled, and then the roar of rounds cut through the air, deep-sixing the satellite dish. *No more cartoons for a while*, flickered in Reyna's mind.

"Hit the dirt!" Val screamed. The hovercraft had topped the rise. Explosions blossomed around them, and the air filled with flying earth and dust. Ellis yelled, hit by shrapnel, and then the mines at the maple tree exploded, overturning the craft and spilling its occupants. They barely made it into cover before it went up. "Hurrah, Dave!" Reyna heard Val call out.

There was silence for a moment, and then a high, thin keening wail rent the smoky air. Sherri was sitting on the bunker top, holding Shango's small, bloody form and sobbing. Reyna reached out from where she lay, tears in her eyes. "Sherri, honey, get back down! It's not safe! Please, honey. . . ." The thin, careworn vampire woman ignored her as if it was merely the wind, keening with her. Blood tears poured down her face, running rivers of scarlet.

Lizard wept too, clutching her gun. "Oh, no, not the kid. Damn them!" Reyna wiped her eyes with the back of her hand, smearing her face with wet redness, and moved forward on her belly to try and get to Sherri before the bounty hunters did.

But Sherri had other ideas. She got clumsily to her feet, a thin figure in her stained housedress. Her lips were peeled back from her teeth and her fangs showed in a snarl. "You took my baby!" she screamed, almost incoherently. Aiming herself at the woods where the invaders had scattered to, she launched herself like a projectile, too fast for human eyes to see. Almost too fast for Reyna to follow, but she managed.

Val found herself lying alone on the ground between two discarded M-28A2's, the dust settling around her.

It was a bloodbath, literally, after Sherri went berserk. They tried to fire a few of the trees, but the frost was too heavy and the flame wouldn't take. They tried to run, but there was no way they could be fast enough. They tried to shoot, but their targets were too fast to take aim. The bloodlust spread like a plague from Sherri to the rest of them, until the trees and the dirt of the trail was splashed red. Reyna found that being hungry was a good thing, at least today. It was a strength. It was a need, and needs fed you.

When she managed to clear her head, she and Lizard and Lance held Sherri down by force and tried to restrain her. She was wild-eyed, foaming and snapping like an animal. "Sherri, it's us!" Lance cried, trying to get her to respond. "It's us, baby, we're not trying to hurt you!"

"Come on, honey, they're all dead!" Reyna gasped, scrambling to hold down the writhing vampire under them. "You've got to stop this now! You've got to come back!" Then, out of sheer desperation, it came to her. She climbed onto the struggling woman's chest, put her face an inch away from the snapping fangs, and *reached*.

It was just one of those things, like blocking a blow instinctively with a move you were never taught. It was as if there was a handle just between the woman's eyes, just behind her skull. Reyna caught hold of it mentally, and held it hard. Sherri slowly quieted, panting. "Calm down now, honey," Reyna whispered. "Slow down. You're okay. Rest now."

Sherri's eyes were glazed. "I'm okay," she said woodenly, lying completely still. She stopped breathing and closed her eyes. Reyna climbed off her chest and looked up to see Lizard and Lance staring at her in mixed awe and dismay.

"What did you—" Lizard began, and then broke off, turning her eye contact away. Lance avoided her gaze similarly, and scuffed the dirt with the toe of his sneaker. Reyna felt rather than realized the shifting of authority, the distance suddenly between them. She sighed, and turned to stumble off into the woods, restless and twitchy with a hunger that blood and carnage had not satisfied.

What am I becoming? she said to herself through a haze of confusion. It was as if the tendrils of her mind had suddenly outgrown her skull and were casting all around her like a net. She felt a flock of crows settling into a tree above her, and as she brushed that touch across them, they rose again and flew off, cawing, she imagined, their derision at her.

"It's over," Joachim said, wiping his nearly-scarlet eyes with the back of his hand. "I got to get some sleep, or I fall over where I stand, man."

"That goes for all of us," said Lance, busy with Ellis's wounds. Lizard had carried Sherri's limp form into the bunker, and she was staying with her. Tamlaine, Dave, Samantha, Jao, and Dorothy had taken Shango's body away to the woods for burial. Val leaned on her new gun wearily, wondering how it could possibly have taken only a few hours.

"Where's Reyna?" she asked again for the fourth time.

"Told you," Lance said, not looking at her. "She wandered off into the woods after they were all killed." He paused, as if wrestling with something. "What happened to Sherri . . . that was real hard on us," he said finally. "I guess we didn't know what we were really capable of."

Val got to her feet. "I'm going to go find her," she said.

Lance looked up, quickly. "Don't," he said. "She'll come back when she's ready. It might not be . . . very good right now."

The dark-haired woman looked at him scornfully. "I know my mistress. She'll need me now, more than ever. Don't even try to tell me what to do. I don't answer to you, Lance."

He shrugged. "Have it your way." Val slung the torch gun over her shoulder and strode off.

It was easy to track the trail at first. The carnage helped. Val shuddered when she saw it. It was coming home to her for the first time that she lived with a houseful of vampires. Then the trail faded away, and she didn't know which way to go. "Reyna!" she yelled. "Reyna!" *Let them all be dead, let there be no more who might ambush her. Or me.* "Reyna, love, it's Val!"

A figure moved in the haze across the clearing in the tall pines. Val lifted her gun instinctively—and then lowered it as she saw the grimy black bandanna. Reyna's eyes were wide, staring, glazed; her face and leather jacket were marked with blood. *Oh, please let none of it be hers,*

Val prayed. Her undead lover looked up, and their eyes met.

Val felt herself seized by the force of Reyna's will. It was like being a fly caught inevitably in a web of fatalism. All thoughts of Shango and Sherri vanished; even the attack seemed like a vague memory. Nothing existed but Reyna, and her need. Val dropped the gun to the dry leaves and walked toward her mistress, walked into her embrace and trembled in her arms.

Reyna pointed upward and Val wrapped her arms tightly about her lover's neck, burying her face in the worn leather jacket. The taller woman jumped up—Val trembled again at the ripple of strength in that motion—and caught a tree branch some fifteen feet off the ground. Hand over hand, she climbed toward the crest, carrying both of them, until she reached a sturdy fork about forty feet up.

Val kept her eyes closed. It was easier not to think about anything, easier to let herself be dragged along inexorably by Reyna's coercive power. The cold edge of a knife blade traveled along her throat, down her sternum, and dipped under her T-shirt. The fabric pulled, ripped, exposed her to the cold air. Her nipples hardened and she shivered, making a discomfited puppy-noise. Her hands were yanked above her head and tied to the tree limb with her shredded T-shirt; the bark scraped against her back. *Don't open your eyes*, said the last small voice of independent ego in her head. *Don't look down*.

Hands pulled off her boots, unbuckled her belt, and removed her jeans, tossing them to the far ground below. Cold. Bark rough against her bare ass. No way to squirm into comfort. The blade traveled down her inner thigh like a concentrated spot of coldness and danger, up her belly, across her breast, back to her throat. Then Reyna's kisses followed the trail it had blazed.

The first bite was just above her left nipple, and she cried out. The wonderful, brutal mouth left her breast, and she heard her lover say, "Shut up." Then it was as if her vocal cords had frozen; she could no more make a sound than she could fly away. The kisses resumed, this time on her inner thigh, her tenderest place. The bite, ah, the pain, the sweetness. Reyna was just teasing her, taking surface bites, not taking the large blood vessels. Hands spread her legs even wider and a warm tongue flicked her clitoris, teased it out of hiding. Lips formed around it and sucked, sucked until she was writhing and choking on the command that gagged her, and then just as she was coming the teeth came down on her. Oh, no, not there, not there, oh no, oh yes, do it, do it, ohhh. . . .

The wave of her orgasm subsided as she strained against the cloth binding her wrists, and then she relaxed, panting, not caring about the rough bark under her any longer. Reyna's nails traveled up her body, those nails that had grown thick and hard and curved since her change, and Val gasped, sucking in her stomach. The sensation changed from light scratching to painful gouging and she thrashed, trying to find purchase with her dangling heels and failing. The pain started to arouse her again, in that terrible, twisted way it always did. She felt a denim-covered knee between her thighs and pressed against it, desperately.

There was the sound of a zipper coming down; Reyna straddled her bare thigh and ground herself into Val's hip. One hand got a purchase in the shoulder-length dark hair that she had forbidden Val to cut short; it felt too good to grab it and force her head back in order to gain access to that tanned throat. The other hand took Val's face by the chin and turned it to receive her kiss. It tasted of blood; the tang covered her lips and chin as Val quested with her tongue. The lips moved to her neck and she felt Reyna's hips buck against her, harder, harder, then a long shove that pressed her brutally into the conifer at her back. Still expecting the violation at her carotid, she turned her head farther and arched her neck, but then Reyna backed off and let go of her, physically and mentally.

Reyna rubbed at her face as she carefully zipped her jeans over her still-sensitive genitals, suddenly exhausted. She realized that she'd only had about three hours of sleep, and the sun was burning overhead. She was sated, though, from other throats; there was no need to take more from her lover. Val, naked and still bound to the tree, began to shiver violently. "Mistress," she said in a small, high voice, "please get me down from here. I hate heights."

Her head was clear; all the spiraling tendrils of awareness seemed to have withdrawn back into her head. Suddenly she realized what that meant, what had happened. "Oh, fuck," she moaned, scrambling to cut Val loose. "Oh, baby, I'm so sorry. I . . . I didn't realize . . . shit, I think your jeans are on the ground down there." What had she done? Somehow the killing, the bloodshed, all the rest seemed insignificant next to the way she had taken Sherri by the forebrain—and then Val.

The smaller woman opened her eyes. "It's okay, love. It won't have hurt them. Just get me down." She rubbed her freed hands, trying to get some feeling back into them. Why hadn't she noticed when they went numb? Wrapping her naked body around Reyna's, they went down the tree. Val felt a rush of relief when her feet touched the brown leaf-covered ground, but her knees buckled when she tried to walk. She was freezing, and her teeth chattered uncontrollably. Reyna wrapped her leather jacket around her and picked her up effortlessly, carrying her toward the bunker like a baby. *This was one of the good parts of the deal*, Val thought to herself. After the fear and the rush of desperate activity, it was good to just curl up and be Reyna's slave again, with no responsibility and no control . . . no control . . . She blinked several times. "Reyna?" she asked in a small voice. "What—"

Her lover wouldn't meet her eyes. "I don't know. I didn't know I could until. . . . Sherri . . . I wasn't quite all there, I guess, I . . . just did it without thinking."

Val gazed up at her, her eyes large and dark. "Did it bring you back . . . what we did?"

Reyna drew a deep breath and let it out. *Remember to breathe. It's so easy to forget when you don't need to do it.* "Yes. It did." She paused to mount the hill. "Thank you. As always."

"Then it's okay." Val turned her head and buried it again in her lover's shoulder.

Reyna's voice was anguished. "Val! No, it's not okay! I didn't— I mean, consent has no meaning if I can just—"

"Stop that." Val sounded tired. "Put me down, okay? I think I can walk now." This time, when her feet touched dirt, her legs seemed ready to bear her, but she leaned against Reyna for a moment longer. "I don't have time for guilt about my choices, and neither do you," she said quietly. "We've come this far. We'll get through whatever we need to. So stop worrying and get us both home; we can experiment with this new thing tomorrow."

Reyna stood still, stroking her lover's hair. "That's all? You trust me that much?"

"I trust you. It's the only thing I do trust in this damn world. Let's get home, okay? I think they're all wondering if you've gone berserk like Sherri and run off."

She let out a shaky laugh. "No, thanks to you. I'm all right. I'll always be all right in the end. Thanks to you."

Val took a step and realized that her boots were still somewhere in the woods. Sharp twigs crunched under her bare feet. "Maybe you ought to carry me back after all, love. Mistress." She rubbed her head against Reyna's chest. "Please? May I have the privilege?"

"You've earned that privilege forever." The vampire swept her lover into her arms again and set off down the path. "You know," she added. "if you stopped loving me, I'd be devastated. This leash has two ends."

"I know," said Val. It seemed the sensible thing to admit it. "I know."

Desolate Dance

Steve Eller

"This is important to you, this . . . image?"

"What else is there?"

I pondered her strange question while she undressed. Truth, I thought, might be an appropriate answer. Perhaps reality, as well.

And I wondered why would she want this elaborate masquerade, when she had the soft warmth of her flesh, the taut strength in her slender limbs. Why would she desire so desperately to create such an illusion when she possessed the true moment in all its stark beauty?

As I watched, she slipped the ragged shirt over her head. The dark fabric fluttered to the floor, melting into shadow. Silently, she drifted close to me and placed her tender palms against my chest. She pushed me, gently, and I allowed myself to be moved back until I felt

something solid behind me. Turning my head, I saw a
sheet of glass rising all the way to the darkened rafters of
the ceiling. I pressed my shoulders against the icy pane,
gazing at her as she backed away, so slowly. Her glittering
eyes remained locked on me the entire time. It seemed
endless.

Twisting strands of moonlight glistened across her bare
skin as she stood before me. The sight made me miss a
breath. Radiant and unashamed, I thought. Her shoulders
gleamed like pale marble. Tiny hands of the same shade
began to drift over her body, caressing. Her eyes closed. I
heard her faint sigh echo in the cavernous room.

I resisted the urge to share her thoughts, allowing
myself only the briefest of tastes. I felt my heart's pace
quicken as her dream bloomed in my mind. An intricate
fantasy of seduction and surrender, of succumbing in
wanton release. The heat of the passion in this tiny
creature enflamed me.

I had no need for this game; I had reality. Still, as I
savored her thoughts for a moment more, I found
something strange beneath her meandering dream woven
of blood and abandon. I realized she didn't really believe
it. To her, this was all image and illusion. In her fevered
mind, we were both merely playing our dark roles.

I withdrew from her thoughts. Her face was lowered
now, alabaster features traced in harsh brushstrokes of
shadow. Her slender fingers worked at the silver buckle of
her wide leather belt. A moment later I heard it clatter to
the darkened floor at her feet. She was already unfastening
her shimmering skirt of transparent blood-red fabric.

But my gaze drifted to her bare head, shining in the pale
light. The shape of a gothic bat was tattooed onto one side
of her shaved scalp. On the other side was a tangle of
thorny vines, etched into her skin in dark green. The two

dark figures were the only blemishes I could see on her perfect, pallid skin.

I heard the soft hiss as her skirt fell to the bare wooden floor. Closing her eyes, she took another step away. Her fingers came up and locked around her smooth skull. They flowed back, as if she was brushing a tumble of hair. I heard her moan softly , and fought against the urge to touch her mind again. Instead I stared at her slender body, drinking in each detail. Her limbs were thin and wiry, feral. And I saw hints of the other things drawn into her skin, images in vivid colors, dark words traced in secret places once hidden by clothing, now half-hidden in shadow. I wondered again why she needed any more than this. Until I remembered she didn't believe any of it was real.

She came to me. Her warm hands brushed my face, the scents of her body still clinging to her fingers. One hand wandered across my lips and I opened my mouth, tasting. Her other hand drifted down, opening my shirt, tracing fiery circles across my skin. The sensations, and her closeness, were so delicious, so agonizing. My nerves crackled beneath my skin, the torturous pleasure burning in my brain like a blinding sheet of heat lightning.

A heartbeat later she was behind me, drawing the shirt down my back. Her arms closed around my chest. I felt her hot cheek pressing between my shoulderblades, her hardened nipples raking the tender flesh of my back. Her hands moved lower, unfastening my pants.

Time became meaningless as we embraced, a series of portraits painted by a godlike artist. Some moments seemed endless, spanning ages. Others lasted a mere heartbeat. Crushed in each other's arms, we tumbled onto the bed. Her hands drifted down my back to my waist. As they moved toward the front, I stopped her.

"No. Only you."

Sighing, she rolled onto her back. Her slender arms slid up past her head, fingers lacing into the wrought-iron headboard. Her knees rose, her legs opened. I knelt between. As I lowered my face to her body, I could see more words, more of the images drawn into the tender flesh.

Droplets of sweat trickled over her belly, sparkling in the frail moonlight like crystals of ice. But they sizzled against my tongue as I licked slowly up. I followed the delicate curves along the underside of her breasts. Her skin was soft, yet fiery. I could hear her breaths, quick and ragged, as she writhed against the twisted bedsheets. My mouth closed around her breast, my tongue licking tiny rings. The nipple rose higher. I closed my teeth around it, gently. With the slightest of pressure the skin broke, a single drop of blood searing my tongue.

Laboring against the desires of my nature, I moved upward. The flesh of her throat was flushed and damp. I tasted the sweat pooling beneath her chin. Heavy and salty, the musky flavor enflamed me. I could feel her arteries pulsing as I rounded her neck and licked at her ear. I sucked the lobe into my mouth, holding it for the softest of love bites. I savored another taste of her blood. My lips closed on hers, a moment later. I wondered if she could taste herself, as our tongues tangled. Taste her own blood.

It was ecstasy and misery as I tore my lips away from hers. My tongue wandered languidly down her body. I felt her fingers fluttering light as feathers against the back of my head as I tasted the skin inside her thighs. I closed my eyes at the maddening mingling of softness and warmth and wetness.

Her fingers suddenly curled, tangling into my hair. Guiding my mouth. My tongue drifted across wiry hair, matting it down with saliva. The texture and taste sent my thoughts spinning out of control. I forced my legs back, off the bed. I knelt at the bedside, reaching out for her. My hands closed around her waist, drawing her closer until her hips rested at the edge. I cupped her buttocks in my hands as I lowered my face again. I realized that her fingers had never left my hair. I wondered why she needed any more than this.

Then there was nothing but heat and wetness and silken skin. I licked harder, deeper, and found more warmth, more softness. I felt myself shivering, my pulse thundering in my ears, my nerves skittering. My hands slid upward, grasping the tender skin behind her knees, opening her further. Somewhere deep inside the burning, velvety skin I found a tiny hardened bud of flesh. My tongue caressed it. I became lost, disembodied, in her scents and tastes. I groaned with pleasure at the whisper-tang of old, life-rich blood.

An eternity later I heard her quick intake of breath. She moaned, almost as if in pain. Her fingers tightened against my head, the nails scraping. Her entire body seemed to tighten, and I felt tiny ripples arcing through her. Her touch softened, her fingers falling. Breathless, I tore my lips away.

Moonlight gleamed along the liquid curves of her body as she rose silently from the bed. Crossing the room, she disappeared into shadow. I heard a door opening in the darkness, then the wispy rustle of heavy fabric. As she stepped back into a jagged patch of light, I saw her spread a flowing white gown across the bed. Next to it was a wig of tangled blonde curls. I drew in a sudden breath.

"Why all of this?" I whispered.

"To make the dream real."

"But you don't need the dream. I am real. Why don't you believe?"

"I believe that you believe. It's the same to me. And it's enough."

I gazed at her as she sat on the edge of the bed and began drawing the long gown over her slender legs. Her strange words swirled in my mind and I struggled to understand what she meant, what she felt. There was something here, I knew, something real, something to be learned. But it was elusive and alien. Perhaps it was something I had known as man, but had forgotten as cold centuries shaped my new nature.

The girl stood, fastening the tight bodice around her chest. The contrast of the shaved and painted head atop the elegant gown halted my thoughts for a moment. Emotions rushed in to take their place. I felt a sharp ache in my heart, a longing. The girl was so passionate about her dream, and her role in it. It was almost like pity, what I felt, but more desperate. The lusts of my nature bubbled beneath the surface of my emotions, coloring my mind. I was strangely jealous of the devotion she held to her fantasy. There was something unique about her. She stirred something in me. But I had known she was unique the moment I paused in the darkness, hesitating to take her life.

I watched her come out of the club and walk straight into the shadows, unafraid. Blue and red neon light pulsed over her bare limbs as she drifted into the darkened alley. I wanted her so much at that moment, to run my icy palms over her delicate shoulders, to kiss her defiant little face. It was so flushed and fiery with blood. Almost as if her skin was merely a thin mask, holding back the surging blood beneath.

I ached to touch my tongue to the salty beads of sweat trickling in the patch of shadow between her breasts. I could smell it, coating her skin, still warm from her night of dancing. My veins drew into cutting wires. My mouth dried, longing to fill with her. With blood and flesh.

Before I could move, she stopped and looked directly at me. Her eyes held me in an embrace as fiercely fatal as the one I wished for her. She stepped closer. It was as if she had known I was here, and was coming for me. Almost as if she wanted me as desperately as I wanted her. Her scent was maddening as she pressed her damp, wiry body against me. I couldn't move.

"Are you a vampire," she asked. "Are you real?"

My heart thundered with desire, threatening to leap up my throat and out of my mouth. I clamped my teeth tightly, clenching my jaw.

"Yes," I hissed through rigid lips.

She made a soft sound, almost like laughter. Her gaze was so full and deep, as if all the wisdom and all the pain of the word tangled together to weave the shimmering darkness in her eyes. And in a moment of perfect clarity, it seemed to me that pain and wisdom were meant to be forever tangled together. What does she know, I wondered. If I fall into those eyes, will I ever surface again? I wished, for a moment, that I could see my reflection in them.

"Will you make it real?" She whispered. "Just like my dream?"

"I don't understand. I . . . "

"They always say they're real. But they can never make it right. Can you?"

"I am . . . real . . . I . . . "

My mind struggled to find words but I heard only shapeless sounds as my tongue flopped in my mouth like a sliver of meat. Her closeness, her smells, her words, sent my thoughts into a whirl. In confusion, I brushed her mind with mine, something I always waited to do until the absolute moment of death. I considered it the most intimate of acts, a way to taste both the giving and taking of life at the same instant. But I needed to share her thoughts. To understand.

Swirling threads of thought burned across my mind. The sheer intensity of her fantasies stunned me. She was both the seductress and the breathlessly seduced. I was to be the dark stranger, a dangerously erotic mingling of faces and scenes from books, and movies, and dreams. Both of us taking, both yielding. An exchange of warm blood. Dreams of eternal life borne out in acts of love and heat and passion. Until final forgiveness in the pale light of morning. When the precious fantasy becomes a lie. The belief, the moment, enough. The bitter aftertaste of blood.

"Will you do it for me?" Her eyes were so dark and deep. "Can you make me feel it?"

"Yes."

She took my hand and led me out of the alley and down the darkened street. Past dark shapes lurking in the shadows, all glittering eyes and glowing limbs. Creatures draped in black, their pallid faces following us. I could feel the jealousy in their minds, in envy of the heat we would share together. Strange, tender, empty, young humans.

As we walked together in silence, I wondered what I was going to find in the desolate dance of her fantasy. Within her. Within myself. What will I learn? Or remember.

I was trying to remember something. But thoughts of the girl swept it all away. She was twirling, arms out, spinning around the room. Her head was thrown back and she was humming a song. The sound was frail in her pale, arched throat. I listened to the soft rustle of the material, the dry rasp of her bare feet against wood. She was lost in her dance, in her abandon. Heating her blood for the culmination of her dream.

I tried to remember. There was something here. About dreams, about their meaning. And she knew this mystery, the thing I was unable to understand.

Have I lost my dreams, I wondered, now that I no longer dream? Do I still have the ability to imagine? Or have I become a hollow thing of sharp instinct and hunger and pure thought? Is that my nature now?

I wondered if she stirred some lost part of me. The human part? Am I now only a dancer in my own masquerade? Then what do I hide behind my mask? Have I truly lost something, or do I seek to find something else?

The girl tumbled back onto the bed, breathless, laughing. I watched her grip the golden wig and spring back up. She dashed to the mirror, pulling the false hair on. Giggling, she lifted a silver brush and began making long strokes with it, straightening the tangled curls. Her eyes were closed, as if in ecstasy. I stared at her with something close to panic burning in my chest. What is it that she has? I must know. I must have it, too.

I felt my body moving, sheer desire animating my muscles. One step, two. My arms came up, hands cupping as if to hold some unseen, precious thing. My jaw fell, and my breaths came hot and ragged in my gaping mouth. My heart fluttered. The insides of my mouth throbbed, laced with dry threads of agony. So close now, the mystery. The secret locked within that fragile life. The burning, bloody, fleshy life.

My fingers touched her warm shoulders, and I squeezed. Gazing into the mirror, I saw darkened imprints in her perfect skin, as if her flesh was being molded by invisible, ghostly hands. I shuddered at the sight of the violent tremble tracing down her throat. She raised her head, and her eyes opened. I saw her deep eyes grow bottomless as she looked into the mirror and saw nothing behind her.

Her scream echoed in my ears, and her silent screaming thoughts slashed into my mind. Instead of the mingling of dream and truth I had found before, there was only fear and confusion. The intense conviction she had felt was gone, replaced by a gnawing dread. Her dream was lost in the wake of reality.

"No," she whispered. "I can't see you. You are real. But you can't . . . "

"This is what you dreamed. To make it real. Now it is."

"No, please. Don't hurt me. I don't want this, not like this."

"Then what? When it was only fantasy, you wanted it to be real. Now that it is, you want the veil of your fantasy again. I don't understand. Do you know so much more than I do?"

I pulled her up and away from the mirror, searching her glimmering eyes for the depth of understanding I sought. But only terror swirled there, tears sparkling in the pale light. She shivered in my hands for a moment, then her body grew cold and limp. A heartbeat later her eyes rolled back and her mind went away.

"No! Tell me why you love this dream. I need to learn about this illusion that burns brighter than what is true. Tell me!"

I shook her. Her tiny limbs flopped and her head rolled on her fragile neck, but she didn't awaken. I flung her down onto the bed.

"Why the images? You longed for the barren reality of my nature, you burned for it. To kill without remorse. To live forever without the need of redemption. But when you had it in your hands you wanted this precious fantasy, this false scene of seduction. 'Make it real,' you said. And it became real. What is the lure of this illusion? Why is it so vital?"

I gazed down at her. She was perfect in her tender flesh, in her strange strength. Why was it not enough for her? She was beyond beautiful in her wild and weird way. Why would she want to be taken in any other manner, than with her fragile limbs tangled into mine? Staring at me with those glimmering eyes as she died? She was almost too real.

I reached down and pulled off the wig. Her head slipped to one side and I saw the tangle of thorny vines twisting around her ear. Why was appearance so important to her? I pictured her sitting before the mirror, brushing her false hair, smiling. Preparing herself. Imagining herself. To look like her dream.

Was that it? Beyond the sharing of blood, beyond the offering of flesh and passion? What was this power in the image of self? I tried to remember being human. Was the conception of self so powerful to me then? Have I forgotten as I become a changeless thing of eternal instinct? I turned to the mirror, and saw nothing.

A dream of my own bloomed in my mind, and I felt a strange longing that I hadn't in centuries. To see myself. Perhaps if I saw my own image, I would know if it held the mysterious power that had driven the girl to such vivid fantasies.

I grabbed her by one of her slender shoulders and drew her closer. Bending over her, I tore at her throat with my teeth. The hot blood sprayed, then bubbled out, running into the folds of the twisted bedsheet.

I held my hands close to the wound, cupping my palms. They quickly filled with the warm flow and I spun back to face the mirror. I raised my hands to my cheeks.

Slowly, I worked the hot blood over my face, letting it run into every curve of my flesh, letting it trickle over my lips. I spread it over my eyes and chin. And I saw my own image beginning to take form. The steaming blood was visible in the mirror, tracing the ghostly features beneath.

Again and again I went back to the bed and returned with handfuls of the living blood. I slathered it over my lips and neck, over my forehead and temples. I streaked it through my hair and let it flow over the back of my head.

I gazed at the dull red mask hovering within the mirror, glistening in the moonlight. Floating near the disembodied face were two crimson hands, drifting, dripping. I stared at my face, a thing I had not seen for so very long. My heart tightened in my chest.

Perhaps, I thought, there is something to this illusion. Maybe reality can be strengthened by the occasional dream. Maybe that was the mystery the girl knew. Maybe that was what I had forgotten. And she had shared the precious secret with me in her fiery blood.

I watched as my crimson lips quivered, twisting into a crooked smile. But within my mouth was only darkness. I would need to paint my teeth before I could see them. I turned back to the bed to gather more blood. Then I stained the teeth red, letting the needs of my body burn, forgotten for a while.

Vox Vampirica

Alan Smale

"Hello?"

"Hello, Jennifer, you still there?"

"Yes, here I am. I was praying we wouldn't get cut off . . . you wouldn't *believe* how many times it happens, switching from the party line to one-on-one. I used to think maybe it was my phone, but it seems to happen to everyone."

"We're alone now? Just the two of us? I've never done this before, I can't tell."

"Yes, yes, just you and me, Roland. I really liked what you said out there. About pain and pleasure, and the passing of the years? Well, that's kind of how my life's been too. I don't want to talk about it now, of course, but it struck a chord with me. Just listening to you made me shivery, and I knew we'd be good together, you know?"

"I'm glad . . . because that pain is a part of what I am, Jennifer. A small part, I hope, but nonetheless a vital one."

"You sound . . . wise. How old are you?"

"A gentleman doesn't tell, and a lady wouldn't ask. . . . Old enough to know a few things about the world. But no gray hair. No paunch. Still supple."

"D'you work out?"

"I don't need to. I just stay in pretty good shape. You have a sweet voice, Jennifer. Tell me what you look like."

"Me? Darn, I was kind of hoping you would go first. I feel a bit shy, actually."

"Don't be. Don't be frightened that I won't want you. I want you already, just from hearing you."

"Why?"

"Ah, now you're stalling."

"Well, maybe I am. Shy, like I said."

"All right, then. Your voice is . . . rich. Full of life. A harmonic voice."

"Ooo, harmonic. That's nice. You're smooth. Okay, then; I'm about five eight. Maybe a little heavier than I'd like. Not fat, exactly, but not a beanpole either, if you know? Good childbearing hips—wasted on me, I'm afraid . . . no kids, no desire for them either. But listen to me, telling you all my flaws first. I guess I'm not very good at this. Maybe you should have called a 1-900 number."

"No, no . . . I wanted a real woman, and you sound very real. You know how party lines are. It took me a long time to find you, Jennifer, and you sound just fine to me."

"Ooo, I just got goosebumps. Your voice is so— seductive. I'll bet you're a real charmer."

"I like to think so. But you were telling me about yourself."

"Um, okay. Let me tell you some good things, then. I have red hair to my shoulders. Kind of curly, wavy really.

It's natural, I've never permed it. And my face is cute, well, I think so . . . good cheekbones, green eyes."

"Mmm, green eyes, excellent . . . Tell me about your skin."

"I like my skin, too. I'm a redhead, so I have to stay out of the sun or I freckle up. My skin is creamy white everywhere, even my shoulders. It's very light. Soft. Nice to touch."

"Ah, a great prize for a caliph. I'm sure you'd look stunning in jewels and silks."

"What's a caliph? Is it like a sultan?"

"Close enough."

"Maybe. Is that what you'd like? To be my sultan? Would you like that?"

"Mmmm. I could give you an order, and you'd have to obey. You would dance for me, hips swaying, those green eyes locked on mine. Yes, I like this. My harem is in attendance, kneeling in two lines along the walls of a great baroque hall. It's my private audience chamber. Glazed blue and gold tiles cover the walls and floor with abstract spiral patterns. The Hall is lit with candles and lamps, and a cool night breeze drifts in through the open arches. It's a splendid place, but I'm looking only at you. You're wearing only a light, almost transparent belted skirt and a jeweled top that makes white domes of your breasts. Your shoulders and stomach are bare. As you dance, a thin film of sweat appears on your neck, damp against your white skin. I *adore* white skin, Jennifer. Then you kneel before me, and in front of all my wives, you—"

"Sounds like you've really been there. The mysterious East."

"Somewhere similar. When I was much younger."

"Well, hold your horses, or your camels, my prince. You haven't even told me what you look like yet."

"Me?"

"Sure. Hey, you don't want to tell me? I was honest with you."

"Yes, yes, I will. I was just thinking. Where to begin."

"Well, do you have a mirror there? Tell me what you see."

"No, I don't have a mirror . . . do *you* keep a mirror by the bed?"

"Well, actually I do. When I touch myself, inside? I like to hold a mirror down there, so I can watch."

"Are you touching yourself now?"

"Tut tut, not so fast, my lord."

"Mmm. Well, all right. I suppose I'm about the same height as you. Perhaps an inch taller. Dark hair, very dark eyes, but I'm very fair-skinned, like you, and I keep out of the sun as well. Almost entirely."

"You don't *sound* five nine. Your voice is so deep . . . so *muscular*, almost. You have the voice of a big, powerful man. One who'd have strong hands."

"Five feet nine inches was considered tall four hundred years ago. It just depends on your outlook."

"I didn't mean that *I* minded. You're not shorter than me, that's all that matters. And you sound striking . . . light and dark, sort of gothic."

"I suppose. So I should tell you that I'm wearing a crimson shirt and black pants, in pleated cotton."

"Wedding ring?"

"No ring."

"Good. But, boy, do I feel like some kind of slut now. You have all your clothes on and everything. And me, well . . . "

"Really? What are you wearing? Or not wearing?"

"Well, I . . . no, I'm not even going to say, till you take off some of that stuff."

"All right."

". . . Hey. Tell me what you're doing."

"Oh, sorry. The phone is in my right hand. I'm lying down on an ottoman, by the way, a full length one. It has a dark green covering, maybe like the green of your eyes, and carved wooden arms in polished mahogany. It's a nice piece. Anyway, my shirt is open now, to the waist. I'm unbuttoning the pants . . . first the big button at the waist, then that smaller backup button on the end of the little tongue of fabric that keeps the pants hanging right."

"Is there a zipper?"

"No, just more buttons. I'm undoing the fly now, popping them one by one. Tricky with only one hand. There. All undone now."

"What's underneath?"

"Black shorts. I'm old-fashioned, I can't wear briefs. I'm lifting up my hips so I can ease the pants out from underneath. Sliding them down my legs now. My thighs and calves are well-formed. The muscles show. I'm moderately hairy."

"Oooo."

"The pants are off. Now the shirt . . . there, I'm just wearing the shorts. I can see the outline of . . . what's underneath."

"Are you . . . aroused?"

"Yes, but, I'm not big, if that's what you mean."

"Turned on, but not . . . "

"That's right. Jennifer, I need to tell you . . . it's been a long time since I made love to a woman. A very long time indeed."

"Um, that's okay, look, you don't have to tell me anything you don't want to, you know."

"Ah, you think. . . . No, no no no, no, that's not it. No. I've always, oh, greatly preferred women. Especially women like

you, Jennifer; strong, voluptuous women with pale, soft skin
. . . and I have high hopes of you, I can feel myself wanting
you. It's just that I made a decision a long time ago not to
have that kind of relationship with a woman anymore."

"Priest?"

"Good grief, no. Far from it."

"Anyway, now, you want to have 'that kind of
relationship' again."

"Yes."

"And you're worried that, perhaps, you won't be able to,
um. . . ."

"Exactly. I've tried, Jennifer, but when I'm with
someone, even someone like you, something happens that
. . . makes sex impossible."

"Shhh, now I understand."

"I doubt it."

"Well, anyway, let's just see what happens, shall we?
I'll tell you what I'm wearing, okay? But you're not to
laugh. I'm wearing a push-up bra, and stockings, sheer, in
dark green, like your ottoman and my eyes . . . it must be
fate, don't you think? Green looks good on me. But, I
know nobody's going to *see* me when I'm on the phone, so
there are other things I like to wear to be comfortable and
sexy. So. I'm wearing silk boxers, not panties. I like the
feel of the silk on my thighs, but I like to be able to reach
in, you know? And do things to myself, without having to
take them off. And I've got a black shawl around my
shoulders, because a guy I once adored gave it to me, and
it's a little cool in here with the window open. And black
three-inch spike heels, because they make me feel slutty,
and I don't have to *walk* anywhere. And. . . ."

"Yes?"

"I have some, ah, toys here, too, Roland. I'll tell you
more about those later, maybe. But there's one thing I'm

already using, it's a little dildo, real small and thin, and I like to . . . well, let's be honest, it's up my ass right now, actually. It's small enough not to hurt at all, but big enough to fill me up. I can feel it when I reach in at the front. And when I lie on my back and rock on my ass, it moves around. It's nice. Mmmm, I like just telling you that it's there. Are you shocked?"

"No. No, it sounds wonderful. I can imagine you, in your emerald finery, squirming while you talk, and. . . . Are you in bed?"

"On top. Black silk sheets. I like to be good to myself. My white skin against those sheets, it's like I'm shining, glowing against them."

"I can *see* you on those sheets, it's like I'm there with you. Keep talking, keep talking."

"Okay. Well, I'm lifting my left leg, pointing it up, bending it at the knee now. I have a headset, so both my hands are free, both hands just stroking my thighs while I rock on my little ass-plug and think of you. Little thrills inside of me. Hey. Lift the waistband of your shorts and tell me what you see. Hurry."

"Too dark in there to see anything, I'm afraid. . . . No, I'm just teasing. I'm reaching in now. My cock is still soft . . . it's lying there curled against my left thigh. I'm touching it now. It's smooth, about five inches long. Thick in the middle, but it tapers at the end."

"Five inches, soft? Now, you wouldn't lie to a girl, would you? Tell me the truth, darling, it's always more fun than a tale."

"Well, as tails go . . . no, it really is that size, I promise. Just lucky, I guess."

"Touch it all along its length. Cup your balls. I'm still rocking. My right-hand middle finger is pushing up into my slit now. The silk is getting damp. Ooo, are we in the great Hall again? Are your wives watching?"

"My wives, yes. More women file in and kneel to watch, these are the serving girls and maids in waiting, they all want to see you. There are forty women now, all tanned, dark, Moorish-looking, in purple and gold and red headdresses. Little bells ring when they move their heads or shoulders. They're all watching you, Jennifer. They're beautiful with soft bodies and white teeth, and their eyes are riveted on the pale sheen of your skin, the flame of your hair. They've never seen anything like you, and you're dancing for me again, and me alone, but you feel their eyes feasting on your body. Do you like that?"

"Mmmm, yes. They all want me. All of your wives wish they could strip me and lick me and have me themselves, but they can't—"

"Your white body is making them crazy, but they have to sit quietly and watch. You're a houri, you can touch yourself, but they, no, they just have to be horny as hell and sit quietly."

"There's going to be a damned orgy in the harem tonight, you can bet—And when I kneel after the dance I'm touching myself, fingering myself through that thin gauzy skirt, and your wives can see me moving but only you can see what I'm doing and how wet I am, and my lips are apart and full, and my green eyes are wide. . . . I'm breathing hard. My cheeks are red. You can see that I'm hot. The shawl is off, here, by the way; bare white shoulders, creamy skin . . . "

"You're kneeling on the tiled floor, Jenni, rubbing yourself, and the good feeling is growing. You're melting inside. I'm standing before you in my robes. I take a step nearer, and you feel my fingers in your hair as I tilt your head back, to better see the curve, the waterfall of your neck, tiny veins throbbing, your red lips parted. . . ."

"Um, I'm panting now, you can hear me wanting you. There *and* here."

"I'm getting big, Jenni."

"Where? I mean, in the Hall, or. . . ."

"Here. I *am*."

"Really?"

"Really . . . I can't believe it. It's a pole, a tower . . . *shaitan*, so *big*, I haven't seen that for centuries, and it's so . . . the tip, so *sensitive*."

"Should I touch it?"

"No. Yes."

"All your wives are watching me as I reach out and—"

"My wives . . . they're telling me. . . ."

"What, what?"

"My other hand . . . my fingernails are long, I reach out and sink my nails into your skin, that white flawless skin, and pull four deep furrows. Four long scratches from your chin down that sweet neck to where your breasts start to swell, and blood beads up in four divine lines and flows down your chest as your strong heart pumps it out. . . ."

". . . Oh my God. . . ."

"You're tingling now, Jennifer, crackling from your neck to your toes. The heat surges along your limbs, and the three things you need the most are for me to drink deeply from the dark cuts in your flesh, and to come, and for my wives to watch you as it happens."

"Oh, ooo."

"But you have to ask me, Jenni, you have to invite me and beg me for it."

"Drink me. Drink from my *neck*. Oh. Ohh. . . ."

"You're still touching me, I'm still big, you're still moving your other hand inside yourself, and my *wives*, chanting Drink, Drink. They're so *loud*. I bend over you."

"Oh, yes."

"And I sip your blood, wanting to savor it, but it's so *good*, hits me like a jolt, your energy and life spark against my teeth and lips. Blood rich and deep, like your voice, and creamy like your skin, and coppery, so that my throat just burns and I suck deeply of you . . . my mouth is on your neck and your heart is pounding, *beat, beat*, your whole body is a pulse, and you're burning from your chin to your toes. The heat surges along your limbs. And I reach down between your legs and push your hand aside. My fingers go into you, and the pulsing becomes—"

"Oh, oooh. Ahhh. Uh, uh . . . yes, suck it, bite me, bite my *neck*, take it, everything you need . . . Oh . . . oh, oh. . . ."

"Are you . . . ?"

"Yes, my fingers are pushing and I'm rocking, and it's starting, it's building . . . oh, uh, uh, uh . . . Yes! . . . Ohhhhh. Oh my, oh yes."

"Tell me, tell me."

"Ah, I'm done, it's over, love, and I'm creaming, foaming everywhere. Oh, that was *intense*. Wow, I'm shaking. And my butt, jeez, that's sore."

"Jennifer, it's my turn, Jennifer . . . "

"Yes, it is. I pull your robe aside and your cock is standing up like a tower. Your wives all gasp and sit back because there it is, big and strong and *they* could never make that happen."

"Uh. . . ."

"You have a fever, a blood fever, you want me so hard. It's like my blood is swirling around your feet, and I dislocate my jaw and take you for one wet, delicious second all the way down into my throat."

"And your teeth close on me."

"No, they don't."

"Hurt me, Jenni, use your teeth or your nails, but you need to hurt me, *now*—"

"No, I don't do it."

"But I want it like that, it's what I *need*. . . ."

"I draw away and smile. You stand there, shaking, with blood on your lips and a hard, glistening rod."

"Jennifer, it's been such a long time, you *have* to. . . ."

"In the Hall, and in your room now, I tell you to take your tower in your hands. Stroke yourself gently. Do it, while I smile at you, sitting back on my heels, hands on my hips, red hair in a cloud around these creamy white shoulders. Blood is smeared on my neck. It's pooling between my breasts. I'm beautiful and I've got all you need, but I don't give you release."

"I can't come like this, Jennifer."

"No, you can't, can you? You have to ask me, don't you? You have to be invited. You can't come till I give permission, and you have to beg me to hurt you, or it won't happen."

"I *am* begging."

"No, Roland, I mean you have to fly over here, right now, and bite me a little. Then you have to let me chain you, and *then* you can beg me."

"What?"

"Fly over, Roland. In real life. I know you can."

"Uh. . . ."

"Here's the address: 9601 Brentwood. Got that? How fast can a bat fly with a hard-on?"

"Jennifer, I can't. It's too . . . it's dangerous. For you."

"No, it isn't. I have something you need, don't I? Roland? Say something. What did you decide?"

"Why are you doing this?"

"Silly creature. . . . Because I want a powerful spooky being to kneel at my feet and beg, of course. What could be nicer? Oh, and there was something else, what was it now . . . ah, yes, immortality."

"Jennifer . . . how did you know?"

"I knew what you were before we even transferred to one-on-one. It's in your voice, dear. You can't disguise it."

"Jennifer, I'm so big. And aching. I'm on fire."

"Then you'd better get around here quickly. The window is open."

"All right. All right. I'm going to hang up now."

"Be quick. I want you here. In my neck . . . and on your knees."

"Ten minutes, Jennifer. I'll be there in ten minutes."

"I'll be waiting. Hurry, Roland. Hurry."

The Razor's Edge
Kymberlyn Toliver-Reed

The shadow world of Perilous Gard.

The setting is almost medieval in tone. Velvet tapestries line the walls, of mythological beasts and beautiful men and women under their dominion. Stone gargoyles gaze sightlessly at the revelers, certain in their power to terrify. Discordant chants, sinful madrigals echo the seductive screams of the damned. People move as if wraiths; the silks, satins and velvets of exquisite gowns barely make a sound. Voices are low whispers as if amongst the wind. Crystal goblets tinkle, filled with vintages rare and precious. The food is a delight even for the most discriminating of tastes.

Those considered Masters and Mistresses of Perilous Gard are highly sought. They are at the very height of their decadence, moral only when it suits their purposes.

Unlike many of their kind who see a slave only in terms of a willing body to be used or discarded at whim, they tend to form lasting attachments to their slaves—many of the slaves at Perilous Gard bear the mark of ownership, either brands or rings. Love between the two is certainly not uncommon. The more pragmatic, however, see the bond as a means of securing total and abject devotion.

The slaves of Perilous Gard are highly trained, pampered, and prized all over the world as the most obedient. They are not picked for beauty alone, for all know well that beauty fades over time. They are striking creatures, no doubt, but are chosen for their intelligence, as well for their capacity to transcend the boundaries of pain.

Sometimes cruel, almost godlike in their demeanor, the masters and mistresses of Perilous Gard expect nothing less than total worship.

And, nothing else is given.

I

She is Regine d'Florentaigne—known to all as The Countess: a name, whispered in adoration and even tender affection by those who can but love and worship her from a distance.

Those who know her well—and there are but few, for The Countess does not take her attachments lightly—they say she does not merely walk—she stalks, panther lean, senses attuned. Cool, haughty, regal, and highly disdainful of those around her, be they master or servant.

She is dressed in a gown of ebony velvet, close-fitting at the torso, the cinched leather bodice compressing and pushing her breasts up and out. From the waist down, the gown falls in a graceful shower of black, sweeping the floor. She wears no jewelry at the throat. Underneath, leather boots with six-inch heels caress a pair of voluptuous thighs that none dare dream of possessing.

Her short dark hair is pulled away from an earth-brown face, emphasizing a seductive innocence that belies the heart of a skillful whip hand. The full, lush lips are reminiscent of ripe plums.

At her side, a leather riding crop dangles from slender fingertips with their perfect half-moon nails, the thin snakelike tongue supple from much use.

Regine is restless tonight; she has been for several nights past and many here are aware of it. While many are more than familiar with the cause, having at one time or another experienced it themselves, none would dare to presume upon her willing submission.

Regine seeks one who will take her far beyond the Rubicon of pain, past where it crosses over into pleasure. She has not yet savored the feel of giving up control, of being at the mercy of another's caprices, and she feels denied, incomplete. Her last slave left unsatisfied, complaining that her mistress's punishments left little to be desired. Regine has been a domme for so many years, and it no longer excites her. She is consumed by the need to belong, heart, mind, body and soul. . . .

She wants to walk on the razor's edge.

II

He stands in a corner, in the shadows, his eyes blazing in the semi-darkness. Regine is aware of him long before their gazes meet. To some around him, he is a mere shadow image, created by flickering wall sconces; to others, he simply isn't there at all.

He is dressed like an eighteenth-century man of leisure, in tight fitting trousers, gleaming knee boots, a brocaded waistcoat—all black. A silk shirt, almost blinding in its stark whiteness, lays casually open at the throat. Around his neck is a leather collar with the familiar d-ring.

Regine moves closer, captivated by sea-green eyes, coldly sensuous, the feral glint of a predator. His hair is waist-length and silky straight. There is a timeless androgyny about him: high cheekbones, thinly arched brows, long sweeping lashes.

In spite of the d-ring that marks him as a submissive, Regine is more than sure that he has never submitted to anyone. The aura that surrounds him is jet black, dangerous. To master him would take more power than even she possessed. Everything about him was dangerous, unpredictable—the type of man a woman like Regine cannot resist. Danger makes the blood flow faster, the heart beat a frenetic tattoo. Caution is thrown to the winds.

Their eyes are level as she stands in front of him. He stands a few inches taller, yet his presence makes him appear more than he is. His gaze is disturbing.

"Who are you?" It is The Countess who speaks now. Her voice is low pitched, velvet iron. Those who are familiar with it know that it is a voice to be disobeyed at one's peril.

He regards her with aloofness, looking her up and down, unimpressed. Taking her measure and finding her wanting. At first, she is angry. Who is *he* to look upon her in such a way? Then, curiosity overrides anger. She has never been appraised quite so frankly.

"I am Lord Astin Prescott, Viscount Sothern, and I am not, nor have I ever been, a slave," he replies, his voice deeply resonant, the English accent elegant and highborn.

He was a man more than used to being obeyed at all times.

Regine raises her crop, pointing to the d-ring that encircles his throat. He shrugs casually, dismissing it. "Not everyone who wears a ring is a slave. I prefer it. People stare. They wonder whom I belong to." He gazes at her, lust and conquest clearly written in his eyes. "As if I would allow myself to be owned by these pretenders, who have precious little in the way of imagination. Their petty little punishments would bore me to tears."

There is an underlying menace in his voice which draws her further into his web of seduction, all done without the slightest touch. Everything is inflection, the look in his eyes, his body language. Astin folds his arms, circles Regine like a great hunting cat, predator and prey.

"So, it seems the so-called 'mistress' of Perilous Gard has come full circle. How wonderfully novel. And, how unexpected." His laughter is sardonic, full of malice and anticipation.

"Know that I am not one to show mercy easily. If you choose to come with me, everything you have belongs to me. Every moan, every ounce of pain I choose to bestow upon you." His eyes bore into her soul. "Your pleasure . . . and your life, if I so wish it."

Every fiber of her being screams warning. Regine knows that she should not go with him, that they haven't negotiated the scene. He does not know her limits.

And neither does she.

"You have no limits, Regine d'Florentaigne." Astin's hand reaches out to cup her chin. His fingertips connect with her skin. She shudders from the contact.

He smiles wickedly, showing teeth perfectly white against the pale of his skin. The canines are long sharp points, lethal, animal, able to rend and tear through flesh and bone like a knife through paper. Regine knows what he is. She does not turn away; Astin can indeed compel her to obey him, although a slave under compulsion is little better than a mindless puppet. But, he does not have to compel her—her mind is open to him.

Terror and arousal war for dominance.

"You know what sort of being I am. You have a choice—turn from me, and I will not harm you. Come with me and your fate rests in my hands. This perhaps might be your last night upon this mortal earth."

Her decision takes mere seconds, and there can be no regrets. Silently, he takes Regine's hand. She has acquiesced and there is no turning back.

No one notices their exit.

III

There are candles lit, seeming hundreds of them, their flames reflecting onto the highly polished surface of the hardwood floor. The dimensions of the room are lost upon her as shadows leap and pirouette in the flickering light. Regine gazes at Astin from under heavily lidded eyes. She feels almost dreamlike. Her rational mind tells her to be frightened, to escape this madness, and this man who is no longer mortal. Astin is a vampire. He is beautiful to look upon, as beautiful as the fallen angel, Lucifer, was reputed to be still, yet he can take her life without fearing the consequences.

How many others have come here with him? And what befell them afterward?

He takes the crop from her hands, fits the handle into his palm. It belongs there. Naturally.

The supple tip rests against her throat, and slowly trails downward.

"Shall we dispense with the niceties, my lady?" murmuring the question. "Undress!" the command given with all the potency of a lash. He then changes his mind. "Leave the boots on. They lend a certain allure to your nudity."

Regine obeys, a little afraid of undressing before him, but fear is part of the game. In this case, the fear is no game. Moments later, she stands in the middle of the room, naked except for her boots, the heat of her body surpassing that of the candle flames.

"Spread your legs," he orders quietly. Regine does not obey this time. She wants to see if he can make her—a foolish gesture, perhaps, knowing what she knows. She wants to see how far she can push him.

Astin knows all this, he is more than familiar with this game. His smile is malevolent; he is looking forward to disciplining her—among other things.

"You know I have the power to force your mind, but why should I? You want to bear no responsibility for your actions, is that it?." He asks, purring sensuously against her ear, the salt tang of his breath overwhelming her senses. "You need to believe that I compelled you. However, you forgot one small detail, my sweet slave," and here his tongue snakes out to taste the salt of her skin. "I didn't compel you, Regine, and I won't. You are here of your own volition, and that is what makes this more interesting for me. Besides, why should I hurt you now? I have plenty of time because this room is spelled to remain in perpetual darkness. And, it is far more arousing to smell your fear as well as your lust and to know that I am its cause."

His fingers tug harshly at her swollen nipples. The sensation slowly builds into a pulling, then his teeth biting at them, careful enough not to break the delicate skin. His tongue senses the blood racing to the aureoles. Regine throws her head back and moans deeply.

He stops, anger on an angelically perfect face. "I am not the least interested in your desire. Be silent!"

"And if I'm not?" she challenges, heightening the tension between them, her breathing keeping pace with the rapid beat of her heart. Defiance, while part of the game, takes on an added dimension. How much defiance is too much?

"Then I stop, and simply sate myself upon your body, which I might enjoy for a fleeting moment or two, but can quickly lose its appeal, especially once I have drained you. I can feed upon anyone. What I plan to do to you is something else entirely. And, trust me, you want this more than I do."

The threat excites her. Regine feels the wet between her thighs. It comes unbidden, yet welcome.

The tip of the crop continues its slow, tortuous exploration, resting at the juncture between her legs.

"Spread your legs!" he commands. "Now! And do not attempt to try my patience."

Regine obeys, catching his gaze. His eyes burn her.

"Very good, my sweet. It appears that you do know how to obey your betters. Now, hanging above you is a silk tassel. Grasp it with both hands, wrap it tightly around your wrists, and do not let go of it for anything. I'm simply not in the mood to cater to your whims. I may appear civilized, but that is merely an illusion I can project at will."

Regine reaches up, the silk soft as she wraps it around her wrists.

What does he see, Regine wonders. Does he find her beautiful, her dark skin glittering in the candlelight, standing in the middle of the room, arms over her head, bound by choice?

"You are quite beautiful," he says softly, answering her unspoken question. "And by the time I'm done with you, you'll be stunning. Because you'll belong to me, one way or the other."

"I don't belong to anyone." Regine says quietly.

"But you want to, don't you?" Astin begins pacing around her, the crop and his fingertips caressing her, driving her insane. Every pore is electric, pulsing. The lightest touch sends her into a frenzy.

"You want to belong to me, body and soul, don't you? Perhaps I choose to deny you? Will you beg, Regine? Yes," he hisses, his face inches from hers, taking on a more animalistic quality. "You will. And I know why . . . because you want this. You've been seeking me, whether you know it or not. I've seen your dreams, and I've been in them. No mortal man, no matter how skilled, can possess you the way I will. I can drain you to the very last drop of blood, and you'll allow it."

The crop lightly flicks against her ass. The leather slides between the firm round cheeks, down between rosy lips. He withdraws it, satisfaction as well as amusement clear on his face.

"What, my sweet whore, wet already? Imagine how wet you'll be when I've done with you."

His fingers find their way between her legs. He is close to her, lips barely touching her skin. His hair, the scent of flames and sandalwood, but strangely not of the charnel house. His breath, hot, flows around her. A finger parts her swollen pussy lips, pulling back the hood that conceals her clit. One finger slides inside, then another joins it. A third. A fourth, until his entire hand has penetrated her. He begins a savage dance inside of her, in and out, deep yet slow, and there is no resistance to his invasion. His fingers clench, his arm, like the rest of his body, sensitive to the flow of blood, even here. For a fleeting instant, Astin wished she were on her monthly courses; most vampires disdain feeding from a woman's menstrual flow, but to Astin, the hot iron saltiness was a drug beyond intoxication.

Against Astin's wishes Regine cries out at the sensation of being ravished. He removes his fingers quickly, then smacks her hard with the crop on her thigh.

"You, were told to be silent!" Astin hisses, striking her again. "You forget yourself 'Countess' Regine. I own you now!"

"You don't have what it takes to own me." Regine is baiting him, knowing that he will punish her for her insolence. Hoping that he will punish her. But she cannot surrender so easily, even to one such as he.

Astin laughs. He is pleased and says so.

"Ah, my lovely victim, I could spend all evening proving just how wrong you are. Look at you, begging to be hurt. Begging to be fucked. My entire hand was inside your dripping cunt, and you throughly enjoyed it." Without warning, his hand penetrates her again, thrusting deep into her womb, heedless of her pain, but very aware of his savage delight in causing it. Regine moves against him, willing to take all of his arm if he so chooses.

"Not so haughty are we, Mistress d'Florentaigne, with a man's fist between your netherlips." Astin moves within her in a slow, steady rhythm, feeling her open up to him like a hothouse flower. The pleasure of him is too much and again, Regine disobeys by crying out for more. He gives her more, hard and fast and cruel.

Astin suddenly tears out of her, not caring if he has hurt her in any way. He raises his free arm, the crop whooshing through the air; the blows, evenly spaced, leave welts on the back of her thighs.

No sooner than the blows land, he is down on his knees, kissing away the pain. He bites her roughly and Regine gasps as teeth sink into the raised welts, feasting on the hot racing blood. Nothing has prepared her for an experience like this, frightening and arousing both at once. His hands on her cheeks, parting them. His tongue explores her, licking, tasting, sucking greedily, her juices flavored with the taste of leather and pain and her life force.

Regine writhes, moaning, deep throaty animal cries. Astin will strike her again; she is past caring.

He does. The sound of leather on flesh echoes within the silken silence of the room. Regine strains against the bonds, forgetting that it is she who holds them, that she has imprisoned herself.

Astin is fascinated with her. A thin trickle of blood stains the brown buttocks. Such a magnificent beauty, in such exquisite pain. It seems a shame to mark such lovely thighs, he thinks to himself.

Still, can't disappoint the little wench.

More blows, latticed symmetrically across her flesh. It takes skill and concentration to make the leather fall in such a way.

A hand softly caresses the places where he has struck. The flesh is scalding hot to the touch, and Regine groans, choking back sobs.

"I wish you could see it, Regine," Astin draws the tip of the riding crop along one of the welts. "Such artistry, if I do say so myself. I love marking my victims this way. I pride myself on possessing a certain amount of creativity, flair, if you will."

"Besides," and he strikes her again. "I find that doing so heightens the victim's pleasure a thousandfold." He strikes her again. "Doesn't it?"

Another blow falls. Regine tenses, relaxes; the pain washes over her. Astin spaces each, wanting her to savor it, to memorize it.

He stands in front of her, arms crossed over his chest, the crop held carelessly in one hand. His erection strains against the confines of the trousers. It takes all the control he has not to strip and fuck her. He cannot let the game end so soon. He enjoys it far too much.

He knows that she does too.

A thin sheen of perspiration lends a copper cast to her dark skin. Her nipples thrust out, drops of solid chocolate kisses. He watches the steady rise and fall of her chest. She opens her eyes, slightly clouded with passion haze.

No tears.

Yet.

"Tell me something, Countess," the sarcasm in Astin's voice is obvious. "Have you ever engaged in anal play? As the recipient, of course."

Regine tenses up, as if he has already invaded her. "No," comes her reply, barely a whisper.

"Do I take that to mean 'no,' as in you've never been fucked in the ass, or 'no,' you'd rather I not. Not that it matters, really. You resist me, and the pain will that much worse. Not that a bit of pain doesn't excite you, am I correct?"

A small flicker of defiance manifests itself on her face. "You can do whatever else you want to me, but not that."

A finger reaches out, tracing a line from her cheek to her lips.

"You, my sweet slave, are acting like you have a choice in the matter."

"I think I do. What about safewords? This is against the rules." The moment the words fall from her lips, she realizes the absurdity of the notion.

Astin laughs, a sound both erotic and threatening. "Excuse me, but you should have thought of that before you followed me here. I play by a whole different set of rules. Mine. I am above such trifling concerns as 'safewords.' After all, I am lord and master here."

Regine tries to wrench away from him. Her struggle amuses him. It excites him. He finds the irony of her situation delicious. She can end this if she wants to, simply by letting go of the silk.

Predator he might be, but he has never forced anyone. He has never had to.

"I do not care if you fight me or not, Regine. The result will be the same. Your body belongs to me, even if you don't know it yet." Astin's face moves closer to hers. His breath is warm and sweet, slightly spicy, slightly metallic from her own blood.

"I truly own you now, Regine."

His lips capture hers in a rapacious kiss, claiming her mouth and tongue, tasting blood. He presses the back of her head with his hand, insuring that she cannot escape. He bites her bottom lip, swallowing and savoring her blood with all the delicacy of a connoisseur of fine wines.

She cannot breathe. She is drowning. His kiss drains the life from her body.

It is a kiss that she returns willingly. The kiss is a raging, uncontrollable torrent of possession. Regine flows into the swirling rapids of his domination. If she has to die, then let it be like this. A wild kiss from Astin, a being who holds her very self in thrall.

Astin. His name reverberates through her mind like the thundering crash of cymbals.

"Astin." She whispers his name into his mouth.

He pulls away slowly, the taste of her lips forever imprinted into his mind. Her lips are stained with blood.

"Do you realize what this means, my dear countess?" His voice hardens ruthlessly, "Know that you are responsible for what has happened up to this point, and for what will happen. Of how much pain I can inflict upon you, and that you will not deny me anything . . . including your immortal soul."

Regine's heart races. "I do."

"We shall see. Come, Regine, walk the razor's edge."

Astin spins Regine's body around, her back to him once again. The blows fell on the firm flesh of her buttocks, each stroke causing the skin to ripple. Regine cries out, panting, pleading. This time, Astin does not chastise her for not remaining silent. Her voice, her agony, is thrilling to hear. The sweetest music. His senses are wide open now as Regine opens the floodgates of emotions never brought to the light of day. Such forbidden and dark desires from a mortal woman.

"Beg for it, Regine," he whispers, his lips lightly nipping at her ear. "Beg for me to continue. Not that it matters—I just want to hear you plead."

Her head rolls back, lips parted invitingly. Each hot kiss of the riding crop blends into the one before it, scarring her body and searing her soul. Regine is too far gone to want to stop. Nothing matters now, except this moment. If he stops, she will go mad.

"Astin." The words come out in harsh sobs. "Astin, please!"

"Louder, countess."

Regine screams her desire, tears of lust and pain and hunger and need streaming down her face. "Oh dear god . . . please. . . Astin!"

The leather is like fire, burning. Regine flows into it, totally consumed. Astin's hand is steady, but just so. He, too, is consumed. He realizes that he cannot go on much longer. His body demands that lust and hunger be assuaged.

He suddenly tosses the instrument aside, unable to withstand the calling of his nature. He sheds his clothes quickly. His cock is taut, stretched to the limit, painful to the touch.

He rubs his cock between her legs, coating it with her wetness. With a finger, also slick with her, he parts her ass cheeks, burning hot from the beating. He works it inside of the tight passage.

There is resistance. Regine tries to push the intruder out. Astin slaps her hard with his other hand. "Give in to me, Regine. You don't have a choice any longer."

Regine sighs, goes slack, letting him do as he will, knowing that she wants this as much as he, or perhaps even more. She has dreamed of such total surrender.

For Astin, the mental war continues. His mind urges him to take it slow, to teach Regine to relax, to open herself up to him. His body screams in frustration, feeling itself thwarted. The ache in his groin is near unbearable.

Somehow, he finds the strength to resist his body's singleminded insistence for a few moments more.

He guides himself slowly, inside the lube-slicked passage, impatient to be inside, aware enough to be gentle. Regine gasps, arches to take it all in, knowing that she wants this even if it feels like she is being ripped in two.

Astin feels her stretch and open around him. He goes slowly, sinking into her, grasping her hips, pulling her to him.

He pulls out slowly, then in again. In. Out. Swept by a tide of sensory overload, Astin thrusts, impaling her fully, pulling her to him, sinking his teeth into her neck as he fucks her hard and deep, drawing forth her blood, thick and hot and flavored with sex and her desire to walk the fine line between fear and eroticism. He sucks at the pulsing vein greedily, his tongue lapping at the twin punctures. Regine shudders, her heart pounding in furious cadence.

A single mental command and the silk that binds her hands drops to the floor. She is free, but only just. One arm fastens tightly around her waist, binding her physically to him. Astin bends Regine forward as the other arm makes its way between her legs, his hand entering her again. In sublime rapture, Regine screams, her body sweetly violated in ways unimaginable. O death, how sweet thy advent.

"I will not take your life, Regine," Astin says, his voice a sibilant whispering harshness that captures her mind as he has captured her body. "I will take you to the edge, but I will not let you fall."

Sublime pleasure suffuses them both, slaves to the mindless, heedless emotions of lust and surrender. In and out, slow strokes as hips raise and lower to counter each thrust.

Time stops. Astin's body moves faster, slamming harder inside, himself close to climax. Regine, all semblance of control gone, opens herself fully, her heart beating loudly in the dark silence. Her song is one of triumph as well as capitulation. She writhes against his cock and his fist, both of which impale her and bring her such decadent ecstasy.

With one last powerful surge, his cry loud and exultant, Astin explodes deeply within Regine. His seed, not surprisingly, is as red as the blood he has taken from her.

IV

Regine awakens against the softness of cotton sheets, freshly laundered. Her eyes adjust to the hazy light of midmorning, the sun hidden behind heavy clouds and streaming through Venetian blinds.

Her gaze falls upon him seated comfortably in a padded wing chair, clad in a thick terry robe, his hair faintly damp from what? A bath? The green eyes regard her with cool amusement.

A vampire who likes water.

"Simply because I have been dead for several centuries is no excuse to give up the more civilized amenities of existence. I have many sins upon my soul, Regine d'Florentaigne, vanity being the least of these."

It occurs to Regine that she is taking her situation rather well, considering that she is in the presence of someone who can read her slightest thought—and who needs blood for sustenance.

"Perhaps I know little concerning the behavior of vampires, but I thought your kind couldn't function sexually in the way the rest of us do. I thought the taking of blood became the sexual act itself."

Astin smiles enigmatically. "You ought not to believe everything you read or hear about us, my dearest Regine. Those who write about us more than likely assume that we do not exist. And, as to being able to function sexually, you have my assurances that I function more than adequately to suit anyone's needs. Including yours."

Regine sits up, doing her best to ignore the stiffness of her legs and the slight throbbing of her buttocks. She is puzzled at just how good she actually feels; there should be a certain sense of weakness. She has no idea of just how much Astin took from her last night.

"Not as much as it seemed," he answers matter-of-factly. "I have excellent control over my hungers, even when it seems that I do not. What wounds you suffered, I used my powers to heal. I cannot have my most lovely possession strolling through Perilous Gard looking as if I'm some type of savage. You are aware that you do belong to me, correct?"

She returns his look guardedly. "That is a matter open to discussion. Now what?"

Astin stretches his long legs out in front of him, a Cheshire-cat grin crossing his face. His fangs are barely visible, and the effect is dazzling. The light of the false day finds him even more beautiful than the night.

"You rest. When you feel up to it, I'll draw a bath for you, then a massage. Then," and the look darkens faintly, "I'll take you again. Not as harshly, just as a reminder of your new status. You are now the sole property of Lord Astin Prescott, Viscount Sothern."

"I'm flattered."

Astin dismisses her flippancy. "And so you should be. In life I was fastidious to the extreme, a bane to all the fashionable women in Society, and in un-life, my standards are still as exacting. I consider myself fortunate to have found you amongst those jaded pretenders who frequent Perilous Gard."

"And, in spite of a title that may no longer exist, if I should refuse?"

"You won't," Astin assures her with certainty. "You can't. You've given yourself to me, Regine. For as long as I want you. And," he adds, gazing directly at her, eyes full of amusement, "the title indeed exists. You may check *Debrett's Peerage* if you like."

When at last Regine answers, there is no defeat in her voice; in fact her voice is one of curious triumph. "I have. Haven't I?"

"Completely. I'm wielding no force over you. I am what you need, and no one else can satisfy your craving, without forsaking their humanity. Since I am no longer human, except in appearance, I can fulfill your deepest, most decadent fantasies. But who knows," he says smoothly. "Someday, you may be able to top me. I may even let you."

The thought brings a slow mona-lisa smile to Regine's face. Oh, the pain she will inflict upon him will be like nothing he could ever conceive of.

How, indeed, does one top a vampire?

Dark Freedoms
by Jim Lee

The two of them stood silent for a time, watching the door close and listening to the exhausted, retreating shuffle of Mother Frederick's feet.

Her angular and jet-black face impassive, Clementina's gaze returned to Annie. Her lips, full and prominent and purple enough to approach the stereotypical, pursed. A single brow arched, requiring an immediate response.

Annie Court winced. Her pale cheeks reddened, her body began to quiver. *Amazing,* she thought. *How easily she does it! Makes me want and even need to fall on my knees before her. To beg forgiveness; to atone, singlehanded, for all the crimes—crimes of either act or attitude—committed by my people!*

"I'm sorry," Annie whispered.

Clementina stared back at her for another moment.

Then she gestured, dismissing the matter as too trivial for comment.

Her turbaned head swung in an impossibly graceful arc and she regarded the fevered, dying figure on the bed.

Annie, still captive to the human need to apologize, reached out but Clementina turned her hand aside with smooth indifference. Iris, Annie's childhood friend and Mother Frederick's only surviving daughter, moaned and resumed her mindless, tortured thrashings.

"Oh, God." Annie sobbed, bit her lip. "Help her, please? Soothe her way, at least?"

Clementina nodded, gave Annie and then the door a sharp glance. Annie's head bobbed and she remained to guard the doorway. It wouldn't do at all for one of the anguished family to walk in on Clementina's sort of mercy.

Besides, it might be something worse than childbed fever. Unlike her so-called owner, Clementina was quite immune to the all-too-common diseases. She touched the senseless woman's bare shoulder without fear and firmly, efficiently drew the rumpled bedding aside. Iris calmed measurably, as if the cool ebony flesh itself was able to siphon off the dying woman's agony.

Iris wore but a single white chemise as a nightshirt, and though it clung, stained and pasted to her clammy flesh by perspiration, Clementina freed her from its confinement without difficulty.

Annie stood by the door, watching Clementina's thorough and deeply sensual, even sensuous, examination. She watched and sobbed, remembering the past. The innocence, the carefree and unknowning sweetness of childhood. Annie Court watched and struggled with shocking, mixed emotions.

She watched her friend, dying from infection only days after losing a son in childbirth. She watched Iris, being touched and probed and then slowly, effortlessly being fed upon by the dark and mysterious ruler of Annie Court's soul.

Annie's gal. An ordinary, if strangely dignified and intelligent, slave—according to most anyone else.

Clementina.

Now that her Father was gone, only Annie knew the truth. It was a truth she guarded jealously, as much for her own sake as for Clementina's.

Annie stood there quivering, her nipples hardening against her bodice and her frilled underclothing endangered by the pulsating moisture between her legs.

And she watched Iris calm completely. She watched Clementina raise one of her friend's doughy white breasts and move into place, the retractable and delicately threatening fangs emerging to pierce Iris.

Annie Court watched as her beloved vampire fed, leaving only tiny marks along the underside of a breast, where no-one would see. She watched the gentle, blissful smile on her friend's face—and she tried her best not to envy the doomed but now-quiescent Iris.

Annie cringed. She felt angered, yet compelled; proud and jealous and fascinated. Even somehow honored—to be allowed to witness something this profound!

It was always like this when she watched Clementina feed upon another. The memory of that first time, nine years and countless feedings, countless moments of searing intimacy later, came surging up. It engulfed her once again.

She could smell the arid sweetness of the hay quite clearly. Could see the slow pirouette of dust illuminated by the angled rays of sunlight as she crept into the barn. She heard the muffled sounds once more, could sense the intense and mutual need above her.

Yet again in memory, Annie scaled the ladder. She winced, remembering the splinter in her hand, received halfway up the ladder and dripping blood thereafter. In her mind's eye, she saw herself continue. She saw herself peer into the shadowed loft and she gaped dumbstruck at what, at who she saw.

Father. The word, the image still resonated in her head. She had been 18, had never seen a fully naked man. Let alone one with an aroused, rhythmically surging member. But then, there he had been, in shocking and vivid detail. His back to her, Thank God!

And beneath him, legs canted wide in acceptance and also stark naked, had been Clementina.

The passion of that embrace had been undeniable, yet there had been more to it. Silent and bewitched, Annie's eyes had drawn upward, past the undulating confluence of groins. Her gaze had settled on the other, even more extraordinary point of joining.

Her father's arms had been downthrust in support, his head raised and neck exposed. Gratefully, eagerly exposed. His face was blissful as Clementina's long dark fingers dug into his shoulders. Her blunt-tipped breasts wobbled as they squirmed and bucked together. She rose up, flashing her fangs and clamping down again. Yet it was the way this man—who pretended to be her Master—gave his blood that shattered the last of young Annie Court's illusions. Quivering, gasping meekly in delight.

Annie had watched them. Black and white. Male and female. Apparent slave and true, exultantly powerless bondsman.

She watched as they joined, shared. Exchanging one vital essence for another. And exchanging far more. She watched and yearned, as she never had before.

Ten days later, Annie had come to Clementina. On her knees. Somehow it had seemed the only proper way. *The proverbial moth*, Annie remembered thinking even back then. *Drawn to flame, to the promise of its own destruction. Yet glad for the danger!*

Returning to the present, Annie watched Clementina straighten. The vampire adjusted the simple homespun of her dress. She eased an unmoving Iris back into the stained chemise, positioned the bedding as before. Her left hand moved, effortless and discerning as her fingertips brushed along the dying woman's arm.

A head turned, independent of its supple and ageless body.

"You can come close now," she told Annie. "I'm finished and it's nothing you can catch. Childbed fever." Clementina snorted, shook her head. "So unnecessary! If your jackass doctors would only learn to wash their damnable hands!"

Annie paused, frowned.

It was a puzzlement. She was used to the dark immortal's salty private language. *Another thing of hers that only I am now permitted to know!* "How could such a simple thing . . . ?"

"The how or why, I'm not sure of." Clementina allowed herself a look of mild amusement. "But I know the washing helps. Hands, instruments. You come to see what works and what doesn't readily enough, in the course of over twenty-two hundred years!"

Annie shivered. *She was centuries old when Christ walked upon the Earth!* Annie would never, surely never, grow accustomed to that basic truth. And yet she never doubted any of Clementina's stories and experiences. Not for a single moment.

She came near, staring at a paler, placid Iris.

"Is she dead?"

"No." Clementina frowned. "You know I don't do that! Too risky." They watched the faint but unmistakeable pulse of the dying woman's nostrils. "I took enough to settle her. She will die in any case, but with far less pain. That is what you wanted?"

Annie nodded, went on staring.

She started back, even though Clementina's touch was as gentle and as expert as ever. Then Annie sighed, relaxed. She found her body craving the flattened palm and the splayed, ebon fingers. They swept up her torso and lingered to caress the bare flesh of Annie's neck. She allowed her ageless lover to play servant for once in private.

Clementina guided Annie into a chair and held her through the night, kissing her brow and soothing the mortal woman when she wept. The day dawned slowly, as if reluctant.

Iris was still alive, weak and mercifully unaware, when her Mother came to thank Annie once again. "It was so good of you! Her Father cannot face this and Captain Smith's so far away, fighting that devil Sherman. I could not have sat there another night, yet to leave her alone—" The old woman shook her head. "However did you calm her, dear?"

"Clementina is a most accomplished nurse. Has a way with the gravely ill."

"Oh?" Mother Frederick turned, as if only now realizing the slave's presence. Her smile was grateful and looked honest, yet the words were still addressed elsewhere. "How good and thoughtful of you to bring your gal along! I'm in your debt, Annie Court. Truly in your debt."

Annie's face flushed, but she took her example from Clementina's regal calm.

The Frederick family carriage was brought around and Annie stepped into it, aided by the aged black driver. Clementina followed, without assistance. She sat to Annie's side. She was, after all, 'Annie's gal.'

They barely spoke as the carriage took them to the farside of Mobile. The driver kept his eyes straight ahead and said little.

The women held hands. They looked out across the Bay at the forts that still grimly defended the Confederacy's last great port city. A Confederacy, a nation that was dying, as surely as lris Frederick Smith.

Back at the Court Mansion, Clementina left the carriage first. She looked about as if considering, then turned and helped Annie down. It was clear that serving the white woman was no more than an afterthought, a duty to be performed in public but lacking any deeper meaning.

Annie thanked the driver, sent him on his way.

Word came just after noon: Iris was gone.

Annie sobbed when she heard. She pushed Clementina's hand away, then gladly folded into the embrace and followed the ageless figure up the winding, ornately carved staircase.

Hours later, Annie sat on the bed to watch the sunlight fading. She turned her head, extended her arm and ran her fingertips across the unfailing round perfection of a jet-black breast. "I'm glad the stories aren't all true. I love to see the glisten of the sun upon your skin."

Clementina smiled, eased into place at Annie's side. Her eyes invited the mortal to caress both orbs at once and Annie did so, with a faint smile. "Like most hunters, we're at our best in the dark. And there's something about the transformation. We're more sensitive to direct sun than you."

Annie nodded, thinking. "Even from the first? Down in Africa?"

"That's right."

They kissed. Then Annie dipped her head. She began to swab the flat of her tongue back and forth across Clementina's breasts. They both were ready and sensed each other's readiness as well.

Clementina undid the stays and untied the knots holding Annie's corset in place. It slipped away and, with patient movements that had Annie panting throughout, the ageless beauty removed her latest consort's last three petticoats.

Exposed and almost equal in their shared nakedness, they folded together onto their backs. Hands moved, caresses were exchanged. *I love you*, Annie thought. *I need you! I can't wait another second!*

The mortal woman rose up. She straddled her lover, her darling and the very center of her universe. Annie stretched out, lowered herself, face-to-groin and groin-to-face.

Slow caresses, gently probings, short licks and long, tender kisses brought the two of them to ecstasy as one.

Sighing, Annie allowed herself to be toppled over.

Clementina turned, dragging a sweaty and yet still-cool thigh across Annie's face. They faced each other on their sides and their tongues took turns, carrying each other's sweet essences back and forth.

"The one who did this," Annie murmured. "Made you this way? Was he really an Egyptian?"

"Ethiopian," Clementina corrected patiently.

"But he was an advisor to Pharoahs?"

"Ethiopia invaded, ruled Egypt for about fifty years. My mentor fled when the last Ethiopian Pharoah was deposed. About six hundred B.C., from the present calendar."

"And he was . . . ?"

"Like me. A taker of blood. A quiet ruler of men's souls. It was another three hundred years before I was born and he found me, in a minor village of central Africa. I was his slave, both literally and in the other sense, even after he made me immortal. He taught me the value, the freedom of ruling without seeming to."

Annie nodded, touched her lover's hip. "Your first white? A Roman soldier?"

Clementina let out a deep breath. "I had left my first Master. Took a mortal, a merchant from what became the Empire of Ghana. We went north. The last Punic War had just ended. Carthage was gone. I was hungry and my consort lured a soldier from his post, with the promise of his black whore's attentions for a few coins."

"And you let him?" Annie gasped, her heart pounding as it always did.

"Him and the merchant and countless others across the centuries and continents!" Clementina's voice rose, irritated by the mortal's excitement and moral questionings. "I saw the founding of Timbuktu and Great Zimbabwe at its peak! I was with Mansa Musa's caravan to Egypt in the thirteen hundreds and met the first Portuguese ship to come up the River Gambia. That ship's first mate was the first white man to know the honor of pretending full ownership of me! For the next four centuries, I traveled the world—owned by Frenchmen, Spaniards, Englishmen and others. And yet I was always, always, in control!"

Annie tried to turn away, but Clementina's hand jerked her around by the chin. The earthy scent of the immortal's perspiration invaded Annie, as it always did, more spellbinding than any mere perfume.

"I made a worthless, blackskinned brute of a slavetrader into the virtual ruler of Gabon. I thought to stay among my own in Africa a while, perhaps to turn this traitor into one of value. But 'King' Denis proved as low and vile as any, including the white men he dealt with. I saw it in eighteen thirty-nine, when he allied himself with the French. It was easy enough to include myself, as an unwritten extra in that treaty!"

Annie blinked, hearing something new and understanding another part of Clementina's epic story. "That's how Monsieur Bayard became your Master?"

"And how I came to America." The immortal shrugged. "I told him I was ready to leave Africa, again. To try somewhere new to me. We traveled your South for several years, until he grew too feeble for my requirements."

"Then Father bought you."

"Then I *arranged* for your Father to buy me. Just as, a few years further on, I *arranged* for you to see us together!"

Annie gaped. She sat up suddenly and withdrew her hand. Her mouth curled, almost spat the next words at Clementina. "You planned that? Goddamn you. I was shocked, horrified! Goddamn you straight to Hell, Clementina!"

Her hand swung forward but stopped just short of the immortal's knowing, wise, untroubled countenance.

Clementina's voice softened, slowed. Her touch returned, feather-light and reassuring. "I must be cruel at times, sweet Annie. Ruthless, just to survive and be safe. Tell me, truthfully. You saw him, feeding and fucking me. Which sight troubled you more?"

"Mother hated you, " came the muttered reply. "Never spoke of it, of course. But she thought Father loved you more in the end than her."

"She was correct."

Annie winced, but there was no denying Clementina's total honesty. It commanded the same in turn.

"I envied him. Both ways." Annie bowed her head, shook it slowly. "As I've envied all your consorts, living or dead. Even Iris."

"I was never with your friend," Clementina assured. "Only last night, when we both knew she needed me. And it was your idea, remember?"

"I know." Annie sobbed. "It was a kindness and I do thank you. But still. . . ."

"I think it's time," Clementina muttered.

Annie paused. "Time for what?"

"Time that I bred you." The words snapped out, sudden and cruel. Exactly how some whites might speak about one of their 'property.'

And whatever else she was, Annie Court was in fact under Clementina's absolute control. Willingly, even gladly. But she, Annie, was the real slave here and sometimes the vampire insisted on reminding her.

"I can't marry," Annie protested. "He'd find out about you—about us!"

"Yes, I'm sure he would. And then I'd have two regular sources for what I need, rather than one!"

Annie gulped. Her body shook.

"Is the prospect of a man's embrace so unpleasant?"

"I—no."

"Yet you have given every man to approach you the mitten, in no uncertain terms."

"I thought to protect you. Your secret." *And my exclusive place in it*, Annie admitted to herself.

"It's time." Clementina kissed her softly. Their noses remained together, rubbing delicately. "Shelby Jackson might be the best choice. He's still about, waiting for his parole to expire."

"I know." Annie thought about Shelby. Decent and strong, intelligent and not unhandsome. He'd been captured after Vicksburg and released in the usual way, on his signed promise not to fight until officially exchanged for a Yankee POW of equal rank. She felt drawn to him— not as strongly as to Clementina, but truly drawn.

Twice already, she had found herself in romantic and private situations with him. Twice, she had been tempted and he had been clearly willing. But twice, she had begged off.

Annie blinked. "You arranged it? The time in the woods and at the theatre? You want me . . . him . . . us?"

"I've been slave to more mortals than I can count. It's been the perfect cover, a way to have control without being seen and to feed without risking the hunt! But the world is changing, maybe for the better. Slavery is dying here, Annie. It's dead already in most other places."

"What has that to do with me and you and Shelby?"

Clementina sighed. "I needed you, when your Father's health began to fail. Soon I'll need Shelby in addition to you. And you'll both need me, too. The easy life of slaves and privilege you've known all your life is *over*."

"I'm not a fool, Clementina." Annie Court glanced at the window, at the darkness ahead. "I know it's over. They say Richmond will be lucky to hold out another six months! And the Federals. . . ."

"Slavery will be gone." Clementina gathered Annie to her bosom. Her embrace was comforting, if lacking some of the bodily warmth of a mortal. "But people will rebuild. Strong, vigorous and young people like you and Shelby Jackson. You'll have no slaves. But you'll have each other. And you'll have one loyal, but now free and paid, servant."

"So I'm to marry Shelby? Share my life—our lives— with him?"

Clementina nodded. "I'll be good to him. And to you, as always. And to your children, when the time comes and if they're willing."

Annie stiffened. "This arrangement sounds so . . . perverse. Everything I've been taught says this is wrong!"

"Who taught you it was right to lie beside another woman, Annie? And a black one, no less, who drinks your blood and who some legal papers say you *own*, courtesy your Father's estate? Oh, I have done things you cannot begin to *imagine*, girl!

"I have been with men and women both. Loved them and used them. I shall again, no doubt. But they have known the joy of my embrace and a rare sort of freedom— a dark and odd freedom that comes of willingly, consciously *deciding* to serve another!"

Clementina paused, looked deep into Annie's eyes with their foreheads pressed together.

"Tell me, mortal. Am I evil?"

"I don't know." Annie Court trembled. "I don't care. I love you and I agree. If I come to love Shelby, I'll marry him and share everything with him. Including you. But . . . if the emotion is not there, I'll find us someone else. Agreed?"

"Of course." Clementina smiled. "Surely I'd never argue such a point with one who owned me!"

They laughed and then they settled, wiggling beneath the silk sheets together. The silence between them was profound. Profound and comfortable.

Shadows

Lela E. Buis

The old house was haunted, they'd told me in town. When I had looked at it that first time, I could see why people might think so. It stood at the end of a long, ragged drive, backed up against stark woods. Scraggly weeds obscured what must have been the lawn, and a good-sized oak tree had shoved over the garden wall. Heavy shadows darkened the house even at noon, and the sun picked out a morbid rot infecting the gingerbread trim. The inside was open to the elements, spiderwebs on the mantel, filth on the stairs. The second floor bedrooms had been violated through broken casements, and bird's nests and bats' droppings cluttered the floors.

Retreating to my car again, I dusted my hands in dismay. It would need a lot of work to get rid of the rumors. Still, I needed a project just then, and an old house was certainly that. A money pit, didn't they say? Aside from my consulting, I had enough from Milo's life insurance to cover it. I forgot my hands were filthy then, and smeared dirt across my forehead and into my eyes.

The various workmen took care of the weeds in the yard, trampling over them with their tools and heavy boots. I did a lot of the yard repairs myself, as much as I could, anyhow. The physical labor was something I had needed.

Was this a personality flaw, my wanting to live in the past? Or did I just want to hide from my friends?

Whatever, I was moved in now. The finished house was staidly Victorian. Seen from the yard, it had a somber clapboard spine barely softened by the rounded, ornate porch. Leaded-glass windows cast a shifting, ghostly pattern on the pastel walls inside. The stairs had turned out mahogany, a convoluted swirl of patinaed wood and carved balustrades that rose into the dim glow of the second floor hallway. I'd furnished the place with period antiques and carpets to match, but still it was lifeless, because Milo wasn't there.

Well, hell. Standing there in the shifting, dying light of the upper hallway, it struck me all of a sudden—the effect of finishing the job—a terrible angst that had been lurking in wait for me all this time. Milo and I had always meant to retire here. We'd argued about it for years, put money away for the work. And now it was just me, coming to live here by myself—and sooner, rather than later.

I shuddered, wandering back downstairs and through the cavernous parlor, touching things, glancing over my shoulder now and then. Since I was here and solitary, the place had a questionable ambiance, as if I'd imported shadows with my things. Well, dammit, of course I had.

I fended off the urge to spend another night in town. For a while I sat on the new wicker furniture of the porch with my feet up, not sure I was pleased to see the sun disappear into the deep tangle of surrounding woods. Finally at dusk, I shivered briefly from the chill, and retreated from the mosquitoes to see what I could find to eat.

I was ravenous, just digging canned salsa and chips out of the grocery bags when a knock came at the kitchen screen. A man's shoulders darkened the last of the twilight. I had an instant of reserve from recent city living. Still, it wouldn't be good to get off on the wrong foot with the neighbors, so I crossed to the door. Seen closer, he was a reassuring silhouette, youngish and not overly large or hulking.

"Come in," I said, and shoved against the door spring.

"Thanks," he said.

The world tipped as he came into the light, slid sideways. He didn't seem to notice.

"I was just walking in the woods," he said, "and I saw your lights come on. Didn't know anyone was living here yet."

"I just moved in today," I said, with a certain difficulty. For a terrible second, I had trouble getting my breath. I'd thought he was Milo—a ghost suddenly materialized. I got a grip on my nerves. "I'm Lora Stansic." I nearly choked as I held out my hand.

"Giancarlo," he said. "Also, Stansic."

I stared, forgot to take my hand away. He was indistinct with the light behind him, an inch or so taller than me, slender and dark-haired, dark-eyed. China pale skin, gorgeous in that chiseled, eastern European way that had first attracted me to Milo. He was wearing a navy sweater and jeans, nondescript boots, and he smelled somehow of earth, old woods, and old houses. His hand felt wide and strong, very cold. Chill from the woods, no doubt. Or maybe it was my own hand that was cold. I let it fall, took another breath.

"I didn't know any Stansics still lived around here," I said and eased backward against the counter.

The house came from Milo's family, an older aunt that had died and left it years before. She'd been in a nursing home for years, and the house was already decrepit by the time she was gone. Milo had come up and taken care of things, sold her furniture—fallen in love with the house. Maybe I'd meant this as a memorial—I'd never seen it until after Milo was dead himself. Damn lucky the local kids hadn't vandalized it worse. But then, it had that reputation.

And now, here stood someone who could be Milo's ghost.

"I do," he said, answering my unasked question. "My friends call me Carlo."

A cousin—it had to be. His smile was faint, a delicate curve to his mouth. A darkness touched his eyes, a deeper dusk than the shade gathering within the house.

"You're Milo Stansic's widow, aren't you?" he said. "I'd heard he died, but not how."

His voice was a smooth tenor, oddly attractive. I turned away sharply, back to the groceries. "An accident," I said. "A car crash on the New Jersey Turnpike. Do you live close by?"

"Well, yes," he said. His eyes were opaque now. "Within walking distance, anyway."

"Would you like to stay a few minutes?" I asked. "Have some coffee?"

He looked at the cans spread over the counter, identified the jar of instant.

"I'll pass this time," he said, and flashed me a real smile to soften the refusal. He glanced at the clock above the sink, presenting an angular, dark-edged profile. "I should get going." His midnight eyes came back to me. "I just wanted to say 'hello.'"

Sudden panic shuddered through my veins. I wanted to keep him here. I wanted to ask him about the family, whether he'd known Milo. I gasped for another breath, choked, desperate, but then I pushed it all down. Don't scare the man away, Lora. There'll be other times.

I held out my hand again, hoping he wouldn't feel it tremble.

"Well, um, thank you for stopping by," I managed. "I'll have some real coffee next time."

A curious vapor was already rising from the woods, a breath of ground fog from earlier rain. He dissipated into it like mist himself.

Dammit, I thought, *dammit, dammit*—feeling the desperate loneliness crash down in his wake.

I opened a can of soup for dinner, ate in the kitchen alone. The rabbit ears on my TV didn't bring in much in the way of reception. High as the house was on the hill, there were higher ridges around me. I'd have to see about getting cable hooked up.

I drifted upstairs, stroking the banisters, trying not to think how empty and cold the house still seemed, trying to ignore the shadows that flitted away when I tried to look at them directly—another unhealthy symptom like staring at strangers and seeing someone else. Moonshadows flowed through the beveled panes upstairs, shattered into obscure patterns, nearly blood-colored. Tonight I didn't like the effect at all.

I showered and shampooed, rinsing off the sweat that I'd accumulated in the day of moving in. The tub was quaint and frivolous, decorated by claw feet and a ring of hanging plastic, ruffled outside with real lace. A big room, big windows, high ceiling. I'd lined half the walls with tile, left the rest with the original dark paneling. Naked in the full length mirror, I looked stark as a ghost myself,

pale and frosted with moisture. I was reasonably slim, but
not as thin as the norm. No gray in my brown hair. Too
young to be a widow, and to sleep in a cold bed by myself.

I yanked a comb through my permed curls, blew them
dry. Well, to hell with it all. The bed had nice carving, and
I'd held out for an authentic feather mattress to make up
for the lack of a husband's arms.

I woke from an erotic dream. It was a problem I'd had
for a while after Milo died, but it hadn't happened to me
recently. It was some time before the cool summer dawn.
I'd thrown back the blankets during the night, and now I
lay naked under the canopy, aroused, alive, quivering on
the tremulous edge of orgasm. The dream had been
confused, immediate, as if I had really felt a man's lips on
mine, his hands on my breasts. Worse, I could feel where
he had been inside me, fitted and tight against that
throbbing, hungry spot that ached to be rubbed, to be
mated and used.

I sighed. My skin tingled, ablaze with fire. I captured a
quick breath, raised my hands slowly, slid them along my
heated belly, over my breasts. The nipples were tight, hard
from the chill air, aroused by that ghostly touch. I teased
the points gently and stretched, enjoying the heat, the
ache. Then I gasped sharply, groaned as the orgasm
crashed down over me, triggered by the movement. I
arched, rose with the tide of sensation, throbbed, peaked—
slid down the other side into sweetness.

It was the best orgasm I'd had since . . . well. After a
while I got cold, and felt around for the blankets.

Later when I opened my eyes in bright daylight, the
whole thing seemed part of the same cloudy dream. But
certainly the orgasm had been real. Checking myself in
the mirror, I had that tousled, satisfied look of a woman
recently laid—only a few mosquito bites the worse for

wear. I'd have to get some bug repellent the next time I went to the store.

I'd need different coffee, too. I poured most of the instant down the drain.

I wanted to get the computer hooked up today, my connection with the rest of the world. I intended to work from right here, so I'd set aside a room as an office, but I still had my files to unpack. I got off to a slow, difficult start, and by night my shoulders ached and burned with overuse.

I fell into bed, had the same dream again, but later this time, in the pale light of dawn—but not the orgasm.

That was unusual two nights in a row. Typically my needs, or maybe my hormones, built up, and then once released, left me alone for a while. Yesterday's mosquito bites had faded by night, but now they were back, dotting my throat and my breasts with red and angry welts. I checked the window screens, but they all seemed tight. Damn, I hadn't realized the things were so predatory.

The local paper had come this morning, its bright wrapper clear in the dawn. I sat on the shaded porch to read it, drank some of the godawful bitter coffee. There was a listing of clubs, a social page. I wanted to meet more of my neighbors, get involved. Still I had work to do around the house, plus a consulting job I'd done the research for and not wound up before I'd moved.

I folded the paper and laid it across my knees, leaned my head back to study the pattern of shade on the refurbished lawn. The woods loomed beyond, thick and forbidding. The roses I'd put in were blooming already, and their perfume seemed heavy, almost cloying on the damp, morning air.

A curious thing. Somehow the dream hadn't completely cleared this morning, and the erotic urge still nagged at me. Not quite an ache, but still a distraction, it was a warm need that resided in the nerves of my inner thighs, a teasing where my nipples brushed against my flannel shirt. I closed my eyes, breathing the rose scent again. Damn. It had been such a long time since I'd had a man. Was it the ghost of Milo doing this to me? Had I brought him along with me, his memory? Or was it something else, something that came with the house?

Whatever, this morning I needed to go to the grocery store. There was a ramshackle shop just a few miles down the road, a combination meat and convenience store with gas pumps out in front. Homely and old-fashioned, it had taken my fancy, and I was determined to shop there instead of making the longer drive into town.

The store proprietor's name was Bogart, I recalled, with maybe the faintest, aging resemblance to the star.

"Miz Stansic," he said, tipping a nonexistent hat. "What can I do for you this morning?"

"Coffee," I croaked, and then I tried to remember what else I needed.

It took me a while to gather up a few supplies and get them back to the counter.

"Ma'am," he said. "You be careful out there in the woods by yourself. Don't you go openin' your door to anybody at night. Things goes on in the woods sometimes. And folks might take advantage of a widow livin' alone."

I had my mouth open to say certainly I was going to be careful, but instead I shut my teeth with an audible click.

Bogart didn't seem to notice. He checked out the groceries on his manual register, turning them over slowly to search for the prices and ringing them up one by one. I watched him, chewing at my lower lip. He'd gotten me to worrying about strangers, infected me with doubt.

"Mr. Bogart, I've been wondering," I asked. "Do any of my husband's relatives still live around this area?"

"No," he rumbled, blinking through half-glasses. "None I know of."

That confused me.

"None?"

"Not since Miz Edda Stansic died," he insisted. "And that was years back. Your husband's aunt, wasn't she? Last of 'em, as far as I know."

"Um," I commented.

He began to bag the groceries, set them up on the counter with a gesture of completion.

"Here you go," he said. Then his face changed, darkened to a frown.

"What's that?" he asked.

"What?" I said, almost startled.

"What's happened to your throat?" His voice had gone gruff.

"Nothing," I said. "It's just a mosquito bite."

Still, in the car my hand strayed upward. The bites didn't itch. Instead they felt tender, ached with a sweet pain that connected in some way with my dreams.

And it seemed Mr. Giancarlo Stansic had lied to me. Still, the way he looked bothered me—too much like Milo. He had to be a cousin. So where was the lie? That he lived around here? Maybe he'd just been in town for a visit, and I'd never see him again. Suddenly I felt the choked, desperate fear recurring that I'd felt as he went out my door—that I wanted to see him again, and I wouldn't. He was the first man I'd really looked at since Milo died. He was real, concrete—I had touched him that night. Or was he? Now I wasn't sure. Somehow the incident had gone confused too, lost in the erotic cataclysm of that next morning.

I was starting a headache, and my ice cream was beginning to melt in the seat. I started the car and drove on home.

A pair of aspirin killed the throb behind my eyes. I studied the marks on my throat in the bathroom mirror, found they were fading already. I dabbed on some Neosporin and went to work in my office, but by two o'clock I had to give up.

I couldn't keep my mind on what I was doing. My nipples itched with the slightest brush of the shirt; my breasts felt heavy and swollen. My jeans were too tight, the seams rubbing hard across my aching flesh. I'd never had anything like this happen to me before, nothing so sweet and full of pain. Not even when Milo and I had first gotten married and we'd spent a week lusting after one another in the Bahamas. And this whole obsession was beginning to center on a face that wasn't Milo's at all. Panic surged through me when I realized that. I thought about masturbating. I thought about about calling the sheriff and asking who the hell was masquerading as Giancarlo Stansic.

That would be downright dumb. People already whispered about the house.

I sighed and snapped off the computer. In the end I didn't take either option. Instead, I spent the rest of the afternoon going through the old family albums that were something else Milo had inherited from his aunt. I dug them out of the boxes, leafed through the pages. The brittle sheets crackled over one by one, the sepia faces staring out from the past.

Nothing.

I don't know what I'd expected to find. The eyes, the jaw, the delicate line of his mouth. Or maybe the dark mole that had stood out on the pale skin of his forehead. And why was I so focused on Carlo's face? No idea. I had barely seen the man. I packed the dusty albums back in their box.

I was starving. I had forgotten lunch, and now it was late for dinner. I had something to cook tonight, made up some spaghetti and a salad, bolted a tumbler of wine.

By then my whole body was throbbing as I thought about the coming night, and the dark empty hours of the morning. Pure lust. Was this something that could be captured and labeled like the wine? Maybe not, but still I meant to try.

I meant to stay awake. I lay there watching the slow march of moonlight across the walls, listening to the deafening rasp of cicadas from the woods. I counted off the minutes, the hours, and finally I felt a dark lassitude sweep over me.

With it came a tension, the ominous stabbing of fear. I didn't really know what the hell I was doing here— playing with the supernatural? Maybe I should have fled back to New York as soon as I realized something was . . . was. . . . But then the thought was gone, sighing away on the shimmer of moonlight.

Something drifted through the screen like windblown mist, took shape, a darker shade in the cloudy darkness of the room. I lay, mesmerized, watching.

And something else materialized, as well. I'd known all the time it was there. It haunted me in the shadows of my apartment in New York, again in the gathering gloom of this house. The ghost of Milo stood between me and every man I'd met since he'd died, a dark, indistinct phantom that warned me away.

But not this time. The air sparked with electricity, exploded in swirls of white-hot cloud. Flames crackled along the ceiling, flaring, hissing where ectoplasms met. I jerked up in terror, cowered against the headboard, clutching the blankets with frozen hands. Wind battered at me, tore at my hair. Fire scalded my skin. A portrait tore loose from the wall and crashed across the room. The frame flew into splinters against an antique chair. A vase exploded with the next slash of fire, and thunder crackled through the billowing mist.

"Stop it!" I screamed. "Stop it! What do I have to do, make a choice?"

Suddenly, just like that, everything was dark and quiet in the room. The house was empty, still—too empty. I huddled against the headboard, heaving for breath.

"Dammit," I shuddered. "Don't both of you go."

A shadow reformed, blocking the moonlight.

He shed the sweater, the solid boots and jeans. His body was paler than Milo's, taller, heavier about the shoulders and thighs. A breeze drifted the curtains. The bed gave, and then his arms went around me.

I sighed, turned my head slightly, felt the sharp edge of incisors within his kiss. His hand drifted over my breasts, and my nipples hardened and rose to meet him. He nipped my earlobe, kissed my throat, and already I hurt for him.

"He's gone," he whispered. "You had to let him go."

"Carlo . . ." I said.

"Wait. . . ."

He caressed me in a way I'd never felt before, his hands like the moonlight, his lips the soft flutter of moth wings, with needles of fire beneath. Every touch inflamed me, until finally I couldn't wait any longer. I slid down flat in the bed, reached for him, and he shifted over me. I caught my breath as he pushed in—gasped at his first thrust into that heated, burning ache. Then I lay helpless and shuddering beneath him, clutching him, moving as he did, my face pressed tight against his ear.

He felt the tide rise between us, pierced my throat as it broke. I had never felt such an orgasm, but I had guessed at it, feeling the pale afterglow that first morning after he'd gone. I rocked beneath him and fell, lay there shuddering in the aftershocks, wondering how much blood he took each time.

I didn't care. I was young, hot-blooded—and dammit, I had the resources to spare. I held his cool body over mine like the missing blankets, breathing in the scent of earth and old houses that still clung to his hair. He stirred finally.

"I was afraid you were another ghost," I said.

He shifted to one side, nipped at my earlobe again. "No," he said, "but I do come with the house." Then he sighed into my ear. "It's been empty far too long."

Cherished Blood
Vampire Erotica

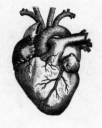

Drink to Me Only with Thine Eyes—

A. R. Morlan

Not very long after making my way to the great, glittering night-jewel of a city known to simple mortals as New York, very soon after I opened my store in fact, I commissioned a fellow artisan to hand-ink a framed scroll which now hangs above the counter located toward the rear of my showroom:

"The Beginning of Wisdom is Learning to Call Things by Their Right Names."

—An Ancient Chinese Saying

Originally, I intended the sign merely to provide a gentle reminder to my customers about the importance of knowing the difference between soft and hard pottery, or of glazed ware from enamel ware . . . for while I am a master of long standing (the longest standing) in the ancient art of creating pottery of all forms and of virtually all historical styles, it still causes me pain to hear someone ask for a "porcelain flowerpot" or "something simple—like a Ming vase, maybe?" Yet, whenever my customers read the sign today, in this time of names more bizarre than any I have previously heard in my many centuries of wandering the ever-shifting, blood-scented starlit darkness—eccentric jumblings of the Anglo-Saxon and the African, Gaelic and Germanic, with scatterings of names purloined from my native Orient—they invariably take my words as an invitation to explain their own idiosyncratic appellations to me, even as they dismiss my own name (albeit a common one among my countrymen long before I ceased to be a member of the Chinese—or human—race) without comment.

And always, when they pause in their perusal of the examples of my art available for immediate sale, and glance up at the inked scroll, they begin their personal litany with some variation of this question:

"'Right names' . . . does that mean some names for things are wrong?"

"A name is considered wrong only as long as its true meaning remains unknown."

That's usually enough to set the customer off on his or her litany of why "my name is just right for me"—and, because (for the time being) that person *is* merely my customer, and not my impending evening's repast (*if* I can abide their continued presence), I fold my hands against my torso, widen the smile on my lips, and nod sagely as yet another potential meal explains the original meaning of his or her first or last name ... or all three given names, if the customer is inexplicably proud of the *combined* meaning of his or her given title.

Personally, I choose to forget the meanings of names given to those customers I later rename "Sustenance" ... and then, for the sole purpose of being able to tell any concerned relatives or friends who might drop by my establishment seeking information about their missing loved one that I never heard of such a person, especially by that name. ...

But sometimes, I remember a name because the person bearing it holds the promise of being more than a nourishing interlude, a means to sate my unending, immortal hunger ... and especially if that person is *not* so readily obtainable for my more personal needs.

Even if she had done no more than mention her name without elaboration, I would have been unable to forget it ... or her; from the soft, petallike sheen of her flesh to the the subcutaneous throbbing of rich, heady blood in her veins and arteries to the guileless shimmer of her pale green-gold eyes, she was the epitome of feminine beauty and submerged passion. Far more beautiful in her unadorned simplicity than any of the wandering Empusae in ancient Greece, with their seductive, blood-sucking ways, or the Countess Bathory in all her blood-bathed glory ... more desirable to me than any concubine from my native China, even in the sunlit days of my life, before the long-nailed nocturnal demon *Kian-si* favored me with a form of half-life after what should've been my certain death at her daggerlike hands.

Spurred on by the unspoken challenge of my sign, she not only uttered her name to me—"Trinette"—but then took pains to explain: "It's French, and means 'little innocent'—my mother, she was really into French culture and all, because she'd taken French in college, but we're really from Northern Italy, the blond part. I think it's a kind of . . . dumb name, but my boyfriend, he thinks it's cool. Of course, with him having a name like 'Cronan,' I suppose anything else *would* sound cool—"

How old can she be? I found myself wondering, even though the question was, of course, made moot by my own advanced sum of years; to me, the most wizened crone still able to draw breath was but a babe when I was celebrating my own several-thousandth (counting them can be far too depressing!) birthday by imbibing the lifeblood of what may well have been that wrinkled hulk's great-grandparent. . . .

Still, the obvious youth and inexperience of this maiden enchanted me, even as it intimidated me—I would, paradoxically, need to be less subtle, less suave than usual, in my pursuit or her, lest she simply not understand my import. Yet, I could not openly take her, steal her away to be my wife, for she was obviously promised to another—the scintillating small stone set in the ring on her left hand was a longstanding sign of her potential enslavement to another . . . this "Cronan" she spoke of so nonchalantly. . . .

"But surely, a name like 'Cronan' must have a right meaning of its own, no? A special meaning, like your name?" (I cringed at my own poor syntax, but to capture, sometimes one must provide suitable camouflage for the trap.)

Trinette smiled at my question, and said as she leaned against the counter which ran between us like a fireproof curtain protecting the fragile parchment from the hungering flame, "It's funny, but his name really does sorta describe him. . . . It means 'little dark one' in Irish, which he is on his mom's side, and it also means 'brown one' in Gaelic, which is what they speak in Scotland, where his dad's from. Like, literally. He was born there."

Moving her thin, delicate arms in a supple pushing motion which made her gently mounded breasts heave and fall under the restraining protective embrace of her blouse, she gracefully backed away from the counter. As she began strolling the widely-spaced aisles of low, glass-topped shelves upon which rested examples of my kiln-fired work, she added, "And that's where he and I will be moving once Cronan gets his degree. . . . He's studying medicine, only not to be a doctor, y'know, like a doctor-doctor, who treats sick people. Cronan's going to be a psychologist—"

As my would-be bride of blood prattled on and on about her earthly love, I watched the graceful, winglike swoop and flutter of her tapered fingers as they moved to almost-caress the surface of a lusterware pseudo-Greek vase, then hovered longingly before a translucent Sèvres plate, before actually descending to shyly touch the surface of a Sung-period (or celadone to people of her time and place) objet d'art—a small goblet, whose soft green gaze shone with a moist-fleshlike sheen in the store's indirect white lighting. . . .

(The image of our night of consummation was so clear to me, the details as sharply defined as one's reflection in porcelain:

(Trinette's bare arm moved languidly down my naked torso, the soft tender skin of her inner forearm brushing my own flesh, as her fingers walked down across my belly, toward my waiting organs of delight. And as gently as one might lift a paper-thin china tea cup, she slipped her hand, palm up, under my low-drooping globes of *yang* essence, then—with one coyly rubbing finger—she stroked the underside of my Jade Stalk, until it slowly stiffened in response to her tender ministrations.

(As my Jade Stalk rose, erect and as firm as the spout of a ceremonial teapot, my Trinette shifted beside me, revealing the long sloping curve of her bare back and globular buttocks as she moved herself into position over my triumphant organ. Carmine-daubed lips parted like two carved arcs of the finest cinnabar, then bent down her head of fiery-bright hair until the ends of her tresses brushed against my tensing thighs. And when her face was close to me, I could feel the soft exhalations of warm air against my throbbing stalk, just before a tongue-tip of exquisite, probing softness began to explore the glans and underside of my Vigorous Peak . . . followed by the sharp-edged glancing contact with her ivory incisors, which made my entire body tremble.

(Then my entire Jade Stalk, from tip to base, was engulfed in a cave of liquid, undulating warmth, caressed with a tongue which whipped from side to side like the lashings of a flicking cat's tail—and soon I felt the rushing warmth of yang essence flowing upward through my trembling manhood. But to squander my essence on a mere act of fellation would be wasteful, according to the old Masters of my race. Yang essence was limited in supply, especially for a being like myself, yet . . . this was my wedding night, to my precious bride of blood, so perhaps a *small* wasting of yang essence would be in order—

(Especially when my beloved's lips and tongue were so indescribably soft, and yet so urgent, in their ministrations. And so I did not go through the prescribed motions, of closing my eyes—for to do so would have deprived me of the sight of my beautiful one—pressing my tongue against the roof of my mouth, bending my back and stretching my neck, prior to opening my nostrils wide and closing my mouth, then sucking in my breath, in order to pull the semen back into my body. I did none of these long-prescribed things . . . but the reward of seeing my Trinette's face bent low over my groin, eyes closed in ecstasy as my yang essence rushed into her mouth, creating a kilnlike inferno around my throbbing Jade Stalk, was far greater than the conservation of my limited yang essence. . . .)

Turning her head quickly, so that her shoulder-length russet-brown hair moved, pendulumlike, in a sheaf of herbal-scented beauty, she asked, "Is this jade?"

Considering that there was now a good fifteen feet of floor space between us, I deemed it to be the most proper time to step out from behind my shieldlike counter and slowly, courteously, make my way toward her. Even from the chaste distance of five feet away, once I finally stood in place to speak to her, I could literally feel the throb of her lifeblood, calling to me in a deep, moist susurration that echoed in my very body. Calling upon my centuries-old reserve of willpower, I forced myself to smile once more, before replying, "No, it is merely a glaze upon the porcelain . . . but you are quite right in your supposition. Many people have mistaken Sung porcelain for carved jade."

(Or in your case, a Jade Stalk, I thought, as ripples of pleasure from my fantasy of her continued to course through my body.)

"Oh, that's a relief. . . . I didn't want you thinking I was dumb." Trinette smiled before moving down the aisle until she came to another, similarly-shaped drinking vessel I'd crafted. She cupped it as tenderly as a concubine cradling a man's Jade Stalk in her pink-suffused palm, and asked, "So I suppose this one is also pottery and not real jade?"

It had been over eighteen hundred years since I'd fired that particular drinking cup, back in the time of the Imperial kilns made available for the use of master potters like myself, yet the silky-smooth green glaze still shone as brightly . . . but only a total innocent like my Trinette (how those syllables rolled so vibrantly in my brain!) would confuse a piece of Han period pottery, with its simple, sturdy silhouette, with the supple, graceful curves of Sung period pottery.

But that ignorance suddenly made me aware of other, more useful gaps which she might have in her knowledge of my craft—not to mention in her knowledge of the center of my existence.

"What do you suppose is the difference between this bowl"—I cupped my hand under a small, glazed-ware piece I'd done as a time-killer while waiting for some Raku to cure—"and this bowl?" I finished asking, as I lifted up a granite-ware ashtray with the other hand. Trinette's liquid-fire eyes darted from one grayish glazed piece to the other, as her delectable mouth formed a small, coral-painted moue . . . then the darting flames of color in her dancing eyes grew warmer, as she replied confidently, "The price!"

The sly girl had peeked under each piece, so as to see the price sticker I'd affixed to the underside of their bottoms—and in doing so, had completely missed the crucial difference between the earthenware bowl, with its relatively plastic clay (which in itself was quite, quite close to soft pottery, save for the addition of a glaze), and the stoneware ashtray, with the greater percentage of strengthening silica in the clay mix—a percentage which ensured that the resulting piece, when fired, would be of close, hard inner texture.

Not an easy distinction to see, but it was a difference as crucial as trying to suck lifeblood from a painted, carved statue of marble, rather than the sleep-stilled neck of a cosmetics-adorned harlot. . . .

True, the upper surface of the bowl was quite similar to the utilitarian ashtray; both pieces were hard, shiny, mottled in color—but the unglazed undersides were obviously unique to each piece, as individual as the varying, sloping curves of a waiting neck. The bottom of the bowl was akin to the flat end of a common flower pot, while the other object's unseen surface was light and flecked with infinitesimal spots of shining silica, much like the small bright glints of light in the eyes of the freshly-bitten. . . .

Warmed by the sanguine self-assurance which suffused through my own rather tepid veins upon this latest revelation of her blissful ignorance of my artistic domain, I bade her to follow me down another aisle, to a low shelf covered with naif-design flower pots designed to appeal to Midwestern tourists and students low on funds. Then—after selecting one of the pots—I gestured for her to follow me up an adjoining aisle, where I'd arranged several of my finest alkaline-glazed Chinese and Japanese-styled teacups, each crafted of clay well-blended with silica and kaolin . . . cups which were exceptional examples of porcelain's resonance and infusibility, their upper rims semitransparent, yet almost diamond-hard.

Gingerly picking up one of the palm-sized cups, I held the pot and the cup before Trinette—

(even as I longed to hold my hands under the cuplike softness of her gently swaying, unfettered breasts, my thumbs lightly teasing her nipples into budding hardness, before nuzzling her bared neck with my probing, pursing lips, and aching, porcelain-tempered fangs. . . .)

—and asked in my most solemn, stereotypically Chinese-merchant, butter-up-the-customer voice, "Touch each of these, and tell me, what is the the difference between them?" while I envisioned her touching parts of my own body, both the soft and the hard. . . .

(Gratefully swallowing down my yang essence with a tender smile, Trinette fondled my gradually-drooping Jade Stalk with one hand, while running the other hand back up my torso, until her fingers rested just below my jawline. Cupping my chin in her palm, she used her thumb to gently move my upper lip away from my incisors, then bent low to kiss me, her mouth still salty-sweet from my essence, her tongue prying itself between my teeth before mine slid forward to meet hers, in a pliant moist embrace—)

Suppressing a giggle, Trinette lightly caressed the unglazed, near-porous surface of the flowerpot, whose exterior might easily have been grazed by the jutting stone in her ring, then ran the same tapered finger over the superbly-glazed skin of the teacup, then shrugged, since I'd made sure that the bottoms, with their price stickers, were angled away from her clever green eyes.

"You can't even guess?"

She shrugged again, creating delicious folds of creamy flesh which briefly rose up to cradle the bottom of her neck, before she relaxed her shoulders.

Tilting the bowl and the pot so that she could see into them, I replied, in my best Chinaman-make-joke accent, "No hole in bottom!"

Her laughter was like glass wind chimes which formed a silvery descant to the throaty warble of the nightingale back in the land of my lost humanity, and I almost shed a tear at the memory of my former warmth and easily-rising passion and then limitless yang essence. But the reality of my current fate, and my unending need for both sustenance and (occasionally) emotional nurturing, kept the smile on my lips, and the twinkle in my eyes.

"That's a good one. . . . I'll have to remember it for Cronan. . . . Speaking of him, that's why I came in here—do you sell wedding goblets?" she asked, confirming the rightness of the plan I'd already begun to form for trapping—and keeping—her as my own.

"I do sell them . . . but first, I have to make them special, for each couple who request them," I replied, consciously slipping into the near-Pidgin dialect which seemed to put her more and more at ease with me, perhaps because it contrasted so well with the erudition of her someday-psychologist fiancé.

"Personalized?" she chirped, and my heart fluttered in time with her warbling voice. "Like with names and dates?"

"With anything they desire . . . any color, and any size goblet. For big thirst, or little thirst—"

"You'll have to make them plenty big. . . . Northern Italians and Scots-Irishman do love their wine." She smiled, and as her lips parted to reveal even, off-white teeth whose surfaces glinted in the store's white light, I imagined them bathed in the wine-red richness of my own immortal blood . . . blood which, when sipped by a mortal, had an effect which far surpassed intoxication, both in duration and in the resulting fire in the blood—

(And as our mouths pressed close in a firm-lipped embrace, Trinette began to writhe against me, her body burning from within as my ageless essence invaded each limb, each digit, with each hard-thudding beat of her heart, until all of her was infused with the most essential part of my being—my wedding gift of eternal life, of a hunger beyond mere physical sating, for my body, my essence. And only in the presence of one who'd partaken of my blood could my blood pulse strongly through my body, my Jade Stalk . . . my only possibility of true consummation was copulation with one of my own kind. . . .)

Even if I could not yet taste her blood, by the time she was lawfully wedded to her beloved Cronan, with the first sip from her special goblet, she would instead be mine and mine alone.

"Do you want your names and the date of the wedding on them?" I asked, suddenly all business (it was either that, or begin to chortle and dance around the aisles from the sheer exhilaration over what would occur during her wedding feast . . . an even I could literally picture in my mind's inner eye, it was so real and so vivid for me.)

"Yeah, but something else, too. . . . Wait a sec, I have it written down—" Trinette began to unzip her fanny pack, then rooted around in the bright green nylon pouch for something, until she gave me another radiant smile, and held up a sheet of paper covered with a couple of neatly handwritten lines, in an obviously masculine, but refined hand:

> *"Drink to me only with thine Eyes,*
> *And I will pledge with mine"*

I couldn't stop myself from smiling as I read those words; I'd been fortunate enough to hear Ben Jonson himself sing them, not long after he'd penned them in England so many, many years ago, and I felt a stab of longing for those gilded, passionate, yet elegant days, even as I felt an unexpected bond of . . . kinship for the man who'd selected the words for his as-yet uncrafted wedding goblets. Trinette's Cronan had to be quite a fine catch, especially for a young woman of her dubious intellectual gifts (bloodlust or no, I did realize that despite her physical charms, she was not . . . the sharpest incisor in the mouth).

"—wants them written or carved or whatever along the rim of the goblet, with the first line on his goblet, and the second one on mine," she was saying, as I forced myself to appear focused on her. "And could you make them red, or maybe even dark red? My bridesmaids will be in red velvet, only the maid of honor's going to be in *dark* red—"

Dark red indeed, I told myself, wistfully remembering the Cinnabar Clefts of my long-gone concubine conquests, as she went on and on about the size and shape of the goblets she had in mind. Oh, I will give you goblets—or rather, a goblet, my sweet innocent, my untasted wine—of a true, deep *blood* red. . . .

Trinette's wedding was to be in one month, more than enough time to prepare the special mixture of the most plastic, easily molded clay I could buy, plus an entire cup's worth (drained slowly, a few drips at a time, and always between my living feasts) of my own blood, and form the goblet by hand, partly by fast-kicked wheel, until it was ready for a glaze composed (again) mostly of my own eldritch blood, mixed with the more traditional glazing compounds. And just before I applied the living deep red glaze, I carefully incised the phrase

And I will pledge with mine

to that convex outer surface, forever marking the goblet as the one intended for my bride of deepest-red delights, that bearer of her own Cinnabar Cleft, a place my own lips would soon caress, even if the days of my last such nether-lipped were as distant as the last period of my own Jade Stalk's porcelain hardness, yet another tantalizing memory, albeit a soon-to-be-revived memory—

(Once Trinette's lips touch the wine-filled goblet, the flush begins with her lips, turning them a bloody-dark crimson, far darker than any modern lipstick, then progresses through her body, limb by limb, until she is covered with a blush of submerged fire . . . and it is with that warmth, radiating for her entire body pressed tightly against mine, that my long-dormant Jade Stalk rises once again, filled with a matching inner flame, the strength of blood seeking like-blood. ...)

—white for Cronan's goblet, I used my finest siliceous clay, and merely the regular glaze. But once I'd fired the goblets, they looked remarkably similar, save for the differing lines of "The Forest: To Celia" that embellished their outer surfaces.

But even after they'd cooled, the goblet which was to caress the lips of my beloved-from-far-away was not quite ready. Inside the concave surface of the goblet, deep within the shadowed recesses of the breast-cupped interior, I used an iron nail to scratch off much of the glaze, so that the slightly porous inner clay was revealed. In turn it would release the essence of my blood, of my . . . uniqueness, into the acidic wine which would soon fill the goblet. Be it red wine or white, the acids in the potent brew would work a form of magic for me, distant, subtle legerdemain of the most insidious, infectious—yet sensuous—sort.

When Trinette's soft lips touched the goblet, and the sweet liquid-and-blood touched her waiting tongue, she would truly be a bride, of the most unholy sort. It was all I could do not to laugh aloud when she arrived to pick up the finished goblets, with her Cronan in tow, for even though he was a most comely young man, fine of limb and manly-fair of face (with his own hidden rushing spring of crimson fire under his fine-pored flesh), he would be no match at all for my plain-faced allure. ...

On the night of their wedding feast, I paced the confines of my pottery studio located in back of my shop in anticipation of the coming of my longed-for blood-bride. True, she was not the first of my ensanguined mistresses of the night, but even for those of my kind, forever can become too, too much to contemplate, and so I'd been "widowed" many times, when those whom I'd converted through the sharing of my essence decided to in turn convert others more comely, or more to their liking, to the life of moon-kissed darkness and even darker desires and needs. But Trinette, my little innocent one, she longed for the kind of wisdom I possessed, the kind of power which comes with centuries of un-life, and the memories of countless nights of submerged passions—for didn't she breathe more deeply when speaking of her loved-one's love of education, of prestige?

For her, I could provide the erudition and status she longed for, plus the promise of life (or a dark-lusting simulation of it) eternal . . . all in exchange for perhaps a century or two of undivided adoration. . . .

Glancing at the ornate Swiss clock on the wall of my studio, I noticed that it was well past the time of the reception. It was being held only a few long blocks from my store, a miniscule walk or anxious run away. I began shivering with anticipation as sensual as any fleshly orgasm I'd once experienced, for I knew that the elixir of my eternity-tainted blood and her wine would prove irresistible to her, and would lure her on just as surely as the curved hook guides the silvery carp through the still, still waters, or the scent of the Open Peony Blossom attracts the ever-seeking upright Red Bird to a sheltering warm home—

The dry, frantic scraping of nails against my studio's alley door was echoed with the soft humming of "Greensleeves" behind that closed wooden barrier, the melody sinuous and melancholy in the night silence . . . and as I opened the door, I reflexively pulled back my lips and bared my porcelain-shiny incisors, in anticipation of sinking them (much like my own Red Bird, from my days of truly living flesh) deep into the bared bosom (in lieu of the Open Peony Blossom) of my blood-mate—

—who in turn was staring at me, eyes bright with bloodlust and eager for that dark consummation of the night . . . only they were eyes of warm amber-brown, under waving short hair of deepest mahogany.

But before I could utter a single word of dismay, Cronan smiled, his lips barely covering the already-growing incisors lightly rimmed with blood-wine, and pantomimed an arms-crossing gesture with his goblet-bearing hand . . . a motion which had brought to *his* lips that goblet formed from clay and blood, and glazed with a coating of my own inner essence, fire-hardened into a glaze of near-diamondlike vitrification. . . .

But yet, when he smiled, his eyes took on a warm, ale-bright glow, one which was even more beautiful than the green-gold fire of . . . of his newly jilted bride's eyes. And as my wine-distilled blood raced through his fine features, and suffused his flesh with a ruddy bloom, I nodded my head in agreement with the wisdom—and rightness—of his name, be it the Irish or the Gaelic interpretation, as I moved my working fingers down his shirt, revealing his well-muscled, darkly-tufted chest button by undone button—and when my hand reached his waistband, he placed both of his warm hands on mine, and fervently nodded his assent as I unbuttoned and unzipped his tuxedo trousers, and let them fall down past his already-erect Jade Stalk with a billowing *shuuush* of black fabric.

And, as my fingers gently eased his Jade Stalk out of his briefs, before massaging it from the base to the throbbing, clear-pearl-adorned tip, Cronan's eyes fluttered closed, even as his mouth gently parted, revealing the growing buds of the ever-lengthening incisors within, while his own seeking hands caressed my bared shoulders, and slid palms-out along my jawline, in a motion so, *so* close to my imagined wedding night with . . . with *her.*

And, as his own fiery yang essence warmed me from within, surging past my aching lips, I realized that once I referred to Cronan as my blood-mate, rather than blood-bride, a most wise choice had been made for me by fate.

For once Cronan knelt before me, and partook of my yang essence, there was no difference at all between the fantasy of a month ago and the reality of this night.

After all, as my sign in the shop says, it's all a matter of calling things by their right name. . . .

Just as a mate might be that of the soul, as well as the body. . . .

Blood Dreams

Susan Elizabeth Gray

The vampire's wife rolled toward the center of her bed. The sheets were cold and her husband's place was empty. She opened one eye and looked at the glowing red numbers of the digital clock. Two-thirty-one. Sunrise wasn't until six-twenty, so it would be at least another two hours until he came home, if not longer.

Theresa stretched, sliding her body over the satin surface of the sheets. She reached under her husband's pillow. The cloth bag of dirt was there, tied with a velvet ribbon. That was just one of many little idiosyncrasies that Theresa had to get used to since they'd met, at last year's Halloween party. Blake was dressed, of course, like Count Dracula. Underneath his cape he wore a white tie and tails, and he even had an ebony walking stick to complete the ensemble. Theresa had been persuaded to go to the party at the last minute, and all she could come up with was a pair of cat ears and a silky black dress. She drew whiskers across her cheeks and practiced a faint meow.

At the party, Theresa stood by the punch bowl, watching the friendly conversation and flirting swirl around her like confetti. Suddenly she became aware of someone standing beside her. He stood as silently as she, watching. Finally, he said, "If I had known the party was going to be this much fun, I would have come earlier."

Theresa laughed before she could stop herself and turned to see if she knew him. His hair was as black as his cape, and swept straight back off his forehead. He was so tall Theresa had to tip her head back to look at him. He smiled, clicked his heels together once and said, "Count Dracula, at your service. Or, you can call me Blake."

Theresa made a mock curtsy. "Theresa," she meowed.

"A pleasure," he said, as he took her hand. He raised it to his lips and Theresa shivered at their cool touch.

They spent the rest of the evening in a corner of the room, talking, and Theresa was impressed by his self-assurance and calm. He seemed to look at the world as she did, a few steps back, apart from the meaningless day-to-day trivia that consumed most of her friends.

He explained that he worked the night shift, but promised to call her on his break the next evening. When she left the party, he raised her hand again to his lips, but this time turned her palm upward and pressed it against his cheek. "You are so warm," he said.

DEAR DIARY: I met someone last night, finally. At the costume party. His name is Blake. I'm afraid to like him too much. I gave him my phone number. I hope he calls.

Three-ten. Theresa pulled the covers around her and turned to one side. She remembered how, at first, she didn't believe him. "You're just teasing," she said. It was only when he pulled her over to the mirror and stood right beside her that she began to believe, to feel the sharp edges of reality blur and soften. She turned to him, breathless, faint with the first stirrings of both fear and desire. She pressed her hand against his chest.

"How?" she asked.

He took her hand and led her over to the couch. Speaking slowly, in a quiet, measured tone as if talking to a child, he explained—explained how he had been born again so many years ago. Born of a woman, yes, but not his mother. How his appetite changed and how he must feed it every night. He tried, he said, to only take from those who wouldn't be hurt, those who were sick and dying anyway.

"But I thought vampires were evil," she whispered.

Blake looked down at her with glittering eyes. "We are," he said softly, and kissed her.

DEAR DIARY: Am I crazy?

The first time they made love, Theresa wept. He was so gentle, his hands so cool against her heated flesh. When she was ready, he paused, leaning above her. "I need to use protection," he said softly.

"No," she answered. "It's all right. I can't. Get pregnant."

"It's not that," he said, and slid to the side of the bed. He reached over and removed a small, foil package from the pocket of his pants. The condom crinkled as he unrolled it, smoothing it over his dark, erect penis.

He bent down and kissed her on the forehead. "You'll be safe," he said and entered her.

Afterward, when they had each been broken on the back of the wild horse, Theresa watched as he removed the condom, its tip full of blood.

DEAR DIARY: He asked me to marry him. I know what he is. But I have never met a man who is so gentle, so careful. He promised he would love me forever. I'm afraid of what that means.

They married at City Hall on a cold winter evening when the sun set shortly before five. No one was invited. The justice of the peace kept glancing at his watch, as if eager to get home to his well-lit house for dinner, a house filled with warm-blooded children and a plump wife. After the ceremony, they went to Theresa's favorite Italian restaurant. Blake, ever courteous, ordered pasta with marinara sauce, and claimed to be too full from a late lunch to finish his meal.

At the table, the wine glowing in the candle light like liquid rubies, Blake looked into Theresa's eyes and said, "I will never hurt you." She was surprised at the small sigh of disappointment rising in her breast.

DEAR DIARY: I cut my finger last night. It was eight o'clock and I was slicing vegetables for a stir fry. Blake is polite and lets me eat first, before he leaves to find his dinner, or should I say dinner partners? The knife slipped and sliced into the pad of my index finger. A bead of blood, garnet red. I could feel him stiffen and draw back, and his nostrils flared like a mad horse about to bolt. I don't know what came over me. I crossed the kitchen to where Blake was sitting at the round, oak table. The blood was still a bubble, thick and round at the tip of my finger. My heart was beating so hard I could barely breathe. I showed him and said, "Do you want to lick it?" He shook his head but I could see the desire rising in his eyes like

mercury in a thermometer on a blistering hot July day. I took
his hand and turned it, palm up, and placed it on the table.
Then, with a boldness I didn't know I had, I squeezed the
drop of blood from my finger until it lay, a small, red pool, in
the center of his palm. I turned, and went back to the kitchen
counter, to my slicing. The sucking sound behind me made
chills run up and down my spine.

**Theresa stirred again, and turned toward the clock. Four-
seventeen. Not long now. She lowered her hand and
pushed up the hem of her thin, silk nightgown. Her sex
was warm and wet, waiting. Once, they had tried to make
love before Blake went out for his evening meal. His body
was cold and his penis felt like a core of ice entering her,
sending icicles of pain flashing through her body. She
pulled him closer, but no matter how tight she held him,
he was still cold. And the way he looked down at her,
with eyes as flat and black as wafers, black and empty....**
"You're so warm," he whispered. "Warm and full," he
said, tracing one finger along the side of her throat. Then
he pulled back, leaving her breathless.
Now they waited until he was full, his skin warm and
rosy from the hot blood of others.
"Do you ever kiss them?" she once asked.
"Not on the lips," he replied.

DEAR DIARY: I hear the flutter of wings while I sleep. I think
it's the others, come to brush against my windows, trying to
get in. He told me his friends didn't understand how he could
be married to a mortal, how they didn't think it possible to
lie down each night next to a heart pumping fresh blood
through veins and arteries, to be that close to living flesh and
not take just one, luscious, mouthful of blood. Blake has told
me the rules, though. They can't come in unless I invite
them, but I'm still afraid. The sound is soft, like thick

feathers brushing against the glass. Sometimes I hear my name. Sometimes I hear them laugh. I wish he could stay home to protect me.

Four-fifty-three. Theresa pushed back the covers and stretched her arms over her head. She hated waiting, never knowing if he'd had an easy evening and would come home early. Or whether he'd be in at the last minute, with barely enough time to undress and slide into bed before the sunrise. She swung her feet to the floor. The bedroom opened onto a balcony and Theresa crossed to the door to pull open the curtains. She pressed her fingers against the glass.

"Come home," she whispered to the night.

DEAR DIARY: I have to leave the house now, when I have my period. Blake said he would go, those few days each month when my body is ruled by the crimson tides of the moon. But the risk is too great, the risk that someone will find him as he sleeps during the day—find him and rouse the sleeping monster to full force. "It's a myth that sunlight melts us," he told me. "It just makes us mad and we have to strike back." So it's me that has to go.

Theresa opened the door to the balcony. The air was cool and she felt her nipples harden against the silk fabric of her nightgown. The moon was like a bowl of milk in the dark sky, and the light poured into the room. She shivered and hugged her arms around her waist. The sound of fallen leaves scuttling across the dry grass made her shudder. It was as if they, too, came alive at night to scratch at your legs.

She closed the door, but left the drapes open. She stepped across to the oval mirror which hung above the dresser. Theresa's hair glowed in the pale moonlight like a red star. She lifted her comb and started to pull it through the waves of her thick hair.

Without turning, she knew that Blake was suddenly behind her; she could feel the warmth rise from his body and smell the coppery scent of his breath. Theresa put down the comb and turned to face her husband.

"I was hoping you'd be home early," she said. Blake kissed her on the forehead.

"Let me wash up first," he said.

Theresa sat on the edge of the bed, listening to the sound of water running in the bathroom sink. She had wondered once, out loud, what would become of a vampire who lost his teeth. Blake stared at her. "We have other ways," he slowly answered.

The sound of the water stopped. Blake came into the room, his shirt already off. He sat down next to her on the bed. Theresa ran her fingers lightly over his bare chest, smooth and hairless, as unlined as that of a teenage boy. She pressed her palm flat against him.

"It's so strong," she said, feeling his heart beat underneath her fingers. "Are you full?" she said.

He nodded and drew her face close to his. "Kiss me," he said.

Theresa pressed her lips against Blake's warm mouth. She could feel the sharp edges of his incisors underneath his lips. Blake pushed gently on her shoulders until she was lying back against the pillows. With one hand, he reached for the waistband of his pants and unclasped his belt buckle. Theresa heard the urgent release of his zipper and moaned at the touch of his penis as it brushed against her leg.

She slipped off her nightgown as Blake reached into the nightstand drawer for a condom. Already, a red dot of moisture had formed on the tip of his penis. Before he could stop her, Theresa took one finger and smeared the blood on her fingertip. She raised her finger to his mouth and placed it between his lips. "Waste not, want not," she said, as he sucked.

Theresa watched as Blake unrolled the condom slowly over his penis. "Do you want me?" he whispered. Theresa reached for his penis. "Yes," she answered and moved her legs apart.

The darkness in the room was softening to gray around the edges, and Blake looked like a shadow as he rose over her and slid into her moist center. Theresa groaned and moved her hips to quicken his rhythm, but Blake stopped. "No," he said. "Not yet."

She looked up into his face. Blake's eyes were stars flickering against the velvet sky of their bedroom. Theresa felt a jolt as the light from his eyes penetrated hers and traveled down her spine. It felt like every nerve in her body had caught fire and small flames were licking her skin.

Theresa pressed against him, her arms clasped around his neck, her legs circling his back. She felt the thin membrane of flesh which separated them start to melt and she was unable to tell where she began and Blake ended. It was as if Blake was both inside and outside of her. She felt him surround her and for a single moment, no longer than the space between the beats of her heart, Theresa could not remember her name.

DEAR DIARY: I can't bear the thought of growing old next to him. I'm still young, but already I can see the lines forming around my eyes, across my forehead. He'll look the same, always. And he'll live without me, forever. I don't know if I can stand the thought of him being with another woman, even after I'm dead. I'm afraid to ask how many other wives he's had. The most he's told me is that he has never married another vampire. Maybe the thought of eternity with the same woman is too much for him.

Dawn was pressing against the edges of the dark window-panes. It was almost time. Theresa went to the bathroom to wash. Blake's shirt was on the floor, the collar flecked with blood. She picked it up and held it to her face. It had a strong smell—sweat, mixed with fear, laced with a sweet perfume Theresa didn't recognize. She slid the shirt over her naked torso and looked in the mirror.

"Could I do it?" she whispered to her reflection. Theresa bared her teeth and ran her finger over the sharpest one. She bit down, hard, and the metallic taste of her own blood flowed into her mouth. She sucked, like a child who has pricked her finger on a pin. Suddenly she felt Blake rise up behind her.

"What are you doing?" he said.

Theresa remained silent.

He placed one hand on each of her shoulders and looked down at her. "Do you want me?" he said. Blake's eyes flashed, like a cat in the dark. Without blinking, he took her hand and placed it on his throat.

"Feel me," he said. Theresa felt the pulse of the vein in the side of Blake's neck. Her fingers rose and fell with the strength of the beat.

"Listen, " he said, and drew her head to his chest. At first, all she could hear was the rhythmic "thump-thump" of his heart, a restless drum that seemed to vibrate even the floor she was standing on. Theresa felt her heart speed up and match the rhythm with its own beat.

"Listen," Blake said again. Theresa strained her ears. At first it was a rushing sound, like being caught in the middle of a river that flowed fast and deep. Then, underneath the fury, Theresa heard the voices, hundreds of voices. "Help me," some cried. "No," others moaned. The rest were sounds, sounds that started out as human and changed into a howl of pain and desperation, loss and emptiness, and finally a terrifying silence.

Theresa pulled her hand from Blake's neck and her head from his chest. She gasped as her heartbeat broke back into its own rhythm.

"No," she said, her voice low and thick in her throat. "I don't want you."

Blake nodded. He smoothed her hair from her face and pressed his cooling lips against her forehead. "Good," he said, and went back to the bedroom.

Theresa turned to the mirror, her face pale, her eyes filled with both fear and knowledge. The taste of her own blood was still on her tongue as she reached for her toothbrush. When her mouth was clean and the shirt back on the bathroom floor, Theresa went into the bedroom. Blake was under the covers, his hands straight out along his side.

As she did each morning, Theresa pulled down the shades and made sure the drapes were securely drawn. Blake was drowsy, his eyes barely able to open. The sun was minutes away from breaking the horizon. This was when they were the most vulnerable, Blake once told her. That time between sleep and wakefulness, when the edges of dreams start to fade and reality came into focus.

"If you ever want to kill me, do it then," he had said.

Theresa leaned across the bed and gazed at her husband's high forehead, the brow smooth and unlined. She tucked the comforter close around his body. Blake's eyes were closed now and his breathing barely perceptible. Theresa traced the outline of his mouth with her finger.

"Not yet," she whispered. "Not yet."

Symbiosis

Rhomylly B. Forbes

The city belonged to Graciela. No other of her kind had come forward to challenge that claim in a quarter of a century, perhaps longer. This was not unusual; it was primarily a matter of preserving one's territory. For the sake of custom and safety, one Child of the Night was quite sufficient for any major metropolitan area; more might arouse detection by the Children of the Day.

Consequently, the red flyer with gothic black lettering taped to the inner window of Dragon's Tears Bookstore announcing, "VampireCon! Celebrate the night and take over the Washington Hilton . . . For more information, call . . ." most certainly caught Graciela's attention.

Vampire . . . Con? In my city? Who dares?!? **Graciela** thought, the unfamiliar emotions of worry and anger wrinkling her smooth ivory brow. *No, it could not be so. I would sense . . . I shall go and teach these usurpers a lesson.* She set her mouth in a grimace. *They will learn that this is not their city . . . and that it is mine!*

Graciela's preternaturally sharp fangs flashed once in the light from a sputtering neon sign as she faded into the dark streets with a swiftness and agility born of long practice.

No one paid the slightest attention to the tall, pale woman in impeccably neat but somewhat old-fashioned garments, long auburn hair tumbling free about her waist, prowling about the lobby, ballrooms, and hallways of the Washington Hilton. Days later, when she had time to think on it, Graciela allowed herself a moment of surprise that she had, in fact, not attracted undue notice. Almost everyone else she encountered sported black, old-fashioned clothing, full black capes, and black hair—some obviously, and poorly, dyed.

But nowhere could Graciela smell another true Child of the Night.

What is this? A film? Not one of them is real. Graciela shrugged her shoulders as yet another youngster in badly-applied white pancake makeup and black eyeliner raced by. She had not hunted in two or three days. At her advanced age, Graciela no longer needed to drain her chosen victim to the point of death. However, most mortals were neither eager nor willing to "donate" the relatively small amount of fresh blood she occasionally needed to survive. This was a nice, clean hotel. It was unlikely there were any rats about.

But maybe, just maybe, she could make a fantasy come true for one of these pretenders. Graciela had read quite a bit of popular fiction about her own kind; she knew what humans desired, or at least what they purported to desire. Not that she had any intention of transforming her prey

into a Child of the Night, but perhaps she might find and
seduce an attractive, willing victim for a quick . . . taste.
Tomorrow night, away from this bizarre parody, she
would fully satisfy her mild hunger. Graciela chuckled
low and deep, with a hint of irony. *But what a perfect
place to hunt! These strange mortals masquerading as
vampires do not recognize me as the real thing. And even
if they did, they would likely beg me to perform the rite
of blood sharing with them rather than attack me with a
wooden stake. How completely odd. . . .*

Her mind resolved, Graciela decided to explore this
strange gathering more thoroughly. Hundreds of years of
honing a Child of the Night's natural swiftness and agility
allowed her to enter a large, crowded place called
"Huckster's Room" without the benefit of a "Con Badge."
She puzzled over a display of small metal disks covered
with writing that proclaimed KISS ME, I'M BATTY! and
VAMPIRES DO YOU TILL YOU'RE SUCKED DRY and GO FANG
YOURSELF. She had no idea what they meant, but they
seemed very popular; there were more humans clustered
around this booth than any other. Perhaps they were
religious slogans of some sort.

A few tables sold clothing similar to what Graciela had
seen on the humans in the hallway: full black capes, black
wool pants, short black leather skirts, long black frock
coats. In her soft burgundy velvet smoking jacket, crisp
white tuxedo shirt (unbuttoned low enough to show a hint
of cleavage), and faded blue jeans, Graciela felt positively
underdressed. She looked down to find she was the only
female there not shod in black pumps with stiletto heels.
How, she wondered crazily, *could they ever catch their
prey in those? I would fall down like a fool if I tried.*
Graciela gazed fondly for a brief moment on her own worn
but still sturdy black Reebok hi-tops. *Much more*

practical. Comfortable, too. If these mortals were true Children of the Night, they would starve within a week.

A woman in the requisite black garb and white makeup walked up and asked her a question. "Excuse me?" Graciela asked politely. She had no little difficulty understanding what the woman was saying.

"I thaid," the woman lisped slowly. She wore some small plastic device in her mouth, giving her the appearance of having greenish-white fangs. It also made the woman spit horribly; Graciela desperately wanted to wipe her own face dry, but was afraid that would be considered rude. "Do you know when the danth ith thuppothed to thtart?"

"Death?"

"Danth! Danth! Wock and Woll! You know, dithco!" The woman had the nerve to look at Graciela as if she were the idiot.

"Oh, dance! Uh, no. No I do not. Sorry."

The woman shrugged. "Nithe fangth," she said as she moved away. "They look weal."

Real? Of course they're real! Oh, never mind. "Thank you," was all she said to the woman's retreating backside.

Graciela decided she'd had quite enough "Huckster's Room." She slipped into something called "Art Show" when the pale man in an ill-fitting tuxedo who was guarding the door became distracted by a wandering teenage girl covered only by a few sparse bands of leather and black spandex in strategic places.

Wandering the makeshift aisles of what she discovered was some sort of temporary gallery featuring very strange art, Graciela marveled anew at the fascination, sometimes obsession, that mortals had with her kind. She gaped in disbelief at a collection of cartoons featuring cute, furry ferrets with sharp fangs and black capes, wondering if she had missed some hidden profound message or meaning.

There were pictures of vampires sitting in front of computers, vampires flying spaceships, vampires watching television, even one of a vampire "moonbathing" in the nude.

I do not understand any of this at all. Why do these particular mortals . . . idolize us so? There is nothing glamorous about being a Child of the Night, nothing exciting. It is lonely, it is dangerous, it is . . . Graciela sighed, searching for the right word. *Empty.*

She came to the end of one of the aisles and stopped; the large oil painting hanging there immediately commanded all of her attention. Moonlight illuminated a tall, handsome, male vampire astride a black stallion. The vampire was kissing the hand of a lady vampire standing in the snow at the horse's side, her cape billowing in the cold night air. Both wore the tenderest expressions Graciela had ever seen on any face, mortal or no.

Long ago, when Graciela was a newly-made Child of the Night, she used to dream of such a scene as this. Love among her kind was a very rare thing, and she had quickly learned not to yearn for it. But this painting, the adoration depicted on the lady vampire's face, renewed those centuries-old desires. Suddenly Graciela ached with loneliness. Turning, she fled "Art Show" in blind sorrow with all the swiftness of which she was capable.

In the relative safety of the lobby, Graciela paused for a moment to restore her customary calm, then decided to peruse the smaller rooms down the hall from "Huckster's Room" and "Art Show." Perhaps a likely victim could be found there.

The first room contained a small group of people sitting crosslegged on the floor, paying rapt attention to a stocky, bearded man who looked and smelled as if he hadn't bathed in weeks. He was strumming a slightly out-of-tune guitar and everyone was singing:

And there was Brown, upside-down
Hanging like a bat among the beams.
"Blood! Blood!" the townsfolk cried
As they filled our ears with screams.
Oh, don't let 'em in til we've all drunk up.
Somebody shouted "Hey Vampire!"
HEY VAMPIRE!
And we all sucked blue blind paralytic blood
Til the castle walls caught fire.

Graciela shuddered, and quickly closed the door behind her.

The next room was empty.

The third room was filled with very solemn looking people, all wearing formal, black clothing with accents of red and white. At the front of the room stood an imposing figure, pale as linen, with a black velvet robe and ropes of cheap garnets strung about his neck, presiding over a very nervous-looking couple.

As Graciela opened the door, the young lady was saying, "I, Akasha, take thee, Lestat, to be my lawfully undead husband. . . ." Graciela vaguely recalled reading some very popular books a few years ago that featured vampire characters with those names. She didn't remember much from the books, but was pretty certain that "Lestat" had weighed more than ninety pounds and usually wore pants with legs long enough to cover his bony shins. Also, if she recalled correctly, "Akasha" had neither blonde roots in her hair nor braces on her teeth. Graciela fled this room even more quickly than she had the singer's.

Now what? Graciela was pondering her next move when all of a sudden a horrific noise filled the hallway. It started as a strange metallic screech, then became a crash that was followed by something that sounded as if a dozen Siamese cats were being murdered.

The Undead Dance had officially begun.

Graciela peeped into the darkened banquet hall that had been pressed into service as a discotheque, unable to see much because of the strange flashing lights, artificial fog, and crowded, jiggling bodies. She circled the perimeter of the room and gazed at the wildly hopping dancers in stunned fascination. She was not paying much attention to where she was going.

"Oof! Oh, gosh, I'm so sorry!" The person she had just walked into had to yell to be heard above the unbearably loud music.

"No, please. It was my fault. I should have looked . . ." Graciela bellowed in response until a careful look at the person made the words falter and die in her throat.

It was a young woman in her mid-twenties, with unruly blond curls that tumbled past her shoulders, and a body that would have made Rubens fall to his knees and pray for permission to paint it. Unlike practically everyone else Graciela had seen so far, she was dressed in clothing that actually fit. It also flattered her solid frame, although the long, full, rust-colored skirt topped by a complementing floral lace-up bodice was hardly daily street wear, at least for these times. The ivory peasant blouse underneath the girl's bodice drooped seductively off her ample shoulders, nicely exposing her cleavage and the top of her soft breasts. Graciela felt faint stirrings of hunger, both for blood and . . . well, Graciela hadn't felt stirrings for that in over two centuries.

But she was certainly feeling them now.

And she had no idea what to do.

Fortunately, the young mortal saved the situation. "Wanna dance?" she shrieked.

Dance? Me? Like that? I . . . I don't know how. I'll look foolish. I have no sense of rhythm. Ohhh, how did I ever get myself into this? **Graciela took a deep breath and hollered the only thing she could, under the circumstances. "Yes. I would like to dance."**

They moved out onto the floor, amid a sea of bouncing, jerking bodies. To her eternal relief, Graciela found that her dance moves looked no more awkward than anyone else's. In fact, once she relaxed and actually listened to the music, she started to enjoy herself.

The next number was a slow, romantic ballad, and before Graciela could even think, the young woman was snuggled in her arms, her head nestled trustingly on Graciela's shoulder. Graciela could feel the girl's breasts crushed against her own chest, and somehow, even through the many layers of clothing the girl was wearing, Graciela could feel a heat, a need, emanating from her groin. At the end of the number, Graciela lifted the girl's chin with her finger and kissed her long and slow and deep, gently cupping the human's face in her hands and taking care not to let her sharp fangs hurt the girl. Not yet.

In the quiet lull between the end of the song and the beginning of the next one the girl said, "My name's Joanie. Would you like to go somewhere quiet—to, um, talk?"

Graciela was beginning to get a little confused. *I thought I was supposed to be the hunter, here. This girl— Joanie?—is making all the first moves, and I'm letting her!* "I would like that very much." She followed the blond human out of the hot, noisy banquet hall.

"I have a room here at the hotel, if you'd like . . ." Joanie was blushing slightly.

"That would be fine." If vampires had that ability, she'd be blushing also. *This is ridiculous! What is going on here?*

As they waited for the elevator, Joanie asked, "What's your name?"

"Graciela."

"Pretty. French?"

"No. Italian, actually." *What am I doing? I never give my real name to prey, much less tell them where I come from!*

Joanie reached over and gently laced her warm fingers around Graciela's cool ones. They entered the lift, still holding hands.

Joanie's hotel room was at the very end of a well-lit, carpeted hallway. On the way from the elevator they passed several rooms whose open doors revealed loud, raucous gatherings. Graciela had heard the term "party animal." A few glances at the individuals attending the gatherings taught her its meaning.

Mercifully, the heavy, closed door of Joanie's room muffled most of the sound. Joanie quickly walked over to a rather large portable object that Graciela knew was commonly called a "boom box." "Do you like classical?"

"What?" As her experience with hotel rooms was rather limited, Graciela was taking the opportunity to explore her surroundings. At the moment she was trying not to wrinkle her nose in distaste at the ugly, impersonal decor and disinfectant smell. "Oh. Yes. I like classical."

Joanie touched a button on the box's surface and the opening bars of Beethoven's Egmont Overture filled the space, effectively masking the remaining sounds of Bacchanalian revels from the hallway.

"Nice."

"Thank you." *Stop stalling, Joanie! You know what you brought her here for!*

Graciela caught a glimpse of herself in the mirror. Even allowing for a Child of the Night's natural pallor, she

looked pale and nervous. *Stop stalling, Graciela! You know what you brought her here for!*

"I . . ." they both said at once. Joanie recovered first. She let out a soft chuckle, and opened her arms invitingly. "Come."

With a low moan, Graciela crossed the room to take her place in Joanie's embrace. She lowered her lips to meet the girl's, her hands buried in Joanie's thick curls. Graciela cradled the human in one powerful arm, with her other hand she loosened the front lacings of Joanie's bodice, her fingers deft and sure even though it had been many centuries since she had handled such clothing.

Never had Joanie experienced such a kiss. It made the one they'd shared on the dance floor seem fleeting, shallow, in comparison. She closed her eyes and let herself thoroughly explore Graciela's mouth, her tongue and teeth, and allowed Graciela to explore hers in turn. She felt as if her very soul were being pulled into that kiss.

Joanie reached up and began to tug at Graciela's jacket until it was a small pile of burgundy velvet on the carpet. Joanie's bodice soon followed. Without the bodice to hold it up, her peasant blouse fell almost to her waist, baring firm yet ample breasts and full, pink nipples. Joanie quickly unbuttoned Graciela's white, pleated shirt, and allowed it to join the other garments on the floor. She grabbed Graciela by the shoulders and gently but firmly pushed her down until she was sitting on the edge of the bed, then swiftly removed her own skirt and blouse. A few moments later, Graciela's sneakers and jeans were added to the pile of discarded clothing.

Before Graciela had a chance to protest, much less assume control of the rapidly evolving situation, she found herself lying naked in Joanie's arms, her skin tingling from the feather-light kisses Joanie was planting all over her body. Within moments, Joanie began to gently knead, nibble and lick Graciela's firm white breasts and light brown nipples, and for the first time in over two hundred years, Graciela groaned softly with desire.

Slowly, tormentingly slowly, Joanie kissed and licked and suckled her way down to the soft crease between Graciela's thighs and torso, missing not an inch. Pink skin mingled freely with alabaster as Joanie gently spread Graciela's thighs and settled herself comfortably between the vampire's long, muscular legs. Joanie teased the top and inside of Graciela's thighs with her soft pink tongue, swooping down every so often to brush the outside of the vampire's nether lips, making Graciela clutch the thin bedspread beneath her with rock-hard fingers. Before she could stop herself, Graciela began to writhe and twist her hips, desperately trying to make Joanie's tongue touch her long-neglected clitoris by accident. It didn't work.

"Please," Graciela whispered, too consumed by need to care that she, the superior being, was begging a mortal for sexual release. "Oh, please."

Joanie gently parted Graciela's outer lips with her fingers and began to lap softly at the unusually salty but not unpleasant nectar she found there, before working her way up to the vampire's hardened button. As Joanie's tongue made first contact with that sensitive nub, Graciela gasped. Joanie flicked her tongue hard and fast against Graciela's clitoris, then changed the rhythm to soft and slow, licking the area on either side of Graciela's tiny organ with her firm tongue before sliding back down to her sweet opening for another taste and driving Graciela nearly wild and to the brink of orgasm in the process.

Joanie sensed that her new lover was on that edge, because she pulled back and lightened her tongue touch, forcing Graciela to push up with her hips to maintain any contact at all, until at last Joanie took pity on her and plunged her moistened face back into Graciela's warm slit, licking it with a fury until Graciela reached a shattering release, arching her body off the bed and nearly breaking Joanie's nose by accident on the strength of her bucking hips alone.

When Graciela could see again, Joanie was holding her gently in her arms and looking somewhat smug. "Long time?"

A brief, sorrowful look crossed the vampire's features. "Longer than you could know." Then she brightened. "So . . . ?"

Without another word, Joanie grinned happily and settled back on the thin comforter. Starting at the tops of Joanie's feet, Graciela kissed, caressed, explored, and gently licked her way up the girl's body. Joanie tried not to giggle when Graciela reached her kneecaps, but it did tickle a little.

Graciela found and lightly caressed every sensitive spot: the inside of Joanie's elbows, the small of her back, pausing her intense explorations every so often to tease Joanie's nipples to erection with lips and tongue. *Amazing. I haven't forgotten how to satisfy a human woman after all. Although I cannot recall that any of the others satisfied me first. . . . I could easily grow accustomed to that. . . .*

And whenever any part of Graciela's magnificent body was in reach, Joanie's fingers and mouth were busy exploring also. Joanie discovered that Graciela had a particularly erogenous spot at the base of her spine, and another one right above her left hip. Thigh, stomach, and breast, light tan and pale ivory, all blended together to form a wondrous whole.

Graciela could sense the musky dampness gathering between Joanie's legs. Slowly, almost teasingly, she slid down the girl's body, nudged her legs apart and gently spread her moist, rosy labia and began to circle Joanie's clitoris with sensuous thumb strokes, sometimes trading it for tongue and lips in the oldest act of love she knew. Joanie's breathing was becoming heavy and ragged when Graciela smoothly shifted position, her mouth positioned over the curve formed by the union of Joanie's neck and shoulder, leaving her fingers to coax even more sweet honey from Joanie's warm slit. Graciela's hunger for blood was almost as strong as Joanie's need for orgasm at that moment. *Yesss. It is time.*

"Oh, yes!" Joanie growled, turning her head and brushing a few stray curls away to expose the vulnerable area further. "Take me! Oh, bite me, please!"

Graciela' fingers increased the rhythm and pressure on Joanie's throbbing nub and slowly, delicately, pierced the tender pink throat flesh with her needle-sharp teeth. Instead of struggling or fainting like all of Graciela's previous prey, Joanie screamed Graciela's name in ecstasy. The familiar, warm waves of orgasm rocked her body as she clutched Graciela's head to her shoulder and held on for dear life, her soul dancing in joyous oblivion.

The sudden rush of pure orgasmic energy that poured into Graciela via Joanie's blood completely satisfied the vampire's hunger even more quickly than usual. Confused and slightly embarrassed, she pulled back shortly after Joanie relaxed in post-release contentment, unwilling to meet the girl's earnest gray eyes. Joanie languidly lifted one hand to her neck, staring in mild amazement when the fingers came away smeared with blood.

"So. Now you know." Graciela rose from the bed and began to rummage about on the floor for her clothing, intending to dress and flee the girl's presence as quickly as she was able. It was a large city; she was a very old, highly skilled vampire. The girl would never see her again and, in time, would most likely relegate this entire episode to the realm of dream, or fantasy, or both, and Graciela would once again be alone. But Joanie's soft words stopped her.

"I already did."

It is not easy to surprise an eight-hundred-year-old Child of the Night, but Joanie had just done it. Graciela quickly sat down in an overstuffed chair, clutching her smoking jacket about her like a shawl. Joanie slowly eased herself up until she was sitting against the padded headboard, resplendent in her nakedness and terrified of saying the wrong thing that would drive this exquisite creature from her life forever. Graciela took a deep breath. "How?"

"Three things, actually. The biggest clue came when we were kissing earlier. I've seen a lot of custom-carved fangs in my time, but I've always been able to see, or at least feel, the seams where they fit over the person's real canine teeth. Yours don't have any seams. Plus, your skin is too cold and too white for you to be anything else."

"And the other?"

Joanie's eyes grew soft and even more compassionate. "I noticed you earlier in the Art Show, and I saw how you reacted to my painting."

"Your painting?" Graciela was confused.

Joanie gestured to a scattered pile of matted prints covering the top of the low dresser. "I'm a semiprofessional artist. That's why I'm here. That large oil painting, it's one of mine. Most people see it as the ultimate fantasy; you saw it as a shattered reality. I could tell by your face."

Graciela nodded and swallowed—hard. "Why . . . why did you paint it?"

"I'm not sure. It's part of why I'm attracted to the whole vampire role-playing subculture, I guess."

Finally, the chance to ask the one question Graciela had been aching to ask a human for years. "And why is that?"

Joanie smiled and snorted softly. "There's probably as many answers to that as there are humans playing the life. For me. . . ." She paused for a moment, trying to find the right words to explain. "My parents died when I was a little girl, and I was handed around from relative to relative while I was growing up. I've always been attracted to vampirism because it seemed to have such a strong sense of . . . permanence, I guess, something I needed pretty desperately. Also, the idea of not dying and not losing any more loved ones to death also had—has—a lot of appeal." Joanie started to blush. "Plus, as you've seen, I have some, ah, unusual tastes in lovemaking."

"Women?"

"Well, that too, but I meant, um, being bitten. Blood."

"Oh."

"Speaking of which, are you sure you, how do I say this, got enough?"

It is even harder to surprise an eight-hundred-year-old Child of the Night twice, but Joanie had just done it again. "You enjoyed that?"

Joanie's smile looked quite satisfied. "Oh God, yes! You couldn't tell?" Graciela shook her head no, too dumbfounded to speak. "I've gotta tell you—your teeth didn't even really hurt. Not like a human's at all. In fact, I was kinda hoping we could do it again sometime. Soon. Often." She looked at Graciela pleadingly and was surprised to see the vampire's dark brown eyes well up with blood-tinged tears. Joanie leaped off the bed and knelt at Graciela's feet, gently covering the hands that were still clutching the smoking jacket. "What's the matter? Did I say something wrong?"

"No." Graciela wiped her eyes, then wiped them again. "I am not accustomed to bringing such happiness, such pleasure to my prey. It is not the usual way of my kind. I would . . . I would very much like to share lovemaking

with you again." *And for a brief while, my little Golden One, I will not be alone, I will not be empty. This is too much to hope for.* **"But I do not understand. You wish me in your life?"**

It was Joanie's turn to become teary-eyed. She nodded. "I . . . this sounds silly, I know, but I've dreamed about finding someone like you for a long time. Let's just take things one day, oops, sorry, one night at a time and see how it goes. What do you say?"

Graciela smiled, the first time she could remember doing so in decades. "I say yes. But tell me, Joanie," The name was already a caress upon her still-bloodstained lips. "From what I have read and all I have seen tonight, I am surprised you do not immediately ask for the rite of blood sharing. Why is this?"

Joanie paused for a minute, then an impish grin slowly spread over her features. "Well, don't you think it would be kinda foolish to ask to spend eternity with you when we don't even know if you can get along with my cat?"

And even an eight-hundred-year-old vampire had to acknowledge the wisdom of that.

El Tigre

Catherine Lundoff

I have but recently arrived in this new land, sent from my home in disgrace for believing the seductive words of a young noble from the court. He took advantage of my naivete, and now both my child and I will pay the price: she raised as a bastard in the convent in Spain, and I sent to this cursed land conquered by barbarians who call themselves my country-men. I was told that I am to be the new "companion" (a term that I believe to be synonymous with "maid") to a Doña Fernanda, a widow related somehow to the Viceroy, as well as distantly related to my cousins and myself. It is hoped by my cousins, the only family that I possess, that here in Mexico, far from my disgrace, I will find a suitable marriage. I hate them all.

Closing my diary, I find my gaze drawn out out the window to the courtyard below. Dimly lit archways open onto a dusty open patio, circled by some small orange trees, with an even smaller central fountain, a sad replica of the great palaces of the Moors in my beloved Spain. I lean on the edge of the window, inhaling the warm evening air in great breaths as I try not to weep. A noise below causes me to pull back into the shadows. In the dusk, I see a cloaked figure emerge from one of the archways on the floor below and walk swiftly toward the stables. Surely it is some other servant of the elusive Doña Fernanda, whom I have yet to meet in my two days here. A servant on an errand, yes, that's it; thus, I try to dismiss my curiosity. But my gaze follows the figure as he emerges, leading a black horse, mounts, and rides rapidly from the courtyard. What errand could call for sending a man out onto the dirt roads outside of Veracruz, just as night falls?

I ponder this question as I draw the shutters closed. There are many such thoughts for me to mull over, first and foremost concerning the purpose of serving as a "companion" to a woman I have not seen. At least my room is plain and comfortable—far from luxurious, but better than the convent. The bed, with its carved wooden posts, seems large enough for two, and there is a strange and beautiful woven cloth draped over the wardrobe which holds my attention each time I approach it.

I bow my head for the prayers that do not come before the image of the Santa María which rests on the carved wooden shelf on the wall opposite from my bed. Then, placing my rosary on the shelf before her statue, I read the Bible in the wide bed with its woven coverlet until I fall asleep, one of the few things that I can thank the nuns for teaching me. I wake with a gasp many hours later, my nightdress open at the throat, shivering in the night breezes from the open window. *But surely I closed that*, I think to myself as I dash across the room to shut it again.

It is only when I return to the large soft bed that I remember my dream. A dream about a woman, wearing the clothing of a man(!), standing over my bed, and gazing down at me. She is tall and lean, wearing a long black cloak and carrying a sword. Her high cheekbones and long black hair mark her as *mestiza*, one whom my countrymen see as "tainted" with the blood of the unfortunate indios of this land. She is beautiful and even in my memory, I am drawn to her. Drawn to her, perhaps, more strongly than to the young lord whose words brought me here. I find that I want to taste her lips, as thoughts that had been carefully forced down in the convent return once more. I remember lusting after Sister Teresa, the strongest and most comely of the nuns, remember desiring her attention, even her punishments. Here is another such a one to awaken that desire I thought long dead within me.

My awareness shifts as her hand brushes my hair away from my face in this dream of mine, the most vivid I have had in some time. As her hands brush my face and neck, I find my lips caressing them. I blush somewhat to think of it, but only a little, for I am a fallen woman, even at only eighteen summers, not some convent innocent who has never known carnal desires.

I draw her onto the bed in this vision of mine, reaching out to pull her lips to mine for a kiss. Even though it is just a dream, I feel the heat rush through me as I remember the imagined touch of her lips. Her lips part and she showers my neck with kisses, as she unfastens the top of my nightdress to expose more of my shoulders and neck. In this dream, I know that I will give her anything she wants, though I should burn in Hell for eternity as the priests told me. I feel her bite my shoulder, then a dreamy lassitude overtakes me and I fall into a deeper sleep.

Having remembered, I lie awake until the first birdsong drives me from my bed to gaze out the window.

My hands go to my shoulder and looking down, I can see a bruise with two small cuts where I was unmarked the night before. I shiver superstitiously and cross myself more from habit than belief. The sainted *iglesia Católica* never did aught for me but tell me that women who bore bastards were doomed in the hereafter. Nevertheless, I fear this unknown mark as I fear the heat that she awoke. I try to pray as the only comfort left to me, but find that my thoughts will turn only to the night before and to my daughter.

The tears come, unwanted, when I think upon my little one back in Spain and the fact that I will never see her again. That thought pains me more than the realization that I am alone and unprotected in a new land, with strange marks upon my shoulder. I hastily wipe my eyes as one of the servants enters silently to tell me that the Doña will see me after I have eaten my evening meal. She exits swiftly back into the hall.

It strikes me as odd that all of the Doña's other servants are so very quiet, so sullen, so quick to disappear. The majority are old women, with craggy unsmiling faces, garbed always in black, much like this one. Perhaps the Doña's household is still in mourning. What must this woman be like to rule such a house of sorrow? My curiosity consumes me and the day passes slowly until my dinner arrives. I eat the odd mixture of rice and beans quickly and put on my most respectable dress, the finest of the plain black serge dresses that my cousins let me take when I departed. I wear it without adornment in deference to the house, then after a moment's thought, I defiantly fasten my black lace mantilla about my head and shoulders. The lace was my mother's, the last bit of luxury I was able to hide from the voracious hands of my cousins; I will not have the Doña think I have no pride at all. I leave to follow the servant to meet my new mistress.

I am escorted to a room, lit by a single candle, at the back of the house, one without windows in the dried clay walls. The candle barely illuminates the colorful carpet, the heavy wood furnishings and the room's only other occupant. She is heavily veiled, wearing a black silk dress trimmed with lace, and seated in a ornately carved wooden chair. I cannot not see her face as I make the appropriate curtsey, and so I study her curiously, in a manner that many have found impertinent. Somehow, I sense that she finds it amusing. "So," Doña Fernanda's deep voice fills the room, "you are sent to me from our shared cousins in Spain, and I am to feed you, house you, and find a match for you." I nod miserably. "And what will you do for me?" I know now that she is laughing at me.

Indignantly, I raised my head. "I can read and write, as well as play the harpsichord and other instruments. I'm sure my lady will find my abilities to be quite satisfactory."

"Good." That voice behind the veils purrs at me, and I feel a rise of that same heat that I felt last night and once again this morning. I gasp in horror and glance down quickly in hopes of covering my confusion. "I am ill much of the time, which forces me to rest during the day as it is much too hot for me. I would like to see you in the evenings, at which time you can entertain me. Once I get to know you better, we'll see about a match for you. Meanwhile, I suggest frequent baths to keep off the heat. The climate differs greatly from Spain." She rises to press my hand gently. I am dismissed, thinking as I leave that she does not seem much like an invalid.

Several days and interminable nights pass in which I am not sent for to be companionable, or otherwise. I read on

the patio, attempt to gossip with the other servants, and
wonder if my dream will come again. The others are not
forthcoming about our mistress, saying only that she is a
widow, whose husband died several years before. The
Viceroy granted her permission to keep her husband's land
and to not remarry, highly unusual in this land where
wealthy widows are courted assiduously. I wonder how
she did it, and whether I will be foisted off on one of her
unsuccessful suitors. I long for more details about this
woman who weighs so on my mind.

While I learn little about the mysterious Doña, they do
tell me about another local mystery: a strange masked
man, known as "El Tigre," who has been paying nightly
visits to some of the more notoriously brutal landowners
in the region. It is said that they are much kinder to the
indios and peasants who work their land after such visits.
Having heard something of the unchecked abuse by both
Church and nobles, this news gladdens my heart. Perhaps
he will rescue me from my boredom and disgrace, along
with his other good deeds. Or, I dare to dream in my most
secret depths, *she* will return.

In my boredom, I begin to take advantage of the Doña's
library, where I read many interesting and surprising
works. Among the most interesting things of course, is the
existence of the library in the first place. Ordinarily, a
wealthy woman in my country would possess only the
Bible, and would be fortunate to be able to read that. *She
must have been brought up by the nuns as well*, I think,
or else blessed with a remarkable parent. One of the
works that holds my attention is a tome on the forces of
darkness, and how they operate in the mortal world. I read
about demons and succubi, about creatures who steal
infants, and about those who seduce men in their sleep. I
cannot help but wonder if my dream lady is one of them,

but I can find no reference to such a female demon visiting a mortal woman.

I also begin to bathe in the sunken pool downstairs provided for that purpose, as I had been advised. One night, as I lie soaking in my thin, white shift, as all good girls are supposed to do, something the nuns told me often enough, I hear someone enter. Thinking it to be the quiet housemaid, Consuelo, with more hot water, I murmur "Gracías." The chuckle that answers is certainly not Consuelo, and my startled eyes open to find the Doña kneeling next to the pool near my head. Immediately I am torn between wanting her to find me irresistible and wanting to conceal my body, made very visible by the wet shift.

Years of convent training make me draw myself up, instinctively covering myself with my hands. As I sit up, she tilts my head back, and lifting her veil, presses her lips to mine. My wet arm slides from over my breasts and goes around her neck of its own accord, as though I am possessed, as perhaps I am. I feel her hand move down to cup my breast and to caress my nipple. The nuns' distant voices shriek warnings of the eternal flames as my flesh burns to her touch, and I respond, racing far beyond their reach.

My delighted gasp is permission enough for her, and she pulls me onto the towels next to the pool. I am amazed at her strength. In the dim light, I cannot not see her face very well, but her kisses tell me that she is the woman from my dream. I draw back in amazement to study her cold, fierce beauty. "I have dreamt of you. . . ." I whisper.

"No dream, little one. I could not stay away from your beauty. I have known that I must have you since I first saw your portrait and heard your tale. But you must know that I am not like you. Even my very distant cousins would not have deliberately delivered you into the power of a demon." Demon? I study her avidly, heart racing, knowing I must seem wild-eyed with terror.

"I am not mortal, dulce. I will live forever, surviving on the blood of others. The warm light of the sun is death to me, so I must sleep during the days and move about only in the dark. I have been this way for many years, after my husband's bite brought me over." She pauses distastefully on the word *husband*. "I knew nothing of what he was about, having been a convent bred innocent, much like you, *amor*. He fed off me until I became as I am now. I learned enough to hasten his end in revenge for making me a monster. I also learned to savor the joys of a woman's body from one of his erstwhile loves and realized that I was not ready to be completely dead. Now, I find that I am lonely, and longing for the warmth of a mortal lover. But I will not deceive you as I was deceived." She turns to me, eyes glowing,"Will you share my bed, knowing what I am and what I can do?"

My hand strays to my neck, to the marks she left in my dream vision, now made stark and real. "I must draw deeper than that, amor, draining you close to dry before you become as I am. If I terrify you, you have only to say the word and I will find you a husband. I am nothing if not honorable." She smiles a strange, sad, twisted smile. I reach out to that sorrow. *What are we both but women with naught except each other?* I draw her hand back to my bosom.

Her hands are on the strings of my shift, and I am lost in the soft touch of her lips, her tongue as she kisses my neck. Soon my shift is down around my waist and her mouth is on my breast. I feel my back bend as her tongue strokes over my nipples. My hands scrabble at the fastenings on the back of her dress, wanting her to be as vulnerable as I am. She evades me, sliding the wet shift lower as she lays me down on the towels.

She licks her way along my legs, and I am filled with a desperate sense of desire and panic. *What is she doing to me?* Her tongue reaches the space between my legs and I scream with delight, with horror as she sends flames through me. *Truly I am damned now,* I think, *but if this is Hell, Heaven can be no better.* I am swept along by the strokes of her tongue until all my muscles bend at once and I must cry out. She licks her way back up to my mouth and I see that her eyes are larger and darker than any others I have seen before. I pull her to me, but not before I notice something else. Her teeth are long and sharp, and I gasp in terror, marveling that I had not noticed them before. Torn between fear and lust, I hold her off me for a moment. "Do you mean to kill me?" I manage to ask.

"I mean to possess you completely." Her eyes mesmerize me and I fall into them, not caring if she drains me dry or if such desires will cast me from the Church forever. I feel her teeth graze my neck, and I bend my head back so she can reach me, can drink my blood though it means my life. Her teeth sink in and I feel some pain, then a joyous lethargy as I slip into a deep sleep.

I wake somewhat tired, but gloriously happy in the late morning light. If this is what it means to be a "companion," then I shall regret only the loss of my daughter, and nothing else. I do realize that it will not do for the servants to see her love bites on my neck, and I wrap a silken cloth around my throat. Once again, some days pass before I see her again. The others, particularly Consuelo who has served her lady for a long time, warn me not to disturb her during the day, and she does not come to me at night for two nights. *Do I want to be as she is?* I cannot answer this question, and so I am in a fever of impatience, barely sleeping or eating for dreaming of her, yet torn with fear, for I, too, am not ready to be completely dead.

As I stand near the window on the second night lit up by the full moon, I see the cloaked figure once again leaving the house to go toward the stables. One glance and I know it is she, so strong and purposeful is her stride. With no thought as to why she would ride at night, I run downstairs in my shift with nothing over me but a silken shawl. I reach the patio just as she leads the horse from the stables. "Take me with you!" I gasp. "I cannot, my love." I see that she is dressed in men's clothing, wearing a sword and a mask, and I realize who el Tigre must be. I plant myself before her, and without a second thought, I tear my shift open at the neck in hope that my offer will be enough, for I know that men hunt for el Tigre and I fear for her as much as I want her.

She growls and her arms encircle me, lips pressed so hard against mine that my lips feel bruised. "I must feed elsewhere lest I kill you. When I feed from the landowners, I can terrify them into treating the peasants better," she whispers into my ear as she kisses it, her hands running over my body under the shawl, in spite of her words.

"I'll guard your horse and wait for you," I whisper. "Please. I don't want any more nights without you."

She studies me for a long moment, eyes midnight pools that I drown in, long, lithe body graceful and powerful in her man's garb. Finally, with a dry laugh, she swings onto the horse, pulling me up before her and wrapping the cloak around us both. "Very well, dulce. I would be pleased to savor your charms before this evening's less pleasant task." Her arms encircle me while her hands rip the shift further until one of her hands cups my breast. I arch my head backward onto her shoulder gasping as the heat fills me.

The horse takes us where it will, until I look around to realize that it has come to a stop and we are in an old cemetery, some distance from her hacienda. Tall, dark trees surround the stones marking the graves of the dead. It is a strange, macabre sight, lit only by the moon. Some of the stones lay at odd angles as though the dead themselves had shifted them and I shiver at the thought. "Does this spot frighten you, amor? I feel a special kinship to it, and it is undisturbed by those who seek el Tigre. I will take you home if it is too much," she murmurs in my ear.

Something about this place of the dead draws me as well, in spite of my terrors. Suddenly I find that I desire her touch her here, with the eyes of the ghosts upon on us. "I fear nothing while I am with you, mi amor," I whisper in a voice scarcely my own, as I place my hand on hers and hold it to my breast.

She pulls her hand away, leaps from the saddle, then lifts me down to the ground. As I touch her waist, I feel the coil of a long whip at her belt. Without thinking, even as she unclasps her cloak to lay it on a long flat gravestone, I pull the braided leather from her belt. My eyes close as I think back to the convent, to the many beatings that I received from Sister Teresa, to the look on the nun's face as the leather hit my skin and to the way her hands felt as she touched me afterward. I did many things to earn those beatings and that touch. Perhaps . . . I turn to Fernanda, holding the whip out. "I was very wicked to follow you the way I did," I whisper.

Her sharp teeth flash in the moonlight. "Oh, I must remember to thank those cousins of ours for such a wicked companion as they have found me. I have longed for a lover who would indulge all my desires of her own free will." The whip snakes along the ground as she turns me to face a standing tombstone. She shreds the shift from

me and forces my legs further apart with her knee. I am
not so much breathing as I am panting, like a dog, but I do
not care. Nor do I feel the cold, even as her first stroke
pushes me forward so that my breasts touch the icy stone.
My head hangs over the stone as I embrace it. The whip
snaps along my back; the burning of my skin and the
burning in my belly becoming as one. My cries fill the
night.

Five strokes and I can barely stand. I feel her stand
behind me and run the handle of the whip up my legs. My
moans and whimpers are beyond any restraint that I feel
capable of exercising. I feel her lick the small amount of
blood that she has drawn off my back as the whip handle
slides further. She bends me further over the stone and
slips it inside me. As she begins to thrust, my knees
buckle and she has to hold me against her as she pushes
the whip in and out of me. This is what I always dreamed
that Sister Teresa would do, and I am crying, begging for
more, begging for I know not what until my whole body
can take no more and only her strong arms are holding me
upright.

She picks me up and puts me on her cloak, her teeth
finding my neck. I manage to unfasten her shirt to touch
her breasts as she feeds. She pulls her bloody teeth from
my neck as I wrap my legs around her waist. "I must feed
elsewhere tonight, *querida mía*. I do not altogether trust
myself with you." Dragging herself from me with an
effort, she wraps the cloak around me. "Wait here. I'll
return within the hour. Sleep." At her last word, I slip
into that great abyss that such nights with her produce.
Before I sleep, I think I see a great gray wolf running from
the cemetery and down the road.

When I wake, I am in my own bed at the house. I
wonder if I have dreamt it all until I feel the stripes on my
back. For a brief moment, I am afraid that I have gone too

far, that she will kill me in her passion. The thought fills me with only a vague apprehension, something which puzzles me. Does my own life mean so little to me, that losing it is nothing? Or do I trust her, a creature of the night, not even mortal, so much that I will place my life in her hands?

I contemplate how little I know of her, of her life and what she is. I think back also on what my life had to offer before her: disgrace, at best a joyless marriage, at worst a life of dependency upon more fortunate relatives. As I have only my daughter in all the world that I care about other than her, and if I cannot have my little one back, I throw my lot in with Doña Fernanda. Alive, with some small measure of independence, I might yet think of some way to regain my daughter.

With the matter settled for the moment in my own mind, I eat well and rest, saving myself up for my beloved. Somehow, I find that I do not greatly question that I should love another woman, probably because I had seen instances before, in the convent, that led me to believe that such things were possible. She has certainly proven on my own body that she can make me feel as I have never felt before.

Some nights later, I am called to play the harpsichord for Fernanda and some guests who have come from the surrounding haciendas. She sends word of this by Consuelo rather than coming herself, but at least she sends a note as well. The note says, "Querida, I ask your help in entertaining some of my kinswomen. Much will be asked of you tonight. If you wish to please me, leave off your heavy undergarments when you come to me. Trust me and remember that I have some control over both myself and others." I dress in an agony of apprehension and anticipation.

When I enter the room, I see four women, two resembling Fernanda in some way that I only dimly comprehend. I sense, rather than identify, their kinship to her, knowing instinctively that they are like her and that the other two are mortal like me. They are all older than I, and wear the plain, simple garments of spinsters living on their family's largesse. Yet, I am drawn to their power and grace. These are not the sullen, broken women I am accustomed to seeing in wealthy households, but instead are like the abbess of the convent, both comfortable in their strength and somehow otherworldly.

We dine and the others study me almost as assiduously as I examine them. We exchange pleasantries and learn somewhat of each other; the others are all dueñas and companions, unmarried women and widows as I had suspected. The evening meal with its oddly flavored chicken and rice passes quickly. Once we have finished dining, Fernanda dismisses the servants and bolts the doors securely behind them. Smiling mysteriously, she ushers me to the harpsichord.

After I play, which I find makes me more homesick than I expected, Fernanda draws near and gently strokes my hair.

"You look sad, dulce. What is it?"

With little regard for the others who are tactfully engrossed in their own conversation, it tumbles from my mouth, "I love you, but I miss my daughter."

"Where is she?" asks Fernanda as though she has always known. Perhaps our cousins had told her.

"In the convent of the Santa María near Madrid," I offer in a rush.

"We will see what can be done. Now, would you like to help me entertain our guests?"

My heart fills with hope as I gaze up at her. "Anything you want of me, you are welcome to take, even my life."

"I don't want to take your life, but I desire you, your passion, your beauty. I want my friends to see the beauty of your body and your surrender as well," she whispers. "Oh, yes! Take me now!" I find the words pouring from my mouth, any thought of propriety long forgotten. She sits beside me on the playing bench, her hands unlacing the bodice confining my bosom. I hear a gasp from one of the other ladies as Fernanda bares my breast, then bends to take it into her mouth. My arms encircle her neck, frantic moans arising from me as I slip beyond self control. The thought of the other women watching makes me burn with desire, rather than the shame that I should feel.

I gaze back at them in time to see one of the women pull another to the floor in front of her, turning her so she can watch us, and sliding her hand into the other's bodice. I see the second one's look as the questing hand finds her nipple and she moans as she meets my eyes. I am wearing only a flimsy shift under my dress. Fernanda's hands pull the dress off me, leaving me in my light shift to face the women across the room. The woman caressing the other's breasts pulls a sharp dagger from the table and slices the second woman's dress from her with not a scratch. We face each other, each watching the other's excitement as the other two women watching begin to touch each other as well.

As my beloved's hands undress me, she reveals to the others that I am suffering from the curse of Eve. Pulling the rag from between my legs, she growls deep in her throat, and the others draw near, pulled to my blood. Before I can think more about it, Fernanda kneels between my legs and begins to lick me ferociously. Her two kinswomen hover nearby, their companions forgotten for the moment. The thrill of fear only makes the flames within me burn hotter. They could tear me limb from limb at this moment and I could do nothing to stop them. Fernanda lifts her head to gaze at me, eyes burning and mouth bloody. "Share," hisses one of the other women.

She favors them with a sharp-toothed smile. "Are you afraid, little one?" she asks, looking at me. I nod, too overcome to speak. "Do you want them anyway?" I nod my assent again and she moves to hold me as another takes her place. The two human women hover nearby, watching and touching each other, too overcome to resist the sight of my pleasure. The fierce tongue drives me harder and harder until I cry out as my body arches out of control. The third moves to take her place as the second lady returns to the two companions. I hear their moans mixed with my own. My hands grasp her hair as she feeds. Fernanda's fingers tighten on my breast as she kisses me, her tongue inside my mouth. Once again I am transported, crying out into Fernanda's mouth as that insistent tongue strokes and slides inside me and against me. The other woman sits up panting, my blood on her fangs.

She watches me for a moment more, then bows to Fernanda and moves to join the others; plainly, she commands them. One of the human women has pinned the arms of the other, now stripped of her dress, while one of the vampire ladies caresses and kisses her. She begs and moans, arching her back and opening her legs to express her desire but the kissing and biting continues. The sight arouses me again and I reach for my beloved. Her fingers slide inside me. Her other hand turns my face toward the women as one of them pulls a leather belt from her dress and begins to lightly smack the bared legs and back of the woman who is now kneeling before her. I squirm against Fernanda and she pinches my breasts hard. "You're very wicked to want another, my sweet," she growls in my ear.

She pulls me from the bench and across the room in a single movement. I am pushed to my knees, my face between the legs of the woman I have just seen whipped. "Lick!" Fernanda's order could not be denied, and I taste another woman for the first time. The belt's sharp smack on my buttocks distracts me for a moment, only to have the woman catch my head and pull my face back into her. "I'll stop if you don't please her." This threat serves only to inspire me further. As the sting of the belt warms me, I move my hand up to her, part her with my fingers and push inside as Fernanda did to me. Her fierce cries of joy warm me until I beg for my loved one's touch, her hands, even her teeth.

As the other woman holds me in her arms, kissing me fiercely, I feel Fernanda's tongue begin to follow the welts made by the belt. She laps the blood from my thighs like a cat as I crouch over the woman on the floor, passionately returning her kisses. I see Fernanda's hand go to the table and take something from it. Her finger pushes into me. I spasm with pleasure, moving my legs further apart for whatever she has planned for me. Her finger moves and I push against it, feeling a new sensation of pain and pleasure. A second finger joins the first and I begin to rock backward against her hand. Then she pulls them out, heedless of my disappointed cry, and pushes something hard inside me. It fills me, stretching me farther than I thought possible, all thought of anything except taking it all in gone from my mind.

Her finger enters my other opening and I enter a world of pleasure that I never imagined before. My moans and cries are pulled from my throat as I surrender all control to her, my demon lover. She possesses me utterly until I collapse upon the woman under me, whose hands touch and fondle me the whole while. Fernanda's hand roughly catches my hair, bending my head back as her teeth sink into my neck. "Make me yours," I whisper. "You already are," she whispers back as I fall away into unconsciousness.

When I recover my strength some days later, I find that she has booked passage on a ship to Spain for me, as well as providing an armed escort to guard my virtue. She gives me documents authorizing the adoption of my daughter by some relatives of the Viceroy. They will keep her nearby, and I can see her grow up as a relative at least, if not as her mother. I cannot keep her myself because an unmarried lady would not be permitted to keep her child. Still, it is more than I dared hope for. As I stand on the ship's deck feeling the uneasy rocking under my feet, I think back to my parting with Fernanda.

"Will you make me like you when I return?" I ask, filled at once with trepidation and desire.

"Do you want to live forever?" she responds, eyes blazing.

"With you," I answered from my heart.

"Perhaps when you return, el Tigre will require some assistance. We will have to see if you are worthy."

"Let me prove it to you," I whisper, stepping closer.

"When you come back. . . ." her fingers pass gently along my cheek, and she vanishes with a swirl of her cloak, leaving me on the dock where I first came to this land. I have only my thoughts of her to warm my bed on the cold shipboard nights. Those and the two punctures in my neck which stay strangely hot to my touch. . . .

A Moment in Time

Deb Atwood

"These habits of yours have got to stop."

Laurie chuckled at the expression on his brother's face. "Really, Jeffrey? And what habits are those?" Standing slowly, he walked over to the bar in his office and calmly poured himself a brandy from a crystal decanter. He offered the bottle to Jeffrey, who refused with a wave of his hand and an expression of disgust. Laurie's smile widened. "So, what is it that offends you? My habits of drinking and eating something other than blood? I realize I no longer need it for sustenance, but I find it a delicious pleasure, difficult to cure myself of." He sipped at the brandy slowly, savoring the taste. "I find it a pity so few of our kind can still enjoy the lovely tastes of this world."

Across the room Jeffrey Cuthbert scowled at his younger brother. "You know that is not the habit of which I am speaking." Crossing the room, he snatched the glass from Laurie's hand, spilling the contents onto the rug. The wet stain spread across the Oriental design as they both stared down at it.

Slowly Laurie raised his eyes to meet his brother's. A faint hint of anger was banished quickly. "Really?" His voice was deceptively mild. "One could never tell by your actions. Do you realize what it will take to clean that stain?"

"Buy another."

Laurie frowned. "You have never had an appreciation for the finer side of life." He reached for the glass still held loosely in Jeffrey's hand, stopping only when the other man clenched his hand shut, tiny shards of glass joining the stain littering the carpet. Laurie shook his head, refusing to meet his brother's eyes. "Overly dramatic. One might almost think you have been persuaded to take up acting."

"I am not here to speak of myself, but of you, Lawrence." Jeffrey brushed the shards from his hands, the cuts healing quickly as he walked away. Laurie merely poured himself another glass. When Jeffrey turned back, the younger of the brothers was seated again on the sofa, legs crossed, the glass already half-empty and held loosely in one hand.

"Ah yes, concerning my bad habits." Laurie smiled. "And exactly which habits were those?"

"The way you involve yourself with mortals is distasteful."

A single eyebrow rose. "And your habits are not?" It took no more than that hint to remind Jeffrey that Laurie knew all his secrets.

"What I do does not matter!" Jeffrey bellowed, losing his composure momentarily. "London is my city, and I

am in control here. You answer to me." He reminded
Laurie of a dog defending his territory.

Laurie shrugged. "And you find my involvement with
mortals a problem. C'est la vie." He finished the final
swallow of his brandy, and stood, walking over to open
the door to his office. He smiled politely at the slim, dark-
haired girl in the hallway. Turning back to Jeffrey he saw
that his brother had managed to compose himself once
more, his expression the usual calm mask. "I believe
Karen is waiting for you, brother."

"If I find that you have allowed another mortal to
glimpse the truth about our kind, brother," Jeffrey said
darkly, "I will be forced to take action, no matter what
your connections with the elders of our race. It is I who
hold power here, and it is I who decree what is proper
behaviour."

"Of course, brother." Laurie bared his teeth in a dark
imitation of a pleasant smile. "I'll do whatever you want,
whatever you desire. I live to serve you."

Both heard the sarcasm. Both chose to ignore it as
Jeffrey left. Laurie shut the door, his lanky body dropping
back onto the sofa, head cradled in his hands. "Damn you,
Jeffrey," he muttered. "Just because someone decided to
make sure we couldn't die doesn't mean we can't care
about those who can." It was a longstanding argument
between Laurie and his brother. The elder vampire had
never understood the ties Laurie felt with his mortal
friends, his enjoyment of their lives. Laurie sighed with
frustration. He would never endanger his race by allowing
a mortal he did not trust to know the truth about himself.

"Are you all right?"

Laurie's head snapped up at the sound of the voice. His
assistant stood in the doorway, her hair pulled back in a
ponytail. She was still dressed in running clothes, and a
light sheen of sweat was visible on her forehead. He had to

smile at the worry on her face. "Yes, Melody, I'm fine. Just another argument with Jeffrey."

She came up behind him, her fingers digging soothingly into his taut shoulder muscles. "Over what this time? How you run the school? Or is Eric coming to visit again and Jeffrey can't stand the thought?"

Laurie allowed a shiver to run through his body at the sound of his sire's name. "God forbid Eric drops in again. A century without him would do me just fine." He sighed with pleasure. "Mmm, don't stop."

Melody laughed. "Hedonist. You just keep me around because I give good backrubs."

His head dipped, allowing her better access to his shoulders. "No, I keep you around because you are the most gifted human mage I know in this forsaken land. And despite what Jeffrey thinks, our kind cannot do without humans."

"You argued over me?" Melody stopped in surprise, fingers resting lightly on his shoulders.

Laurie gave her fingers a reassuring squeeze. "Not you in particular. Just my tendency to become . . . involved . . . with humans in general."

She walked around the couch to sit beside him. "He doesn't seem to me like someone who should throw stones."

"He's not," Laurie agreed. "But he has always been the sort to act as if he were always right. Even when we were children." He sighed, then stood. His desk was spread with papers—students' grades, new admissions to his school. He barely looked at them as he began to file them away. "Melody, do you think you can handle things around here on your own for a while?"

"Don't let him scare you off." Melody's green eyes glittered angrily. "You have just as much right to do what you want in London as he does."

"Of course I do," he replied easily, loosening the tie he had worn in honor of the business meeting with his brother. "Which is why I'm going to go on holiday. Right here in town. Nothing serious; just a bit of a fling." He grinned. "I don't give up, Melody. I thought you knew that."

She found herself grinning back. "I didn't think you would. Take your time; I'll keep everything under control."

"Thanks, girl." He dropped a kiss on her forehead and hurried off to pack a few necessary items.

"Can I get you something?"

The girl's dress was cut low, giving Laurie a broad view as she leaned over the table suggestively, her breasts almost brushing his arm. He smiled distractedly, muttering, "Red wine," as he waved her away.

She pouted, straightening up. "Will that be all, sir?"

He glanced up, seeing her smile at him and pose. "The wine will be all," he said firmly. She frowned and walked away, leaving Laurie to survey the club again.

It was a typical club in this new era of darkly Gothic music. Laurie felt this new generation was the most comfortable he had found since his birth time. With his pale skin, long hair, dark clothes, and flowing poet's shirt, he fit in as if he were born to this time instead of centuries before. The music swirled around him, an underlying rhythm almost like a heartbeat seeming to crawl inside his soul. So many people . . . so fragile.

"Here's your wine." The glass was set down with a slight thunk, and the girl waited only long enough to get her pay before hurrying off to a more accommodating customer. Laurie didn't even notice her leave.

He reached into his pocket and withdrew a vial, emptying it into the wine. He swirled it with a finger as the deep red liquid grew cloudy and thick. He sucked the finger clean, watching the dancers speculatively. Spotting his quarry among the throng around the bar, he quickly downed the contents of the glass. He left the empty behind on the table as he walked away, licking his lips clean.

"Would you care to dance?"

The young man looked up, surprise mirrored in his chocolate eyes. Laurie smiled reassuringly, "Of course, if you would prefer not to . . ."

The man smiled then, sliding off the bar stool. "No, actually I'd love to."

"Well then." Laurie held out a hand, clasping the stranger's firmly in his own. He drew him out to the dance floor, already moving to the slow beat of the music.

The young man had dark hair, cut shorter than most of the others in the club, and deep chocolate eyes. Laurie had to smile at his quarry. He slid his hands around the other's back, pulling him closer as they swayed to the beat.

"Isn't this where you deliver a corny line?" the stranger inquired, chuckling. "Or shall I play the dominant and do the honors?"

Laurie frowned, stepping back slightly. "Just because we are both men does not mean we need to play at any roles." Perhaps Laurie had made a mistake. But he had been watching the man for several nights before deciding to approach. He had considered every option, and this seemed to be the correct one. Had he been wrong?

The stranger shook his head, smiling ruefully. "I'm sorry. I'm not very good at this."

Laurie began to move off the dance floor, drawing the other man with him to a table in one corner of the club. "Perhaps we should talk." If he were wrong, it would be better to find out now, rather than later. And only honesty would tell. "Do you drink brandy?" At the stranger's nod,

Laurie caught the waitress and gave her the order, before settling in at the table. "Where should we start?"

Dark eyes blinked once, and then looked away, off to the dance floor. "Maybe we should start with introductions."

"Lawrence Cuthbert. Most people call me Laurie."

The other man smiled. "Ryan James." He looked just a little more comfortable, and Laurie began to relax. He was moving too fast. He hadn't made a mistake, just a miscalculation.

"Tell me a little about yourself," Laurie encouraged.

Ryan shrugged. "There isn't really much to tell. I'm a student at the university. Majoring in biostatistics. It's a good enough field." He seemed to be defending a choice he hadn't made.

"Good enough," Laurie agreed. There was a long silence, as Ryan toyed with his drink. "Can I be honest?" Laurie finally broke the silence. "Would you prefer if I let you alone?"

Ryan glanced up sharply. "No. It isn't that at all." His eyes softened as he looked at Laurie. "Actually, I . . ." He shrugged. "It's just that I had a companion, and he only moved out about a month ago. I guess I'm not as over it as I thought."

"It does take time," Laurie agreed, reaching out to take Ryan's hand. When the other didn't resist, he squeezed gently. "I'm sorry to have moved so fast."

Slowly Ryan's other hand stole up to cover Laurie's. "It's all right. I was just a little scared for a minute there." He stood, still holding Laurie's hand. "Let's try this again. Would you care to dance?"

"I'd love to." Laurie smiled, allowing himself to be led to the dance floor.

As they danced, Ryan relaxed, his body swaying closer to Laurie's until the two relaxed together on the dance

floor, moving easily in synch. Laurie ran a hand over
Ryan's back, drawing it up over his shoulder, then
touching the pulse on his neck. It fluttered quickly under
his fingers, as Ryan's head fell to Laurie's shoulder,
exposing the neck to his touch.

Laurie licked his lips, trying to hold the hunger at bay.
The night was growing late, and the hunger came more
from desire than any true need for sustenance. Gently he
pressed a kiss against the skin just below the curve of
Ryan's jaw, feeling the pulse jump as the other man
sighed. Then he drew away. "I think perhaps it is time for
me to go," he said softly.

There was a flicker of regret as Ryan said hesitantly, "I
don't live in the dorms. I have a private flat now that
Evan's left."

Laurie allowed his own regret to reach his eyes. "It's
too soon. You need more time." He slid his hand away
from Ryan's neck, over his shoulder, down to his hand.
With a gentle squeeze, he stepped away. "Perhaps
tomorrow evening you'll be here again?"

Ryan relaxed slightly. "Perhaps." There was a teasing
glint in his eyes.

"Then perhaps so shall I," Laurie teased in return.

It wasn't until the doorbell rang a second time that Laurie
woke. He blinked twice into the darkness, hand swinging
out automatically to switch on the light. A glance at the
clock confirmed his suspicions . . . daylight still lit the
outside world. The sun would be setting soon, but it
seemed far too early to him. Grumbling, he threw a robe
over his shoulders and stumbled into the living room of
the small flat he had rented for his holiday.

He leaned heavily on the intercom button. "Yes?" His
voice was still hoarse with sleep.

There was a pause, then the distinctive beep telling him the button downstairs had been pressed in response. "I'm sorry, did I wake you?"

Laurie tried to recognize the voice, but couldn't. Salesman, most likely. "Something like that, yes. Is this important?"

Another pause. "I'm sorry," the voice repeated. "I'll come back later if you'd like."

"No, I'm awake now." Laurie sighed, and slipped his arms into the robe, fastening the belt about his waist. "What are you selling?"

"I'm . . ." This time the pause seemed to go on forever.

"Yes?" Laurie prompted, beginning to grow impatient.

"I'm not selling anything." The words seemed to tumble out in a jumbled heap. "It's Ryan."

Laurie relaxed against the wall, a half-smile lighting his face as his hand reached for the buzzer. "Come on up."

He could hear footsteps moving slowly up the two flights of stairs, then approaching his door. He swung it open before Ryan had a chance to knock, motioning for him to step inside. Once the door had shut behind him, Ryan simply stared quietly at Laurie, taking in the robe, the disheveled hair, and the imprint of the pillow still on his cheek. With all the shades drawn, Laurie stood half in shadow. Ryan shrugged helplessly.

"I really am sorry. Melody warned me that you're not usually up until six o'clock or so, but I got impatient." His voice trailed off toward the end, like a boy caught with his hand in the cookie jar.

Laurie flashed him a reassuring smile, while wondering how Melody had managed to get on a first name basis with his new friend already. "It's quite all right. Why don't you fix yourself something in the kitchen while I go shower?" He pointed in the appropriate direction.

"Would you care for tea?" Ryan called after him.

"Yes, no sugar or cream," Laurie called back, then shut the door to his bedroom. He took the cordless phone into the bathroom with him, and started the water running before dialing.

"Hello?" Melody sounded a bit rushed.

"You've met Ryan," Laurie said flatly. "Not to mention told him where I'm living. Would you care to enlighten me as to how this came about?"

Melody chuckled. "Well, you did tell him your real name. He's a bright boy, and an attractive one at that. He did a little research, found out about the school, and showed up on the doorstep late this morning. When he asked for you, one of the students sent him to me, since you're officially on holiday. He didn't want to say how he had met you, but I figured out enough to realize that you've already fascinated him. Not bad for a few days' work."

Laurie scowled at the phone. "Thank you for your opinion."

"Any time." There was a pause before Melody asked, "You aren't simply using him to pay back Jeffrey, are you?"

"No, I saw him for the first time a while back," Laurie admitted. "I had been thinking about it, and I just needed to get away from things right now, and Ryan seemed like a pleasant way to do it."

"He seems vulnerable."

Laurie remembered the look on Ryan's face when he talked about his last lover. "Yes, he does. But don't get all mothering over him. I'll take care not to hurt him."

"I expect as much from you, but I wanted to check." She hesitated a moment, then added, "Take care of yourself, Laurie."

"I will. And you do the same."

"Of course."

Laurie set the phone down on the sink, then stepped into the shower. He washed quickly, and toweled dry, his long blond hair hanging loose down his back. He threw on a pair of dark gray sweats, then rejoined Ryan in the living room.

"You look much more awake." Ryan's gaze flickered quickly over him.

"I feel it," Laurie admitted. The phone call and shower had given the sun time to set completely, and he felt much more awake. Seeing Ryan sitting there reminded him that a drink would be in order when possible, but now just wouldn't be a good time. And Ryan wouldn't be a good victim.

Yet.

Laurie accepted the cup of tea Ryan offered, and sipped at it slowly, not certain where to start. Ryan perched on the very edge of the sofa where he sat. He held the teacup in one tense hand while the other hand toyed with the handle of the cup. Laurie avoided sitting on the sofa with him, choosing a nearby chair instead. "Now." He smiled pleasantly. "What is it that I can do for you?"

Ryan blushed lightly. "Actually, I don't go to that club very often, but I hoped . . . that is, I wanted to get together with you anyway."

"Do you like the theatre?"

Ryan cocked his head. "Love it. But I don't have a budget that allows me to go."

Laurie picked up the phone, already dialing. "Thankfully, I do. As well as a friend who has been trying for weeks to get me to see her latest show." He paused while the phone rang, then smiled when he heard his friend's voice. "Remember those tickets you keep trying to force on me?" He chuckled at the response. "All right, all right. You're not trying to force them on me. Would you perhaps be able to set me up with two seats for this evening?" His smile grew. "Under my name at the box office? Thank you, I do appreciate it." He set the phone down and took in Ryan's wide-eyed look. "All settled. We've got an hour or so before we should be there, so would you care to go out for a bite first?"

"Love to." The younger man stood and walked over to face Laurie. "I hope you haven't thought I'm being forward about all this."

"Not at all," Laurie assured him. "It rather flatters me. At my age, I'm not used to being chased."

"At your age?" Ryan laughed. "You must be older than you look. If I didn't know about your position at the school, I'd think you were hardly older than myself."

And with many more mistakes like that, I'll not make it to much older, Laurie cautioned himself. "I'll just be a moment while I change." Back in the privacy of his bedroom, he looked in the mirror. Tall and slim, his features were those of a man in his early twenties. But Laurie had already lived for centuries when Ryan was born. He had watched humans live and die, and had even seen other vampires die. He shook his head, partly dried strands of hair flying wildly. It wouldn't do to think of death at a time like this. It would only depress him, and destroy his evening with Ryan. He quickly changed into something more appropriate for an evening at the theatre, dropping the sweats and slipping on black slacks, a ruffled white shirt, and a gray vest. He tied his hair neatly back in a ponytail, and composed his expression. No more thoughts of death, only life.

When he returned to the living room, Ryan was scanning one of the few books Laurie had brought with him to the flat. He set it down. "Ready to go?"

"Yes." Laurie's smile didn't reach his eyes. Memories intruded, despite his resolve, and he found himself thinking of Jim's Aztec features when he glanced at

Ryan's dark eyes. It had been a year since Jim's death in San Francisco. Since Laurie had returned to London afterward. Obviously he hadn't buried the pain far enough.

"Is something the matter?" Ryan paused at the door.

Laurie shook his head. "Nothing. Just a little tired still. Give me a few moments and I'll be wide awake." He ushered Ryan down to the car.

The exchange left a feeling of friction between the two. Ryan was worried he had done something wrong, and Laurie wasn't quite sure how to relax and begin to enjoy the evening again through the memories. But by the time they finished dinner and reached the theatre, running late after slow service in the restaurant, they had both relaxed and begun to enjoy the evening again.

The lights were blinking, signaling the show was about to begin, as Laurie and Ryan slipped into their seats. The opening music stole over them, and Laurie rested his hand on the arm of the chair between them. By the time the first line was spoken, Ryan's hand had covered Laurie's, and the two sat through the show with fingers entwined.

As the lights slowly came up for intermission, Laurie reluctantly disengaged his fingers from Ryan's. "I'm going to get a bit of something from the bar. Would you care for anything?"

"White wine would be nice," Ryan decided. "Thank you."

Different, Laurie decided as he walked away. Ryan was definitely a breath of fresh air for him. He was nothing like the others Laurie had associated with in recent years, either male or female, and for that he was thankful. He wasn't looking for anyone to replace the others. He wasn't sure what he was looking for, but he hoped he had found it in Ryan.

"You do realize, you are doing exactly what Jeffrey did not want you to do."

The voice was slightly breathy and low, and held a hint of steel. Laurie turned to find Karen standing just behind him, elegant in her low-cut navy evening gown. In her heels she stood tall enough to look him in the eyes, and her gaze was calm and even.

"Is my brother here as well?" Laurie inquired mildly.

"Thankfully, no," Karen admitted. "And I'll even offer to keep quiet this once."

"For a price," Laurie muttered.

"It is a simple one," she agreed. "Stop seeing that mortal."

"Can you prove he is mortal?" Laurie knew that with his magics it only took him one look to know a mortal from a vampire, but for Karen it wouldn't be so easy.

"In time, but he would likely be dead by then, and the point would be moot." Karen paused significantly. Her expression was carefully light. "Would it not?"

She truly was his brother's child, her lazy smile mocking him. He could win, he knew, but did he really want Ryan to be the chess piece in a game between himself and his brother? That had never been his intention. An escape, some peace and quiet, and a loss of bitter memories. Why couldn't it be that simple?

"Well?" she prompted.

Laurie's eyes narrowed as he moved up to the bar. He glared at her briefly, then turned to order two glasses of a good white wine. Accepting the glasses, he raised one between himself and Karen. "To my brother. May he never find out about my companion. The war we would have over your mind would be terrible to behold." He took a sip, watching her eyes.

She took a slow, deep breath, only for show. "You may have a point, and you may not. For now I will not tell him. But in time, never fear, he will learn on his own."

"I don't doubt it," Laurie agreed. "But then it will be between him and me. This is an argument that you and Ryan have nothing to do with." He raised a hand to catch her arm, fingernails biting into the soft flesh. "And you should remember that little detail next time you approach me. If you attack those who are in my protection, my brother can afford you little protection from me in return."

Karen's blue eyes darkened. After a moment of locked eyes, she angrily yanked her arm from his grasp. Angry red marks stood out against her white skin, and thin rivulets of blood ran down to her elbow. "Agreed," she hissed. "You may war with your brother all you like. Do not involve me."

"Agreed." Laurie sipped at his wine as she walked away, her back stiff and heels striking the floor sharply. Such a pleasant girl, in some ways, and one of the more skilled actresses he had known. But she deserved his brother, and Jeffrey's straitlaced ways. Her spirit wasn't free enough for independence.

The lights were already flickering when Laurie slipped back into his seat, handing Ryan's glass to him. Neglecting to let go, Laurie held the glass to Ryan's lips, tipping it slightly while the younger man sipped at the wine. "I am sorry to take so long," Laurie whispered. "I met an old acquaintance in the lobby, and the conversation took longer than I would have expected."

"That's quite all right." Ryan licked a stray drop of wine from his lip, extracting the glass from Laurie's fingers, then turning back to face the stage. "I saw an acquaintance of my own."

Laurie watched the other man carefully, following his gaze. Perhaps a few rows down, and several seats off to the left, a stranger turned and glanced in their direction. Brushing his brown locks out of his eyes, the stranger nodded politely, briefly, then turned away. Laurie felt Ryan's body stiffen next to him, and a bite of jealousy shot through him. "Is that him?"

"Who? Him?" Ryan nodded in the direction of the stranger. He blushed slightly. "Actually, yes. That's Evan. I . . . I think I mentioned him to you last evening?"

"Yes, I believe you did." Laurie's voice masked his emotion, sounding dead even to his ears. "Is he with his new companion?"

"He claims it didn't work out." Ryan's voice sounded slightly choked. "He's with his sister tonight."

Laurie sat silently, turning his concentration to the stage before him. The curtain rose and the characters were still there, and just as believable as before, but it seemed something was missing. Technically, it was an excellent production, and Janine was in her element in the starring role. He would have to introduce Ryan to her after the show. Perhaps. . . .

He glanced over to see that Ryan seemed to be having as much difficulty concentrating on the story as himself. "You miss him," he whispered softly, his hand covering Ryan's on the arm of the chair between them.

Ryan shrugged. "I suppose I do." He bit his lip, and glanced again at Evan, whose dark head was bent in conversation with the girl sitting next to him. Ryan's eyes hardened slightly, and his back stiffened. "But it was his decision, and it was probably for the best." His hand turned under Laurie's, ending up palm to palm, fingers entangling together. "After all, if he hadn't walked out on me, I wouldn't be here with you."

The jealousy seemed to subside somewhat, and Laurie took care to squash it completely. He raised Ryan's hand to his lips, gently kissing the fingertips. "I'm sorry to say it, but I'm glad he walked out on you then."

Ryan's eyes shone as he smiled in return. "Then so am I."

Their attention turned back to the stage, the story engaging their interest again. When Laurie glanced back at Evan one last time, the other man was staring back at the two of them, his expression unreadable in the darkness. Smiling to himself, Laurie released Ryan's hand, and dropped his own arm around his companion's shoulders. A gentle tug, and Ryan leaned into him, head dropping onto Laurie's shoulder.

As Laurie watched, Evan turned away again. Laurie relaxed in the comfortable feeling of Ryan nestling against him, and resolved to enjoy the rest of the show.

"You brought me a gift!" The beautiful blond swept Laurie and Ryan into her dressing room, enveloping Laurie in a warm hug. The silk of her dressing gown tickled his face as she drew her hand over his cheek and chin. "How wonderful of you." She then turned her attention to Ryan, grasping his shoulder firmly, and surveying his face and build. "An attractive one as well. Is he mine to keep?"

Ryan paled, and Laurie bit back his laughter. "No, Janine, he is my companion for the evening. I knew you would never forgive me for seeing your show without stopping backstage, so I persuaded Ryan to accompany me." Stepping forward, he gently disengaged her fingers from Ryan's shoulders, and pulled him back, sliding one hand down to catch Ryan's fingers with his own.

Janine pouted. "You are no fun, Laurie. You never were."

Laurie's smile was fond with remembrance. "Then your memory is failing, my lady."

Her momentary lapse was replaced with a sunny smile. "You are quite right, Laurie. You can be more than fun when you want to be." Her attention snapped back to Ryan. "Keep him, child. He will amuse you and enjoy you."

Ryan's face flooded with color. "I . . ."

"Don't listen to her," Laurie whispered, barely loud enough for Ryan to hear, the warm breath softly tickling his ear. "Janine has always run off at the mouth when she shouldn't. Just pay her no mind, and you'll be happier."

"Are you going to introduce me properly?" Janine asked cheerfully, as if she had no idea what Laurie had just said; both knew that she had heard it perfectly well.

"Janine Sanders, please meet Ryan James." Laurie gave Ryan's hand a gentle squeeze. "Ryan, Janine is one of the foremost actresses of the era."

"Your show was wonderful," Ryan enthused, beginning to relax.

"Really?" Janine had never been one to resist praise. "So tell me," she motioned to a couch, and both settled down, "what did you think of the staging in the scene where . . ."

Laurie stepped away as the two dropped into an enthusiastic discussion of the production. While Ryan obviously had no background in the theatre, he knew what he enjoyed seeing, and had very definite opinions. And Janine, of course, loved to play to an audience, and Ryan was momentarily captive.

After more than an hour, Ryan glanced over to where Laurie stood, a half-smile on his face as he watched the pair chatter. Laurie's smile broadened at the look of dismay on Ryan's face. "I'm so sorry. I believe I was distracted."

"Janine will do that to anybody," Laurie assured him. "If I hadn't expected to spend quite a bit of time backstage, I never would have brought you here."

"It has been a lovely visit." Janine languidly rose from the couch, one arm outstretched to Ryan. He helped her to her feet, gently kissing the back of her hand. "Please, do bring your companion again." Her voice was light as she said it, but it held the sound of an order to Laurie's ears.

He cocked his head, eyes narrowing slightly. Following her gaze to Ryan's neck, he shook his head slightly. Janine began to pout, but pushed Ryan toward Laurie. Ryan, oblivious to the byplay, merely walked over to stand by the door. "I'd love to come by again, sometime, Janine, if you wouldn't mind."

"As soon as we get the chance." Laurie ushered Ryan out the door before Janine could protest.

"You sound upset."

Laurie's eyes widened, surprised that Ryan had caught that. Then he frowned to realize the jealousy that must have displayed so briefly on his face and in his voice. "She would eat you alive," he muttered.

"I doubt that." Ryan laughed.

"You'd be surprised." Laurie's voice was too low for Ryan to hear. "Would you prefer me to admit that I'm jealous?"

Ryan stopped walking, turning to face Laurie. "Are you really? Why?"

Laurie shrugged, and simply drew Ryan toward him, kissing him gently. He stepped back, trying to measure the bewildered expression in Ryan's eyes. *So young, so alive.* There was a hint of bitterness as Laurie said, "I'm not sure why I'm jealous. But I am."

Ryan turned away, and began walking again. He was silent until they reached the car, and Laurie began to drive away. When he finally spoke, his voice was low. "Have you slept with her?"

"Janine?"

Ryan nodded. "She seemed . . . familiar."

"We've known each other a long time." Laurie's fingers tightened on the steering wheel slightly, thinking just how long that time was. "And yes, long ago in our past, we were rather intimate."

Ryan was staring out the window, the back of his head to Laurie, gazing into the darkness. "It couldn't be that long ago."

"Long enough." Laurie tried to put an end to the queries with a note of finality. It worked, and the silence grew uncomfortable.

Laurie reached out, fingers falling softly on Ryan's shoulder, until the younger man turned to face front once more. Laurie let his hand fall down over his shoulder, clasping Ryan's hand in his own. No response. Laurie's hand fell to the seat between them, and he started drum his fingers against the leather seat.

"I don't know how you do it."

"Do what?" Laurie kept his voice casual, wishing he dared look inside Ryan's mind, but hating the idea of invading his privacy that way.

"I think I'm jealous," Ryan admitted. "I keep thinking of you and Janine, and wondering . . . why did you stop seeing her? How can you be such good friends now? I don't think I could ever be friends with Evan again. And. . . ." his voice trailed off, and there seemed to be a small catch in his throat. "If you had a relationship with her, a normal relationship, whyever would you want one with me?"

Laurie's hands clenched in surprise. He couldn't keep the anger from his voice. "What the bloody hell do you mean by that?"

Ryan shrugged, turning to look back out the window again. "If you sleep with women, if you can sleep with women . . . I just don't understand what you want with me."

Laurie jerked the steering wheel hard, stomping on the brakes to skid to a stop at the side of the road. Luckily, at that late hour, it was nearly deserted, and the one lone car behind them swung around easily. He gave himself a few seconds to calm down. "What, exactly, is it that you are trying to say, Ryan?"

Ryan swallowed hard. "Do you have to make this so difficult? You know what I'm like, what my preferences are. I thought . . ." he blushed, barely visible in the darkness. "I thought you were the same. But I guess you're not."

"Are you saying that because I have, in the past, had a relationship with a woman, that I'm not good enough for you?" Laurie's voice was dangerously low.

"No!" Ryan's voice echoed in the confines of the car as he shouted his surprise. "It's just that a man wanting a woman is normal . . ."

"Are you trying to say that my wanting you is not normal?"

"It's perfectly normal, for me," Ryan allowed, "but not for you."

"Oh, bloody hell," Laurie swore. "Look, Ryan, there are a lot of things you don't know about me, that you may never know about me, and that you may not understand." Running his fingers through his hair in frustration, his fingers caught in the ribbon holding his ponytail and he yanked it out. Long blond strands framed his face, slightly tangled from the ribbon having been removed. "Ryan, my relationship with Janine, or with anyone else in my past, has nothing to do with might happen between us. Nothing."

Ryan's chocolate eyes reflected in the lights of a passing driver, and Laurie read confusion, insecurity, and a glimmer of hope. He sighed, deciding to forget talking about it. Reaching out, he clasped Ryan's shoulders and pulled him close, kissing him gently. "There," he said softly, "does that make my point?"

Ryan sat back slightly, a quirk of a smile barely beginning. "I think so. Care to reinforce it?"

And Laurie did.

"Would you like to do something this evening?"

Laurie yawned, hiding the soft sound from the phone. Even after two weeks, Ryan still called him before sundown. Someday, perhaps, he'd change, but Laurie enjoyed his enthusiasm, and his company. "Did you have something in particular in mind?"

"Well," Ryan hesitated. "We've done something just about every night, going to the club, and the theatre, and . . ."

Laurie frowned. Ryan's insecurity must be wearing off on him, he decided, as he asked, "Have we been spending too much time together?"

"Not at all!" Ryan insisted. Laurie could almost picture him grinning on the other end of the phone. "I was just thinking that perhaps it might be nice to have a quieter evening. I could pick up some fish and chips on my way over, and a bottle of good rosé. What do you say?"

"Sounds wonderful," Laurie agreed. "Give me a half hour to crawl out of bed." He was still smiling at the click of the phone, then yawned again. Slowly he climbed out of bed, forcing himself to stay awake. It wasn't long until dark, but it was hard to stay awake during even the shortest of daylight hours. A slowly warming shower helped, as well as the eventual setting of the sun.

He dressed carefully, but casually. Gray slacks, a black T-shirt. He didn't bother to dry his hair, simply tugging it back with a leather strip. No socks or shoes either. He always preferred his freedom, and if they weren't going out, there was no need for formality.

When the doorbell rang, he hurried to get the buzzer. Ryan's footsteps moved slowly up the stairs, and Laurie had the door open to greet him. At the sight of Ryan, Laurie forgot what he had planned to say. "Hi."

"Hi yourself." Ryan stopped a short way from Laurie, smiling shyly. "Well?" Holding out a bottle in a bag, he added softly, "Here."

Laurie stepped back from the door, motioning for Ryan to step in as he took the bottle from him. "Not bad," he decided, scanning the label quickly.

"I've got dinner as well," Ryan reminded him.

"Wonderful." Laurie watched as Ryan moved to the table and began to lay out the meal. Ryan was comfortable in Laurie's flat already, finding the plates and silverware easily. "Wineglasses are above the sink," Laurie offered, when Ryan faltered.

"Thanks." Ryan walked back, slipping the bottle from Laurie's hand. "Would you care to join me?" He filled both glasses, then handed one to Laurie. "You're being terribly quiet. Is something the matter?"

Laurie shook himself slightly. "No, no, nothing." He forced a smile to his face, trying to shake the nervousness he felt. Ryan was one more man, one more relationship. One more meal. After centuries, that was the only sane way to see it.

Ryan raised his glass. "To two weeks."

"Two weeks, and more," Laurie agreed. Stepping forward, he took the glass from Ryan, kissing him quickly. "Let's get to dinner before it gets cold." He smiled softly. "It's always best to eat a meal hot."

Both were silent during the meal, Laurie reflecting on his plans for the evening, and Ryan silently observing. Once everything was finished, the table cleaned, and the dishes taken care of, Laurie felt a familiar hunger and an equally unfamiliar set of nerves fall over him. "Perhaps you'd care to watch the telly?"

Ryan shrugged. "It's up to you. To be perfectly honest, I just couldn't stand the thought of spending another evening wearing something dressy and uncomfortable." He gestured at his jeans and T-shirt. "As much as I've enjoyed the theatre and shows and dinners, I'd much rather just spend time with you." He blushed slightly.

Laurie began to relax. "Then perhaps a show or two." Snagging the remains of the wine, and the glasses, he led the way into the living room.

Reclining on the couch, Laurie draped an arm about Ryan's shoulder, enjoying the feel of the younger man cradled against his side. As a comedy droned on across the room, Laurie ignored it, gently stroking Ryan's neck, feeling the pulse jump under his fingers.

"Much better," Ryan whispered. His hand had settled on Laurie's knee, and stayed there, fingers splayed over the leg. "Don't stop." He sounded surprised when Laurie's fingers left his neck.

Laurie chuckled. "Don't tell me you have a sensitive neck." He could feel the heat rising under his fingertips as Ryan blushed.

"Hell, yes."

"That could make the evening very interesting. You might say I have a fondness for necks myself." Laurie sat up, turning to face Ryan. He took the younger man's chin in his hand, tipping his head back. "Now, where is best to start?" he mused.

Laurie began to nibble just below Ryan's ear. He worked his way down, licking at the side of the neck, arriving finally at the crest of the collarbone. Ryan sighed, his head dropping back, exposing more of the tender flesh. Laurie drew back, and held his breath, bringing the sudden hunger back under control.

Ryan's eyes flickered open, and he pulled himself forward to glare at Laurie. "Don't you dare stop again," he ordered. There was a sudden confidence in his voice as he pulled Laurie forward, kissing him firmly. "You started this," Ryan muttered against his lips, "and we're going to finish it."

Laurie smiled. "Damn straight." And then he bent back to what he had been doing. He could feel the hunger still, but something else interfered. No matter how strong the thirst was, the desire was stronger. As Ryan's hands gently, then roughly, caressed his body he realized that Ryan was far more than another simple mortal.

Laurie worked slowly, unbuttoning Ryan's shirt a single button at a time, trailing his fingernail across Ryan's chest. He untucked the tails of the shirt from Ryan's jeans and then slid it over his shoulders. He then moved slightly so that he sat behind Ryan on the couch, and nibbled on the back of his neck. Ryan swayed back, leaning against him, one hand stroking Laurie's leg.

"I like it," Ryan murmured.

"That's the point," Laurie chuckled. He reached around and unzipped Ryan's jeans, one hand sliding inside slowly. The muscles under the skin jumped as Laurie's hand slid over Ryan's stomach, then he sighed deeply as Laurie's pale fingers curled around the darker length of Ryan's cock. "And let me guess, you like that as well," Laurie whispered.

Ryan didn't bother to answer out loud, stretching back to allow Laurie easier access to his body. His hips began to move gently against Laurie's questing hand, until the vampire laughed. "Not yet, luv." He pushed Ryan away. "Stand up, and finish getting yourself undressed."

He enjoyed the show as Ryan slid his jeans over slim hips, his briefs following them quickly as he kicked them across the room. Shoes, then socks, then Ryan stood there, hands on his hips, glaring playfully at his lover. "Seems a bit unfair," he grinned. "Me standing here in the buff and all, while you're still dressed."

Laurie stretched languidly along the couch, hands behind his head. "So do something about it."

"With pleasure." Ryan tugged the T-shirt over Laurie's head, throwing it off to one side. Then he knelt on the floor and carefully touched the bulge under Laurie's slacks. With one hand, Ryan reached to loosen the zipper, his other hand caressing Laurie through the strained fabric. Laurie raised his hips, allowed Ryan to slip the slacks over them. His cock made a tent in his boxers, and Ryan smiled as he slipped those away as well. "Much better," he whispered, lowering his lips to engulf Laurie's hard length.

"Oh. . . ."

Ryan's tongue swirled around the tip of Laurie's cock, tasting it gently, then he roughly engulfed it, pulling hard. All the while one hand dipped below to cradle and stroke his balls. Laurie groaned as Ryan bent before him, tongue working magically over him. The vampire's fingers tangled in Ryan's short chocolate locks, begging him not to leave, until with a final moan Laurie pushed him away.

"Not yet." His voice was hoarse as he motioned for Ryan to join him again on the couch. "Here, sit on my lap."

Ryan raised an eyebrow, curiously, but did as he said, settling back against him. He could feel the hard length nestled between his cheeks, and he rocked back slightly against it, until Laurie's hands on his hips stilled him.

"If you keep that up," Laurie whispered, "I am going to lose control. And I don't want to lose control"—He paused significantly—"yet." His hand dropped back to stroke Ryan again, while he claimed the younger man's lips with his own.

"Please, Laurie," Ryan whispered. His lover didn't have to ask what for, stroking him. Ryan was breathing hard as Laurie pulled him up, moving so that Ryan was kneeling on the couch.

"Stay right there," Laurie whispered. He held one hand out to the side, and in a flash of magic a small foil packet appeared between his fingers. He tore the wrapper, quickly sliding the condom over his erection. He stroked along it, taking the lubricant to smooth into the crack of Ryan's ass.

Laurie knelt on the couch behind Ryan. Positioning himself carefully, he slid into the other man's ass. Both men groaned with the sensation.

"Lean back," Laurie ordered softly. Somehow they managed it, maneuvering carefully until Laurie sat again on the couch, and Ryan was on his lap, with Laurie still buried inside of him. Laurie's hips began to rock slowly, as his hand echoed the motion on Ryan's cock.

"Now, Laurie," Ryan urged. "Please!" He was breathing in short gasps, his head falling back against Laurie's shoulder, baring his throat. His hips bucked forward, clenching around Laurie's length even as Ryan thrust his own cock against the vampire's hand.

Laurie set his lips against the soft skin of Ryan's neck, feeling the pulse fluttering there. Ryan sighed, his eyes closed in passion. Laurie couldn't restrain himself any longer, neither his hunger for Ryan's body or for his blood. As his teeth slipped into the vein, he could feel Ryan's body shudder against him as Laurie's own tremors began.

Laurie gently licked Ryan's neck, feeling the wounds close beneath his tongue. Slight tremors still shook his mortal body, and Laurie simply held him, waiting for the tremors to die down.

The sounds of the telly still sounded across the room; one show ended and another began before Ryan stirred and sat up. He disengaged himself and began to move around the room, silently picking up discarded clothing, sorting out the items.

"Going somewhere?" Laurie asked mildly.

Ryan glanced over in surprise. "It's gotten pretty late. You usually kick me out right about now."

Laurie stretched lazily along the couch, drawing Ryan's attention easily to him. He smiled and licked his lips. "What if I asked you to stay tonight."

"I'd ask if you're sure," Ryan told him, his chocolate eyes serious.

"Dead serious," Laurie assured him. "Do you have anything to do tomorrow? I'd love to keep you to myself tonight."

A slow smile began to spread across Ryan's face, the light reaching his eyes quickly. "And I'd love to stay."

Laurie stood, taking the shirt from Ryan's hand, dropping it back on the floor. Taking his hand, he drew him towards the bedroom in the back of the flat. "There's only one condition to this," he cautioned. "Don't you dare wake me up during the day tomorrow."

"Agreed."

Laurie laughed at the answer. Thankfully, all the windows were magically barred. He doubted Ryan would ever keep that promise. And he didn't care. He'd taken care of his thirst. Now he wanted to spend the rest of the night enjoying his time with Ryan.

"I'm in love." Laurie's voice fell flat into the silence.

"You don't sound happy about it," Melody commented drily as she looked up from her stack of paperwork. Catching sight of the expression on his face, her eyes widened slightly. "Oh my, you don't look happy either."

"I'm happy," Laurie muttered, dropping his lanky frame onto the couch in his office. "And I'm not happy." He ran his fingers through his hair, drawing the long strands back, then dropping them so that they hung over his face. "Dammit, I just wasn't expecting to fall in love."

Melody walked over to the couch, settling carefully next to him. "I take it this is that fellow who stopped by a few weeks ago?"

"Ryan, yes," Laurie agreed. "We've gotten quite close since then." He leaned forward, chin on his hands. "The thing is, Melody, Ryan's mortal. Therefore, he's dinner. And that's all he should be to me." Leaning back again, he sighed dramatically. "A damnably attractive goblet of blood."

Melody chuckled. "I'm mortal. Am I just dinner?"

"While I have nibbled on your neck on occasion," Laurie told her, "you're not just dinner to me. But I wouldn't say I'm in love with you, either."

Melody considered him as he sprawled across the couch. His face was paler than usual, and his clothes were wrinkled. The shirt looked slept in, and his eyes were drawn together in a deep frown. It almost looked as if he had worry lines by his eyes. "This is really bothering you, isn't it? You really are upset that you're in love with him." She covered his hand with her own, squeezing gently. "Why is it so bad?"

"He's mortal, dammit!" Laurie jumped up and stalked away, pacing around the room. He gestured broadly as his voice rose in his agitation. "Vampires can't fall in love with mortals. It just doesn't happen. It isn't worth anything. Mortals die."

Melody didn't try to hide a wry smile. "And vampires don't."

Laurie crumpled, as if he'd been struck, ending up semi-seated on the floor. "No, you're quite right. Vampires most certainly do die. And almost as unexpectedly as mortals do."

The thought seemed to hang in the air between them. Laurie had been despondent when he returned from the States nearly a year before. His relationship with Jim had still been new when the Aztec vampire had died in a firebombing. It had been months before Laurie could stop his frenzied work long enough to confide in his partner.

"I'm sorry."

Laurie sighed. "I deserved it. You are right. I shouldn't hold it against him that he's mortal."

"You don't seem any happier," Melody observed.

"No," he sighed again, "I'm not. I'm almost beginning to wonder if Jeffrey is right. Maybe I should stop involving myself with mortals."

"Close the school? Abandon me?" Melody teased.

"I already told you, you're different. You don't count as a mortal."

"I'd love it if you'd remind the deities in power of that when it comes time for me to die," Melody quipped.

Laurie forced a smile. "I could fix that mortality problem of yours in an instant."

"You could do the same for Ryan if you wanted, as well."

"If he wanted," Laurie looked away. He walked over to the window, and stared out into the cool night. "I've never discussed it with him. It just hasn't come up."

"You haven't . . ."

"I've tasted his blood, yes," Laurie answered her unasked question. "But we haven't talked about it. He hasn't asked any questions, and I haven't felt like volunteering."

"How long?"

Laurie shrugged. "A week. It's . . ." He drew a deep breath, filling his lungs slowly, feeling the pressure of the air inside. He didn't need to breathe, but it still helped calm him, letting the air out little by little while he tried to put his thoughts together. "I can't resist him. I barely tasted him, and he is so . . . his neck is so sensitive, he's so responsive. The reaction he has to everything is part of what I love about him. I want to keep giving him that joy."

"So do it."

"How?" He felt helpless, confused. Melody suddenly sounded far older than him. "I don't know how to do it, without changing him somehow. I have to explain everything to him, and I'm afraid it will make a difference." His fingers tightened on the windowsill, nails digging tiny half moons into the wood. "I've never actually had a relationship with someone who didn't know who I was, or what I was, before it began."

"Does he love you?"

Laurie shook his head. "I don't know."

Melody approached to stand behind him, hands on his shoulders, rubbing gently. "Have you told him you love him?"

Laurie's head dropped forward, hair shadowing his face. "No."

"Then what do you think your next step is?"

Laurie straightened, shrugging her touch off. "You really believe in honesty, don't you?"

"Lying is making you miserable," Melody confirmed. "I'd rather have you sitting here telling me you love him and being happy about it, instead of worrying about what he's going to do when you tell him you're an evil creature of the night. So just go and do it."

Laurie walked over to the desk and yanked a drawer open, pulling out a brush. He tugged it through the tangled strands of his hair, grunting with the pain as it resisted being brushed. Finally the long locks hung straight around his face, and he dropped the brush back into the drawer, drawing out an elastic instead. He quickly braided his hair, and twisted the elastic firmly around the end. A single strand escaped, falling across his nose when he turned back to look at Melody.

"Fine, I'll do it your way." His back was stiff and resolute as he turned to leave. "You're right. Whether he rejects me, or agrees with me, or. . . ." Watching, Melody saw his shoulders suddenly slump, then Laurie turned to face her again. "Whatever he says, you'll still listen to me, right? Even if I did say you didn't count."

"I'll still listen to you." Melody smiled encouragingly. She had never seen Laurie this nervous, this insecure. "That's what friends are for, to pick up the pieces."

Laurie clasped her hands, squeezing tightly them tightly, then releasing her. "Thanks. Wish me luck."

"Good luck." Melody smiled at the closing door. "But I doubt you'll need it."

Laurie hit the buzzer to let his guest in. Whistling, he strode to the door, and whipped it open. Footsteps were still coming up the stairs. "Hello, Ryan," he called out cheerfully.

"Is that his name?" Jeffrey's voice was dry and his expression sour as he came into view. "I take it you are expecting his company this evening."

"As a matter of fact, I am." Laurie turned on his heel and walked away, leaving Jeffrey in the doorway. "Come in," he called back, "and shut the door behind you. Both of you."

Jeffrey stepped inside, and motioned for Karen to follow. As he removed his gloves, Jeffrey surveyed the flat, while Karen hovered near the door.

"You don't have to be on guard duty," Laurie told her. "No one is going to be attacking you here. Ryan isn't a hunter."

"You trust mortals too easily," Jeffrey reminded him. "What evidence do you have that he can be trusted?"

"None at all, without going into his mind." Laurie's eyes hardened suddenly. "And don't order me to do that, Jeffrey. Because I won't. I do trust Ryan, and that is something you will have to learn to understand."

A hint of bitterness crossed his face as he turned to Karen. "As for yourself, I thought you had made me a promise."

She lowered her eyes. "I had agreed not to tell Jeffrey, that is true." Laurie saw the flash of anger in his brother's eyes, but Karen carefully did not look at either of the men. "But I also agreed that while I would not aid him, neither would I hinder him."

"You are a vampire," Jeffrey reminded him. "And he is human. He is cattle, good only for manipulation or dinner."

Laurie raised an eyebrow, a bit of humor returning. "Oh? And what would you do during the day without your human servants? Do you trust them?"

"I control them."

Laurie shuddered delicately at Jeffrey's statement. "You would have done well in the feudal age, brother. What a pity you can't return London to that time." He walked away, and busied his hands arranging a setting for two on the table. "But whether you control the mortals who protect you during the day or not, the fact remains, you cannot control me. And as I am my sire's child, I doubt you wish to cross me, either." While Laurie had never liked his sire, he recognized the use of Eric's standing within their race. "I will take any action against Ryan as a direct action against myself." Laurie's expression was mild as he turned to face Jeffrey once more. "Is that clear?"

"And should you reveal yourself to that mortal, I will accept that you have endangered all our kind and deal with you accordingly." Jeffrey's voice was deep and solemn. "I believe our elders will agree with any action I might take."

Eyes locked, neither would look away. "My sire might have something different to say," Laurie said simply. He held his brother's gaze a moment longer before purposefully turning his back. "May I get you something?"

He heard a small sound, as if Karen began to speak, but Jeffrey interrupted. "No, we will be leaving soon."

"Not soon enough," Laurie muttered. He didn't care if he was overheard; Jeffrey already knew his opinion.

When the bell to the flat rang, Karen reached the door before Laurie could, swinging it wide.

Ryan stopped in the doorway, looking curiously into the apartment. "Am I interrupting something?"

Laurie sighed. "No, come on in. I've got everything set up for dinner, if you don't mind eating in."

"Not at all." Ryan stepped in, and watched as Karen closed the door behind him. She merely watched him in return, a slight smile on her face. Looking away, Ryan stepped close to Laurie. "Are you certain I'm not interrupting? I can always stop back later." He chuckled softly. "And after I was so careful not to call and wake you up this evening, too."

Laurie stifled a groan at the frown on Jeffrey's face at the last comment. "They were on their way out anyway." He motioned toward the couch. "This is my brother Jeffrey, and the lovely young lady at the door is his companion Karen." Laurie slid an arm around Ryan's waist, tugging him gently closer. "Brother, this is Ryan." Laurie smiled at his companion, then kissed him, deepening the kiss as Ryan responded.

Ryan drew back after a moment. "If we start now, we'll never have dinner," he reminded Laurie. After a glance at Jeffrey, he added, "And I don't think your brother approves."

Laurie hid a smile at his brother's glowering expression. "My brother has never approved of my lifestyle," he agreed. "And he likely never will. He will simply have to learn to agree to disagree."

Jeffrey stood, tugging black gloves over his hands. "Perhaps," he acknowledged. "But that is something we can discuss later. For now, you would do well to remember what we have already discussed this evening."

"As would you," Laurie agreed. He watched as the door swung shut behind the other two, then slowly dropped his strong hold on Ryan. "As would you," he repeated softly.

"I'm not causing you any family problems, am I?" Ryan's chocolate eyes mirrored his concern. "I'd hate to think I'm coming between you and your family."

"You would not be the first thing to come between us." Laurie sighed. "My relationship with my brother has never been a good one, and the years have only made it worse." He flashed a bright smile and drew Ryan to him. "But that has little to do with tonight. Did you have any plans for the evening?"

Ryan laughed and grinned, eyes dark with desire. "Dinner, and maybe dessert." He frowned as Laurie abruptly pulled away from him, turning his back. "What's wrong?"

Laurie kept his back to him, tongue running over his sharp canines. It took a minute before he was under control again. "Nothing." He managed to keep his voice from shaking. "The argument with Jeffrey must have bothered me more than I thought."

"Are you certain you want company this evening?"

Laurie didn't say a word, merely walking into the kitchen and returning with a tray. "And let my home-cooked meal go to waste? I hardly ever cook, so you must at least try it." His grin showed his return to good humor. "After all, I may not cook like this again for years."

"It looks wonderful." Ryan took the plate of fettucini from the tray and set it on the table. Moments later they were seated, and Ryan made a noise deep in his throat as he tasted the meal. "This is wonderful. What do you mean you won't cook again for years?"

It would be the perfect moment. Laurie slowly chewed, swallowed, and tried to work up the nerve to say it. Then a sip of wine. When he looked at Ryan, he was waiting patiently for an answer. "It's an exaggeration." Laurie sighed, mentally cursing himself. "I'm an excellent cook, but I so rarely do it. My friends say it's like I cook only once every decade." *Which is true,* he admitted to himself.

Ryan accepted the answer, silently finishing dinner. "I hope I'm around the next time you decide to cook, then." He flashed a quick grin, then disappeared into the kitchen with the dirty dishes.

Something turned over in Laurie's stomach. Next time . . . he liked the idea. Standing, he shook his head. Melody was right. He had to talk to Ryan, and soon.

"Where are you wandering off to?" He hadn't even heard Ryan come up behind him. The other man slipped his arms around Laurie's waist. "You look like you're a million miles from here."

"Just thinking of you." Laurie sighed as one of Ryan's hands caressed his chest. He could feel Ryan's body against the length of his back, cheek pressed into Laurie's shoulder. "Where do you want me to be?"

"Here," Ryan whispered. "In my arms. Now." He groaned softly. "Please?" He easily untucked Laurie's shirt, pulling so that Laurie had to lift his arms and allow it to slide over his head. Then Ryan's hands sought the zipper. . . .

Laurie turned in his arms, forgetting everything else. "Damn." He kissed Ryan, nibbling on his lower lip and caressing his ass until Ryan began to moan. The fair-haired vampire stepped back long enough to allow both to shed their clothes quickly, then their bodies entwined again.

"Please?" Ryan's voice was choked, barely a whisper.

"No." Laurie slowly pushed Ryan down to the floor, covering his body with his own. "Not yet."

Skillfully he stroked Ryan's body to the breaking point, not allowing him his release. He ran one fingernail across the sensitive balls as his teeth nibbled gently at Ryan's cock. He began to slide his mouth along Ryan's hardened length, sliding it in and out as his tongue swirled over the knob at the end. He flicked his tongue, tasting the salty drop from the tip, then drew back slightly. He moved down to Ryan's knees, kissing the backs gently. Ryan moaned as Laurie's lips and tongue traveled upward, swirling little whirlpools of sensation across the other man's thighs.

"Please. . . ." Ryan moaned.

Laurie didn't answer, allowing his tongue to come close to Ryan's balls, then close to his cock, but not reaching them. His hands were clasped with Ryan's, holding both out to the side. Nothing touched Ryan where he desperately desired it. Nothing. Ryan's hips thrust ineffectually against the air.

"Goddammit, Laurie, please!" Ryan groaned. Laurie obliged then, taking one of Ryan's balls into his mouth, rolling it around, then slipping it back out so he could take the other one. Then he moved back up to the cock that had stroked his cheek as he caressed the balls with his tongue.

Ryan was whimpering, alternately pleading and damning Laurie with every breath. The vampire moved up over him, planting his knees on either side of Ryan's head as he lay back on the rug. "Take it," Laurie ordered, and Ryan did, reaching up and drawing Laurie's hardness into his mouth. He sucked frantically, begging for more, as Laurie reached back behind him, continuing to stroke.

Laurie felt his balls tighten, and he jerked back roughly. Ryan groaned, and reached for him, but Laurie slipped quickly away to lie next to him. He felt Ryan's hands curl around him, stroking and pulling, as he did the same to him. Laurie moved up over his lover, dropping light kisses on his lips, across his cheek, then down to his neck. And when Ryan could only whimper incoherently, Laurie finally gave in, sinking his teeth into the vein as they both slipped over the edge.

Laurie lay half on top of Ryan, his head cradled against Ryan's shoulder, one leg and one arm splayed over the other man's body. With one hand, Ryan gently stroked Laurie's hair.

"I wish it could be like this forever."

Laurie suppressed a shiver. "Just like this?" He chuckled. "Do you want to live forever?"

Ryan was silent a moment. Then he sighed. "It's a nice dream, isn't it? Never dying, I mean. Never having to grow old and die."

Laurie slipped away and propped himself up on one elbow. "What if it were possible, I mean. Would you want to live forever?"

"It's impossible." Ryan discounted the idea.

"But what if, Ryan?" Laurie smiled, and poked him in the ribs, getting a laugh in response as Ryan tried to move away from the tickling. "Play the game. What if it were possible to live forever? Would you?"

Ryan locked his hands under his head, elbows out, staring up at the ceiling. "Is there a price?"

Laurie shrugged. "There are a lot of different ways to be immortal. According to fiction anyway." He took a deep breath. "What if you were a vampire?"

"A vampire?" Ryan sat up suddenly, laughing. "You mean the kind of chap who runs around in a cape saying, 'I vant to suck your blood'?"

"Well, the bloodsucking type anyway." Laurie frowned as Ryan started to laugh again. "You're not playing the game, Ryan."

"All right, all right." Ryan swallowed and managed to stop laughing. "I'll try to take you seriously." He sat and thought, chewing on his lip. Laurie watched him, catching his eye long enough to catch fleeting thoughts and emotions.

"I. . . ." Ryan hesitated.

Laurie felt a sudden fleeting moment of horror from Ryan.

"Would I have to kill?" His voice dropped to a whisper.

Laurie shook his head. "No killing. Just small sips of blood." He licked his lips unconsciously. "Your victim probably wouldn't even notice."

Ryan was silent for long enough that Laurie wished he dared peer inside his mind to see what he was thinking about.

"I don't think I'd like it."

Laurie hid his disappointment. "Why not?"

"I'd hate to see everyone I know die. I'd hate hurting people just so that I could live."

"What if it didn't hurt them?"

Ryan rolled over, his back to Laurie, curled up in a ball. "It wouldn't matter if it hurt them or not. I'd still be robbing them of something they couldn't live without, just to sustain my own life. It wouldn't be right."

Laurie stroked his back, his expression sad. "It's only make believe, Ryan." He tugged on his shoulder until Ryan turned to face him again. He smiled reassuringly. "Vampires aren't real."

"I know," Ryan admitted. "All those thoughts of losing people, and dying, and killing . . . it gets to me."

"Don't." Laurie shushed him with a kiss. "Don't even think about it. This is life." He allowed his hands to wander across his lover's body, bringing Ryan quickly out of his depression.

This time when he drew out the lovemaking it was slow and languid, no hurry, no fever pitch. A strong reaffirmation of life and the living.

"Maybe not forever," Ryan whispered when it was over. He didn't try to suppress his yawn, curling his sated body into Laurie's.

Laurie sat up, his hand still stroking Ryan's side. In moments Ryan was asleep. With a little effort Laurie slipped inside his mind to read a few residual thoughts. Ryan was horrified at the idea of vampirism, at the idea of what Laurie did.

"I love you." Laurie brushed away the tear that fell onto Ryan's back. With another few moment's effort the vampire was inside Ryan's mind completely. Everything was laid bare before him. He didn't look, couldn't look. Didn't want to know how Ryan really felt about him. It didn't matter anymore.

Ryan would never understand who Laurie was. He couldn't tell him; he couldn't not tell him. If he kept him, Jeffrey would use him. Laurie shivered at the image of Jeffrey with his lips at Ryan's neck.

It would be better this way. Better to end it now, before the caring got to be too much. Better to let go.

Laurie sat at the desk, a mound of paperwork before him, the pen dangling between his fingertips. Melody hadn't bothered to knock before walking into his study, and he hadn't even noticed her arrive. She stood there, watching him as the cap of the pen slipped between his teeth and he gently chewed on the tip, brows furrowed in concentration.

"Hard at work?" she broke the silence.

His head snapped up. "What in bloody hell are you doing here?"

"Checking up on you," she admitted. "You've been a bear the last few days. Last I knew you were in love. Want to talk about it?"

Laurie leaned back, placing the pen between his teeth again. Seconds later he yanked it from between his lips and slammed it down on the desk, glaring at it. "I think I need a drink," he muttered. "Want to go with me?"

Melody looked him over. Physically he looked fine. Better, in fact, than he had since coming back from the States a year ago. But his eyes were shadowed. "Let me get my coat." She stood, then paused. "We are talking about alcohol here, right?"

"Just get your coat."

He met her at the door, and walked her silently to the car.

"Where are we going?" She waited for an answer, more concerned when he was silent. His face was unreadable as he drove. "What did Jeffrey have to say yesterday?"

Laurie's back stiffened. "Nothing important." His fingers tightened on the wheel.

It had been a short visit, Karen hovering in the background like a dutiful shadow, while Jeffrey loomed large in Laurie's study. "I see you are back at work." Jeffrey's voice was cool, clipped.

"Yes," Laurie admitted. "Is that good enough for you?"

"Until you step outside the bounds again."

The brothers had stood nose to nose then, and Laurie's eyes darkened with crimson anger. "Leave Ryan alone. He is no longer a part of this."

"Agreed."

Now Laurie's fingers loosened again from the steering wheel as he pulled into the parking lot. The neon sign above the entrance glowed garishly into the darkness.

Melody reached out, her hand light on his shoulder. "Are you sure this is a good idea? Isn't this where you said you met . . ."

"Yes." He didn't let her finish the thought, remembering that first sight of Ryan with painful clarity. "I want a drink. Maybe a dance." He smiled wryly. "Humor me."

He slipped out of the car, walking around to get Melody's door for her. As they walked into the club, she reached for his hand, their fingers entwining.

The music surrounded them, enfolding them in the pulsing beat. Melody squeezed Laurie's hand as he silently led them to a table in a corner, within easy sight of the dance floor. "Two glasses and a bottle of red." He waved the waitress away quickly and settled in, slumping down in his chair.

Melody tried to talk, but he refused to answer, staring at the dance floor. When the wine arrived, he poured two glasses, handing one to her, and toying with the other, barely sipping at it.

She followed his line of sight to the twisting bodies on the dance floor. The music settled into a slower beat, and slowly the bodies resolved into couples, bodies linked and swaying. And everything made sense.

She had only met him once, but she knew who Laurie was watching. She reached out and covered Laurie's hand with her own. "Who is he with?" she whispered.

"Evan. He had just left Ryan when I met him." He slipped his hand free from Melody's and quickly downed his glass of wine, pouring another.

Out on the dance floor, Ryan caught sight of the table in the corner and smiled. Laurie couldn't help but smile in response. Ryan tugged at his companion's shoulder and they stopped dancing. It took a moment while Ryan drew Evan behind him through the crowd. Laurie took the time to compose his expression and his thoughts.

"Hi, Laurie." Ryan's voice was cheerful above the din of the music. "Evan, this is the wonderful friend I told you about."

"A pleasure." Evan's eyes reflected his confusion, a slight recognition of Laurie mirrored there. "Ryan told me how you encouraged him to give me a second chance. I'm grateful."

"Is it all working out?" Laurie was surprised his voice didn't sound more choked. It felt as if his throat were closed.

"Wonderfully." Ryan gave Evan an impulsive hug, his chocolate eyes showing desire. "It's better than before, and everything is out in the open." Evan smiled in response and their eyes caught. Laurie turned away slightly, unable to watch the silent exchange.

"I was overreacting, nervous," Evan admitted. "But I realized how much I missed Ryan, especially when I saw him at the theatre with you. I was so relieved when Ryan told me it was nothing serious."

Laurie quickly finished his second glass of wine. Melody frowned at his pale face, the faint red glow in his eyes. She poured him another glass of wine and quickly wrapped his fingers around the stem. His voice was soft, "I'm glad it's all going well."

"Thanks to you." Ryan slipped out of Evan's embrace. Giving Laurie a quick hug, he dropped a kiss on his forehead. "I really do appreciate everything you did for me."

Laurie reached up, his hand trailing briefly over Ryan's cheek before he jerked it away. "It was a pleasure." He swallowed hard. "If you need anything, you know I'll be there."

"I know." Ryan drew away, moving back close to Evan. As he slipped his arm around Ryan's waist, Evan leaned down and whispered something into his ear. Ryan's eyes lit up and he smiled back. "Let's dance," he whispered throatily.

"You okay?" Melody asked softly. Laurie's eyes were still fastened on the two men who had moved back onto the dance floor, bodies seeming glued together.

Laurie shook his head. "Let's dance." He dragged her out to the floor, fingers digging into her wrist. She slid into his embrace, wrapping her arms around him, hardly flinching when his arms pulled her roughly against him.

"I'm going to miss him." His words whispered softly against her cheek.

"I know," she said. "What happened?"

He shook his head. "I couldn't do it. He hated the idea of what I am. I had to let him go."

"He seems so . . ."

"I erased . . . changed how he felt about me." A tear rolled
down his cheek, falling against Melody's. "I had to."

Melody caressed his back. "You still love him."

"Yes."

She pulled his head against her shoulder. Her hands
stroked his back, comforting, drawing out his emotion.
She could feel his shoulders silently heaving, the tracks of
his tears soaking her blouse. While the music turned fast
she continued to hold him and simply sway.

His Name Was Wade

Gary Bowen

His name was Wade, and he was tall and lanky and played guitar like no man I ever saw. But when he opened up his mouth and started to sing, that's when I lost it. I believe in giving the Devil his due, and so I will say that Wade was a handsome young man in a untutored, ranch-hand kind of way, which of course the ladies liked. He was tall, yet not over tall, he was lean, but not too muscular, though his arms were ropy; and he had sandy blond hair and an easy smile. It was the smile that really did it. The rest of his features were pleasant enough, and many a cowboy with a decent face and a sweet voice has tumbled many a maid, but none of them could match Wade, though at first glance he seemed to be yet another one of them.

Like I said, it was the voice. I was standing there at the bar, doping myself with beer in order to withstand the coming amateur night, not expecting anything good at all. This bar wasn't even on my list, it was simply the place closest to the hotel. It was a coincidence that it happened to be having an amateur night and that I happened to be a talent scout/independent producer. Wade came out and took his place on a wooden stool with a microphone and acoustic guitar. One spotlight was on him, but nobody paid him any mind; there weren't more than a dozen people collected about the tables. None of them was there to hear some local boy with delusions of grandeur sing to them.

But they noticed. Not right away. They were slower than me. As for myself, all I can say is that when he moaned out the opening words, "Don't make me come to Dallas," a shiver went down my spine and a jumble went through my mind, which was half composed of, *I ain't going to Dallas for no man*, **and** *Damn, that boy's got a voice!* which then got melded into, *Gee, I wish somebody would sing that way for me.* I picked up my drink and ambled over to the stage, took a seat right at a front table, leaned back, and watched him sing.

He closed his eyes, didn't look at anybody, just leaned over that guitar like it was the only thing he loved and his fingers flew and strummed while the rest of him was so liquid it's a wonder he didn't slide right off the stool.

I know talent when I see it, and that boy had it raw, in spades, stacked to the ceiling, however you want to put it. I sat there with my heart in my mouth praying to God that he had more than one song in him. God knows how many promising boys and girls I've seen sing one, two, maybe even three pretty good songs, then punk out and flounder. A pretty voice sure is nice, but it don't pay the rent. Not all by itself it doesn't. There needs to be something extra, something that keeps them going, an obsession almost. Without it they might as well be singing in the church choir, because they aren't going to survive the record business.

The chords died away and the smattering of applause went up. I clapped harder than everybody, waiting with baited breath to see what he had next. He didn't disappoint me. Now that he'd hooked us all with the smoky power of his voice, he straightened up, looked me right dead in the eyes, and said, "Let's rock this joint." Maybe he looked at everyone in the house that way. In fact, knowing him now as well as I do, I'm sure he did. And that was the key to his magic; no matter how many people were in the room, no matter how absorbed he was in his music, he would give each person that piercing look that said, *This song is for you.* How they loved it. Women, hell, men, were sending him proposals for everything ranging from midnight trail rides to marriage and things that would get your arrested in fourteen states just for mentioning them. Sitting there in that bar my fingers itched for paper and pen; I wanted to sign him quick before he got away. I didn't examine my own motives too closely; the boy could sing, that was good enough for me. The rest was up to the starmaking machinery.

He had four songs, the maximum anyone was allotted in that place on amateur night. He played them all, and then he took his bows. His eyes raked over me like a poker raking up coals, and he then stepped down. The women mobbed him, but I was right up there with them. He gave me a cool look and accepted a lady on each arm. Pointedly turning his back on me he walked toward their table. I was not about to be rebuffed. I took a business card out of my wallet, and stepping around the redhead, I stopped in front of him and extended my card. "Call me if you want to make a record," I said. He looked at me, looked at the card, and didn't let go of either woman. "What kind of record?" he asked suspiciously.

"A hit record," I replied. "Ten thousand on signing. But I leave town tomorrow morning. You make up your mind." I tucked the card in his shirt pocket. He gave me a dirty look like he didn't like me getting that close to him, but he didn't say no. I touched the brim of my ten gallon hat, said, "Good night, ladies," and walked away.

"A record contract!" I heard one of them squeal. Then both of them were gabbing away at him.

I paused at the door and looked back in time to see him fighting his way clear of the women and retreating to the men's room. I stopped at the bar and ordered another beer, willing to linger long enough for him to catch me once he'd studied my card and decided I was for real.

I waited a long time. After half an hour I got worried and went to the men's room myself. He wasn't there. The hallways contained a door with a sign that said, EMERGENCY EXIT ONLY—ALARM WILL SOUND. I didn't try it, but I was willing to bet the alarm was turned off. *Damn. Now why would that boy run away from ten thousand dollars and a record contract?* I went back to the bar and asked the bartender, "What was that boy's name?"

"Wade," he answered. "Not sure what his last name is."

"He been here before?"

"Nope."

"He gonna be here again?"

"Maybe."

I was there for the next three amateur nights in a row, but Wade didn't show up. I cussed my luck and hated myself for not kissing up to him the way he seemed to have wanted me to, but damn, you can't kiss up to every two-bit talent that comes along because it doesn't pay off. But my bones were telling me that if I could land Wade it would pay off—big. If this boy turned out to be the next

Garth Brooks it would be worth all the ass-kissing. Real stars are highly individual, temperamental people. You have to take 'em that way because their strangeness is the seat of their genius. You take ordinary people, you get ordinary music. But damn, it sure was easier to deal with somebody sweet who could sing a pretty song. People would buy their albums, they just wouldn't buy as many as if the singer was something hot.

Then again, the hot ones had to be rescued from marrying their thirteen-year-old cousins and had to be bailed out for doing drugs and otherwise making life hell for their manager and ruining their label's wholesome image. Anybody who thinks Country-Western stars don't drink, do drugs, run around, cheat on their taxes, get in fights, wreck their cars, and hit their wives are dreaming. They just don't do it on stage like some other folks do. Not yet, though the way things have been going I expect to see it soon. Too many bad boys.

So I cussed Wade-without-the-last-name and told myself I was better off without a temperamental idiot that would drive me to distraction because no amount of money is worth that much aggravation. But I didn't believe it.

After I washed out three times at amateur night I started hunting him in earnest. Finally, a number of weeks later, I spotted the redhead he'd had on his arm oh-so-briefly, and tipping my hat to her said, "Honey, I remember you. You were with Wade."

Her eyes went all dreamy and she said, "Yeah." Her friends gave me funny looks, but she didn't seem to mind my intrusion.

"Do you know where I can find him? I'm with the record company."

She grinned happily and said, "He doesn't need a record, he's just *fine* in person." Her girlfriends tittered.

I pulled out a twenty. "Let me buy you all a round of drinks."

She took the money and said, "He's singing over at the Little Texas on Tuesday and Thursday."

The Little Texas was medium large for a dance hall and saloon. Wade was coming up in the world. He was still working the off nights, bracketing the Wednesday night karaoke, but that wouldn't last long. There was no cover fee; Wade was just some guy they'd hired so they could advertise LIVE MUSIC! He was their lip service to truth in advertising, but boy oh boy, they had hit a gold mine. The place was full, with only a few empty tables near the back. Definitely a good crowd for a Tuesday.

He sat up on his stool and a guy with a piano and a guy with a drum set backed him up. He wore a red satin cavalry shirt with shiny gold buttons and had a new black low-crowned cowboy hat on his head, but his black jeans were seriously worn and his boots were scuffed. I forced my way through the throng of admiring women and found myself standing along the wall with the men. Like I said before, women admirers were in the majority, but there were plenty of men who liked the way Wade sang. Or maybe it was the suspenseful way his torn jeans creaked as he moved. I discovered I was holding my breath in fear (or was it anticipation?) that the fabric would burst and he'd pop right out. Women singers had been playing that trick for years, so much so that when I met a woman in a gossamer lace top that seemed about to explode I paid it no mind because of course it never did. I don't know what they made women's things out of, but it only *looked* flimsy. In reality it was made of steel net, and however much a man might hope to get himself an eyeful, he never would. It took a long slow time before it percolated through my brain that Wade was playing the same game—and it was working just as well, on me and everybody else.

Wade held the microphone close to his lips and crooned, "Do you wanna dance?"

"Yes!" the women shouted back at him.

"Do you wanna dance with me, tonight, under the stars?" Maybe it was ad-libbed, or maybe it was carefully calculated. Whichever, it made the women go nuts, climbing up on the chairs and waving their hands, reaching out for those torn jeans that were just beyond their grip. Later we went on tour, and night after night he'd pull the same stunt, hunching close to the microphone, eyes heavy lidded, smoky voice asking, *"Do you want to dance with me?"* and every night it had the same electric effect.

Yes.

I was more than a little embarrassed to discover I had a hard on.

They played three sets. Mostly they covered popular hits, but added the raw sensuality most stars were too reticent to record. The piano player was competent; he banged out the honky tonk parts with vim. The drummer was good; he kept the rhythm—but neither of them was special. They followed Wade slavishly, simple accompaniments to his voice. After a time their inadequacy began to rub on me because there was nothing they were adding to the show except backup for the Voice. He didn't need them to do what he was doing, but he did need them because that's the way the business was. Guys just don't get up on stage all by themselves and sing. They have to have a band, a light show, a sound crew, they have to *entertain*. That was where I came in. But dammit, I had to catch him first.

So Thursday night I lay in wait for him, arriving early and camping in a dark corner until he and the other two guys showed up and set up. Women were there, too, with their discomfited boyfriends trailing in their wake while the women fawned on Wade. He left the setting up to his cohorts while he joined the women at their table and let them ply him with drinks. I watched him carefully, and discovered another trick of his: he never swallowed. Instead he poured beer down one woman's bodice, making her squeal. Her nipples stood up hard beneath the stretchy green fabric and her boyfriend gave Wade a look that said he was going to be dead in the alley in five minutes. Then he licked her neck clean. He nuzzled her neck long and hard and her eyes rolled up in her head. She slumped against him, dreamy eyes gazing blankly. He smiled, tapped her lips with his finger, then rose from the table and went back to the stage. She lounged in her chair, smiling like an idiot, blond hair sticking to the wetness he'd left on her throat while her boyfriend glowered at her.

I stepped onto the stage. "You need a bodyguard, loverboy," I said. He looked around at me, glanced over his shoulder at the jealous boyfriend, and said, "I'm doing fine."

"What about that record contract?"

"No."

"No?" I gaped at him. "This lousy dirtwater band is bringing in this many people and you say *no* to a record contract? Are you crazy? Just think what you could do with a real band!"

"I have a real band, and we do just fine. You can't do what we do and have it come out right in a recording studio. We're a live band." He ignored me real hard, and I felt like I'd turned invisible. His back was turned to me, and I was looking at broad red shoulders and a tight ass in tight, worn jeans. His boots were silent as he cat-footed across the stage trailing an electrical cord.

Then the drummer was at my elbow asking, "What contract?"

"I offered him ten thousand dollars last month."

"If he signs, do we all get signed?"

Not on their lives. Riffraff like them were a dime a dozen. I thought my answer over carefully. "If that's what he wants, that's what he gets." Now they would be on him like ticks on a hound, and they wouldn't let up until they had drawn blood.

The four songs he'd done at the amateur night were the only four original songs he had. Not enough for an album, but that didn't matter. I went back to my hotel, called Sully, and had him fax me three lyrics with melodies. When I got back to the bar, I folded them up and laid them on the floor by the drummer's foot. His eyes glowed like ball lightning and he almost missed a beat. I went back to the hotel and banged on my laptop until I had the contracts right. I was taking it upon myself to buy the rights to the songs from Sully, and it was going to cost me a pretty penny, which I was sure Wade would never reimburse me for. But I was willing to make an investment.

I didn't go back to the bar until Tuesday, Wade's next performance. I was dying to know how the drummer had made out; were they fighting over the new songs? Were they wearing him down, telling him not to blow his big chance? Or did he wad them up and flush them? Dammit, what did the man want?

Tuesday the place was packed. People were standing in line to get in, so I joined them and paid the cover. Yeah, management had wised up. They had even hung a sign on the front, WADE RAWLINS AND THE PARTY TIME BAND. Yeah, that summed up the act just about perfect. You wanna party, you wanna dance, you wanna rock this joint? Wade's your man. All those baby boomers fed up

with the nihilism of rock would jump ship to party with
Wade. I was about to burst an artery; I could taste the
success. So close. *Sign, Wade, sign.*

Wade came out on stage in a different pair of torn blue
jeans and a red satin shirt with white fringe on it. Same
beat up boots; this boy knew how to blend country hick
with city boy and they ate it up. I raced three other guys
for a vantage point near the right corner of the stage, and
by virtue of being bigger and older than any of them,
claimed the spot. I was chain-smoking cigarettes, a filthy
habit that would kill me if Wade didn't kill me with
musical blue balls first. Wade's eyes flicked across me and
I knew he knew I was there. He fiddled around on the
stage for awhile, then standing up at the microphone,
turned his head and looked right at me, those black eyes
nailing me to the spot, "This next song is in honor of the
most persistent man I ever did know." Then his eyes left
me and I could breathe again. He started singing *"Never
say no,"* the tag line from one of Sully's songs. Just him
and that glorious voice in a bar packed with silence. He
sang the refrain once through, then the drum rolled
underneath his voice, and suddenly the guitar wailed and
we were off on a completely different arrangement than
the one I had sent him. He'd taken a lovely ballad and
turned it into the wail of the damned, and I'd never seen
anything like it. My jaw dropped, my ears ached, and
every eye in the place was glued to him, and I don't think
anybody dared breathe. What had been a fairly clever song
about a young man desperately trying to talk a girl into
dancing with him became a whole lot more, and when he
got to the final line, *"You never said no, but my heart
said yes,"* the women started screaming. They never shut
up either.

After the show was over he walked across the stage and
said, "I want to talk to you." I nodded and he climbed

down. He never looked back, and I glanced at his cohorts. They were staring after him, worried looks on their faces. I'd be worried if I was in their shoes too; Wade might sign without them, or he might blow me off yet again. Either way, it didn't look too good for them to catch a ride on the magic carpet.

I followed him as he walked out of the bar. He ignored the people reaching out to touch him and offer him drinks and kisses. I followed along in his wake, gulping in cool night air when we reached the parking lot. "Take me to your hotel," he said.

I unlocked the rented Cadillac and he climbed in the front seat, then I let myself in. I didn't dare speak, I was pretty sure he was going to sign and I didn't want to do or say anything that would make him change his mind.

"You're a strange man," he said at last.

"Me? I don't think so. You're the strange one."

"You have no idea."

"I think I do."

"Do you? Do you know why I don't want to sign?"

My heart hammered in my chest. "No. I confess, I don't understand that."

"Because I'm a fraud. I'm only good in person, up on the stage. Did you notice the crowd as we left, how it got thinner at the back, how the people up front were practically slobbering on me while the guys in back didn't even notice me walk past?"

Now that he mentioned it, I sorta had. "That's obvious. The biggest fans always crush to the front. The crowd sorts itself out."

"I don't think I could please a crowd much bigger than that one. I certainly don't think you can record that kind of effect on an album either."

"Recordings never do justice to the artist," but I was pondering what he said.

"I don't think I could handle the energy of a larger crowd even if I could please one. It's a two-way street. I get energy from them, and I give it back. It's such a personal thing. I don't know if you understand that."

"I understand." I was sweating under the sport coat. I'd felt the power of his eyes, and now, with him caged in the interior of the car with me, I felt the power of his body. Magnetic. I wanted him to sign the damn contract and a whole lot more. Which was strange of me, because while I've got no objection to what other people do, I never thought I'd be tempted that way myself.

"Do you?"

"Yes, I do. It's why I want to sign you. You've got that intimate primal connection. You're afraid you're a freak. Well, maybe you are, in the sense that you're different from ordinary people. Stars always are. We can handle it. You'd be amazed at what you can do in a studio. It'll translate."

"Maybe that would be a real bad idea. What if whatever it is I've got can be packaged and sold like a drug? What then? You've already seen the Wade junkies."

"Everybody has groupies."

He was looking at me doubtfully. "You act like you've seen it a million times before, but you haven't. Trust me on this one. You have no idea what you're chasing."

I was pulling into the hotel parking lot. "Come upstairs. Sign. I appreciate you being honest about your doubts, but I know the score. Every new act is a risk, and most of them fail. One record, then poof, they disappear. But hell, even if that's your fate, wouldn't you rather give it your best shot than to spend the rest of your life wondering what you could have done if you'd gotten the chance?" He got out of the car without speaking. He followed me up to my room, his satin flashing under the fluorescent lights. It almost seemed to be reflecting, as if he was a puddle casting back the light he couldn't absorb. I unlocked the door, and he stepped past me into the room. I stepped in and shut the door, the lock snapping shut automatically. When I turned around again he was stripping off his clothes.

A good many things went through my mind, not the least of which was pleasure, followed by panic in close second. "You're queer?" I asked stupidly.

He glared at me and stretched his catlike body out on the bed. "Do I have a choice? Everybody wants me. Especially you. Well, now you've got me. What are you gonna do?"

Run like hell, the wiser part of my brain said. His eyes blazed at me. My cock was twitching, and I didn't run. "You misunderstand me," I lied. I had a lump in my throat, and another lump lower down.

He smiled that slow curving I-have-what-you-want smile, and I crossed to the bed and sat down. Then he was kissing me, and it was like making love to a jaguar: quick, lean, and fierce. He hurt me in several small ways, then in one large way, but it didn't matter because his mouth was on my neck and his weight was on my back and I was coming with an intensity the like of which I had never known before. I lay limp, incapable of moving, eyes staring dreamily. My neck stung faintly, and I knew he'd done to me whatever he'd done to the women.

I dragged a hand up to my neck and pressed it against the tiny wound. He dressed quickly, glancing at me. "You'll live," he said as if to reassure me. It hadn't occurred to me that I might not.

I dragged myself into a semi-sitting position. "What did you do to me?" My lips were numb as if I'd been shot full of Novocaine. He watched me warily as if he wasn't used to his prey getting up after he'd—he'd what? Fed? He had his jeans and shirt on and was pulling on his boots right quick. "Don't leave me."

"You'll be okay. You'll sleep it off. You'll have a headache. I didn't harm you." He was rushing to the door. Not that he seemed to hurry, maybe it was my own sense of time that was screwed up. "Sign, dammit," I said.

He stopped short. "Sign?" he asked in surprise.

Limply I pointed at the papers laying on the table. My head was reeling in a way that might have been pleasant if I was trying to get drunk. Slowly he returned to the table. He gave me a dubious look, then started reading the papers. I wished to God he would just sign the damn thing, but he didn't. He was going to continue torturing me with delays.

"You sure you want me to sign this?"

"Yes."

His hand hovered over the pencil. "Don't you want to know what I am?"

I was curious, but in no mood to let myself be distracted. "Sign, then we can talk."

He signed. I sighed with relief and flopped back down on the bed, feeling much too old and paunchy to be taking on a hellraiser like him. He straddled me, sitting on my pelvis, and opened his mouth. He stuck out his tongue and a stinger or fang like a very thin wire unfolded from under his tongue. He lowered it and touched it to my nipple and an electric shock bit my nerve. I jumped and twitched, then he worked that stinger all over my nipple. When his mouth finally closed on it, cloaking the nerves with warm soft relief, I discovered I had another hard on. This time when he slid down my body he let me feel his stinger as much as his kisses, and when he took my cock into his mouth I screamed. He didn't let go, and it hurt so good my hands tore the coverlet.

"Wade," I said afterwards. "You don't have to fuck your manager to get a contract."

He lay down beside me. "It's what everybody wants. I always had a pretty good voice and could play a guitar, but when this happened to me, well, hell. Sex." What he said was true, his fans were all made horny as sin by his voice and every one of them would gladly be in my place. Except me. I was a little sorry I'd let him seduce me like that, but I was also certain that I wouldn't have believed or understood how it was with him if he hadn't. I suspected I wouldn't have been able to resist, even if I had really wanted to.

"What happened to you?"

"Pretty much what I did to you. But it was a woman that did it to me. Why none of my partners wakes up with a stinger in their mouths I don't know. Maybe it's like getting pregnant: it could happen any time, but it really only happens once in a while."

I checked my mouth quick. "Don't you believe in safer sex?"

"It's kind of hard to stop having a mouth."

"Well, you shouldn't fool around so much."

He sighed heavily. "I can't eat anymore. When I sing, they come to me. I take a little bit from each one, and that's how I live. It goes to my head sometimes. I don't want to hurt anyone, and I don't want to lose control. Any bigger crowd—"

"We'll keep you fed. There won't be any reason to lose control."

He rolled over and pressed his mouth against my shoulder. The stinger jabbed and I flinched. It looked like I was the main entree until I figured out a way to keep my strange star satisfied. "I want you in the studio on Monday." Faced with the impossible, my brain took refuge in solving the merely difficult.

"Whatever you say," he mumbled against my chest. Then his tongue was dancing across my pecs, alternating kisses with stings. I was already worn out from his advances, but he seemed as lively as a puppy chasing butterflies. I was definitely too old for this. But like it or not, I'd chased him and now he'd caught me. I let him do what he wanted for the rest of the night. I wished I could say I didn't enjoy it, but that wouldn't be the truth.

Dedicated to Wade Hayes, my genuine cowboy man. It's a good thing they can't bottle that Voice, or I'd be drunk every night.

Katje
David May

As the serpent said, "Why not?"

—**George Bernard Shaw**

When Uncle Bas died and left his little house in
Amsterdam (just south of the Jordaan and west of the
Prinzengracht) to his nephew in America, the news was
greeted among the cousins with knowing looks, the
nodding of heads, and countless shrugs. Barry, after all,
was "like his uncle," wasn't he? This was certain
knowledge for Barry, like his uncle, had never married,
but had for years brought the same young man with him
whenever he visited his family in the Netherlands.

Since Barry had clearly been Uncle Bas's favorite, no
one questioned the terms of the will, but discussed instead
whether Barry would move all the way from San Francisco

to the wicked city of the north, or ask one of his cousins to act as agent in the selling of the house in order to pay the heavy taxes on such an inheritance. The news of his decision to come and live in Amsterdam, after having received a huge sum in life insurance from the death of his "friend" (more than enough to pay the taxes and live comfortably for some time), was greeted with less than unbridled enthusiasm. Still they accepted it with the usual best wishes, however formal, they'd offer anyone, American cousin or not, who came to such good fortune through the misfortune of others.

Barry moved into the little house, only a few meters wide and perhaps twice as deep, with more luggage than seemed necessary to his more austere relations, explaining that some other things (his books, his CDs, and the odd bit of memorabilia) were being shipped. The furnishings and appointments of the house, he explained to his disappointed relations, he would keep as they were for the time being.

Barry insisted on speaking Dutch now, wanting to improve his grasp of the language he had learned in the nursery but had never taken further than the kitchen. He practiced speaking in the shops he frequented in the Jordaan, learned to ask for so many kilos of fruit or cheese, greeted the woman in the coffee shop on the corner, hoped each day to chat with the handsome man who lived across the street and undressed each night in front of his open window.

A small flower garden, narrow but long enough to get some afternoon sun, lay behind the house. A small tree grew there, old and solid, whose branches reached past the bedroom window on the second floor. In this garden, true to his mother's heritage, Barry spent much of his time raising flowers and preserving the work Uncle Bas had done there over the years.

Neighborhood cats came and went, passing through the garden without comment or even responding to his call of *"Poes, poes, poes."* One cat though, a handsome brown tabby, would come to him, often without being called. More endearing still, he would jump from the tree through Barry's open bedroom window and sleep with him. Being lonely, having just lost the love of his life and knowing no one in the city but a favorite aunt and a handful of cousins that he'd never much taken to, Barry welcomed the cat's visits. He guessed the cat had been friends with his uncle, and greeted the visits as a bridge between them, a continuity between the generations.

Working in his little garden one day, he looked up to see the cat sitting on the fence and staring at him, slowly blinking his great orange eyes in greeting.

"Hey, *katje!* Glad you're here. Tell me," he whispered as one conspirator to another, "did I make a mistake coming here? I wanted a new start, but I forgot how hard it is to make friends in a strange city. And I'm not a kid anymore, *katje.* I'll be forty in a few years. Maybe I should go back to California? I still have a few friends left there. What do you think?"

Blinking his orange eyes, the cat walked casually towards Barry and rubbed against him. Then, with a few graceful leaps he was up the tree and meowing for Barry to open the bedroom window for him. Barry laughed as he got up to obey the cat's demand.

Maybe a few months was too soon to tell whether or not this was a good idea. He needed to give himself some time, he reasoned, time to make new friends and find his niche in the city he was now calling home. After all, it had only been a year since Josh had died. He and Josh had talked a lot about living in Amsterdam, and now he was living out their dream alone. For Josh's sake, at least, it seemed right to stay. Besides, he reasoned, climbing the narrow staircase, he'd already buried Josh's ashes in the garden and it would be such a bother to move them again.

Opening the bedroom window, Barry leaned out to appreciate the breeze gently rocking the leafy branches of the tree. With a small meow to warn his host, the cat jumped to the window sill where he sat looking expectantly at Barry. Stroking the cat and looking out towards the rooftops of Amsterdam, he felt a stirring deep in his gut, a longing for the companionship of the men who'd died and left him behind. That night, he decided, he'd meet a man and hold him close again, even if it was only for that one night.

He decided to live.

It was sometime before midnight when Barry was walking down Saint Jacob Straat and saw Ander leaning against his bicycle in the narrow street. Ander was as dark as Barry was fair, bearded, with a compact solid body, a youthful face and ancient eyes, eyes not quite natural even in the dimming summer twilight.

They nodded to each other, each saying hello.

"I'm Barry."

"You're American but you speak Dutch?"

"My mom's Dutch. She came to the States after the war with my Dad. My dad's Irish, which makes me American," he added proudly. "And you?"

"I'm Ander," he said after a pause, as if pulling the name out of the air.

"Can I buy you a beer?"

"*Alstublieft.*"

Once they were inside the Web, Barry leaned over the bar, automatically stroking the resident cat sitting on the stool by the cash register.

"*Twee biertjes, alstublieft.*"

Barry handed the beer to Ander.

"Your Dutch is very good."

"Not really. I don't speak it nearly as well as I'd like. I understand it pretty well, though."

They raised their beers in a toast.

"Groetjes!"

Barry continued to casually stroke the cat as they spoke, ignoring Ander's wary glances in her direction. It wasn't until later, when Barry reached over to kiss Ander and the cat hissed, striking at Ander, that Barry even noticed Ander's aversion to the creature.

Ander jumped back from the attack, smiled awkwardly and said, "Cats don't like me."

"Really? Then let's move on."

Out again on the narrow street, Barry did kiss Ander, felt his own blond beard rub Ander's black beard as their lips touched and their tongues tangled together.

"Where are you staying?"

"Near the Jordaan. I have a place there."

"Your own?"

"Inheritance," shrugged Barry. "Uncle Bas never married, so. . . ."

"How fortunate."

"That he left it to me? Yes. Rather like meeting you."

Ander's eyebrows arched in answer, as if to say, *You never know.*

They walked the moonlit streets to Barry's house, stopping occasionally to kiss in the shadows left by the moon wafting through the trees lining the canals.

Barry led Ander upstairs and stripped out of his clothes as soon as they were inside. He wanted to feel all of Ander, all that had been promised in Ander's kisses. Now naked, he saw how Ander's olive skin was covered with dark hair, his dick and balls pendulous as if bursting with seed even when soft, filled with the stuff of life. In all his years, Barry had never known such desire, a desire not so much for Ander, whose beauty was obvious but not irresistible, as for the ecstasy promised in all the kisses they'd shared since Saint Jacob Straat.

Their bodies lunged together, Ander's kisses spurring Barry on, clouding his mind with the need to possess Ander, to consume, and then be a part of him. He was trembling with excitement, fumbling with the condoms in the dark. He started to put a condom on his turgid cock when Ander's hand stopped him.

"No," said Ander. "It must be real or not at all."

"But you don't know me. I'm—"

"It must be real."

Startled, Barry obeyed even though he knew better. Maddened by desire, he could only comply with Ander's demands. He lifted Ander's legs over his shoulders, aimed his long, erect cock at Ander's butt hole, and entered him in a single magnificent stroke. The tight hole wrapped itself around his cock, sucking and pulling on it with an unnatural control.

Barry fucked Ander, fucked him with a fury and a passion. Their mouths met again and again to kiss as they fucked, the kisses spurring Barry on to fuck Ander harder and longer. Finally, unable to hold back anymore, Barry exploded, felt his balls burst as his seed poured out of him and filled Ander's ass. He collapsed on top of Ander, felt Ander's kiss as their lips met again. And then he saw Ander's satisfied smile, the smile of beast of prey content with his kill.

That night Barry dreamed of Ander.

Ander lay naked in the darkness, illuminated by the moon, his body stretched across an invisible surface. A huge snake wrapped itself about Ander. At first Barry thought that the serpent would kill Ander, strangle him in its death grip, absorb all his body heat. Barry wanted to call out to Ander, to warn him of the danger. But when Ander's eyes opened, his eyes were like the snake's. Then Ander turned into the snake himself and slithered away and out of Barry's dream.

Barry woke with a start, sweat pouring over his body and soaking his sheets. He looked about the room in a panic, not sure where he was or what time it was. A moment later, as his breathing quieted to normal, he was able to orient himself to his surroundings again, to remember where he was as he forgot the dream. Sunlight poured through the window, telling Barry it was already late afternoon. The cat sat on the branch outside his window crying to be let in.

Stumbling to the window, he saw that it was open a few inches already, even though he remembered closing it all the way to keep the cat from disturbing them. Forgetting his puzzlement a moment, he lost his balance, almost falling to the floor. Then, recovering himself, he pulled the window open only to fall back on the bed exhausted from the effort.

The cat jumped through the window in a single self-confident leap. Yowling his annoyance, the cat searched the room, then ran down the stairs to inspect the rest of the house, returning a moment later to Barry's bed. Nuzzling Barry's face, licking the damp skin, and purring loudly, the cat egged Barry out of bed and down the stairs, circling his feet until they were in the kitchen. Thinking the cat wanted to be fed, Barry offered him some cheese. The cat only cried again and again, staring at Barry with his huge orange eyes. Only when Barry sat down to eat himself did the cat sit quietly.

"Why am I so tired, *katje*?" asked Barry a few minutes later as he sat down to coffee and toast. "And where did Ander go?"

The cat hissed.

"Okay, *katje*. Sorry."

He got up to pour himself some more coffee.

"Cream, *katje*?"

A small meow.

"He said he didn't get along with cats. Nothing personal."

He sat down and watched his friend lap up the cream. All the while he ate, though, the cat kept an eye on Barry.

"Why am I so tired? Wasn't I supposed to do something today? Oh yeah, I'm supposed to meet *Tante* Dora for dinner. But I'm so tired, *katje*."

Another meow.

"I suppose you're right. I better shower first, though."

It wasn't until later, when he was walking toward Leidsekruis Straat to meet his aunt, that he realized that he'd been having a conversation with a cat. Even more puzzling was finding that the front door was still locked from the inside, leaving Barry to wonder how Ander had let himself out.

He greeted his aunt with three kisses, saying in Dutch, "Tante, sorry I'm late. Please forgive me."

"Of course," she answered in English.

"Nederland, Tante. Alstublieft."

"As you wish," she answered in Dutch. "Are you all right? You don't look well."

"Just tired, I think. Maybe I'm working too hard."

"Working at what? Have you a job?"

"No, Tante. I mean working on the garden, the house."

"Yes, of course," she answered unimpressed.

The waitress came and they ordered their meal.

"No, you don't look well, at all, dear," said Aunt Dora a moment later, reaching across the table and touching his face. "You feel clammy and a little warm."

"Maybe I caught a little cold last night. But it's nothing to worry about. I'm okay, Tante, really."

She took his hand across the table.

"I have to worry, dear. You're mother's not here to worry for me."

Barry smiled at his aunt a moment before changing the subject.

"Did Uncle Bas have a cat?"

"No, I don't think so. Why?"

"There's a big tomcat that likes to visit me sometimes. He acts like he belongs there so I let him come and go as he likes. I just thought maybe he was Uncle's cat."

"Probably just a neighborhood cat your uncle fed sometimes," said Aunt Dora. "He always had a soft spot for strays."

"Like me, Tante?"

"Well, you needed a new home didn't you?"

After dinner, Barry walked his aunt home before heading back to Saint Jacob Straat. It was early yet, the twilight still an hour or two away. He walked up and down the street a few times before heading back to the house. He'd come back later, he decided, and find Ander again. He felt the logy feeling that had been plaguing him since he'd woken up fade away. He brightened thinking of Ander, thinking of how much he wanted all that Ander had to give him.

Ander appeared from the shadows near the Milk Maids' Bridge. Stepping from behind a tree he came toward Barry, smiling, his eyes almost glowing with pleasure.

"Are you happy to see me?" asked Ander with his seductive smile.

"Of course!"

"Good!"

Ander's mouth reached up toward Barry's, his tongue darting forward as if seeking the warmth of Barry's mouth. For less than a second Barry remembered an image from his dream the night before. He started mid-kiss, then shook off the remnant of the lost memory as he lost himself in Ander's kiss.

Ander pulled Barry into a narrow side street and deep into its shadows. Wordlessly, he undid Barry's trousers. A moment later he was kneeling in front of Barry, sucking on the stiff cock sliding in and out of his wet, silky mouth. Too startled to resist, and excited by the circumstance, Barry held the back of Ander's head as he fucked Ander's face.

Barry shuddered each time Ander's tongue tickled the underside of his cock, gasped when Ander's throat opened and closed around his member, effortlessly enclosing its considerable length and thickness. Again, Barry tried to hold back, tried not to come so soon. His body shuddered as he clenched his butt and slammed his crotch against Ander's face. He felt himself shoot, lost in the sweetness of the orgasm, felt Ander swallow each shot of semen as it filled his mouth.

Then, just as he felt himself sink once more into oblivion, he heard a scuffle, the sound of a cat snarling in the darkness. Ander cried out in pain, and as suddenly as he had appeared earlier, slipped noiselessly into the shadows.

Barry slumped to the cobbled stones of the street and searched the moonlit darkness for Ander, whose kiss he already wanted again. Then he saw him, there on a doorstep, quietly washing his paws and glancing in his direction, a huge marmalade cat with luminescent green eyes.

"*Poes*?"

The cat stepped over to him at a relaxed trot. He looked up into Barry's face a moment before touching Barry's nose with his own and giving it a lick.

"*Dank, poes.* But what happened?"

The marmalade tom continued to nudge him until he got to his feet, then trotted along beside him until they crossed a bridge. With a small mew, the cat turned back to his own territory, leaving a large but dainty calico to lead Barry the rest of the way to his house.

"*Dank U, mevrouw poes,*" said Barry, unlocking his door to discover his own katje sitting on the stairs in anticipation. "You two know each other or something?"

The cats saluted each other with raised tails, touched noses, and rubbed against each other. Then, as if on cue, the calico disappeared into the night.

"I'd like to know what's going on, *mijnheer kat,* but I'm too tired to understand anything that's happened to me tonight."

Exhausted, Barry climbed the narrow steps to his bedroom, followed by the cat.

The next morning he was shocked to see twice as much gray in his hair and beard than had been there a few days before.

Barry didn't see Ander again. Weeks passed into early autumn. He finally met the man across the street, whose name was Jan, and found himself slowly forming a friendship with him. Jan was taller than Barry, just as fair, handsome and leanly muscled. He was clean shaven but had the heavy kind of beard that showed stubble a few hours after shaving. His yellow-green eyes sparkled when he laughed, or when he talked about Barry's uncle.

"You know," ventured Barry rather cautiously one afternoon over coffee. "I can see you when you undress at night. Not that I mind."

"Yes? Your uncle always said he enjoyed watching me. Do you?"

"Very much."

"What should we do about it?"

"This?" Barry leaned across the kitchen table and kissed Jan, slipping his tongue into Jan's waiting mouth.

"You have safes?" asked Jan a few minutes later between kisses.

"Upstairs."

Running up the narrow stairs, they stumbled onto Barry's bed, undressing each other between kisses, pulling on each others' clothes. Rolling naked together on the bed, their muscular frames and thick cocks open to the other's caresses, each sought the secret spot that would drive the other over the edge, giving him the power. Jan won.

Nibbling and sucking on Barry's neck flipped the switch, sending waves of pleasure over Barry's body and forcing him to open himself up to Jan. Jan's hand found its way to Barry's fuck hole as Barry thrashed under Jan's hard, furry body. Spreading his legs apart, Barry wordlessly begged Jan to fuck him. Answering Barry's silent plea, Jan pulled a condom over his fat, uncut dick, then greased his cock with one hand while he prepared Barry's hole with the other. Lifting Barry's legs over his shoulders, he entered Barry.

Arranging his body so their faces touched, Jan moved his hips in and out, plowing the tight hole, filling it again and again with his prong. Barry threw his ass into the air, trying to hold onto Jan's cock with it, not wanting to ever be without it again, his head rolling back and forth in time to Jan's thrusts. Finally, grabbing Barry's face in a kiss, Jan slammed harder and harder inside Barry's hole, releasing the kiss only when he arched his back, and with a growl, filled the rubber with cum. Seconds later Barry's seed splashed all over them, sticking to their sweaty bodies.

When he finally got up to towel off, Barry could swear he heard Jan purring.

It was raining when Barry got in that afternoon, so he shut the bedroom window without thinking of the cat and hurriedly toweled the floor dry. He'd spent the afternoon helping Aunt Dora with a few repairs around her flat near Leidse Straat. He was running late now and needed to get ready for his dinner date with Jan. Aunt Dora had greeted the news of Barry's new romance cheerfully enough, saying she already suspected something of the kind. She even suggested that they all have dinner together next week some time. Thrilled at his Aunt's good will, Barry could hardly wait to tell Jan about it.

Just as he was getting into a clean shirt, there was a knock at the door. Thinking that it might be Jan coming by to collect him rather than meet him at the restaurant as planned, Barry threw the door open prepared to wrap his arms around his new love. Instead of Jan, there stood Ander.

"Miss me?"

"Ander, I . . ."

"Can I come in? It's raining."

"Of course, but . . ."

Ander quieted him with a kiss as the door closed. The kiss filled Barry with all the longings he'd felt before, all the unquenched desire burning deep inside him again. Mindlessly, he led Ander upstairs to his bed. Once in Barry's bedroom, they undressed quickly without talking.

Unable to think at all in Ander's presence, Barry followed his impulses. He rolled Ander over onto his stomach and entered him in a single smooth thrust, not bothering to lube his cock first. Giving in to the need for

Ander's flesh, for Ander's kisses, Barry fell into the abyss. Unable to control himself, a few minutes later he was shooting deep inside Ander's round, furry butt, screaming in pain as he felt his entire being being sucked through his dick. Ander only smiled.

Barry looked into Ander's strangely reptilian eyes for only a moment before he blacked out.

Barry didn't hear the phone ring or the knock on the door a few hours later. He slept feverishly through it all, waking now again to find Ander's smiling face. He'd summon all his strength to reach up and kiss Ander's cold lips, then lay back exhausted. More hours passed and Barry woke to find his hard cock in Ander's mouth. Unable to resist the force of Ander's ministrations, he grabbed the back of Ander's head and fucked the warm, wet mouth until he came. Passing out again, he glimpsed his own hand, now covered with liver spots, like that of a very old man.

Hours passed into days. The phone rang and went unanswered, likewise the loud knocking at the front door. Barry roused himself only now and again for Ander's kiss, or to cum again in Ander's mouth. Even as he felt his life being drained from him, he could do nothing to resist the only comfort now afforded him.

He woke one afternoon to find Aunt Dora shaking him awake.

"Barry, you look awful! How long have you been sick like this?"

Barry tried to form the words to explain but couldn't.

"Drink this."

Barry sipped the warm broth being offered, smiled his thanks and drifted back to sleep. Whenever he woke up now he found his Aunt where Ander had once been. Each time she offered nourishment and each time he managed more of it, staying awake longer each time.

"I must have gotten the flu or something," he said when he was at last able to speak. "I just remember laying down and . . ." He faded off, not wanting to finish the thought, not wanting to remember what had actually happened.

"That's enough, sweetheart. I met your Jan today. He came to the door and I told him you were very sick." She looked down on Barry and smiled. "Your parents are coming, too, dear. They'll be so glad to see you looking better."

Barry turned away, pretending to fall asleep so she would leave the room, knowing that she was lying about his looking better. He could see his aged hands, feel his sagging skin and tired limbs. He'd seen his reflection in the mirror and knew how much he'd aged since he first kissed Ander. He was dying and knew it.

He heard his aunt get up and open the window, letting the late afternoon sunshine warm the room, and left. Barry inhaled deeply, enjoying the sweetness in the autumn air filling the room, and fell back asleep.

Later on it cooled and he wished Aunt Dora would come and close the window. He was about to call her when he heard an odd sound, a slithering and an almost silent hiss, then the sibilant call of his name. He turned in his bed to see Ander sitting in the window, naked, staring at him with his yellow reptilian eyes.

"One last kiss, my love, and it will be over."

Barry could only stare, certain he was hallucinating.

"Your kind is always so sweet, but you, Barry, are the sweetest," Ander went on. "The sweetest soul I've ever tasted. That's why I've taken so long. You're too delicious to rush. But now, sweet Barry, it's time."

With a sudden chill, Barry remembered his dream now, remembered and understood it. To his horror, he saw Ander become a snake, some eight feet long, almost a foot wide where it was thickest. He wanted to scream for help but couldn't. Instead, he curled into the far corner of the bed, waiting.

Then he saw the cat in the open window, tried to tell him to stay away with a wave of his hands, to at least save his uncle's friend. Just as the snake's almost smiling face appeared over the edge of the bed, Ander's yellow eyes now unmistakable, the cat streaked across the room like silent lightning. Attacking the serpent almost too quickly to be seen, the cat sunk its fangs below the snake's head. The cat shook the snake in his mouth, knocking over furniture, banging the snake's head against the wall again and again.

Suddenly the cat and the snake were both men, Ander and Jan. Jan tore at Ander's throat with his bare hands, breaking the neck, then tearing it off the body. Barry watched wide-eyed as Ander's severed body returned to its snake form, then shriveled to a mere pelt. Jan stood over his opponent, wiping his mouth with his pawlike hand before turning around to Barry.

Barry felt his strength returning, looked at his hands and saw the liver spots fade. Touching his body, he found the same hard musculature of years before. Strong enough now to sit up, he could see his reflection in the mirror across the room. The rapidly accumulated gray now faded to reveal the ash-blond hair and beard of his youth. Too startled to understand any of what had happened, he could only look about in confusion.

"Barry," said Jan leaping across the bed to hold him close. "Barry, you're safe now. He's dead."

"What was it? What are you? Have I died?"

"Quiet, sweetheart. Ssh. Rest. You need to sleep to recover. Daylight will be the final cure."

Whether from exhaustion or shock, Barry would never know, but he fell asleep in Jan's arms and stayed there the whole night through.

Jan woke him just before dawn.

"Come see," said Jan.

Turning back into a cat, he took Ander's snake head in his mouth and with a few leaps was on the roof across the way. Going to the window, Barry watched in awe as the morning sun crept across the rooftops. The cat Jan pushed the snake head into the sunlight, stepped back expectantly and watched as it burst into flames. A moment later Jan was back to fetch the pelt and do the same with it. Another burst of fire and it was over. Jan returned the second time smiling, pleased with his conquest.

"What was he?"

"I don't know what they call themselves, but they're as bad as bloodsuckers and live until they're killed by something stronger. Sometimes they even kill each other. I only know that they came from the desert like my folk. And like us they've followed humankind from place to place."

"And you, Jan? What are you?"

"I'm a cat," he said simply.

"Yes, but—"

"Ssh. Your aunt's coming."

Barry returned to bed as Jan quickly righted the furniture that had been knocked over in the struggle hours earlier. When Aunt Dora came in, Jan was a cat stretched across the bed and Barry was sitting up, bright eyed and alert, suddenly cured.

"Tante, I feel so much better today. And hungry. May I have a pancake for breakfast? You know how I like them, with apples and cinnamon?"

A few hours later, Jan came back by way of the front door, freshly dressed and shaved. Overcome with Barry's sudden recovery, and emotionally exhausted from thinking she was about to lose her favorite nephew so soon after she'd lost her brother, Aunt Dora gladly turned Barry's care over to Jan and went home.

"I still don't understand, Jan," said Barry looking into the mirror yet again, mesmerized by his sudden youthfulness. "What happened to me? I look even younger than I did before I met Ander."

"Some things don't need to be understood, my love, just appreciated."

"But why me? Why did Ander want me? He said something about my 'kind.' What did that mean? And you, why did you decide to watch over me like this?"

Jan looked at him a moment before answering, clearly puzzled.

"You really don't know, Barry? Your uncle understood, and he was only *fee* on one side. You're fee from mother *and* father."

"*Fee?*" asked Barry, in English this time. "You don't mean fairy?"

Jan nodded.

"You never knew?" asked Jan.

"This is just like the stories Granny Butler used to tell me. Maybe it explains why Josh and I . . ." He let his voice trail off, remembering how unlikely so much of his life had been.

"Then it is good you are here, *feeje*. There is much for you to learn. And as for why I'm here, I promised your uncle to look after you. And. . . ."

"And?"

"And I fell in love with you."

Jan kissed Barry on the neck as he said these last few words, touching that sweet and secret place that made Barry shiver. Barry automatically spread his legs apart as Jan's hand found his fuck hole, sending more shivers up and down his spine as Jan caressed it. A few minutes later they were naked on the bed, Jan's sturdy cock poised to enter Barry's tight hole.

Grabbing Jan's face as he was entered, Barry kissed his lover hard on the lips.

"Fuck me hard, *katje*! Fuck me hard!"

Jan smiled, purred, and obeyed.

A note about Dutch: Most of the Nederland (as Dutch is properly called) in this story is pretty self-explanatory, especially if you know even a little bit of German (though you should never confuse the two under any circumstances.) The Dutch have a charming habit of creating diminutives and endearments with the addition of je on the end of a word. Kat, or cat, then becomes katje, or kitty. This is done with many everyday words, my favorite being when they turn twee (two) into tweeje when referring to a married couple or a pair of lovers.

The Lunar Eclipse

Thomas S. Roche

The door to the Gallery is open to the street. Dark breezes blow through, rich with lilac blossoms, pregnant with the fruits of a Midnight Spring. The wind wanders aimlessly through the Gallery, caressing velvet draperies and black lace curtains, stirring ancient rose petals and dessicated leaves amid roaming ghoul girls and skeleton boys, will o' the wisps and Elviras, sprinkled liberally with art critics and the nouveau riche. The incense burner near the back gives off the odor of a Catholic funeral. Shimmering moonlight slants down from the paneled windows high above the Gallery floor. Gorecki plays from hidden speakers. Somewhere in the night a star has gone supernova and vanished, its death wail a pulsar beacon bathing the Gallery in radio waves. A poisonous spider spins its web behind the Gallery door.

A man in a black wool blazer and a turtleneck sniffs disapprovingly at a painting of a naked white-skinned beauty with eyes and hair the color of coal. The woman on his arm tosses her hair, removes her sunglasses, and peers forward, studying the oil painting with a collector's grace, a critic's distance, an echoing hint of enthusiasm.

Her eyes narrow to slits; she thinks *such sadness* as if to say it, then refrains. The wind picks up slightly. Rose petals scatter about her feet.

"I like it," she says absently, as if to herself.

"Oh Marguerite," says the man, rolling his eyes. "Puh-leeze!"

Marguerite shrugs and the two of them move on.

The CD player has shifted to Haydn, playing *The Seven Last Words of Jesus Christ*. Occasionally the cry of a bat splits the night, mingling with cello and viola. High above, there are leathery wings and tiny claws upon the windowsil. Overhead the heavens spin in tortured anticipation, rapturous preapocalyptic foreplay, for tonight at 3:04:57 the city will experience its last lunar eclipse of the century. Shadows flicker through the Gallery.

Underneath, before a painting of a haunting ghoul girl, a man in a trenchcoat and Roman collar crosses himself. There is the distant sound of weeping.

The Gallery of Despair is open for business.

She wanders the darkness, drinking her fill of the lush beauty of nightmares. She casts the paintings aside like dead roses, her feet stirring their remains on the black-painted floor.

The woman is shrouded in shadows and a black Chanel overcoat, her black hair topped by an antique sort of pillbox, her eyes and her face down to her lips covered by the barest whisper of a fishnet veil sprinkled with black baby's breath. Black lace mourning gloves cover her white hands.

The girl stands motionless before the painting, her eyes distant and moist.

Her hands are clasped before her. Her black dress swirls in the wind. She clutches an Addams Family lunchbox. She has black hair and pale skin. She is perhaps twenty-three. She is not quite weeping.

The woman stands just behind her and to the left, regarding the painting as well. The girl seems to sway before the work of art, as if hypnotized.

"Such sadness," murmurs the girl, as if to herself. She looks back over her shoulder briefly and sees the woman. Blushing red, she steps aside. "I'm sorry," she says nervously. "Am I blocking your view?"

"Not at all," says the woman, watching the girl. "My name is Cassandre."

"Cassandre," says the girl. "Do you like the painting?"

"Perhaps," replies Cassandre. "Perhaps not. It depends on how you look at it, as most things do."

"I suppose that's true," says the girl, as if it was an important truth. "My name is Andrea."

The woman nods, her full lips pursed underneath the black veil. "And you, Andrea. Do you like the painting?"

Andrea thinks a moment, and then she speaks as if in a trance. "The sadness is crushing. . . . It causes my soul to ache. It makes me feel my soul will be extinguished, the very life snuffed out of me. It is as if all life's subtle agonies and misfortunes are summed up inside it. . . ."

Cassandre watches, mesmerized. Her black lace fingers are crossed as if in prayer. Her eyes study Andrea, fascinated and enthralled. Her lips part slightly as if in the subtle prelude to a kiss. "Is that a yes?"

Her trance broken, Andrea blushes a still-deeper red. "I like the painting very much."

"You know . . . what happened? After the painting's completion?"

"Oh yes," says Andrea softly. "Such sadness."

"She was my sister."

Andrea's eyes are wide, the whites luminescent in the darkness. "The woman who—"

"The artist. Her name was Miriam."

"Of course, Miriam Sacramente. Your sister! How tragic for your family. . . ."

"I'm the only one left," says Cassandre sadly. "For the moment." She raises her hand to her temple, then quickly bites one finger as if wrestling with tears. "Our family has always been haunted by tragedy. But Miriam and I shared a bond. The mourning I feel is immeasurable." She sighs. "My sister was a . . . disturbed woman."

"And the model—?"

Cassandre shrugs. "I didn't know her."

"I think her name was Loren," says Andrea. "A friend of mine was in her acting class. Such sadness. . . ."

"Yes. Sadness. I miss Miriam most acutely. Some days I think I will shatter for want of her guiding hand. She was my elder sister, you see, and very much my mentor . . . though my sister and I differed on certain fundamental matters of artistic philosophy."

"You are an artist, as well?"

Cassandra smiles vaguely. "If you like."

"I'm studying at the University. But I fear I won't ever be this good. Talent like this is so rare. . . ."

"Skills can be learned. Miriam taught me so many things."

"But you differed with your sister? On matters of art?"

Cassandre regards the painting. "More on matters of . . . morality. Basic and fundamental morality."

Andrea's chin inclines, her eyes narrowing. She studies the woman, her body stiffening slowly as she processes the statement. Andrea nods gradually, turning to look at the painting, finding her gaze straying periodically to the back of Cassandre's head, the slope of her neck, the fall of the black hair on her collar. The woman is very expensively dressed, though with impeccable restraint. The black fishnet veil makes it plain that she is in mourning, not merely indulging in a fashion statement.

Andrea feels her breath coming quickly and imagines the glass of red wine that she and Cassandre might share in the Gallery Café across the street.

But alas it seems impossible if Andrea has correctly inferred what Cassandre's moral differences with her sister may have been—

"You differed from your sister," says Andrea sadly. "On moral grounds. . . . That must have been very difficult." Gently, fearfully, she asks, "Was this a . . . religious difference?"

Cassandre turns her head, eyes Andrea at a subtle yet distinctive, unmistakable angle. Faintly, she smiles, mischief twisting the edges of her full lips. "Perhaps it was, after all, a religious issue. Or, more properly, spiritual. We differed almost solely on issues of morality."

Cassandre's eyes hover darkly behind the veil. Her smile disappears and she tells Andrea, very softly, "On matters of taste, my sister and I were virtually identical."

Andrea finds her hand straying absently to her throat.

The seduction is achieved with a minimal number of words exchanged, a soundless apocalypse. Andrea orders red wine, Cassandre absinthe. The bored punk girl at the counter is listening to a very loud Rachmaninov, perhaps the ideal accompaniment to an irresistible invitation to a shared midnight of mourning. Andrea sips her wine as she and Cassandre quietly discuss art and experience—in vague terms considering the subtleties of various shades of

black and the beauties of the midnight wind, sharing
whispered speculations of the promises of lush mortality
within the corridors of the Gallery of Despair. Andrea's
second glass of wine remains untouched on the bistro
table as she feels Cassandre's fingertips travel onto her
wrist with an admirable subtlety. Andrea inhales, smelling
Cassandre's warm fragrance, a subtle mélange of exotic,
nameless wood scents and the perfumes of necrotic
flowers from genera long thought extinct. It is a
bewitching olfactory symphony that causes Andrea's nose
to tingle, awakened. With the finesse of an artist,
Cassandre touches Andrea's flesh, applying only the
lightest of touches, causing Andrea to goosebump all over.
The sensations of Cassandre's fingertips on her forearm
make Andrea's belly flutter, her throat tighten, her pulse
start to race. Andrea loses herself in the texture of the
seduction, recalling yesterday's sumptuous nightmares.
She becomes acutely aware of the proximity of Cassandre's body to hers, the pressure of Cassandre's bare
knees against her own. She feels the tension growing
between them over a progressively smaller space. She feels
the tangible desire welling in her body and conjures a
silent prayer that that desire is mirrored in Cassandre's.
And yet her whole body seems drugged, as if she is in a
delicious but frightening dream. The fear is almost too
much to bear, and Andrea continues staring down,
unwilling to break the spell Cassandre has cast by her long
silence. When Andrea does finally look up, Cassandre's
face is mere inches from her own, with blackberry lips
parted and tongue-tip extended almost imperceptibly—
and Rachmaninov surges in that final tempestuous
explosion as hopeless souls arrive on the bleak shores of
the Isle of the Dead, and Charon deposits them, laughing
cruelly; the souls, abandoned in a desperate orchestral
summoning, serve a delicate counterpoint to Cassandre's

lips locking magically onto Andrea's and parting just the appropriate amount. Cassandre leaves a bill on the table, giving the punk girl a large tip.

High above the city in Cassandre's rented loft, Andrea finds herself deliciously undressed. The huge loft is unfurnished except for a black-framed futon with a red velvet bedcover, a single white candle, and a tiny cassette player that issues forth a tinny rendition of one of Beethoven's string quartets. Cassandre has disrobed, except for the black lace gloves. First Cassandre's long lace-clad fingertips unfasten the front of Andrea's dress. Moonlight shimmers across the futon and the flesh of the naked Cassandre. Skilled fingers peel back Andrea's black lace dress and the black slip underneath, ease both over her shoulders, expose the white expanse of her throat, the slope of her breasts, her firm dark nipples with their steel rings. Cassandre's two suitcases are opened on the floor by the futon, containing scatterings of black lace and red velvet, with her black overcoat hanging by the door next to Andrea's leather jacket. The dress comes down easily, amid a gentle squirming of Andrea's body. The slip follows more slowly, accompanied by a faint prickling of Andrea's skin as it excites. The uncharacteristically haphazard manner with which Cassandre discards the dress and slip onto the floor heralds the approach of her ardor. Breezes stir the winds of the room, excite the flesh of Andrea's breasts, swirl Cassandre's perfume around Andrea's face. Surging forward, Cassandre takes Andrea's face in her hands and kisses her: insistently, demandingly, tenderly. Their tongues entwine and Cassandre feels the cold steel of Andrea's piercing.

Deliciously, she draws back at the summit of the kiss, creating a tension that grows as they regard each other.

Perhaps an inch now separates them, lips and eyes aching to touch.

Cassandre's fingers find Andrea's breasts, touching the nipples gently.

Andrea, dressed now only in her panties, reclines into the sumptuous red velvet bedcover as Cassandre rises to her knees and flows over her, not quite touching Andrea, not quite sliding on top of her. Instead, Andrea finds herself stretched amid red velvet as Cassandre's fingers entwine with hers, as their arms touch, as the fingers of Cassandre's other hand draw a path from Andrea's breast to her throat and then to her chin.

Cassandre lays on the bed beside Andrea, the length of her naked body very close to Andrea's but not quite touching. Andrea feels the touch of the fingertips on her chin, the inspecting caress of the path traced down, up, down, up, then down again, then finally up as Cassandre's fingertips take Andrea's chin and push her face, demandingly, to one side.

Andrea whimpers softly as she feels her throat exposed, feels the surge of blood and fear along the path Cassandre's fingertips have traced.

Then gradually, yet suddenly, comes the aching moment, the frozen seconds as Cassandre's mouth gradually descends, her blackberry lips parting sumptuously as their edges twist, her eyes sparkling. Cassandre savors the moment of surrender, the tension between their bodies explosive in the moonlight. The moment lasts for perhaps ten seconds in torturous and erotic desperation, but even so Andrea finds herself unable to scream.

The touch of Cassandre's mouth upon her throat is perhaps the most intensely spiritual sensation Andrea has ever known. The pain of the penetration feels inexplicably like ecstatic pleasure, and the warmth in her throat is unmistakably sexual while retaining a certain religiosity. Beside Cassandre and unrestrained, Andrea squirms, her body writhing freely on the bed, until Cassandre begins to stroke her smooth stomach gently; momentarily, the motion of Andrea's squirming body subsides.

Cassandre's left hand entwines Andrea's black hair and takes a firm grip on it, holding her tightly in position. A single bead of red makes its way gradually down Andrea's throat and onto her breast, pausing at the swell of her nipple, to be followed by the path of a second bead of red. Both rivulets then fall despairingly onto the bedcover.

Eagerly: Violin, second violin, cello. Viola.

Subtly, with the distinct but flattering taste of an afterthought, Cassandre's hand moves lower on Andrea.

Afterward, Andrea finds herself staring into Cassandre's expressionless face, seeing no trace of her blood on the vampire's lips. She recalls being dimly aware of the gentle stroke of a warm sponge on her breast, then on her throat. The sharp smell of antiseptic and the feel of the adhesive bandage brought back memories of childhood sickbeds. Cassandre's eyes flicker darkly in the starlight, for at this moment the moon has experienced its only remaining total eclipse in this century. Her fingertips trace the outline of Andrea's slightly parted lips; her tongue aches with the memory of the girl's taste and the texture of her surrender.

"You understand now," whispers Cassandre, "how I differed substantially from my sister on matters of morality—but certainly not on matters of aesthetics."

Andrea nods, faintly, her body very weak. She tries to speak, but it only comes out as a deliciously tortured moan. Cassandre lays a single finger gently on Andrea's lips and whispers, "Rest."

Morning finds the sunlight streaming through the
skylight, caressing Andrea's body. The warmth dispels the
weakness inside her, but slowly. It is not quite sleep that
she experiences until late in the morning, but a delicious
kind of trance, the sensation of her soul having been
somehow purified of the indulgence of conscious thought.

Cassandre has left, offering only a note on parchment,
written in fountain pen, cryptic only in its directness:

*The loft belongs to a friend who is not expected back until
early next month. Please stay as long as you like; there is food
in the refrigerator, though you will find that my tastes run
distinctly toward the sublime. I mustn't return—not for a time,
at least. My thanks and affection always. C.*

Andrea lifts the note to her face, inhales deeply of
Cassandre's scent—indescribable, subtle, seductive. She
lays on the bed, the parchment across her breasts, feeling
strangely unbetrayed, yet oddly unfulfilled. There was,
after all, no agreement, no suggestion of lovemaking to
come, no promised nights of ecstacy and sanguine
spiritual enlightenment underneath the lunar eclipse.
Never an implication that any part of either of them
would belong to the other, except for the blood which
passed between them and the passion that blood had
wrought. There was only the frozen moment when
Andrea understood her devourment and knew, with a
certainty that struck to the core of her being, that she was
not going to be harmed. It was a certainty that Loren,
Miriam Sacramente's beloved and unfortunate model,
may have had at one time, but that certainty was
unfortunately in error, as so many certainties are. This is
perhaps the moral lesson that Andrea would have offered,
given the chance to compose her own epitaph—but,
thankfully, she was not yet offered that chance, nor that

necessity, for Cassandre differed significantly from her sister—in matters of morality if not of art. And gothicka by moonlight offers its own kind of epitaph: a taste for the undead and, perhaps, a lingering appreciation of Rachmaninov. And what the hell, maybe a haiku, since it's morning:

> She was kissed
> beneath the catharsis
> of the lunar eclipse.

The Blood Hustle

Raven Kaldera

So I don't usually go under for johns, all right? I mean, I don't have reactions that are based in reality. If I get a hard on for them, it's because I'm thinking about something else. If I make noise, it's because I figure they want it. I do what they like, and I collect my pay, which isn't in money.

In a way, the only thing I do that's real is when I collect; I get my hands on their throats and get my fangs into their carotids so fast that they can't change their minds and stiff me. It's that bare minute of sincere pleasure as their lives flow into me that really turns me on, that gives me a hard on that isn't faked. I can never seem to control that desire, no matter how hard I try. Sometimes, when I pull away, I see a flicker of uncertainty in the trick's eyes, as if the reality of what I am—and what I'm not—has just flashed momentarily across their minds. All it takes is a touch from me, though; a softly spoken word, a caress, and they're back to their comforting illusion, the uncomfortable possibilities forgotten. Which is what I want, since illusions are my stock in trade.

More often I pull away to see their eyes glazed and gasping, especially the ones who've never been under the bite before. They might have heard about how good it feels, how you can get addicted to it, but they didn't really understand it. I never take anything that comes out of their mouths for the next hour seriously; they'd promise me their first-born children until they come down. The ones with a taste for it aren't as gullible, of course. They may want it bad, but they kick me out afterward to enjoy their nod in privacy. They know better. So it's what I do; I'm a very special kind of whore, but don't you think it's all that different in the end.

So I showed up at the hotel room to meet this guy— Tenny brokered the arrangement, told me he was OK— and waited. I was early; another appointment had fallen through and all the buses actually came on time. I ran through the Black Sun mantras in my head, the ones I learned from my sister in the discipline training of her religion. Yeah, that's right, DarkMother's Children, the Zavaret's little cult. *Thou shalt not kill except in self-defense, thou shalt not feed without consent,* and all of that. Or the "vampmonks," as the others call Black Suns. Of course, they have to hunt down their prey; mine sign up for the privilege. And they don't have our learned control; they're more prone to go crazy, kill people without meaning to. I don't always agree with my sister's rigid ethics, but I'm just enough of a control freak not to want to be ruled by the Urge.

It was getting late and I needed to stretch my legs. I got up to look out the barred window and was staring out at the street when he came in. I heard him approach the door and turned around, leaning up against the wall, hands shoved in the pockets of my leather jacket, weight slightly to the side, hips thrust forward. The pose of a thousand James Dean fakes for sale on La Posse street, sure, but guys fall for the old stuff, the fetishy tried-and-true. My ripped cutoffs and black T-shirt with the print of Saint Vlad, the jacket and harness boots, the black bandanna around my forehead, all worked for queer guys the way push-up bras and garter belts work for straight ones. Women are harder to please; I have to guess and figure out what they like, or hope they can take me in whatever gear I happen to be in.

He was short, slight, ordinary-looking. White-collar, at a guess, maybe educated, dressed down in newish jeans. He caught his breath when he saw me—good sign—and then ducked his head and hurried to the armchair across from me. I stayed standing. Let him get a good look. "So I'm here, man," I said softly, unthreateningly.

He cleared his throat and crossed his legs, just after I caught a glimpse of what he was hiding between them. "You know how you're getting paid?" he asked, his voice cracking.

I nodded. "Do you understand what that means?" I threw back. Best to get this part over with quickly.

His nostrils flared. "You tell me."

I looked away, phrasing my words carefully. "You don't get my blood," I said, toying with the Black Sun pendant around my neck. Tenny would have explained what it meant. "Believe me, you don't want it. I don't do piss, shit, or animals, and I don't do anyone else unless I negotiate with them separately." My gaze slid toward him; he nodded briefly. "And you're safe with me; I won't hurt you. You were told?" Part of what allowed me to do this job was the thoroughness with which I had put about my reputation as a DarkMother's Child, and my absolute adherence to those tenets. It wasn't nearly as absolute as my rep might suggest, but no one needed to know that.

"You had references," he said, and then there was silence as he looked me up and down more openly. "You must need it bad," he said, and I resisted the urge to roll my eyes. I was never hard up, but he wasn't the first trick who it suited to believe that I was starving and desperate. "How long has it been for you?" he asked

I bared my teeth in something that might have been a smile but wasn't. "None of your fucking business," I said pleasantly.

He looked startled, and then laughed. Good, a sense of humor. A rare find in johns. "You're hot," he said, a thread of longing in his voice. "I haven't been with a guy since high school."

"Why?" I asked, shifting my pose to show the outline of my cock against the denim cutoffs.

"None of your fucking business," he retorted, and then stood up and came toward me. He was hard, all right. "What are you hiding back there? Turn around, I want to see you," he ordered. I grinned and did it, letting him get a view of my ass and my waist-length hair. He came up behind me and ran his hands through it, buried his face in it. "Gorgeous," he mumbled. "You smell so good."

"Not at all like the grave," I quipped, looking up at the ceiling. He seemed a little unsure of what to do next, so I put my back to the wall and pulled his hips to mine. I let him lean into me, let the front of his jeans press against mine as he kissed me. He smelled of toothpaste; I was touched.

The guy clung to me like he hadn't had human contact in years. Hell, maybe he hadn't. His tongue explored my mouth, but fortunately my fangs weren't unsheathed. My hands drifted from his ass to his hard on, and he groaned, so I turned us around and pushed him up against the wall; then I went down on my knees and opened his fly.

There are several ways to get through a blow job without massacring your throat; for example, after a while it gets easy to tell if whether a guy is the type who shoots off right away or takes his time. This guy was definitely in the former group, and he had a little dick too, small enough that I could nearly cover it in my hand. I know queers are supposed to like big dicks, but the only place I like a huge salami is on myself, which fortunately I was blessed with. Feeling charitable and pleased with this trick, I gave him the standard all-out deepthroating, keeping one hand on his ass while I unzipped my cutoffs and got out my own cock with the other. I don't think it took him more than three minutes to give a hoarse cry and shoot off in my mouth. Good, This would be an easy one.

He was still panting and gasping when I stood up and removed my cutoffs, and this time I leaned into him, letting my cock brush his. I was conveniently hard, mostly from a little judicious fantasizing while I had been slurping his dick and he got hold of it and stroked it gently. I actually like a little harder stimulation than that, as mine wasn't as sensitive as his obviously was, but I let myself be teased by the light touch. "What else do you want?" I whispered. "You're paying for the fuck."

"I want more of what I see now," he whispered back. "Lay down."

OK, I got it. You'd be surprised how many tricks want to suck cock, as well as or even instead of being sucked off themselves. Especially the ones who are weird about being queer, so that going down on some guy is the ultimate taboo, one they have to pay an anonymous stranger to experiment with. Not to mention that a guy who's getting paid isn't going to complain about their technique. My trick took a deep breath. like he was nerving himself up, and then sank his mouth onto me. Unlike the nearly effortless blow job I'd given him, he had a little more trouble with my size and his obvious lack of experience. My cock, however, is well-trained enough to come almost when I tell it to, and on all kinds of stimulation. Since I died and came back, it isn't quite the center of my sexuality in the way that it used to be, and I have more control over it. Or I like to think so, anyway, most of the time.

Somewhere along the line, he got a finger between my ass cheeks and tickled the fur on my butt, and that put me over the edge with a suddenness that startled me. I don't ejaculate, and he looked a bit surprised as he came up off me. I lay there bemused and wondering what had just happened. "Turn over," he said, an excited gleam in his eye. He was hard again. Yeah, this was one of the Alexander Portnoy types, shoots off in three minutes and gets hard again in another three, makes up for lack of staying power with continual repeat ability. I got on my knees, ass in the air, which is as much a part of the fetish for these guys as the leather jacket and the attitude. The ones who wanted delicate fresh young things with trembling lips weren't going to want to fuck a vampire anyway. The badboy act was part of the heat; I knew that better than anyone.

Unfortunately, tonight my cock had a different idea.

The second he got a lubed finger into my asshole, I got hard again. This wouldn't normally be a problem, but the odd thing was that I was getting into the idea of being fucked. I usually preferred to let my mind drift while it went on, keeping my sphincter relaxed and letting the get it over with, but tonight some wanting-to-be-mounted urge was getting the better of me in embarrassing ways, and it was all I could do to keep myself from squirming against his hand. He took a long, careful time lubing me— in his inexperience he seemed really worried about hurting me—and by the time he got two fingers in and touched my prostate, it was starting to get frustrating. I growled in spite of myself and thrust backward.

"You really want this, don't you?" he teased. "All that cold contractual stuff, and underneath you really just want this." *Shut up, damn you, and fuck me! It's embarrassing enough as it is.* "Tell me what you want," he ordered.

Bullshit. I was not going to play this game. "Is this about what I want, or what you want?" I grated out.

"You know what I want," he said.

"Then do it!" He kept messing around with his fingers, as if he hadn't heard. I reached down and took hold of my cock; it was rock-hard. What was worse was that my fangs were unsheathing themselves. I bit at the pillow in annoyance and wanting. All right, fine. After as many years as I'd had in this business, you'd think I wouldn't have any pride left. *It's just a trick,* I told myself. *It doesn't matter. You can say anything you want, as long as you get paid. You'll probably never see him again.* "Fuck me," I said between clenched teeth.

"What?"

"Fuck me, dammit!" I yelled, and, thank the gods, he didn't say another word. I felt his thighs line up against mine, and then the head of his cock slid into my sphincter, which hardly objected at all. I pressed myself back until he was in me to the hilt, and proceeded to beat off onto the bedsheets. He fucked me for a fairly long time considering I'd had him pegged as the fast-coming time, and then came while pressing his face into the leather on my back. I could hear him sniffing it, rubbing against it.

We pulled apart and lay on our backs, him still making moaning noises and "Oh God," and me staring at the ceiling. *Thanks a lot,* I told my asshole. *I really needed you to do that to me with a trick, and a first-time trick at that.* I felt his hand on my arm, stroking me. "You're so good," he said. "You're so good."

Yeah, I'm a professional, dude. Some residual annoyance with myself made me look him in the eye and say, "I started sucking cock for money at the age of fourteen." He blinked and looked away for a moment, and I sighed. That hadn't been exactly fair. My choices were my own, and he did seem to be impressed.

The guy—I still didn't know his name—buried his face in the sleeve of my jacket. "I have this feeling of wanting to keep you here," he said quietly.

Every muscle in my body froze into steel. Was this a psycho? I found myself remembering the bars at the window, wondering if I could break through them and get to the street below. It would hardly be the first trick I'd climbed down three stories to escape. He raised his head and must have seen the expression on my face, because he rushed to reassure me. "Oh, no, no, I didn't mean—I just want to see you again, that's all! I know I couldn't really keep—I mean. . . ." He trailed off, looking worried, and I relaxed.

"It's OK," I said. "I'm around. We can make another appointment." I looked at him. "So why haven't you been with another guy since high school?"

He flushed a little. "I've just been putting things off. Like my life." Now it was his turn to stare at the ceiling. "I was afraid of making it official."

"So is it?"

"What?" He came out of his reverie and blinked at me.

I grinned at him. "Are you a fag yet?"

"Almost," he whispered. His hand moved mine to his bare ass cheeks.

"I can fix that too," I said. "No problem." He wasn't bad, I thought, in spite of all his little digs at me when I was ass in the air. Not as bad as some. And he did have a nice butt, when it was up and ready for me to fuck. I took as long a time to lube him as he had me, but considering how much bigger my cock was, it was probably a good thing. He groaned the same when my cockhead passed his sphincter as he had when my mouth went down on him. I'll forgive a lot in a trick when I've got them under me, especially if they cuss and yell for more while I'm slamming them back and forth on my dick. Especially if they want it even more than I do.

"God, I needed that," he moaned, lying flat on the bed afterward. I chuckled and turned him over, nipped at his arm and chest, let him see my fangs. I was playing fast and loose with my usual scenario of nonthreatening hustler; any moment now he could get scared and book, and I'd have to let him. It was easier and safer to play harmless and pliable until my teeth were in a trick's neck. He didn't run, though; just stared in fascination as his tongue quickly moistened his lips. "Time to pay, huh?" he asked.

"Yep," I said, and forced his head to the side. Gently, but I let him see how strong I really was. Then I dove for his carotid.

There's no way to explain what feeding is like. I've done crack, back before, and I don't give a damn that it doesn't have any effect on me now because feeding is better. Some of us go impotent after the change, and although I didn't I wouldn't care that much if I had, because feeding is better. It's not an activity where you moan and writhe. Once I start sucking, I'm caught in a dead silent fixation of ecstasy, suspended in time, with only the trained reflex of my Black Sun mantras to keep me from draining someone in a mindless haze. One mantra, two, three, and I'm up off him, gasping like I've come up out of deep water. I'm not the only one who's described it that way.

I paused and calmed myself with deep breaths, the colors dancing behind my eyelids. Everything was suddenly very bright, very loud, very sharp. My trick was looking at me with That Look, the awed eyes of the recently fed on. I realized it was probably time to go. "I've got to shoot," I said, preparing to wrench myself to my feet. "Got to get out before the buses stop."

"Stay." His hand was on my arm. "The room's paid through the day. Or you could come home with me," he suggested.

Oh, right. "You sure that's a good idea?" I asked, glancing at him through narrowed eyes. It's not always smart to be around when they come down and realize it was all just another drug in its own way.

He paused and seemed to check himself. "All right," he said. "Stay here tonight. If I still think it's a good idea tomorrow, you can move in with me."

Now it was turn to blink. The first part of that statement made sense, but . . . "I'm not some boy to do your dishes and laundry, man."

"Do whatever you want. You can come and go, whatever, just. . . ." He trailed off as I deliberately let a thin trickle of spit, stained with his blood, trail down my chin, and then quickly licked it back up again. Remind him what he was laying in bed with. He was giving me the fascinated look again—or was it a scientist's look, someone who wanted me under a microscope? I had him pegged as a nerd, maybe an engineer? It didn't matter; his cock was hard again against my thigh. Liked that little display of theatrics, did you? My not-very-small ego gave a warm purr and I rolled over on my stomach, letting him see my bare ass again. It's good to feel desired, even by tricks, when you're a monster.

He ran a hand over my ass, slipped a finger between my cheeks, and before I know it I was hard again too, and my hole was twitching with that annoying urge. *What is up with you tonight*, I asked my nether region silently. Acting like a fuck-starved bitch in heat, as if we didn't get all the sex we wanted any day of the week. I glanced over at his little cock, which was rubbing itself against my leg. Just the right size, didn't hurt a lick going in. Oh well, if one has the urge, one should give it what it wants and shut it up when it's possible. And he did say the room was paid for.

"Want to do it again?" I asked, turning on my side so that his dickhead poked itself right up against my still-slippery asshole. I grabbed my cock and squirmed back against him, figuring he wouldn't argue.

He laughed and wrapped his arms around me from behind. "You really hate this job, don't you," he murmured ironically in my ear.

"Shut up," I said as his cock slid into me. Taking his encircling arm in my free hand, I sank my fangs into the delicate blue lines in his pale, slender wrist.

What We Are Meant to Be

Robert Knippenberg

Afterward she lies close in the crook of my arm, her hand on my chest, her fingers spread in gentleness. Her breasts are warm against my side and I can feel the deep clean thud of her heart slowing as her excitement ebbs. I lightly stroke her face, pushing back the dark wetted curls from her precious temples with my fingertips. I do it to tease myself, gauging my hunger.

She mistakes my gesture, thinking it only the expression of the tenderness I feel for her. She kisses my chest and presses her damply satisfied pussy ardently against the angle of my hip. I can feel the pulse of her youthful vibrancy in the sweetly puffy lips of her vulva.

"That was unbelievable," she murmurs, and even in those three words I can hear the lilt of her Castilian accent, the soft stirring sound that had first led me to notice her among all the others.

I always ensure that it is "unbelievable," or "fantastic," or "wonderful" for them. It is the least that I can do.

"Will you stay the night?" she says, her lips and tongue tickling my skin.

She looks up at me, her eyes hopeful black marbles, glinting beneath half open lids.

"If you want me to," I say.

She mistakes the huskiness in my voice for the desire she wants to hear.

"I want. I want to snuggle and rest for a few moments. But then I want to do it again. If I fall asleep, I want you to fuck me anyway, as soon as you are ready. I want the feel of you slowly sliding inside to awaken me." She grins shyly at me. I can tell that she is surprised and a little shocked by the things she hears herself saying, that she is, at the same time, happy that she can say them to me.

My heart goes out to her then, as it had not before. Of course, she did not have to tell me aloud what she wanted. I know she wants this, even as I knew when we began, although she had been too shy to ask me then, that she wanted me to arouse her with my tongue. I always know what they want, even when they do not know they want it. It is part of what I am. Sometimes when it is especially good, as it has been with her, it is all that I am.

And as I have done uncounted times, although not always inevitably, I wish it could be different, that there was some other way. Especially when they're so youthful and inexperienced as she, when they are as hesitant at first as she had been. And then, once we began, so trusting, so vulnerable. And finally, so frankly passionate.

Her large dark eyes begin to flutter helplessly as she slips into that state of perfect quiet, the happy peace that follows complete sexual gratification. The "petit mort" the French call it. Although when I am in a woman's or a man's bed, it is a sleep which is anything but small and unimportant. This is the time I prefer to take them, although it was not always so.

In the beginning, I preferred the moment of climax, sating myself at the very instant when their hearts beat most wildly. I was crueler then, but I could not help it. I was what I was, as I am now what I have become.

For most, the question of what I am would largely be answered by my gender. I am, most of the time and at this moment, a man.

And while it's true that I have always found a certain level of comfort with being a male and consider it more or less my normal physical as well as psychological state, since that was what I was in the beginning, this most basic determiner of character is not a valid indicator of the true nature of my being.

"Who are you really?" she asks sleepily.

Her question surprises me. She had not doubted me when I introduced myself as the ship's navigator. And despite her modesty, her reticence, in the ensuing hours in which we'd danced and talked and laughed, it had been easy to make her feel completely at ease with me.

Of course I had by then already become completely the man she wanted me to be. I had let the transformation begin earlier in the evening, while she was still on stage, entertaining the ship's company with the songs of her native Spain. There was something about the way her delicate fingers plucked the strings of her guitar, the way her soft voice first silenced then filled the room. Whatever our gender, whatever our motives, we are all naturally drawn to youth, to beauty, to innocence. But these are not my sole criteria. Beneath her vulnerability I sensed a vitality, a hopefulness. I'd sat down, as helpless as an empty cup—Ah, that first splash, that winey flavor of romantic dreams! She'd filled me up, and I began to change, to allow the heady flavor of her sinless, physical desires to quench for at least a moment the hollowness which is always inside me.

In the few hours we had so far shared we had already been more intimate than some are in a lifetime. But this had not prepared me to expect her question. However, in the wondrous semiconscious dream state that follows a consuming act of love, sometimes the more perceptive will discern that I am not what I appear to be. Such insights are genuinely rare, but when you have lived for as long as I have, almost nothing is new. I have been asked before and it always pleases me.

"It's very difficult to say," I reply, knowing she will not remember my words, but hoping as I had not dared to hope in a long time, that just for once, if I were to let her live beyond the night, she might remember.

Many times before I had optimistically allowed it in certain cases. I was still experimenting then, still desperately unwilling to accept my uniqueness. But always, meeting my lover of the previous night, by chance as far as they knew, I was inevitably disappointed. I found their minds once again clouded over with doubts, the moment of clarity they had displayed during our joyful union gone completely, just as the night had been banished by the morning's light. And then, more sadly than they knew, I would sweep them into bed again, seducing them so swiftly this time they would find themselves confused at being so suddenly naked and overwhelmed by their lust. And I would not hesitate the second time to end, for all eternity, all their doubts, all their confusions.

"I really have no name. I have lived for so long that I have almost forgotten who or what I was in the beginning.

Whoever I am, you will never again meet anyone like me. I know I never have," I say jokingly.

We had talked like this for much of the evening, pretending to be characters from different times and places. She seemed to enjoy it immensely, saying and doing things her natural reticence would not have normally allowed.

It began when we were discussing her songs. She had written some of them herself, remarking that they were based on old stories that her grandmother had told her as a child and when she sang them she often felt as if she were living the lives her lyrics evoked. I too had said that my mother had often read such tales to me as a child and that I had often spent hours acting out the roles of the various heroes and villains as I grew older.

Of course, I said this because I was responding to her romantic nature. Actually my mother had been illiterate, but since the essence of my life is being the consummate actor (or actress, depending on the sexual role my chosen partner prefers) it was actually closer to the truth about myself than anything I could have made up.

Perhaps it was this, or because of something else about her, some emotion in her that uncharacteristically I could not identify, that I began flirting with the idea of being more candid with her than I can ever remember wanting to be with anyone before.

"Well, start at the beginning then," she says, hugging me and wiggling her pretty toes to tickle the sole of my foot. Her eyes are closed tightly now. She seems suddenly less the wanton young woman, more the small child, her cuddling more like a child's sensuality, her sexuality more a yearning for the reassuring comfort of a larger physical presence, her desire more the simple need to be cradled in a parent's arms.

She is just beginning her life and I know from my experience that the beginnings of things are the hardest part of all. I wonder how to begin my story, how to tell her how I began when I do not even believe it myself anymore. Especially since, given my beginnings and all the years and all the lovers, I have come to realize that most of what people take for granted as real is almost entirely superficial. Besides, exactly how I was created is still as mysterious to me as the question of how, if ever, I will end.

"Very well," I say, forcing down my urge to feed, but doing it now to indulge myself. For the moment I am satisfied to feast on her only with my eyes, to drink in the delicious sight of her naked, perfectly proportioned, diminutive body wrapped sweetly around me. I savor the way her hips flare up graciously from her small waist, the slightly shadowed cunning hollow of her buttock, the way her thighs taper down like arrows pointing to her dimpled knee. Then, swelling and slimming again, her leg narrows to the consummate crystal stem of her ankle before blossoming into the shy and dainty flower of her petal perfect foot.

"But I must warn you, some of it will sound fantastic. Although I shall endeavor to tell you the truth, when one lives as I have lived, one is in danger of becoming a myth even to one's self."

I long to warn her further, to tell her that even over the space of a single life span, the human memory is tenuous at best and she must capture every second of every moment, for any one can be her last, or if not, can be a time which she may one day wish she could relive. And even as I long to go on, suddenly wanting to give her advice as a father would his daughter, I am aware that the ache of my hunger is growing and it is this, as much as knowing she has so few moments left, that stops me.

Again what I say to her, I say lightly, not wanting to alarm her. Little does she know that many of my little jokes tonight have been entirely serious, that what I have just told her is another truth which I have told only to a very few before and which none have ever dared to comprehend.

"Ah, you are not just a character! You are a living myth! That explains it. That must be why I find you so utterly enchanting," she says with a sighing giggle.

Her soft little laugh would have been inaudible to anyone with normal hearing. All my senses are, however, anything but normal. Not only can I hear her clearly, but I feel as well the tiny tremors of her body against my side, and hear as well as feel the slight increase in the rhythm of her heart.

All this fans the heat of my dual desires. Everything she says and does, each tiny sound, each little movement, only makes my hunger for her life force grow, thereby adding to her danger. At the same time, these same things make my cock stir and augment my desire to make love to her once more and thereby she prolongs her existence by just that much. Such conflict is rare and I find it delightful.

"It sounds very much as if I am in for a very long story. The story of your life perhaps?" she asks.

"Perhaps, but what is any life if not a story? The question is not whether it is a story, or even if it is a true story, or even how long it is. The question is whether or not it is an interesting story."

"I love long stories. As long as they are interesting," she says, giggling again, this time at her own remark.

"Once upon a time, there lived in a new and faraway land, a bright young boy full of hope, full of promise."

"Once upon a time?" she says, grinning and stifling a yawn at the same moment. "Once upon a time?"

"All the best stories begin that way."

I have been lightly caressing the smoothness of her back as we talk. Now I reach around to cup her breast as I stretch my neck to kiss her forehead. It is what she needs, these little reassurances. I can feel these things even when others are not aware they want them. Such feelings are the essence of my talent for seduction.

She moans a little, hugs me back with her body.

"I thought you were going to sleep?" I say.

"Yes, I'm sorry but I need to. Just for a few moments. I have had so little sleep for the last week, worrying about this trip. It is the first time I have ever been on ocean liner. But only if you promise to wake me up as I asked."

"I promise," I say and suddenly I know I can keep my promise. This exceptional girl has charmed me so that I find a renewed strength in myself and it is easier to hold back my hunger than I had ever thought possible.

"Then tell me your story. And I promise I shall hear it even if I am asleep."

And so I begin again.

Once upon a time—I forget the exact year, but it was in the 1670s—there was a boy in the town of Salem in the Colony of Massachusetts. His mother and father were more religious than most in the community and he was much affected, because of their grim fervor, by serious thoughts. He spent hours contemplating good and evil and wondering about the angels and devils and witches he heard the minister speak about each Sunday in church.

He was a handsome boy, and by the age of fourteen he had already almost attained the physical size and strength of a grown man. But in his heart he was troubled. His developing sexuality battled with the principles his parents and his teachers had ingrained in him so deeply and he felt at war within himself. He often had

spontaneous erections in school and in church, and at
night he found himself dreaming of the girls he knew—
and sometimes even their mothers—undressing for him
and revealing what they looked like underneath their
layers of severe clothes. He dared not talk of this to
anyone; to escape his sinful urges, he would often spend
hours wandering in the woods, mentally scourging himself
and praying to God to be released from them.

To escape his anguish, he began to watch the forest
animals, wishing he had been born as simple and as
innocent as God made them. Soon he became skilled at
stalking and spying on them. But the more he watched
them, the more he realized that they were not at all the
uncomplicated creatures he had supposed. Their behaviors
and the dramas of their lives seemed to echo back to him
the very conflicting emotions he had come to the woods
to forget.

He was shocked but at the same time excited by the
promiscuity of the nesting songbirds and the frenzied
orgies of the rabbits. He was sickened but also thrilled by
the rapacity of the cunning vixen fox, killing and ripping
apart her prey. He was repelled and yet haunted by the
cool evil slyness of the snake, silently robbing the nests of
the licentious birds, devouring fledglings or swallowing
whole eggs with his unhinged jaws.

But most of all he was affected by the haughty spiraling
of the hunting hawks. He would watch them for hours—
listening to their cries, which never failed to send chills
throughout his body, pretending he was with them, high
above the earth, free from doubt and sin. And then one
day one seemed to be calling him. He closed his eyes and
suddenly he saw the world below, small and clear and
perfect in each detail. Then he felt the hawk's hunger and,
when the bird stooped, he felt the wind in his face, heard
the screaming of the air past his ears. And then, the tiny

final, infantile cry and the hot gush of blood through soft fur as he speared the rabbit with his magnificently taloned feet made him sob aloud with a terrible joy....

The first time this happened he was horrified, sure it was only further evidence of his evil nature. But he could not stop and he flew with the hawk again. Then he found he could run with the fox and crawl with the snake as well. He realized now that unlike what everyone believed, the animals lived rich and vital lives. And further, that their vivid feelings and emotions, so real and so like his, were more powerful and real than what he had been taught human emotions were supposed to be. Now he began to question everything he had been taught, and this troubled him even more.

He tried to talk to his father about this, asking him about God's reasons for the creation of the animals and why they were the way they were, but his stern and pious father told him only to go read his Bible, where all the answers to all questions were vouchsafed to the faithful.

Earnestly he re-read Genesis again and again. And then, determinedly, but now losing any real hope, he studied the other books of both the Old and New Testaments. But as he feared, they held no answers to the questions raised by the things he had seen and experienced. He felt more alone then ever in his struggle with the conflicting urges he felt growing inside him. In his shame and doubt he began spending less and less time with his friends and family and more and more time alone.

And so it was that one day he wandered further into the forest than he ever had before, where he chanced upon a little well-kept cottage all by itself in a clearing in the woods. There he saw a woman working in her garden. He observed her secretly, using the stealth he had taught himself while watching the animals. It was very strange for anyone to be living so far away from the settlement, and the only reason he could imagine that anyone would do so was that she was one of the witches that the minister had warned everyone against.

And as he had been drawn to the behavior of the animals, he went back whenever he could, sure that he would eventually catch her performing some evil or unnatural act. Usually she was outside, but sometimes he spied on her through her windows from the branches of the trees. But always the pretty cottage was the picture of everyday goodness and she would be gardening, or spinning, or tending her little flocks of chickens and geese, or carrying out some other ordinary household task.

But the boy could not accept that everything was as it appeared. Not only did she live by herself and seem to be prospering, a thing unusual enough in itself, but no matter what she was doing or how long he watched, she always seemed to sit or stand or move in such a way that her large starched bonnet inevitably obscured her face. Furthermore, no matter what she was doing, she moved with an uncommonly easy grace, almost as if she were naked like the animals instead of being hampered by the thick layers of dark clothes that she and all women wore to disguise their femininity.

He became obsessed by her and by his musings on her true nature. And so he returned, again and again, becoming increasingly frustrated by his inability to see her face or discover anything else unnatural about her and growing more bold and less careful each time.

Finally, unable to bear it any longer, he walked up to her one day as she was hoeing. She had her back to him and he had made no sound as he approached. He was a well-mannered boy and had been taught to wait until an adult addressed him before he spoke. Furthermore he was afraid to speak for fear of startling her, so he stood, wondering what to do, watching the way her back and shoulders moved as she chopped away with her hoe between the rows of lush vegetables and blooming fragrant flowers. Then he noticed that there were no little weeds trying to gain a foothold where she was working, nor for that matter anywhere in her garden, and everywhere the rich dark earth was already loose and fluffy.

"It took you long enough," she said and he could hear her amusement like music in her voice.

She moved to the next row, her back still to him. The boy knew that not only was she aware of him, but that she had always known when he was there.

But this did not surprise him half as much as the sudden realization that he had always known that she knew.

"Who are you?" he said.

"That is difficult to say," she said, stopping finally. She let her hoe drop and she turned to face him. Then she untied and removed her bonnet.

"Who would you like me to be?"

To say that she was incredibly beautiful would be to mislead you. She was, but that was only a small part of what she was.

The boy was stunned by her, for her hair was the same vibrant color as the fox when it ran in the sunlight, and her eyes were flecked with gold like the hawk's and had their piercing brilliancy that saw everything, and her gaze was coolly hypnotic like the snake, and her skin was as clear and smooth as the whitest unblemished bird's egg, and her voice was as enchanting as the most melodious song a bird had ever sung.

And so the boy stood frozen, not knowing what her question meant, but unable to move or even to speak to ask her.

"Come inside," she said smiling. She took his hand and he was released, sure that before that moment he had never seen a smile, had never felt another's fingers.

He followed her as the faithful dog follows his master. Inside he saw what he was always sure was there but had never been able to see from his perch in the faraway tree. The walls of the cottage were lined with shelves of glass jars, earthen urns, little wooden boxes, and small colored stones that seemed to glow with their own internal light. And, their whiteness bright in the dimness, he saw the bones and skulls of small animals and the large white mushrooms that grew on the trunks of rotting trees, and other things he could not readily identify from their shape and color.

Staring around him he managed at last to speak. "You are a witch!" he gasped.

"You may call me that if it pleases you, and I can tell that it does. But why, if I am what you think, are you not afraid?"

She was right, but the boy had no answer.

"You think that witches are old and ugly, but you find me attractive instead. Is that it?"

"Yes. Yes that's true. But how do you know?"

"I know what is important to know about others. I know how they feel."

Then she went to the large wooden bathing tub in one corner and dragged it across the floor in front of the hearth. She picked up two wooden buckets and holding one out to him said, "I even know their most secret dreams. . . ."

And feeling as if he were dreaming, he followed her outside to the well where they filled the buckets, and then back inside to pour the fresh cool water into the tub.

Then, as she poured steaming water into the tub from the large kettle that hung above the fire, she said, "You may take off your clothes now. It's time for your bath."

He began by removing his boots, feeling as natural as if he were at home. But there his mother would leave the room as soon as he did this. It had been so ever since he became old enough to bathe on his own.

For that matter, neither his mother nor his father touched him or even each other at all except when necessary. They believed that the body was only a temporary housing for the soul and that the devil used a person's body to tempt the soul to forget itself, to distract the heart from the path of purity that God had intended.

But she was testing the water, stirring it with her hand, and as he removed the last of his clothes he knew she was not going to leave. Then, his blood pulsing, his breathing quickened, he became aware of his sinful, rising flesh.

Ever since he could remember he had loved his bath. And ever since he could remember he had been unable to resist the sin of playing with himself beneath the soapy water. He would start out vowing not to, pretending it was his mother's hands that were washing him slowly and carefully everywhere else.

But eventually his hand, almost by itself, would slip down and he would already be hard with anticipation. He would begin with the briefest of touches, until at the end, arching his hips up, he would close his eyes, imagining that it was his mother's fingers gripping and tugging on him, that she was forcing the evil fluid to spurt out of him, splash hotly on his belly.

Afterward, he would open his eyes, watch the evidence of his sin float away in small disappearing spirals as he let his hips sink slowly beneath the water. And then, alone in the terrible peace that always followed this inevitable act of release, he would pretend his mother was kneeling next to the tub, hugging him and kissing his cheeks and telling him how much she loved him.

"For a handsome young boy, you are already quite a man," the woman said. She was smiling, looking frankly at his cock. Her eyes and lips made him aware that it was filling, growing. This made his face turn even redder. He stepped quickly into the tub and sat down, but it was a blush of pride and happiness and not shame her words and grin made him feel.

She soaped a cloth and began to wash him. Her touch seemed to excite and at the same time soothe both his mind and body.

Now he relaxed even more as he laid back against the comfortably carved contour of the wooden bath. Her hands felt as natural as the rain as they moved slowly over his neck and shoulders and chest. He closed his eyes, felt the love he had always yearned for in her caress. She washed his legs next and he felt like an infant again as she purred over his toes, kissing them and then the soles of his feet, then his knees.

She told him stand so she could wash the rest of him. Her hands on his ass and balls and cock made him tingle with a lingering intensity all out of proportion to the innocence of her brief touches.

She finished washing him and took his hand, had him step out of the tub. Then, looking at him, and all the while smiling, she undressed before him and she was the perfect physical fulfillment of his dreams.

The boy felt no guilt or shame that the sight of her perfect body made his cock completely rigid. Instead it was as if all his depraved imaginings, all his impure thoughts, were suddenly wholesome and upright. He felt happy and complete being naked in front of her and his cock became the most honest part of his body.

She began to dry him with a soft towel and again he closed his eyes. Then the towel was gone and it was just her hands caressing him gently and intimately. He could feel her warmth as she stood close, her presence such that any moment he was sure the space between them would vanish, that they would become one being, and the thought that such a thing might be possible excited him even more.

Then he felt the warmth of her breath on his face as she kissed him. Her lips moved thrillingly over his neck and shoulders. Her tongue briefly tickled the nipples of his breasts, then moved slowly downward, delighting his belly.

He opened his eyes then, looked down to see her kneeling before him. He saw her close her eyes as she put her hands on his hips and leaned to put her lips on the tip of his cock. She kissed it lovingly for a moment, just as she had his toes, then took it into her mouth. It was as astonishing an act as he had ever seen, something he had never even thought of imagining.

Then she began sucking on him and it was a more marvelous sensation than he had ever imagined. It made him feel helpless and more powerful than he had ever been, and flames of lust flared up from his loins to consume his useless soul. He closed his eyes again, already feeling the need to ejaculate. She gripped him harder now, holding him steady as she took all of him deeper into her mouth. Then, as the head of his cock touched the back of her throat, he began. He could feel as well as hear her swallowing, as if she needed every drop, as if his semen were an elixir she had to have to sustain her life. He could no longer tell the difference between his body and her mouth, between his soul and hers, between good and evil, or God and the Devil, or Heaven and Hell. Everything seemed suddenly to be one and the same thing and he wanted to embrace it all and fling himself into the oneness, the emptiness, to fill it up.

The spasms went on and on, his balls pumping wildly, forcing his burning fluid through the tube of his cock as if he contained the sins of the world and they would flow from him forever—then he knew she was eating him! Not with her mouth and not his flesh, but *him*—his essence, his life force.

He desperately pulled away. As soon as they were no longer touching he saw, flickering in front of him, a thing so hideous and old as to be almost sexless and inhuman. He knew then that everything he had thought she was had been only an illusion.

Her breathing is gentle and deep and this time her soft hand is limp upon my chest. She had fallen asleep long ago and despite her promise, could not have heard my story.

I decide to take her now, to suck her life essence into me, as that creature had tried to do to me so long ago.

Gently, I disentangle myself from her, moving slowly and carefully so I do not disturb her. I lay next to her, to place my mouth on her lips, but then she sighs and rolls over on her back, her small hands open with her palms up and her legs open like a child's. I look down at her, so vulnerable in her sleep and again the twin desires surge, warring within me. If only she had not moved. If only she did not look so enchantingly available.

But she does, and as I look at her I decide there is time yet. I have forever. I can give her a few moments more. Instead I decide to first fulfill my promise to her. It is the least that I can do. Besides, my cock has grown hard and pulses with the sight of her, and this makes my decision easier.

I position my knees between hers, using them to carefully push hers apart.

Then, holding myself up on one arm, I gently work the head of my cock against the pretty lips that guard her precious opening, easing myself in further. Her lovely cunt is warm and still wet. Using both arms now to hold myself above her so our bodies do not touch anywhere else, I move with gentle thrusts until I am in all the way. The way her rippled walls lovingly envelop me makes me tremble and her almost-virginal tightness makes my cock twitch. Then I begin, moving ever so slightly, just as she had wanted. Her breathing changes as her insides respond, welcoming me.

Moments later she moans in her sleep. I have been teasing her, knowing that she loves being smothered under the body of her lover. Now I dip my head to tickle her erect nipples with my tongue. She wraps her arms around me to pull me down on top of her, whimpering as she thrusts her hips up to meet mine.

It took me almost all of the first hundred years of my existence to discover how to gain complete control over my physical body. Now I use my skill at changing shape and she gasps with delight as my cock swells to fit her shape inside exactly. This time I stretch her a bit more and she begins to murmur, small Spanish words that tell me she has never before been filled so wonderfully, so completely.

This time her mood is not one of gentle romance, as it had been when I first seduced her. I respond to her unconscious wishes, putting her arms up over her head, imprisoning her wrists with my hands. I peg her legs apart with my feet and begin to plunge into her, ramming my pelvis hard against her until her body shudders.

This feeds and fulfills her fantasies of being taken against her will. Her trilled, Castilian endearments become a thrilling babble of sweet and wild obscenities, punctuated by the groans she makes each time I penetrate her deeply and stop, make my cock writhe as if it were something alive inside her. Soon she has abandoned the last shred of her inhibitions. She begs me loudly, and in English, to fuck her harder and faster and just like this forever.

At moments like this it is always been as if I am two beings in the same shell—one participating fully in the sexual madness of the moment, feeling a genuine passion, the other aloof, determining my partner's moods and needs and coolly analyzing my own. And now with her heart beating so hard and wildly against me, I can barely contain either of my selves. One moment I love her, the next I want to take her life.

I feel her orgasm building swiftly deep inside her. I ready myself and when it bursts upon her, I know her life force is at its fullest flower. My hunger too is peaking, but once again, something about her holds me back, some quality that I cannot yet identify. Instead of taking her, I flood her with my come, submerging my hunger in the joy she is giving me, in the rapture I am giving her.

Finally her shuddering slows and stops. Sensing the change in her need, I roll away, freeing her to breathe, so she can begin her return to the sad and terrible state that all ordinary human beings take to be reality.

I light cigarettes for us both and we hold hands as we smoke. She turns on the light on her side of the bed, wanting to see the smoke curling up. It is late and has been dark for a long time, but since I can see as well in the dark as others see in the light, I never bother with the lights.

Looking at her, the flush of her cheeks, the softness of her eyes, the lush slackness of her lips, I want to kiss her, but I do not dare.

"Thank you for keeping your promise," she says, squeezing my hand. "It was even better than I hoped it would be."

"And did you keep yours?" I reply, smirking, raising a brow.

"Of course. So what did the boy do after he discovered the beautiful woman was really a witch?"

Now I look even more closely at her. "You heard me even though you were asleep?"

"Not heard exactly. I don't remember your voice after a certain point, but I remember the pictures your words created. Like a movie in my head."

"That is quite a remarkable talent," I say, wondering— because she is grinning back at me like a smug and beautiful cat—what else there is about her that I have yet to learn. And perhaps, just perhaps, if she has something else to teach me.

"I have been able to do it ever since I was a little girl. I so wanted to hear the stories my grandmother was reading to me, so even though I went to sleep, I heard them. And then later I would see them and let them play over and over again in my head. It made me a rather poor student in school, I'm afraid."

"But it gave you a rich imagination. That is far more important than the things they teach in school."

"Perhaps, but an imagination does not help you make a living. Except in the arts. That is why I took up singing and writing songs."

"You have a haunting voice. And your songs are wise beyond your years. And now I find that you make love as beautifully as you sing about it. Such a wondrously candid sexuality is remarkable in anyone, and especially in one so young. Is this too a product of your imagination, or have you had that many lovers?"

"Not so many," she says, sitting up to put out her cigarette. "But they don't count in any case." She snuggles close to me again and is silent for a moment. And then, and her face is against my arm so that I also feel her lips form the words, "You are my first real lover. And you shall never leave me," she whispers.

Her words both warm and chill me. I know I am not the first man she has ever slept with, but neither is what she says a lie. And now I begin to enjoy this odd way she has of making me feel a little unsure of myself, as if everything she's said and done was a threat as well as an entreaty.

And this ambivalence I have been feeling from the beginning takes on a new and deeper meaning, becomes doubly odd, since I know I have nothing to fear from her. Long ago I tried more than once to end my life, but poisons, bullets, fire, water, even leaping from a tall building, never accomplished anything but a temporary agony. I suspect an explosion that would destroy my body completely might work, but I cannot stand the idea that it might not, that I would only experience a much longer and more terrible torture only to find myself whole again and everything the same.

But even though I welcome this unique and unfamiliar mix of foreboding and delight and would love to spend a few more hours with her to find out what it is that makes her so different from all the others, my hunger is making this impossible. It is time to end this, and to this end I reach over her, as if I were merely putting out the light. Then, pretending I am so distracted by her that I have to kiss her instead, I lean down to cover her mouth with mine for the last time.

But she laughs and squirms away. Then her mouth on my cock distracts me from my purpose. She stops after a few moments and crawls back up beside me, lifting my arm and placing it around her so she can nestle beneath it again.

"Is that what I taste like?" she says. Her lips glisten now even more prettily from the combined liquids of our love.

"Yes. Your exquisite little pussy is quite delicious. You've never tasted yourself before?"

"No. There are many things I've never done before. I've never asked a man to spend the night. And I've never put a man's cock in my mouth. I never wanted to until I heard your story."

This much at least was true. "And did you like it?"

"Your cock in my mouth or your story?" she teases.

I have to laugh. "Either one!"

"I liked them both. But the one is not ready to begin again and the other has not ended."

"Would you like to hear the rest of the story while my cock rests until it's ready to give you pleasure again?"

"I will not let you go until you do."

"Do which?"

"Both."

We both laugh and kiss. It is strangely easy to kiss her now and our two tongues share the flavors of both our sexes. Then I light another cigarette and she settles back. I begin again, once more feeling like the father cuddling his sweet young daughter, ready to tell her a fairy tale.

The boy dashed out of the cottage, running as fast as he could through the woods and meadows. He did not dare to look back, but he listened for her footsteps, kept glancing down at his own bare pounding feet, for now he knew the terror of the rabbit and was sure that at any moment he'd see her shadow, that he'd be taken, that her darkness that would descend on him like the final shadow of the hawk's looming wings.

He was so terrified he forgot he was naked until he saw the horrified faces of the people in the street. And when they gathered around him all he had the breath left to say was, "A witch, a witch!" as he collapsed in their arms.

For two days he stayed in bed, seemingly delirious with fever. His body was hot and his face was flushed, but the boy knew this was no ordinary sickness. What had begun as a maddeningly delicious tingling in his now perpetually rigid cock was spreading up his belly and down his legs and the boy believed his sin was still with him, that it was changing him slowly. In penance, he refused all food and drink and prayed incessantly to God to make the feeling stop. Finally his mother became so distraught she actually tried to hold and comfort him. But this made the tingling even more marvelous and his cock throbbed furiously with a life of its own. "Leave me alone! It's too late!" he screamed, sure this was God's way of punishing him.

Terrified and convinced the boy was under a spell, his mother ran to fetch the minister. Grimly standing over him, huge and certain as a tree—for he had seen, he was sure, such cases before—he insisted the boy tell him who the witch was and where she could be found. The boy resisted, questioning now what he had seen in those few seconds before he ran, certain it had all been the evil inside himself, a fantastic dream for which he alone was responsible.

Finally, when the angry minister threatened him with eternal damnation, he broke down and in exchange for the man's blessing he described the woman as he had first seen her and told him where in the woods to find her cottage, sure that they would search and find nothing.

By the morning of the third day the wonderful burning had spread throughout his body. He stopped praying, emptied by the knowledge that God had abandoned him. By that afternoon, the unnatural sensation began to subside and his hunger and thirst forced him to leave his bed at last and dress. He ate and drank then and was feeling almost normal, when, just as he stepped outside his house, he saw a group of men leading the beautiful red-haired woman down the street. She was bound with enough rope to hold three men and had been blindfolded so she stumbled in the ruts in the road. Then as she was led past him, she turned her head and smiled at him, even though she could not possibly have known he was there.

Suddenly the horror of what he had done struck the boy like the lightning cleaves the tree. He went back inside, his heart sick, his mind numb. He complained of fatigue to his mother and returned again to his bed, where this time he lay burning with a different fire, the fire of his love for this woman who would be burned at the stake because of his accusations. In desperation he tried to pray again, but discovered he no longer believed there was anyone to pray to, and in that moment gave up the last shred of his old religion and wept as he had never wept before.

The next day he skulked through the crowd of townspeople gathered in the square, listening to their whisperings. Her trial had been swift and conclusive, as somehow he knew it would be. Some were saying that she had denied nothing, but also said nothing in her own defense. Others said that she had said she could only be what they thought she was, but had seemed confused about what a "witch" was supposed to be. Still others swore that she had admitted to charming the boy, but claimed she had done it not to harm him, but to save him.

The words they spoke made him realize how little all these people cared about each other, how little they understood the nature of good and evil. He hid his face from them and was silent, hating them almost as much as he hated himself. He wanted to run away, to live in the woods forever, or even better, to die there, but he could not leave her. But neither could he look at her until the very end. Then, when he did, he stared in fascination. She was smiling at him through the acrid smoke, the consuming flames, her eyes as bright and golden as they had been on that sunlit afternoon. She did not appear to be in pain. She made no sound at all. Then she seemed to disappear, as if she had turned completely to ashes in an instant. The watching crowd gasped at this event, which they took as proof of the correctness of their judgment, their solution. But it was then the boy realized his mistake, that he knew she had been real, that instead it was he and his mother and father and everyone in the town who was not.

For days afterwards he thought that at any moment he too would vanish. He became thin, vague, as insubstantial as the air, and at the same time wooden like a puppet, his arms and legs and body doing all the things they had ever done, but without caring, without meaning, without a master to pull the strings.

Strangely, everyone in town spoke to him now, as they hadn't before, but to him his fame was ashes in his mouth, reminding him of her, their friendliness convincing him of the truth he had discovered, that everything was an illusion.

He lived like this for many weeks, not surprised that everyone seemed able to forget the incident, to go on with their small and meaningless lives.

Then one Sunday in church as he sat with head bowed, staring at the floor pretending he was praying, he became aware that the young blond boy next to him was looking at him. He looked back, saw that the boy had long dark lashes and large dark pleading eyes.

The boy's fantasy flashed through him then. It was the first time he had ever felt the desire of another, experienced another's hopes and dreams. What the boy wanted was clear and perfect in his mind and, despite its perversity, was exquisite in its guiltlessness. And even more astounding was the fact that it was the first thing, the only thing he felt was real since the day the red-haired woman was burned.

The boy quickly looked away. But as he left the church, he could feel the heat of the boy's body, as though he were naked and carrying him on his back. Startled, he turned to see the boy stop some distance behind him. The hunger sprang to life in him then, the hunger that from then on would be his life. He knew he had been transformed, that he was not himself anymore. Or if he was, he was also something else.

He smiled at the boy and the boy smiled back. He told his parents that he would like to be alone, to walk for awhile to ponder the minister's sermon. They went on ahead and he began to walk again, with the boy following.

Arriving at his father's barn, all it took was a glance and the boy waited outside while he went inside to get the things he needed. The boy followed him again, closer this time, as he took the path into the woods.

After awhile he stopped and turned. Both of them were breathing excitedly now. He told the boy to undress, which the lad did without hesitation. He motioned the boy to come closer, and a hand on his trembling shoulder made the boy kneel. He ran his fingers through the fine blond hair on the bent head before him, tasting the lad's unfamiliar desires, taking them as his, understanding the urgency, if not the why, of the boy's needs.

He opened his trousers, lifted the boy's chin. He stared into his frightened, girlish eyes, soothed him with a touch of his fingers on his cheek. The boy smiled, nervously, hopefully, then leaned toward him. He shivered at the first tentative touch of the boy's warm, rosy lips. His flesh filled, stiffened, becoming something real again as the boy began gratefully to suck him. He felt the boy's twisted love being released, and it made him happy he was able to fulfill at last the boy's wish, a tightly coiled desire so lonely and so yet so compelling that often in despair, the lad had longed for the courage to commit the ultimate sin of suicide.

He stopped him when it was time and pointed to the tree he had picked out.

The boy willingly pressed his face and body against the rough bark while he wound around him the rope he had brought. Then, his blood boiling, taking the boy's excited anticipation as his own, he began using the harness strap he had also taken from the barn.

It was clear in the boy's mind so he knew just how hard and where to strike. He beat him just as the boy's father beat him almost every day, but he did it with love instead of hate, with care instead of anger, with compassion instead of fear, because these were what the boy needed.

Then, when the boy's buttocks were sufficiently warmed and reddened, he worked his hard wet cock against the boy's wrinkled rose. Again he took as his own the boy's yearning, giving it back to him, to first soothe his fear, then to share with his the delightful slow hot sliding. When the young boy's small hard cock began to jerk in release against the tree, he bent the boy's head back and to the side. He kissed the boy's lips tenderly for a moment, just as the boy had imagined. Their mouths became eager, hungry for each other, and just as he began to ejaculate deep into the boy's bowels, he sucked the boy's life inside him.

Afterward, filled with a power he never knew existed, he carried the boy's body easily as he walked deeper into the woods. He could see each leaf on every tree, the vibrant colors of each petal of every flower. The sky was brighter and more vividly blue than it had ever been. Everything around him seemed to vibrate with life, and it was all the same life in different forms and guises. Everything seemed to make sense now, although it was not a sense he could have explained to anyone.

He found the clearing where he had seen the red-haired woman, although the cottage and the garden were not there as he had known they would not be.

He laid the boy down in the sun-warmed grass, watched the bent green blades spring up slowly, one-by-one, as the body faded, disappeared.

Then he walked off deeper and farther into the woods and was never heard from again.

"It's a wonderful story. Sad, but wonderful."

Her eyes are shining. I kiss her forehead. She blinks and the tears run down her cheeks.

"I'm glad you liked it."

"Except they didn't burn witches in America, you know. At least not most of them. They were hanged, or crushed under wooden pallets piled up with stones."

"Yes, I know. But it's much more dramatic to have her disappear in a puff of smoke."

"But otherwise it's true, isn't it."

"Yes. At least I think it is. I suppose some of the other details are made up, but the essence is true. At least I think so. It was so long ago."

"Has it been long enough?"

"Yes."

"You're sure?"

"Yes."

"Then, it's time."

She slips down on the bed and again her mouth takes me in. She sucks me gently, as if she were afraid I would break. Her tenderness and her concern make me grow hard that much more quickly.

"I'm sorry if I'm not doing it right," she says. "I'm just beginning."

"I know. Beginnings are the hardest. Endings are much easier."

"I don't want to hurt you."

"Don't worry, you're doing it just right."

She begins moving her hand on me then, sucking harder. I should have known all along. It was obvious, but it's so seductive believing our own illusions.

She stops, knowing I am close. "Are you ready?" she asks.

"Yes."

She does it quickly then. In moments I feel it begin. It is glorious! An orgasm to end all orgasms. An orgasm that is the beginning of everything, and at last I understand—and with this ultimate gift of purpose she makes me happy at last. She is beginning her new life as I had begun mine, but with purpose, with compassion, with comprehension. She knows that one day she will give all the lives I've taken and all the lives she has yet to take to another, and that they will be passed on to yet another and yet another so that someday one of us will become that which encompasses all lives, the God that all of us were always meant to be.

Afterword

This is the third volume of erotic vampire stories I have edited, and my friends are beginning to wonder whether there isn't something more to my nocturnal work habits than the eccentricities of a creative mind. Let them wonder—that is one activity I encourage wholeheartedly. Let us let our imaginations run wild, wondering just what is going on in the dark. It is that kind of mental activity that leads to this kind of book, a book about the mysteries of sex, a book about fear of the unknown, a book about sinful pleasures and pleasureful sins both real and imaginary.

In real life I am not a vampire, I am an erotic activist. When I stay up late into the night, I am not feeding my carnal hungers (usually), but typing away at essays and stories made to open people's eyes to the erotic world around them. I am producing newsletters and preparing lectures. When I edit, I am nurturing the fantasies of other creative minds, refining them, honing them. We have worked those late hours to bring this book to you, and already we are at work on the fourth volume, *A Taste of Midnight*. And so, until then, I bid you adieu, dear reader. Read well and be well.

Cecilia Tan
October 1997

The Beast Within
Erotic Tales
of Werewolves

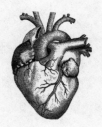

Editor's Note

When I told some people that I was editing two anthologies of erotic fiction, one on vampires, and one on werewolves/wolves, their reaction was "Well, I can understand *vampires*, but why werewolves?" Silly people. I could have launched into a high-sounding diatribe about the powers of lust and our latent savage side. You know. "The werewolf mirrors our own animalistic alter-ego, the creature of the night we become when we are consumed with sensual passions, the transformation that is worked on even the most civilized of humans by sexual lust." Or some nice theory about the parallels between seduction or pursuit of a mate and the hunt, predation. Or even a flip comment about fur fetishes, doggie-style, and so so...

But in the end, of course, these stories say all that and more, and in a much more eloquent and compelling manner. So I just told those people "Wait and see the book!"

Here it is. May you enjoy it to the fullest.

~Cecilia Tan
October 1994

The Spirit That Denies

Jay Michaelson

Using one claw as a toothpick, I worked a bit of gristle loose from between my teeth, flicked it casually skyward, down, down, to land on the roof of somebody's car several stories below.

Lifting my legs I reclined across the ledge, one arm behind my head as a pillow, the other across my chest. I held my right hand in front of my face, its outline blurred by fur as I framed it against the pallid moon. I rubbed my thumb and index finger together, savoring the touch of the leathery footpad flesh that covered my palm and fingers, so different from the softer, fur-covered skin on the back of my hand.

Doing this was my way of recalling the promise I made to myself so long ago; the fleshly oath of my twentieth year. To look upon my Changed flesh each time with reverence and awe; to never let the wonder diminish, as if each time were the first. I turned my hand over in my view, noting the

creases, the way the flesh came together, the super-
position of primate and canine. The thick,
dark-brown hair on the back of my hand/paw, the
skin on my palm leather—tough yet almost as sensitive as it was when I was human. My fascination
extended itself to the tips of my fingers, each ter-
minated by a functional claw, a vulgar, fleshless
extension of the bone. Quite unlike the vestigial
nails I wore in my human guise.

My vision continued tracing its path up my
body; from the tips of my fingers, down my wrist
and the length of my shaggy forearm, past the knob
of my olecranon process, up the bicep, my gaze
halted at last, unable to go past the shoulder, to
take in its own eyes, its own face. I had never broken my promise, despite the passage of the better
part of two centuries. All things considered, I had
come to be comfortable in this flesh, even happy,
after a fashion. I was functional, at least; many
humans could hardly boast the same. On top of
that, I was still enamored of the ridiculous notion
that if I ever broke my promise my esteem would
perish, my body following suit.

I reclined my head against the brick ledge, my
gaze encompassing the rest of the sky and moon.
My hand now scratched idly at my chest. Observing the solemn moon, I sighed, my sigh becoming
a prayer against my wishes. Nonakris! Mother

Night, Thou Nine-Fold Goddess! Mate and Body of Lykaon!

I searched the visible fraction of Her face, finding nought but grey splotches to mar the gleaming white. No answer except the one She always gave; a sullen muteness, Her voice either unwilling or unable to reach me. Pity. I sighed, this time letting it remain a sigh. Thank God the Feast was nearing.

Thinking of the Feast drew my dissolute mind back to Samantha. Thinking of Samantha brought me back to the kill fifty minutes previous. She had looked so *very* much like Sam; her hair long and brown, her height the same...

And there the resemblance ended. The anonymous girl I had killed and eaten in Georgetown was not going to the next Feast, or anywhere else besides the grave.

Nor did she love me.

I skirted around that thought like a scavenger, ashamed of my timidity but unable to confront the feelings it brought up within me. Fear prevents one from joining the fray of life, a distant voice echoed inside me; leaving only carrion while the brave carry off the choicest meats. I was no less ashamed to recall that it was I who originally said that, in defense of my own boldness. It was no less painful for the fact that I who once held that attitude now found myself on the opposite side of it.

On that last, unpleasant note I rose and howled. A longer, less delirious howl than the one I uttered after feeding this evening, but certainly one to stir the dreams of anyone boring enough to be sleeping in Washington, D.C. on a Saturday night.

I staggered after I was done, my senses dulled by drowsiness and blood-euphoria. I couldn't help but recall the taste of blood, the look in her eyes as I leapt upon her...And Sam. I couldn't help but think of Sam as I took the girl's life.

But the girl didn't love me.

"What's-your-problem-Jack?" I growled to myself, my vocal chords emitting harsh sounds that only I could recognize as speech. I know what your problem is, asshole, I said to myself. You're stuck with a girl who wants what you've got, and you're not sure about how to give it to her. I wrinkled my nose with the possibly obscene implications of that phrase. I gripped the edge of the building, clenching my fist hard enough for my claws to score the brick. "What-my-problem-is," I said out loud to none but myself. "is-that-I-am-an-emotional-cripple." I exhaled sharply as the realization hit me that what I had said was true. Watching my cloud of breath dissolve, I felt a sickly twinge in the pit of my gut. What I had said was true.

It took a person with my unique delusion of self-adjustment to complicate things this badly.

Granted, the situation wasn't simplicity itself, but it was one which other members of the Family had dealt with before with more aplomb than I. I catch a woman following me and instead of begging me not to kill her she begs to join the Family. Amidst my snorts of derision she assures me that she's not only got what it takes, but knows more than I realize, and after a quick dose of personal fright, I discover she does know more than any human ever could about us, about me. Besides the patent oddity of the situation it wasn't impossible. Bizarre, yes; but not much stranger than other things that happen within the course of my daily life. I would like to say that the problem resides in my inexperience at guiding someone into the worship of Lykaean Zeus, but before I could give tongue to that lie it turned sour in my mouth. I banged my fist against the ledge. The problem wasn't within the situation; the fault lay with me. Any other viewpoint was self-delusion.

All I have to do is take her to the Feast. Turn her loose. If she lives, great; if she dies, tough.

And then I fucked it up by getting involved.

Heart of stone. Yeah.

I knew I was whining. Up until now all had gone well, barring a few minor disagreements with Human society. Our kind are used to taking a few shells now and then, so that doesn't count. So far,

nothing had disrupted my life in any serious fashion. Then I paused thirty seconds too long before
offing a potential threat. A mistake anyone could
have made. I shifted uncomfortably. I was bitching
about nothing; things are always a sharper pain in
the ass then you're in the middle of them. Emotional overkill. Things would look different at some
future point. Mañana, maybe.

"Enough!" I stretched, unkinked my muscles.
The time I had promised myself to straighten out
my head was being hopelessly frittered. I had re-
tired to this rooftop with some notion of sorting
out my emotions, and that just wasn't happening.
I looked out over the horizon, the low buildings of
Adams-Morgan dwarfed by the government buildings and highrises as my gaze moved towards the
center of the city. I could see lights, cars, people
walking, talking, doing things that ranked high in
importance in their personal worlds; worlds I
would never know. I wondered what time it was,
guessed between two and three in the ayem. I
couldn't honestly say I was still hungry, and since
I was achieving nothing else I might as well head
home. Having arrived at this conclusion I was still
unable to make myself stand up and leave the rooftop. I felt the stirrings of something inside me but
felt entirely powerless to either diagnose or act
upon it.

I knew it was only a short trek across northern D.C., over Stanton Park and back home. All the same I just stood there, hypnotized by the night, the movements across the horizon blending, melding into each other, each individual motion indistinguishable from the items around it, giving the impression that the city itself was seething, was alive. A queer sight, one that gave rise to indescribable feelings. Difficult to express; impossible to ignore.

After wasting more time I shifted on the ledge, dangling my legs and keeping my ears peeled for helicopters.

I've always stayed aware of growing developments in human technology, but I had to admit that the survival value of keeping informed was becoming more pronounced as time passed. It was no longer merely a matter of escaping detection traveling by rooftop, but also a cumulatively losing bet with forensics. What Man won't come up with next. I was still adapting to the idea of Infrared Sights and mercy guns. I used to have bizarre dreams where one day I would be captured by these modern creatures who would lock me in a cage of glass and steel and tell me I was merely a lunatic, a depraved man who thought he was a wolf. Nothing more than a deluded cannibal. But those were only dreams, and the stark reality of feeling my bones warp and shift beneath my flesh as I Changed, the taste of hot blood in my mouth, now *that* was real. Thank God.

I scratched my side, discovering a clot of gore I had missed. I flicked it out to the street, yet another gift for the populace at large.

I stood again, stretched, yawned. I watched the moon casually, just to see what She would do. When She failed to perform tricks for my amusement I turned my attention back to the shimmering horizon. I shrugged. Face it, Jack. Might as well head on home—

Unbidden, a picture of Samantha leapt to mind. I could see her curled up on the guest-room bed in my house, maybe the couch. Her bed—

That hit me.

Her bed.

I hadn't thought about it much until now, but her abandoned apartment was still in the same place I had left it, full of things she had left behind. A quick peek might offer some useful clues. I had been there once, the night when I caught her following me. I had broken in after she had gone to sleep and confronted her; since my main concern at the time was to determine her threat status, I hadn't the time to ransack the place proper, and once she conveyed her good intentions I shuttled her immediately off to my house, keeping her incommunicado to minimize the possibility of damage to my own precarious position in society, should she prove to be a Trojan Horse. After a couple of weeks of observation I had concluded that Achilles had kept his ants and scrap wood to himself, so I hadn't devoted any thought to her abandoned flat. Now, my mind was presenting me with an opportunity to learn more about her, from a different angle. The fact that one could interpret the action as nothing more than crude voyeurism wasn't something my brain presented in the argument. My foremost intent was to gather intelligence, not prurience.

Holding that thought clearly before me like a crucifix to keep recriminations at bay, I embarked upon my journey with the comforting sense of having resolved a course of action. I stood and stretched, ready to go.

With a glance down the alleys on either side of the building I set out northward, crossing to the next roof while mentally plotting my course. Though I didn't know Takoma Park as well as the Dee of Cee, I didn't anticipate any difficulties. Off to Tacky Park I was, and glad to be about it.

About half-an-hour and seven miles later, I found myself in the same neighborhood I had tailed her to that first night. I scrambled across what I knew to be the correct building and from there it was the work of a minute to climb onto what my nose assured me was her third-floor porch. The window was fortuitously unlocked, and in I went.

Her flat was as I remembered it. I walked quietly for the benefit of the neighbors below, padding across the carpet and into her living room. The rooms were permeated with her smell, and I took a strange comfort in this. I scanned the walls, noting the position of each painting and print. In addition to the hellishly surreal Ramon Santiago (which I had noticed before) and the Durer print of a Major Arcana (which I had not) there were also several framed prints that I was completely unfamiliar with. One was of a woman brandishing a sword and seated on a huge bird in flight, another was a man fighting off horrid-looking creatures from a buxom, naked woman chained to a rock. Hmmm.

After surveying the apartment from the living room, I sat in an overstuffed leather chair that seemed centrally placed. It was very comfortable, its padded armrests at precisely the angle conducive to sitting sideways, throwing ones legs over one armrest while leaning back against the other; the perfect position for loafing, in my opinion.

It was several seconds before I realized I was panting. I got up and checked the thermostat,

which registered seventy-two. Must have been the
quick jog over, I thought, and sat back down in the
chair, only to be suffused by another wave of heat.
The chair...

I stood up and studied it carefully. Just an old
leather chair, scuffed and dilapidated. Soft, brown
leather, the frame supported on four thick, wooden
posts. I sat back in it, tried to think into it. Yes...

This was *her* chair. I could feel her sitting here,
viewing her living room and treasured bookshelves;
I could feel her thinking in it, deciding what to do
about something at work, how to deal with a
friend's problem, what to tell her parents when she
saw them next weekend. Or what to tell older werewolves to gull their sensibilities, a nastier part of
my mind added.

But wait: Did I really believe that? It was an attitude that it would be worthwhile to confront
immediately. In summary, what did I know about
Miss Samantha Wingate? She was twenty-six, did
something with computers for a living, was very
interested in the occult and claimed that she had
been guided to me by performing ritual work. She
presented me with intimate information about
myself and my packmates that she couldn't have
obtained in any rational, human fashion, then
vouchsafed herself into my care and power without
a second thought; thirdly, she reacted favorably

when I tested her strength of mind by Changing in front of her. All of this added up to mean something it would take lots of data to contradict; so far, nothing was forthcoming that did. Thus, my cynical statements and overall pissiness were not only undeserved by her but maladaptive on my part.

Having thought my way through that with relative ease, I was now confronted with problems of a more personal nature. Feelings surged forth, percolating through the big fishbowl at the top of my spine, each jeering and cavorting, each saying something different about my internal state of affairs. Did I love her? Did she really love me? What if she died at the Feast? That last though bore with it a rising panic, and I was suddenly struck with the urge to cry. Not knowing whether it was due to the thoughts at hand or self-pity, I stifled it, wresting my concentration back to the matters at hand. I reminded myself that I was here to gather intelligence. Sitting in her chair, I tried to think myself into it, feel her thoughts, her emotions, her ambitions. Who says she was the only psychic in the house?

I settled deeper into her chair and felt the leather, rubbing my furry hide against its smooth surface. I could smell her flesh strongly on the leather, and the thought came to me that she had often sat in the chair naked. I leapt up and looked at it closely. Sure enough, I could see where her sweat and bodily oils had permeated past the curing, darkening the leather in the places of greatest contact. I sat back down and inhaled deeply, my arousal heightened just by the thought of sitting in her chair. I was unsurprised to feel the beginning of an erection.

I sat only a few minutes more, not wishing to allow myself such pleasure; I was here for information, or so I kept telling myself. I got up and strode across the living room, bypassing the bathroom as a source of odors that would only work further distractions, finally settling on her bookshelves as another good place to investigate.

I closed my eyes and pulled a book from the shelf at random, hoping that blind chance could act as the foundation for latent psychism. I opened my eyes to find I held a paperback copy of Martin Gardner's *Fads and Fallacies*. Bah! Serves me right! I stuck it back in its place and employed the more reliable method of reading the titles on the spines. I wondered which books were her favorites. Amidst the more standard books I saw several by Mishima, along with a copy of Genet's *Funeral Rites*. What was the connection? Homosexuality? World War Two?

Near the top of the case on the right was her collection of books by Crowley and other less distinguished authors. On the identical shelf of the left-hand bookcase was a compendious collection of books on mathematics and physics, including Euclid's *Elements*. Beneath those were several texts on calculus, computer functions, transfinite sets, and Von Neumann's book on *Game Theory*.

After removing a few and putting them back I turned around and realized somewhat distractedly that the doorway facing me led to her bedroom. Without pausing to think, I entered.

I came to her bed, knelt, stretching one hand out, my claws dimpling the comforter. I could see the blinds drawn over the large window, smaller bookcases lining the walls. The part of my brain connected to the olfactory sense was screaming all sorts of things at me. Arousal was one of them. For the first time I felt a pang of guilt at my senseless invasion of her apartment, her bedroom especially. What was I doing here? What had I hoped to find, to see? All the reasons I had provided myself with moments before seemed to have evaporated, dissipated as self-deception does, when exposed. I felt ashamed, but even more ashamed that despite my self-realization I wasn't going to leave, yet. I wondered if Samantha was sleeping, or if she somehow knew what I was doing. Probably.

I opened her closet, my nose twitching excitedly as an aroma of perfume, sweat, soap and a thousand

other things wafted out, enveloping me in a cloud
of olfactory bliss. Since most of the clothing she had
taken with her when I spirited her away was casual,
I was unsurprised to see an array of work and dress
clothes in the walk-in. Her shoe tree was covered
with everything from high-heels to high-tops. I saw
a pair of hiking boots in the corner, a trace of mud
around the rims of the soles. I picked them up,
sniffed them. These had seen, among other places,
the sides of Sugarloaf mountain.

I nosed at her clothes, trying to decide which
item she had worn last. I settled on a pretty, red silk
blouse near the center of the left hand rack, the
trace odors less faint than the rest. I pulled it from
the hanger and retreated to the bed. I sat down and
held it in my hand for a few moments, gathering
courage.

I put it to my nose and inhaled deeply. Perfume.
Sweat. Flesh. The tiniest remnant of cigarette smoke
from her office. I could smell her, taste her, my
mouth open as I inhaled deeply. My head swam, and
I recalled something about pheromones from an old
biology text. I breathed again. And again. I could
taste her, and I felt my desire growing.

I removed the wadded fabric from my nose
when I felt the tip of my erection cresting my stomach. I held the blouse away from me, regarding it
with mingled horror and desire. The thought of her,

coupled with the olfactory phantoms summoned... Ah! I lay back on the bed and allowed myself to be carried away with my visions.

First I could see her at work, talking with others, at lunch with friends, coming home and eating dinner. I saw her take her clothes off and change into casual wear, or nothing at all. I could imagine her parading naked through the solitude of her flat. I had visions of her naked body beneath mine, my mouth tasting her nipple. Both my mouth and hands were those of a man—

I realized with a start that I had stuck my nose back into the wadded handful of fabric. I took my snout from the blouse and tossed it aside, feeling both embarrassed and ashamed. It landed on the floor at such an angle that I could see the glinting reflection of a smear of mucus from my nose. My dog nose. I felt another pang of guilt for soiling her clothes, and a wave of something I could not give name to, now or ever. The tip of my penis protruded moistly from its sheath, and amidst my self-recriminations for my sordid behavior, I couldn't deny the taut excitement that lay coiled within me. I rose, knowing that the best way to get my mind off it was to leave.

I didn't dare touch her underwear drawer.

I took quickly to the roof, having barely enough presence of mind to close the window on my way out. I sat on the roof and sniffed at the cool night air, the moon high above, looking down upon me without pity.

I stood, my erection finally diminished, the inside of the protective sheath overly slick with fluid, a tiny, clear drop smearing the fur on my stomach. I wiped it off with my hand, and with a final glance at the moon I started back to my house.

As we left 495 for I-270 towards Frederick, I noticed that Samantha was unusually quiet. Shifting into fourth, I skipped lanes.

"How are you feeling?" I asked. She smiled nervously.

"Okay. Kind of, jittery," She brushed an errant lock of reddish-brown hair from her eyes. "Like butterflies." I smiled.

"This is nothing."

"I know."

"The Feast is more," I groped for the words, glancing quickly in the rearview mirror as I cut sharply into the left lane, accelerated, "—intense. *Much* more intense. This is just a, preview." She nodded, settled deeper into her seat.

I decided the best way to start was with an animal. While a human would have been better, the possibility of disease was an active concern; Sam lacked my immunity to the ills of man and beast. Of course, even with animals there was risk, but since the nastiest parasites were either organ- or host-specific, she could avoid the worst by sticking to the flesh and blood. Hydatid tapeworms in the lungs, flukes in the liver and intestine, et cetera.

We sped up 270 until we came to a place I deemed suitable, several miles up the Potomac, near Clarksburg. I knew this was a good area for herbivores.

I parked the car and stepped out, sniffing the air. I could smell life. Good.

I pulled the car back onto the grass and covered it with some fallen branches, a nearby pine tree donating some fresh ones. I removed the license plates and threw them in the backseat. I locked up and backed off, looking at it from a distance.

"Nobody'll notice that." I turned to Sam.

"Are you warm enough?" She nodded, her coat pulled tight about her shoulders, her hands in her pockets.

"Uh-huh," she said brightly, smiling despite her nervousness. "it's not that cold out."

"Not to me," I snorted. "but I didn't know *you* liked it in the low fifties."

"It's not that cold out," she said with more conviction.

We headed deeper into the forest and I kept sniffing. After walking about twenty minutes we came to a clearing that was remote enough for our purpose. I undressed, folding my clothes in a neat pile.

"Do you have any serious dental work? Bridges? Caps?" She looked surprised by the mundanity of the question.

"Uh— No, not at all. Just some fillings." She opened her mouth for my inspection. I dismissed it with a wave.

"You'll want to take off your coat for this," I said, and she looked forlorn. "But not until I get back. There's no point to freezing you now. Do you meditate?"

"Of course," she said in a voice that said I was silly for asking.

"Then start doing so now. I'm not entirely sure how to go about this. You're going to the Feast in less than a month, and this is to help prepare you. Here's what I want you to do:" I approached her, my face and hers almost meeting. "Think about me. Concentrate on what it means to be a wolf." I tapped my temple. "Try to get inside my head." She stared at me intently, her eyes following me carefully. I could already taste blood, and running my hand over the back of my forearm yielded a greasy feel; the pores were generating oil, starting to Change. "I'm going to Change now. Watch."

I dropped to my knees, my body shifting and stretching. I groaned sharply, my oily flesh sprouting hair, my body itching terribly over every inch of skin. I opened my mouth in agony, drooling inadvertently, my saliva lit with streaks of blood as my teeth reformed, shifted within my skull, pushed out, grew longer. Ahhhhhhh! The Pain! The Torture! My very bones stretching, my frightened flesh screaming with delight. As my skull made ominous pops and cracks, the amplified sounds like explosions in my head, I reflected upon what a masochist I must be to enjoy this, to actually welcome the Change. But I did, as do we all. Despite or perhaps because of the pain it was a tremendous relief to shift back into full form, my true form! Ah, God! Much like the pain of teething, I suppose. A stinging ache, a scrape of flesh and blood, but what relief after! Like the sweetest pain, an aching delight...

Like slipping into a warm bath at the end of a hard day. Only my bath is....full of needles...

I writhed on the ground, my agonized flesh twitching spastically across my doubled frame. My arms and legs changed proportion, the femurs warping within their muscular insertions and origins, grating noisily. I felt like a living marionette, my strings pulled by the harshest hand biology had to offer.

After several minutes of twitching and twisting beneath the assaults of my renegade physiology, I was complete. The death of the man, the Re-Birth of the Wolf. I got unsteadily to my feet, fresh strength coursing through my veins along with a gnawing ache in my stomach, the call of hunger. I stood on all fours, complete, a whole being once again, no longer trapped in that ridiculously limited human frame, nor within my half-man-half-wolf shape. After stretching happily, the fresh cartilage within my spine adamantly refusing to pop, I fell back on my haunches and tossed my head skyward, uttering a joyous howl, my long, white teeth feeling fresh and new, the otherwise pristine enamel streaked with blood. I turned to regard Samantha. I padded closer to her, my lips curved back in the only smile I could make, a carnivorous grin.

"What-do-you-think?" I growled, the words harsh and barely English. It was difficult to maintain human vocal chords within a canine body, and the strain made my throat raw. I could see the sun racing to meet the horizon over Sam's shoulder. A pity. I loved to hunt in the full daylight.

"You are beautiful," she said, her voice soft and awed. She put her hand out to touch my shoulder, her fingers brushing my fur. She looked as though she were about to start crying the way she did the first time I Changed for her. "This is—" she broke off, swallowed hard, started again. "This is too good to be real." I panted at her, my breath still invisible in the cool air.

"But–it–is," I growled. "I–go–now." I said, my throat tiring. Withholding any select organ from change was very difficult to maintain, like balancing precariously on a fence; the first time your attention wanes you find yourself on the ground, a few bruises wiser. I headed into the forest.

"Jack?" she called. I glanced back. "Good luck,"

The first deer I caught was a stag; I devoured him, tearing his throat out and then making short work of the rest. I had the feeling of being under a deadline, because I wanted to finish my meal and catch a deer for Samantha. Maybe that was what was spoiling my normally buoyant mood.

Whatever it was, it didn't last long. After feeding on the stag, I felt the rush of strength and bliss along with the temporary abatement of appetite; satiated, I continued to sniff the wind and follow tracks.

I found another deer soon after. I would have liked to herd her back to the grove, but to do that I needed at least one partner, preferably two. The only way of getting her back alive was to shift to biped, knock her unconscious and carry her back to Sam slung over my shoulders. Despite the waste of time I couldn't see any other way.

I shifted, moving towards her odor when I was done. After sizing up the terrain I dashed towards the doe and she bounded away with almost equal speed, her leaps delicate and precise. I caught her exactly twenty-five feet from where I spotted her, tackling her and clopping her on the head just hard enough to knock her out without killing her.

Shouldering the limp form, I began my jog back to the grove. As I ran I could feel the pulsebeat of her heart warming me between my shoulder blades.

I reentered the clearing gripping the now-conscious and struggling doe by the legs. I strode forward, knowing by smell that no one was there except Samantha. Good thing, too. Sam would have had a hell of a time explaining what she was doing in a grove meditating next to a pile of clothing. Heh.

Despite my innate silence she looked up, her eyes widening as I approached. I knelt down and placed the doe before her on the ground.

"Eat," I said, shifting my vocal chords enough to talk. "You-must-kill-her. With-your-teeth." Sam didn't look at me as she took off her coat. She threw it aside and knelt before the doe, who by this time had redoubled her efforts at freedom. To no avail; my hands remained clamped on her legs, two in each hand. Samantha crouched down next to me, looking to me for guidance. I turned to face her.

"You-must... relish-the-taste-of-blood-and-meat... to-join-Family-you-must-learn. Feed!" I choked out, my voice hoarse. She was listening to me, her attentions torn between the squirming doe and myself. "None of-the-sensations-that-accompany-this-life," I thumped my chest. "will be-buffered. If-you-desire-it-then-proceed." I couldn't bear to tell her, couldn't bear to think that if she failed this test, tradition dictated that I should kill her.

She took her brown eyes from my blue ones, glanced at the doe. Then, without a word, she bent her head to the doe's struggling neck. While I pressed my elbow against the flailing head to hold it down, Samantha placed her open mouth on the doe's flesh, the thick fur insufficient armor against Sam's teeth. As I watched, my heart rejoicing, the doe gave a shrill cry and blood welled up around Sam's mouth, flowing down the side of the deer's neck. Even though Sam wasn't biting in the correct place to cause death, I hadn't corrected her because it would be best if this were messy, if it lacked precision. I wanted her to see the worst side; to feel the grueling labour, not the pleasant sensation of a well-dispatched kill. It was seldom a single act that could be done quickly, anyway; in real life, it was work. A battle between the intensity of your hunger and the will-to-live of the other creature.

After she had taken a bite of the flesh and managed
to work it loose with her teeth she swallowed it,
looking at me with pride.

"Right-here," I growled, indicating it with a
claw, "is-where-life flows. Here-you-must-bite." I
guided her mouth by hand and she bit, her eagerness apparent. The deer let out a terrified shriek
and Sam chewed with increasing viciousness, digging her teeth in, moving her head back and forth
in the correct rending fashion.

As the blood welled forth in vigorous spurts,
Sam tore harder, biting savagely at the resistant tissue. She lifted her face to me, her chin and teeth
streaked with blood, her cheeks smeared with the
deer's moistness, and I realized she was reaching
the tough muscle that enshrouded the deer's major
cables. Soon after that she would be hitting the car-
tilaginous parts of the throat and trachea, and
would have more difficulties owing to the general-
ized nature of her teeth.

While I watched she continued taking small
bites from the doe's neck, the blood welling out in
crimson brilliance and pouring onto the ground.
The doe squealed and blood gushed, and I knew
that unless I helped her we were going to lose that
most delicate pearl of great price, the special
moment when the doe crossed between life and
death. I pulled her head up and tugged the doe's

slackening form closer to me so that we could both partake of her throat. Blood was pumping in weakening surges from the poorly inflicted wounds, the deer's thrombin making itself useful.

"Bite-with-me," I said, pulling her head next to mine on the doe's neck. I could feel her gory cheek pressed against my lips as I sank my teeth into the tender flesh, tasting the deer's death as I pierced her jugular and left carotid. I tasted hot surges of salt iron as I drew my razor teeth through her dying flesh. I could feel Samantha's mouth next to mine, drinking the blood as I raked my teeth away, rending the doe still further, leaving her neck a pulped mess that was more accessible to Sam's small, primate mouth. It was difficult to do, because I could feel the joy of the doe's life gushing out, forcing its way through my nerves, but I wanted Samantha to have it; it was for her. This was her first time.

I withdrew, my mouth ripe with the taste of life, and watched Sam dig her mouth deeper into the deer. The doe's thrashing was weakening enough that I no longer had to hold her legs as Sam tore the remnants of life from her. I watched as she fed, her movements less shaky, her hunger abating. I knew without a doubt that she was of the blood.

Feeling my own hunger rising again, I began tearing at the ribcage with my hands, breaking the bones and stripping the inner meats when Samantha tried to join me.

"No. You-eat-only-the-neck." Without a word she moved back to the neck and continued feeding there.

Together we made short work of the doe, Sam eating her flesh while I devoured everything else. After another few minutes almost nothing remained but the bones.

When we were done I sat back gnawing a femur, satiated. This was the second time I had fed in under an hour. I felt the onset of a drowsy euphoria, my adrenalin pump having dissipated. With a flex of my humanoid hands I broke the bone in half and chewed the marrow thus exposed. I felt good.

Samantha crawled to me, her eyes lit with the euphoria that comes from the direct assimilation of another's life; the joy in partaking of the Sacrament of Flesh, that we of the Family feel after feeding. I reached forward to put a hand on her shoulder. She moved into my arms, the lower half of her face covered with blood, her teeth reddened pearls mounted in ruby gums.

"You-are-of-the-blood," I said, blood singing in my veins. "You will-do-well-at-the-Feast." She looked into my eyes with a feverish intensity, her gaze sighting down my snout and ending in my brain. Then, much to my surprise, she put her mouth to mine and kissed me.

I was both surprised and dizzy; I wanted to back away, to ask why, to request an explanation. Instead I sat there and held her, staring at her with open shock.

She reached up and gripped my head with both hands, her fingers entwining in my fur, pulling my mouth closer. She kissed me again, with more passion this time, biting my lower lip, her tongue touching mine. Even in my distraction I couldn't fail to notice that the wildly disparate design of our mouths presented difficulties. She continued despite the obvious difference of the analogous structures, her determined amorousness brooking no dissension, even from Mother Nature.

She nibbled at my lower lip, then lifted her head and kissed me on the nose, the face, the snout. With a soft groan I met her tongue with mine, gripping her tighter about the waist and licking at her mouth, my own passion growing. She squirmed in my lap as my arousal became more evident. I could smell her sharp pungency and knew that the odor of her sex would enslave me if I smelled it much longer. I had a brief vision of a pack of baying wolves, the screams of the others around me, firelight, blood...She was still kissing me, her hands exploring my body, caressing my shoulders and sides, my arms and neck. I was fearful of what was happening but no longer possessed the strength to push her away. She had removed her shirt at some point, and I groaned as I felt her half-naked body pressing tightly against my furred chest, her breasts soft and arousing. I tried to stand up, knowing I could take no more.

"Oh-God-no," I groaned. "no..." She stopped, taking her mouth from mine and regarding me.

"What's the matter, Jack?" she said, her voice heady with revealed desires. I looked at her with panic bordering on fear, my heart pounding. She reached up and stroked my head, her touch warm and soothing.

"I—We—can't," was all I could say. She kept stroking my forehead, her touch gentle. She looked at me, waited for me to go on. "You-don't-know," I finished in a weak and tremulous voice. She perked up.

"Don't know what, Jack? What don't I know?" She said with surprising vigor. I looked at her with amazement.

"Our-bodies," I managed to choke out. Much to my horror, she gave me a feral smile, stuck her tongue out and touched the tip of my nose. I groaned, moved to even further distraction by her casual manner.

"Is *that* what's bothering you?" She said in gentle amazement. "The difference in our bodies? Don't worry!" She reassured me. I shook my head.

"You-don't-understand," I reaffirmed. "I-
can't—" I paused, my tongue thick in my mouth. I
swallowed hard. "I-can't-do-it-any-other way.
Than-in-the-body-of-a-wolf. I-can't-turn-human-
now. I-can't-even hold-this-form-much-longer." I
said, feeling ashamed, my gruff voice pathetic in my
own ears. She smiled.

"What's so wrong with doing it like this?" She
asked, her voice gentle but distracting. I groaned as
she ground her pelvis against me, her sex rubbing
the furry sheath that housed my penis, her motion
exciting me beyond endurance. I could feel her
moisture working into my fur.

"Canine-physiology," was all I could say, my
voice hoarse, my throat raw.

"Ohhh," she said in a soft voice. "I know what's
bothering you. My silly Jack," she continued stroking my forehead. "You're embarrassed, aren't you?"
I couldn't answer. She kissed me again on the nose.

"You think I don't know about Canine Physiology?" She said, putting emphasis on the last two
words. "Don't know what? You mean I don't know
how it is that you fuck? You mean I don't know that
after you penetrate me the base of your penis," she
grabbed my sheath, her fingers enfolding it. I
groaned, and my erection sprang forth into her
grasp. "will swell once it's inside me until it's sooo
big you won't be able to remove it until you're

done? Done—" her voice became huskier, "—Done fucking me? You think I don't know that after it's," she paused, licking her lips. "fully swollen, you'll turn about and fuck me from behind, facing away from me, our rear ends stuck together like two dogs in—" I howled to silence her. She stopped. I gave a disconsolate groan, my emotions impossible to assess, but including the acute desire to vanish into the ground. My feelings alternating between elation and horror, I wondered if turning to vapor and dissipating in the evening air was too much to ask.

"I-love-you," I growled, only realizing it was my voice as I said it. I felt very strange. With a tender expression she put her hand on my neck and kissed me on the mouth.

"I love you , too," she said and put her mouth to my ear.

"It's not that I know and it doesn't bother me; it's that I know," she nipped the lower part of my ear. "and I want to. I really want to."

I don't remember the rest as clearly as I'd like to. I gave in with a groan and attacked her, licking her face and neck. Not the best way to show my passion, I suppose, but that's what I could do. She resumed her inflammatory motions against me, her legs straddling my waist, her hands working their way around my body.

"Jack?" she asked, her voice tentative. I grunted in response.

"You're hurting me," she said, grabbing my wrists.

"Sorry," I grunted, loosening my grip. I hadn't meant to squeeze her so tightly. She smiled to show me it was all right, and continued moving atop me.

I pushed her down to the ground and crawled atop her. I was Changing as I did so, unable to muster the concentration necessary to hold myself between forms. She noticed, and said:

"It's okay, Jack. It really is," and I finished Changing, her hands playing over my shifting body.

She lay on the ground, watching me as I regained my true shape. I padded over her, my head near hers, and she kissed me again. I whined and retreated until my head was near her crotch. She had removed her jeans while I Changed, and I put my paw to her panties and pulled them down. She spread her legs farther apart and gasped, our mutual anticipation leaving our perceptions flushed, our combined desires almost palpable.

Without further ado I lowered my head to her crotch and gave it the same treatment I had given her face and neck, snuffling at her sex. Her flesh tasted sweet, the tang of her vagina different from but reminiscent of her whole body, her life. She shuddered and moaned as I licked and nipped at her flesh. I looked up at her, stopping to see her reaction.

"Oh God," She panted. "Go on!"

I lowered my head back to her body, planting my forepaws on either side of her. I lapped at her, my big, flat tongue too clumsy to do anything really spectacular to her clitoris. Running my tongue up her thigh, one of my teeth accidentally raked across her smooth skin, tracing a thin welt of blood. She cried out, both hands on my head.

"Jack!" She said, her voice on the edge of delirium. "Don't stop! Oh God!" I put my mouth back to her vagina, her body shivering with taut spasms beneath my lustful ministrations.

I wasn't able to keep this up for very long before I was in a frenzy. Not that I was any too calm to start with, but touching her, smelling her and tasting her was all too much. I stood above her, panting and pawing at her to turn over so I could mount her when she gave me a wicked smile and moved forward beneath me.

My hips were already in motion, thrusting of their own accord at the air. I yapped despite myself as her hand encountered my penis, wrapping around the shaft of my erection, the retracted sheath bunched up behind the growing bulge at the base, exposing the tender, pink flesh to view.

"Ohhh," She said from beneath me. "it's so— different." If I was in human form I would have flushed bright crimson, but all I could manage was

to pant and wish that I could fall into the ground
and have it close seamlessly after my passage.

I whined as her hands stroked up and down,
one hand cradling my testicles while the other
stroked my penis and the surrounding skin. Noticing my discomfort, Sam surfaced on one side of me,
her face flushed and grinning.

"Jack," she said sweetly, "you aren't still embarrassed, are you?" I just looked away, caught
between my fierce biological desire, my feelings for
her, and the last tattered shreds of human pride I
had left. Yes, I was embarrassed.

I felt her hand creeping around my neck, turning me gently back to face her. She looked up at me
and said in a voice I could not doubt:

"I love you," She leaned up and kissed me on
the mouth. "And," she considered, looking into my
eyes, "you love me, whether you can say so right
now or not. Am I right?" I struggled within myself,
trying to fight off my disordering lust long enough
to reform my throat just to say—

"I-do. Love-you. Oh-God-I-do. Samantha." I
said, the words emphasized by the undue harshness
with which I said them. And I did. Love her, I mean.
She smiled.

"Then it's all right." With another wicked grin,
she slid back under me. "And don't be embarrassed.
You're not only beautiful, but you have more to
brag about than any man I've ever seen."

If I could have talked, I would have told her that flattery could get her anywhere, at least with me. Instead I backed up onto my haunches and threw my head skyward and howled. Really howled. The kind of howl that would leave humans shaking in their sleep, warn every animal in a twenty-mile radius that they had better get away from her now and not come back; and (I hoped) display my sentiment at having Samantha stroke my decidedly male ego. She smiled, kissed me again, then went back to fondling me.

She continued studying my anatomy, making appreciative noises at appropriate intervals until I was ready to go insane. My heart was about to tear itself free from my chest while my hips were pumping and jerking despite my best efforts to curb their motions. Samantha was kind enough not to laugh. I finally backed away from her pleasant touch, and growled commandingly. She either understood my growl or saw the feral gleam in my eye, because she immediately got to her hands and knees, presenting me with her ass.

I managed to wait until she had braced herself, her ass lowered a little, her legs firmly planted before leaping upon her, my erection prodding at her vagina, frantic at my attempts to enter. She gasped.

"Need some help back there?" she said, her voice husky with need. In the midst of my ineffective thrusting I felt her fingers on the tip of my cock, her hand reaching between her legs, guiding the tip. I felt my cock in contact with her wetness, tried to restrain myself from too brutal a thrust, failed. She gasped and shivered beneath me. I clutched her waist with my forelegs while my pelvis went crazy. I whined and pushed myself into her, my pleasure increasing a thousandfold.

The first difficulty was when I realized that the base of my penis was already partially swollen, and I would have to force the bulge into her. She knew it, too, and I felt her body tense beneath me as the engorged base bumped against her vaginal lips. I kept my thrusts as gentle as I could, barely in control of the process, and I knew that I was just going to have to let it happen.

Through the haze that was threatening to eclipse my consciousness, I heard her cry out, and realized I had entered her all the way. I hoped I hadn't hurt her, but was unable to think much past that. My cock finished engorging, the bulbous base filling with blood. She gasped as it did so, and I whined as I felt my flesh clasped within hers. Bliss! For a moment, I thought I was dying, my heart pounding within my chest, the whole of my sensation emanating from my loins. I was hardly aware of the tender flesh of my underbelly touching her back and buttocks, the contact feeling both distant and unreal and intimate, as though it were a part of me. I whined incoherently as I felt the tension build within me, listening to her gasps and grunts with growing ecstasy. I felt the familiar tightness in my spine and pelvis; my hips were humping spastically, and I knew I was about to come.

With a groan of happiness, she pushed herself against me, her ass wiggling beneath me. Our motions combined, increased, and I felt an incredible rush of bliss directly up the center of my body, a white-hot current burning into my brain. My flesh was fully expanded within hers, and my body had taken over, all thought erased.

I yelped happily, her groans and cries a counterpoint to my excitement as I moved to extricate myself from above her.

She was still screaming and writhing beneath me as I lifted my left foreleg and placed it on her right side along with my other foreleg, each movement causing explosions of pleasure from my swollen cock, eliciting pained-sounding grunts from her. I gave a tremendous exertion and with a small hop I managed to step all the way over her ass, my final position facing opposite her, our rear ends together. In retrospect, I am grateful that my consciousness was eclipsed shortly thereafter; the thought of getting hung up with Samantha, connected by the genitals in the middle of the woods, was more than my vanity can bear.

Once I was facing in the opposite direction an enormous amount of traction was placed on my cock, my hips going like gentle clockwork, barely moving. I began ejaculating, my penis pulsing as jets of semen entered her body from mine. I was coming....My spine reacted as though a ball of white light had formed at its base...it crept quickly upward, a fluid pulsation of life......it hit my..........brain......Ahhhhhh.................Bliss........My consciousness dissolved, once and for all..............in her........in her body.............I was dying, my mind blissful............*I was*....dissolving......in.....her..... body....I.......was.....We.............Her.............One........ ...God.........

I regained myself about half an hour later, sprawled on top of her, our bodies lathed with sweat.

Sam.

I feared I had hurt her until she opened her eyes and smiled, kissed me. Then it all came back to me...Where I was, what we had done.

"Sam," I croaked, realizing I had reverted to human shape. We kissed again, properly this time, now that I was so equipped.

"Love," she whispered.

"Love," I answered.

I wanted to lay there on top of her forever. She had turned over beneath me, dislodging my limp penis and leaving a huge puddle of wetness beneath and between us. She grinned as I grimaced.

"Sorry," I muttered.

"Nothing to be sorry about," she said in a sincere voice, running her hand across my naked, relatively hairless chest. "it's the way you're designed. Just remind me," she brushed a strand of hair from her sweaty face, and I noticed that patches of hair I had shed as I reverted clung to her sweaty body. "never to let you con me into giving you head." I couldn't help laughing.

"Yes," I agreed, feeling better already. "I'll keep that in mind."

"A question, dear Jack." She said as I sorted her clothes from mine. "Did you actually come all that time?" She paused, "I mean, I know you came, but did you, climax? Did you—"

"You mean, since I ejaculated for almost the whole time, you were wondering if I was also climaxing the whole time, right?" I interpreted for her. She nodded, biting her lower lip, something she did when she was curious. "And the answer," I said, shifting unsteadily on my feet. "is yes." Her eyes widened.

"God," she said appreciatively. "and you're *embarrassed* about this? Most men would be screaming it from the rooftops." She shook her head, stood up, still exuding fluid. I noticed she was none too steady on her feet either, her quadriceps entertaining quick spasms up and down their lengths. "I came the whole time, too." She said as she stretched, sounding very self-satisfied. I helped her into her clothes.

"You've got to be freezing," I said. She nodded, her teeth chattering for the first time.

"Now that you mention it," She said, laughing and shivering at the same timer. After she finished dressing I began donning my own clothes.

"Zip that coat," I said. "you've probably caught your death of cold out here."

"Actually, no." She shook her head. "I wasn't cold at all while we made love. Your hair," she paused, plucked several strands of my hair from where they clung to her neck. "is a remarkable insulator." I rolled my eyes and she zipped her coat. We headed back to the car, leaving the blood-streaked bones where they lay.

"Jack," she said as I slid my arm around my waist. "I love you." I kissed her on the cheek.

"I love you, too." I said, knowing it was true.

The Killing of The Calf

Linda Hooper

Wolves don't like plan-
ning. They don't think much of the future. I was
oblivious to that well-known fact when I planned to
pass my last night with them quietly; I kept to my
room, the room the Clan Circle assigned to me
when I first came to the Keep last spring. Timor was
there with me—it was almost her room as much as
mine—but I thought the time for lessons was over.
I planned on leaving and leaving forever. I knew I
was leaving, because I kept telling myself I was.

I had always liked the room, with its dark
wooden walls almost the color of wine. Tonight, I lit
none of the lamps, but left the room illuminated
only by the fire, warm and low. The windows I had
looked through so many mornings onto the plain
around the Keep I shuttered, and pulled the heavy
drapes across them. As I moved around the room,
my body seemed to have a hard time following, as
if occupied in other duties.

I breathed deeply, to steady myself. Tomorrow would be one of the hardest days of my difficult life, but this night was no longer or short than any other night. I merely had to wait for daylight. I pushed the soft high-backed leather chair close to the hearth. After tossing off my day-clothes, I wrapped a thick robe around my shoulders and fastened it with my belt. I sank into the chair and watched the fire. Timor shared the fire with me; she stretched out and rested her snout between her paws. I thought that we made a rather cozy scene, for a few minutes, but in the sudden quiet I realized that there was nothing cozy about my state of mind.

"What am I doing?" I wailed, surprising myself. The wolf opened her eyes at me with a look that was hard to interpret.

"Why shouldn't I go back?" I asked no one, especially not Timor. She never gave advice about personal choices. No wolf did. Leaning forward, I pulled a log from the pile and tossed it on, even though it was too early for another. Sparks flew onto the hearth. Timor never flinched, but looked at me, narrowed her eyes, and turned away.

"I'll just go back and live in the city like I did before. Just because I've been here doesn't mean I'm all that different. Besides, I love her. I really do," I argued to the back of Timor's head, in that voice humans use when they lie to themselves. "I can't help it if I love someone who hates herself—lots of women hate themselves. She has a reason, she doesn't understand herself like I understand her now. Now that we know who we are, and where we come from, everything will be better. From what I've learned here, I can teach her how to stop hating—herself—and what we are. She'll see." Sure, she would. Denial and wishing the impossible didn't help so I tried giving in to reality. "I keep going back to her anyway, so why should stay... I...." I turned to look at the wolf beside me and took a long breath. "...why should I stay here and... do what you... are suggesting?"

I took another deep, delicious breath and then shook my head to clear it. "Mmm—no!" But I did not stop, I could not ignore Timor's thoughts. The second time I did not shake my head.

I eased out of my chair to embrace the mane of the wolf beside me. "Oh my sister," I whispered, as I lay on the floor beside her, burying my fingers in the fur around her throat. "You hear what I say, but you know how I feel, don't you? And what I am."

Timor licked my lips and nose, then pulled back and looked at me, with an open lupine smile. I licked Timor's nose, then opened my lips to accept her muscular tongue between my teeth. Timor kissed me deeply and I played catch, and tag, with

her tongue. Timor could crush my skull if desired—
but the wolf desired something else, this was
obvious. A lesson. A lesson I hadn't planned on.

Great waves of scent came through the wolf's
warm fur. I stretched out and pulled Timor's body
against my own. My legs pulled Timor's belly between them, and I bent my calves over the wolf's
back. I pulled her chest to feel her fur on my
breasts. Timor's scent insisted: live for the pleasures
one was born to enjoy.

And so we kissed: the strong tongue of the wolf,
licking and licking the inside of my mouth, and my
head thrashing and my throat making little puppy
sounds, opening and playing, running my little
human tongue around Timor's teeth, sucking the
wolf's lips, soft on one side and fur on the other.

Timor's scent pulled me into her like a tornado,
spinning me far away from my little words of a few
minutes ago. If I had truly intended to return home,
I would have left the Keep that afternoon, while it
was still daylight. I must have had some perverse
need to hear little human words of resistance—
humans always resist. I had sensed a place within
me, when I did not leave before sunset, that my
human mind had strongly resisted.

Timor's scent brought me now to that place, at
first a darkness. The light of the fire in the room
dimmed beyond my eyes—I sensed night, and

motion—motion low to the ground, and swift—the running of the wolves. Wolves, running in a pack, scents streaming out behind each one, flooding the others in a steady stream of utter joy, the ecstasy of running through the dark, the dark open plain, toward a wood, and then beyond the trees—the running of the pack, each wolf's singular scent shouting to the rest, an olfactory chorus, I am me! I am here in the pack! The running of the wolves! and I am in the pack!

While Timor and I kissed our kisses inside a human house beside a very human fire, while we lay on the hearth made by human hands, Timor sent out her scent to me, and I took the scent into my body; like the thin clay of an arroyo soaks up the first drops of rain, I soaked up Timor's scent completely, as wholly as I took in her tongue, and shudders shook my body and the scents split into a hundred scents, the dark plain, the motion, the pack, the joy—and each living being in the land around me, the trees, the herbs, the bugs, the mold, the scents on the air, of...

of snow.

When I sensed the snow, I realized again my human nose was such an improperly formed tool for this way of storytalking. I pushed myself up onto my arms, pretending to pin Timor to the floor. Timor snapped my nose and smiled, missing by inches. Her scent changed, the pack running over the dark plain, but now with purpose.

Without apparent effort, Timor raised her head and chest in one motion and, grabbing my shoulder in her teeth like a puppy's neck, tossed me onto my back. Growling as best I could, I tried to toss her back; I kicked with my legs but Timor skipped away from my weak human feet. My open legs released my human sex scent in to the room. Timor turned her head toward my scent, and raised her lips. I kissed her.

Timor put her tongue to my pubic hair and inhaled, sneezed, and sniffed a few times more before making a swipe of her tongue down my hair.

But I wanted snow.

The scent of snow and the running pack, and the shoulders of the pack running beside me, my four pads on the cold earth—and the snow.

Timor and I wrestled; I buried her face in her belly and threw her over using all the strength of my legs. She fell against the chair and relaxed as I kissed and rubbed her belly with my face, sending out my tongue to stroke the softest fur there, edging ever closer to the source of the scent and my visions. I took Timor's vulva in my mouth first and held it there, held it between my teeth. Timor's vulva filled my mouth; scent poured out of her and directly into my brain through the roof of my mouth. I am *With the Pack,* and we are running through the night *together.*

As we leave the edge of the wood at the top of the hill, dawn reaches out to us, and the river valley lies below. It is still night in the river valley where three sharp scents show themselves—a moose and her twins crossing the snow field on the river bank with great difficulty. One calf struggles behind. We run, like a deadly black ribbon, toward them as a single force of nature.

The scent had entered my bloodstream; I felt my vulva rubbing against Timor as I run with the pack toward the calf. Timor lay on her back, and though the fire burned low, I did not feel the cold of the room; my blood flooded hot with Timor's scent.

The cow senses the pack too late; the wind does not favor her this morning. Though she turns to gallop back toward the straggling calf, deep snow impedes her; and our paws barely break the crust. Myself, the wolf lately grown to adulthood and hunting with the pack for this first time, races just behind Timor who grabs the calf's hip and crushes it. I come in next, snap its neck, and blood shoots into my mouth just before we three fall to the snow.

The cow struggles to flail the pack with her razor hooves, but we are too many. She and her stronger calf return toward the river while the pack feed; the calf cools quickly in the reddened snow.

I couldn't stop shuddering, my skin flushed, sweat soaked my hair and wolf fur filled it like wool. Out of breath, I flung off the robe, cinched my belt across my hips, and said the old words as I pressed it to the skin above my womb. The room warmed; I felt the flash, and I lay down beside Timor. The empty human chair watched embers with us. My plans had changed.

Alma Mater

Robert M. Schroeck

Benito thought long-
ingly of his father's forge as the icy wind whipped
the snow around him. The friendly warmth of the
smithy where he had spent his childhood was echoed by the heat that pulsed mockingly in his
forehead and ears. *If the cold does not take me, the
fever will,* he thought, surprised at his own lucidity.

As the wind tore around him, he forced himself
to take another step, and another. *So close to home,
so close. To have survived the Great War, only to
have this happen.* He closed his eyes against the
stinging flakes and, unbidden, the accident re-
played itself in his mind. The wagon ride home,
stuffed in with a dozen other veterans from villages
in the area. The unseasonable cold, even in the
mountains. The sudden squall that blew up out of
nowhere. The wagon overturning, and Benito being
thrown clear—and then awakening much later to

the realization that he'd been abandoned to the storm. Abandoned? Forgotten? Lost? Did it matter?

The crunch of the snow underfoot travelled up his leg, more felt than heard. Another step; another crunch. No, it didn't matter. What did was that he was lost and snowblind. Too many times already he had walked into a tree or bush or rock. It was getting so hard to go on. It would be so much easier to just let go.

Benito paused to wipe his eyes. In the heavy snow he could see little more than a few feet in any direction. He had to find the town, or even the road, as impossible as it seemed. He trudged on, huddling inside his uniform's woolen jacket for what little warmth it could provide, and tried to ignore the fever chills that ran in waves through his body.

His mind drifted as he drove himself forward. Moment blurred into cold white moment, until he suddenly found himself sprawled on the ground. A rough rock wall rose in front of him. He felt a trickle of warmth on his forehead, raised his hand and brought it away touched with a droplet of blood. *Fool!* he thought. *You could have as easily walked off a cliff as into one.* Benito struggled to his feet, ignoring the weakness in his knees. He stretched out one hand to touch the frozen stone and began to stumble along the cliff face.

As he forced himself onward, he could feel the fever throb within him. *Frozen to death, or burned up from the inside?* he wondered. *Which will kill me first?* The thought was strangely passionless. It echoed in his head without the panic and fear he'd expected. *Poppa always said a brave man fought death, but never feared it. Am I a brave man?* He thought of the many risks he'd taken, both in the War and before it, while editing the *Avanti*; soldiers were not safe and Socialists were not popular. Death threatened both. Did that make him brave?

A blotch of dark grey, low against the everpresent white, caught his eye. At first he thought it was just a spot of bare rock. Then he fought the fever-born fuzziness and saw the mouth of a small cave. Slowly, Benito realized it was shelter. He dropped to his knees and crawled in. It was too dark to see, but it smelled... pleasant. A short distance inside, the snow abruptly stopped, and he felt bare stone under his hands. Before he could do more than marvel at his luck, Benito collapsed.

Fever dreams raced through his brain and denied him rest even in unconsciousness. Nightmare images danced behind his eyes faster than he could follow and the taste of iron filled his mouth, making him retch. Sometimes he approached wakefulness, and his mind was filled with vague regrets—*to die without achieving anything lasting...*

to die having wasted my life. He thought perhaps he
woke from time to time, but it had to be more
dreams, for he would find himself suckling at a
woman's bare breast or, to his shock, at the teat of
some grey-furred animal. The taste of the milk
never warned him which it would be, when each
dream began. Only the texture—silky fur or warm
flesh—would warn him before his dream-self
opened his eyes.

Slowly, the nightmares faded, but the images—
bare breast and furred teat, and the feel of each
against his lips—remained. They disturbed his sleep
and the few moments of clarity he seemed to possess. The woman bothered him little, except that he
never seemed to see her face. It was the breast of
the beast that chilled him.

Finally—how long it took, Benito didn't know—
he awoke. He still felt feverish. he lightheadedness
was still there. But he felt certain that he was
awake, and not trapped in yet another dream. He
opened his eyes to see a woman leaning over him.
Firelight illuminated her face, painting it with
glowing tones and casting sharp, dancing shadows,
and revealing the concern in her dark eyes. It took
him a moment to realize that she was beautiful, and
that she was naked. Stunned, Benito recognized the
breasts at which he had suckled in his dreams.

She stroked the side of his face with the back of

her hand, as if to caress him as much as test his
fever. When he seized her hand and brought it to
his lips, she smiled. Her bearing and manner were
almost regal, and somehow, despite her nakedness,
he knew she was no wanton, no whore. But still he
reached out a trembling hand to touch the breast
he thought he knew.

At his touch, she closed her eyes, that serene
smile remaining on her face. Her nipple grew erect
under his fingertips, and he traced around it, feeling the texture of her areola. A low moan of
appreciation rose in her throat, and Benito felt
emboldened. He reached out with his other hand
and took her by the waist, and drew her closer. The
light pressure of his hands encouraged her to lean
over him, and when she did, he took her nipple
between his lips. She moaned again, this time
louder and more insistently. She entwined her fingers in his thinning hair and held him to her body
as he kicked free the animal skins which had served
as his blankets. Instantly, she swung one long,
tanned leg over to straddle him, her sex against his,
separated only by the sweat-soaked cloth of his
uniform.

If this is a hallucination, he thought as he teased
her nipple with his tongue and teeth, *please let me
stay sick long enough to finish it...*

Long, lithe fingertips brushed around the curve
of his ear and down his neck, stopped only by his

collar, as he licked his way into the valley between her breasts. He paused there for a moment to breathe deeply of her. She smelled of musk and grass and animal fur, and over all, he could smell her already-growing arousal.

He slid one hand from her waist to her heavily-furred sex, to find it already moist to the touch. He dared to stroke her, and this time she all but howled in response; she tore his lips from her breast and pressed her own against them. Her tongue drove between them to dance with his own as Benito continued to caress her. When his uncertain fingers discovered her clitoris she moaned into his mouth, and broke their kiss to begin unbuttoning his shirt.

Nimble fingers were interrupted by spasms of pleasure as he played with her clitoris, but she soon had the many brass buttons undone. Benito found himself dragged to a sitting position as she pulled the shirt off him. She flung it to one side and ran her hands up and down his chest as he continued to tease her sex. Short gasps punctuated her soft moans and cries.

Her rising passion seemed to urge her to haste, and her hands flew to his belt buckle. His head spun from the speed with which she stripped the trousers from him, and a small, distant part of his mind thought, *It's a lucky thing my boots were al-*

ready off. But he had no further time to think, for she threw his trousers across the small cave and began to rub her sex against his erect cock. The contrasting textures of rough hair and slick wetness made him gasp, and he reached up to pull her down to him.

As they bit and licked each other's lips, he wrapped his arms and his legs around her lithe body. Almost without realizing it, they rolled over, and Benito found himself on top. He broke the kiss, and stared down at her, drinking her in. Her dark hair splayed wildly against the furs and skins on which they lay, and her dark eyes were glowing with their own fire as she stared back at him. The tip of her tongue, almost blood-red in the firelight, flicked out to lick her lips in an almost kitten-like manner. Benito found the sight incredibly arousing. When he realized that they were panting in unison, he chuckled, then bent his head to her throat.

She closed her eyes and moaned again as he kissed and licked his way from her sensitive neck down past her breasts and across her flat belly. To his surprise, his lips brushed past thin white scars, years old, long-healed and almost invisible, scattered across her torso, but he put the questions out of his mind as he spread her legs and slid down to her sex. Her labia glistened in the firelight, and the taste of her was unlike any woman he had ever lain with before—fresh, clean and strangely *other.*

After only a few moments, though, she pushed
him away. Surprised, he could only stare at her, but
she smiled and caressed his cheek. Then she turned
over onto her hands and knees, facing away from
him. She moved her legs apart, presenting her sex
to him; she glanced back expectantly, then leaned
down to pillow her head on her folded arms.

Benito shuffled forwards on his knees. He slid
the head of his cock up and down along her slick
lips, and brushed it against her clitoris. Her hips
jerked with each touch, and she growled with impatience and frustration. He paused and savored the
moment, taking in the scent, sight and feel of her.
Then, slowly, clinging to her slender hips, he entered her. She was a virgin. Somehow, that didn't
surprise him.

His first few strokes were measured and gentle,
until she began moving in counterpoint to him.
Still, he remained tentative until her own thrusts
backward to impale herself on him grew so frantic
and demanding that he could no longer ignore their
effect on him. He abandoned caution and began to
fuck her wildly. She returned every stroke of his
with a powerful one of her own, until the moist slap
of flesh against flesh echoed off the cave walls.

Benito closed his eyes and tried to submerge
himself in the moment just as she began to make
the noise. It started as a soft, high-pitched

whimper, almost inaudible, interrupted with a hiccup with each slap of loins against buttocks. Gradually, it grew louder and deeper. A gravelly, throaty quality invaded it, transforming it into a sound unlike those he'd heard her make before now. As it changed in tone, her motions grew wilder, almost convulsive. A twist of her hips knocked his hands away; when he blindly grasped her waist again, he nearly drew back in surprise— the texture of her skin had changed. He snapped open his eyes.

Dio mio. The fever still has me.

She was changing.

As he watched, still mindlessly driving into her body, the silver-grey fur sprouted. Something prodded his navel, and he glanced down dumbly to watch the tail grow from the base of her spine, the fur white and silver and bursting out to its bushy fullness in a matter of seconds; she held it curled over her back, out of his way as he continued to fuck her.

Her limbs were almost done transforming, growing slender, their new paws now dark-padded and clawed. Of her face, he could see nothing but the ears framing the black noseleather and fine fur of the muzzle raised with teeth bared. Inside, she was still warm and wet, but the texture was new and different, and she was tighter than any woman he'd ever had before.

Why it was, he did not know, but there was no question of him stopping. A madness had seized him, and all he knew was that they must complete what they had started. He caressed her flanks, revelling in their silkiness as he continued to thrust back into her wolfen cunt. She opened her mouth and howled as her body began to spasm under his. Driven by some instinct he did not understand, Benito fell upon her back and wrapped his arms around her body, and bit into her neck as he came with her.

He awoke to find himself wrapped in skins and furs. Daylight streamed through the long, low entrance, illuminating the cave with a brilliant light. He sat up and looked about him. He was alone—for the moment—but the cave clearly had a human inhabitant. He lay in a rough bed made of more skins and furs laid over a broad pile of dried grass. A firepit had been laboriously hollowed out in the cave floor between the bed and the entrance, and in it crackled a warm blaze. Numerous skin bags hung from the walls, along with colorful feathers and bunches of dried herbs. There was even, much to his surprise, a small, framed picture of the Madonna. Despite its primitive appearance, the cave was meticulously clean, with not even a stray leaf on the stone.

A gust of wind whipped up the fire for a moment, and Benito inched himself closer to the warmth. As he basked in the light and heat of both the fire and the sun, he realized that his mind was clear and calm. The fever had broken. He had survived, thanks to... who? *I'm alive. Someone rescued me. But who...?* Memory rose to answer, with fever-blurred images. A girl? *No, a woman. And... a wolf?* A disturbing vision danced on the edges of his mind, and escaped all his efforts to clearly recall it.

Before he could pursue the memories further, he heard the scratch of claws on stone. He looked up to see the wolf of his fever-dreams standing at the entrance of the cave. The sunlight shining on its pelt gave it the appearance of some otherworldly creature wreathed in silver-gold fire. In its mouth it carried a pair of rabbits, and it was watching him with calm interest.

Almost paralyzed with fear, Benito tried to edge further back into the cave. He glanced at the blazing fire between him and the wolf and thought, *Fire should keep it at bay. I will be safe until she returns. I hope.*

The wolf gave a snort and laid the rabbits gently on the stone floor. It looked up at him, almost expectantly. Benito tried to stay as still as possible, and made no sound. The wolf opened its mouth and its tongue lolled out. It huffed, a sound almost like laughter, and then stood up on its hind legs.

Benito stared in disbelief as the wolf stretched taller and taller, its limbs and body filling out and the face shrinking. Its beautiful grey-silver fur seemed to withdraw into its body, leaving behind smooth, tanned skin. The four sets of nipples on its belly slid together to join and swell into a pair of full, familiar breasts. She shook out the mane of dark hair that had sprouted on her head, and Benito recognized the woman who had nursed him through his fever. *Dio mio. It was no hallucination, the woman and the wolf who were one.* Involuntarily, he crossed himself.

"I am Kala," she said. "Do not be afraid." Her Italian was archaic and strangely accented, but he could understand her—barely. She gestured at the rabbits. "I brought breakfast. Do you hunger yet?"

Benito licked the grease from his fingers. He had been profoundly relieved when when Kala cleaned and dressed the rabbits, then roasted them over the fire. He had half-feared that they would have to be eaten raw and bloody. But she retrieved a steel knife from one of the skin bags and had prepared the meat with all the skill of a practiced hunter. Now, after they had eaten, she curled herself up next to him and answered his questions.

"Mine are an ancient people," she told him. "We have lived here in the mountains for many, many centuries."

"Are you the last one?" he had asked.

She laughed. "No. There are many others. Some live among you. Some, like my line, revere the old traditions, and stay in the mountains to live the life our ancestors lived."

"Not entirely." He pointed towards the image of the Madonna.

Kala shrugged. "Some things change whether we like it or not. But we try to live by as much of the old ways as we can."

"Roman ways?"

"No, much older."

He looked into her eyes. "Was helping me one such 'old way'?"

She reached out and caressed his cheek, smiling gently. "Yes. We have always helped the traveler in need. There is a tradition... it is said that one of our kind fostered the twins who founded Rome."

"Rescued from death to found an empire," he mused, and remembered his feverish regrets.

"We have other traditions," she said.

"Such as?"

"Sometimes we will find a mate among your people." She brushed her lips across his, the tip of her tongue darting between them for an instant. Benito's blood ran hot with remembered and newly-aroused desire. He drew her close, returning the kiss, and wondering what it would be like to stay with her, live with her, love with her, here in the mountains. It drew him, insistent and strong.

But not strong enough. Other fires burned in his blood and in his soul, twin fires of ambition and determination stoked by his rescuer and lover even as she had stoked those of his heart. He held her tightly, and regretted what he knew he must tell her. "I cannot," he finally whispered after many long minutes. She did not reply. "Kala, cara mia, I feel it, too. But I must go. There is a fate, a destiny out there, for which you rescued me. Like Romulus and Remus, I have suckled at the breast of the wolf who saved my life. I now know that I am to build an empire of my own, as great as theirs. After all, there is a tradition..."

As her first hot tears fell upon his skin, he tightened his embrace around Kala and murmured comforts to her. But already Benito was planning the empire that would assure that the name of Mussolini would be remembered until the end of time.

Wilderland

Reina Delacroix

I'm free again. I run across the plain into the wind that whips my ruff against my neck. I brush against the thorny bushes as I lope, to let the sharp branches work loose some matted fur on my shoulder.

The world is full of scent and sound. The pumping musk of a nearby herd of caribou overpowers the tartness of onion grass, and the wind does not quite mask the characteristic clump of their hooves as they move to the riverbank. Summer has come to its full height on the tundra, and my prey are dusty, thirsty, tired and hopefully careless.

The near bend of the river lies over a crest some strides away. I halt, ears pricked to catch the faintest sound of alarm, but they are unaware of my presence. I lower my profile as I stalk to a familiar ledge that overlooks an eddy pool where it will be easiest for the caribou to drink and cool themselves in the water. I can wait and watch until I sight the weakest among them, which will be my target.

The sun has passed from overhead to halfway towards the mountains that form one border to my territory, opposite to the river boundary I crouch near. I know my prey now. It is a caribou calf which stands on its legs steadily enough but nearly falls as it attempts to trot with other calves. Its mother keeps a close, nervous eye on it. Her instinct tells her I am near, prowling, and her offspring is the most vulnerable of the herd. But her instinct is not enough to give an alarm.

I wait, patient as a glacier that moves all before it, for the time to strike.

The sun is nearly to the mountains now; the shadows have gotten long and the light plays tricks. While the caribou are more wary as the light dims, the dusklight offers false security. I am ready to strike from the sunside, the wind in my face. I tense my legs, and spring.

The leggy creatures run in all directions, and the calf gets cut off from its mother in the melee. They bleat to find each other, but my nose finds the calf first. As young as it is, it knows my sharp teeth and claws mean death, and it runs from sheer panic. The treacherous legs give out on the muddy ground, and I close quickly, almost too quickly to clamp my jaws on the throat and begin to tear the flesh—

*   *   *

The scenery flashed white twice and a small red mailbox incongruously posted itself to my immediate right. My computer system at home had just received urgent mail. I sighed and, with my juicy prey still struggling in my teeth, swiped the mailbox twice with a clumsy paw.

Everything went black.

A monitor and keyboard warped out of space and surfed to a stop in front of me. Once stabilized, the monitor linked to my visor and the keyboard to my gloves.

Ordinarily I wouldn't interrupt one of my rare sessions in Wilderland, one of the new virtual reality areas in the vast Network, for anything short of actual world emergency. But I needed a job to afford to enter Wilderland, as well as to provide unimportant things like food and shelter, so I had to pay attention to mundane reality.

to joanna@washline.connect.com
from kate@netware.amaterasu.com

Just saw your old partner Word Smith in the halls, who mentioned that he has taken a freelance offer from Amaterasu to work on documentation for some of our VR offerings and is looking for help. Apparently we're coming out with upgrades to Tourland, Parkland and Wilderland, and when I

mentioned the amount of time you spend logged
on to alternate reality his ears pricked up. So go for
it!! (And don't forget who recommended you—if
this works, I expect a victory dinner.)

Oh, Kate, I thought, if you were here I would
kiss you, and I'm not even a lesbian. And Word
Smith, too, though I'd have to ask Damask's permission first.

I hesitated to log off Wilderland. The excitement
of the chase, the taste of salt and blood on my
tongue as I ripped the throat of the young caribou,
tugged at me. It was the land of my dreams, my true
self, and I hated to leave my kill unfinished.

But the storage charges to save a VR program for
future return at the precise moment of exit accumulated in megabytes per millisecond and mounted
all too quickly to ruinous expense. I didn't have
that kind of money to spare, so I pushed aside my
regret, consoling myself with the knowledge that if
I got the job, I wouldn't have to exist on tuna fish
for a week to afford an hour a day on Wilderland.

Since Kate worked at Amaterasu, I would be one
of the first on the scent... but this was a prime opportunity and there would be others in the hunt. I
had to hurry. I cancelled the rest of my Wilderland
session, pulled up my resume from storage in my
home system, changed my cover letter date to May

13, 2004, and zapped it to Carter C. Smith at both his work and home addresses.

Then I stripped off the gloves and unlocked the VR helmet, an all-in-one assortment of goggles, earphones, and rebreather for rudimentary scent production. The chaos of Dave's Sight & Sound Arcade assaulted me. Machine gun rattle, the ping of crossbows and the snackt! of kung-fu kicks warred with the roar of flamethrowers and sizzle of neon arcs as some ten-year old destroyed the entire Xannax attacking force.

The owner hastened over to take the equipment from me as if it were the Golden Helmet of Mambrino rather than fused sand, wires, and a plastic shell the color of unpainted model airplanes. Dave's plump dark face glistened with sweat despite the air conditioning.

"Any problem, Joanna?" he said as his nervous hands fiddled with the input cable and air hose connected to the Network terminal area.

"No, nothing's wrong, Dave."

"I mean, you stopped early, and I was worried maybe the helmet conked out."

He was a small operator, and the few VR helmets he owned represented a lot of capital outlay. Yeah, they were reconditioned first-generation tech from 2001, but the engraved Roman-style VR inside the Amaterasu sunburst logo attested to their original quality, while the cheap Pakistani knockoffs already lay in piles of silicon slag in the recycler plants.

"Everything's fine. I just got a message over the board there might be a job for me."

"Hey, great!" His smile split the grey stubble on his face. "Don't forget to come back and spend time here. You know I'll always give you what discount I can. I'll even save your favorite helmet for you."

His high school ring rapped on the purple-grey styrene, near the deep scratch I had given it one day as my reflexes followed the in-helmet action too enthusiastically and I sprung...only to collide with the casing of the Intergalactic Wrestling machine.

I grinned at the memory. The thrill of catching my first deer had made the following day's nasty headache worth it. "That's a lucky helmet for me. This time I nearly caught a caribou."

"Working up to bigger game, huh? Rabbits aren't enough anymore. You'll be a Big Bad Wolf any day now, Joanna," he kidded me as he turned to put the helmet in its locker in the utility closet.

"Hey, it takes a lot to feed a growing timber wolf," I retorted. "They don't let us wild animals in the corner market, and I haven't figured out yet how to use my claws to dial for pizza delivery."

I heard him chuckle as I sprinted out the door.

*   *   *

By the time I got home, Word had already skimmed my resume and summoned me to appear at Amaterasu, before he wasted his time interviewing anyone else.

He grinned at me as I navigated through the piles of printouts that mined his office. "I almost didn't recognize you, Jo, you look so strange in that getup."

I stroked the fabric of my lightweight heather-grey wool suit—colored to set off my copper hair and blue-green eyes, and tailored to fit my tall, angular body. "This old thing? Oh, I just had it lying around... in case I was so desperate as to look for work at some place with a dress code. How've you been, Word?"

"Fine, fine." He ran his slender fingers through hair the color of maple syrup. We'd kept in touch over the Network since we'd worked together at Aurora/Phoenix, but I hadn't seen him in some years. He looked great, thinned out a little, brighter-eyed and bushier-tailed than ever.

"Life with Damask suits you."

His hazel eyes greened in intensity. "Jo, I wake up every morning in ecstasy. Damask is everything I ever wanted."

"Good to hear. Where do you wake up, anyway? Last I heard, it was on the floor at the foot of the bed."

He lowered his voice, but his grin widened. "You haven't heard the latest, then. We had a bed specially constructed with a cage hidden underneath. She locks me in there every night. It's wonderful."

"If you don't mind being caged, that is," I retorted.

Word didn't take offense at that, knowing my sense of sarcasm too well. "Hey, I'm a domestic animal, not an untamed creature like you. Belonging to someone is more important to me than being free."

I sighed. "Is it too much to ask for both?"

"Joanna, I'd say you are a hopeless romantic... if I didn't know you'd claw me to shreds for saying it," he added swiftly as I mimed a playful swipe. He swiveled away, the motion a seamless flow into a courtly bow, and the accompanying arm-swing waved me to the only chair in the office that wasn't playing Leaning Tower of Pisa with reams of paper. "Have a seat and I'll go find Darrow—he's the designer/owner of the VR programs, Amaterasu just distributes them for him—to come and meet you. I just need to finish this paragraph."

He bent back to his terminal and busied himself with corrections, muttering curses at the myriad ways techies bent the English language. This familiar scene brought back memories of when Word and I worked together before.

One late night at Aurora/Phoenix we were trying to reconstruct a tech manual that had been
translated from Japanese by way of Xhosa, and we
ended up drinking sake at 4 AM and playing lawn
darts with my beanbag chair. We talked about our
dissatisfaction with our "normal" relationships, and
I became so boldly drunk I showed him some of my
milder erotic fiction.

I had tried to use the jargon of D&s (master,
slave, cuffs, whips, etc.) as a metaphor in stories to
express my own deeper wild-animal fantasies, but
it was an imperfect fit at best. In my stories, slaves
were obedient yet proud, and their masters used
them in ways that enhanced rather than degraded
them.

Word found my lighter fiction much more interesting than I myself did, and shared some of his
more traditional sexual-slavery stories with me in
return. He also told me about the "D-ring-nets",
the Dominance/submission computer networks
MasSlaNet and Dungeonmasters, with their dozens
of sideboards on specific sexual fantasies—bondage, foot worship, piercing, and the like.

I had never dreamed there might be others out
there as imprinted with childhood dreams as I had
been, and the leap of hope I felt frightened me. I
was not as resigned to my solitude as I had hoped;
part of me was still a social animal.

We were just drunk enough that night to dare each other to post our latest works on the nets; once we sobered up, our skewed senses of humor helped us enjoy even the most pathetic and/or obnoxious of our correspondents.

My lighter sex-stories brought some inquiries, but none sparked my interest in return and my replies were polite but negative. My one attempt at something deeper was called "Speaking in Tongues," a story about a werewolf enslaved by a human, filled with violent sex and sexy violence. "Speaking" sank into the nets without a trace, and I never knew if anyone had even read it.

In contrast, Word got lucky within a week and connected with Damask, a tall dominant woman who resembled the twentieth century singer Cher. His intense involvement with her made my own failure to connect with anyone all the more painful, and I split up our partnership to freelance.

Discouraged, I dropped off the public nets completely and narrowed my life to the point of isolation. I worked enough to get by, but my internal world was more compelling than anything outside me... until I found out about Wilderland.

Touted as an alternative to actual wilderness trips for the disabled (or just plain lazy), Wilderland hooked me when I discovered it would allow me to discard my human persona and assume an animal one. My wolf skin fit far better than my human one ever had.

Still, it was a lonely pleasure; even in Wilderland, it seemed, I could not belong to a "pack". In two years, I had never seen another wolf, and I wondered if that was a design in the system, to prevent competition between "players", or just another example of my independent nature subverting my conscious desire.

Or was it as simple as no one else, anywhere, wanted to become a wolf?

Sometimes at sunset, I sat in the high grass above my lair in the mud-brown foothills near the border mountains, and raised my muzzle and howled again and again, in protest at my bitter isolation, and in quest of an answering cry.

Was what drifted down from the peaks then just an echo, or another of my kind straining its voice to reach me through the thin air?

I looked up at that moment to meet a pair of grey eyes set in the unblinking stare of a mature wolf, flat and wary, but curious. I shook my head to clear the cobweb lure of Wilderland memories, but the eyes were still there. They belonged to a thin, loose-jointed man in his mid-twenties, with unruly rust-brown hair and the broad cheekbones of a Native American, who stood in the doorway and watched me while Word's voice rose from its murmur in greeting.

"Darrow, I was just about to get you. This is Joanna McDonnell. Joanna, Darrow Northwalker."

The eyes didn't blink, didn't move, didn't react; he simply stared at me. I suppose I should have been self-conscious, even uncomfortable, under that silent gaze. But I felt no threat from him, only a sense of recognition as he considered me.

So this was the architect of my desire!

"Welcome," he barked, and then the door was empty.

I raised my eyebrows at Word. "Does he always behave that way?"

He shrugged. "Sometimes Darrow can be harder to interpret than his code...but I think that means you're hired."

While my job at Amaterasu helped my bank balance, the day-to-day contact with other people had the unfortunate effect of transmuting my manageable aloneness into not-so-tractable loneliness.

One Friday the scent of Darrow's prized deerskin jacket, dampened by a sudden shower, made both my mouth and eyes water. I felt stirrings in my crotch that even Wilderland could not help me ignore. Though I found Darrow intriguing, I had always followed the time-honored tradition of "not shitting where I ate", or more prosaically, not dating in my workplace. So I went to a human hunting ground.

Squares was a well-attended gathering place for computer folk in Seattle. The owner, a former programmer, designed it to appeal to the computer-friendly: an abundance of video monitors and game machines, free outlets and cables for those who wouldn't leave home without their laptops, networked glassed-over tabletops for those who would.

Eventually I made my selection. Marshall was a technophile, rather than an actual "techfreak" like me. He worked in the marketing department at my old place, Aurora/Phoenix; though our times there didn't overlap, we knew a lot of the same people. He said he liked to hang out with the computer geeks after work as well—told me he found them "creative."

That statement, coupled with his fawn-brown hair, lanky body and a tentative quality I had always found appealing in men, made him a promising target. I cut him neatly out of his group, suggesting we go back to his place because it was closer.

His condo was sterile, like a laboratory. It had bandage-white walls, polyurethaned pine floors, and wire-frame Scandinavian furniture. Everything was so clean I could almost smell the reek of disinfectant. Even his New Age makeout music sounded thin, empty, with no meat coating its synthesized bones. And, in the best tradition of lust-crazed mad-scientists, Marshall liked to experiment in bed... but only in an acrobatic sense. His idea of variety was to change positions every few minutes, and if he'd owned something so ornate as a chandelier, I'm sure he would have suggested we swing from it.

I did come, twice, as he took me from behind, my pubic bone pressed by his athletic strokes into a bunching of the corduroy bedspread, and I bit the pillow to muffle my howls. Yet it was mere mechanics—my wild spirit remained untouched.

He, on the other hand, was impressed with what (to him) were our sexual pyrotechnics, and began to plan future dates with a satisfied smirk.

His assumptions made me feel trapped. I snapped at him, he lashed back instinctively, and the resulting shrewishness reminded me why I didn't try getting laid very often.

His parting kick at me, as I walked out the door, was, "You bitch, you were just using me to masturbate!"

As I trotted the twelve misty blocks to my home, I began to laugh. Marshall was right; of course I had used him (though the same comment could be applied to him as well). But I had been a fool, to imagine that some civilized and hygienic human could ever be the kind of lover my fantasies demanded.

Footsore and heartweary, I unlocked the door to my basement efficiency. I didn't bother with the overhead switch; the glow-in-the-dark stars on the ceiling cast enough light for me to make my way to bed.

"Bed" consisted of a tangle of pillows, blankets, and thrift-store furs over an area equivalent to a full-size mattress. I crawled into them, and reached under the pillow backrest in the far corner for my collection of playtoys. I kept them in the beaded canvas parfleche which I had handcrafted long ago in my Indian lore class, a neat package which my fingers could untie and unfold from memory.

My tail was a small latex butt plug with a padded wire affixed to the flange end by epoxy; knotted into the padding were hundreds of horsehairs. I slathered the plug with lubricant and pushed it into my asshole so that it would swish from side to side as I twitched my rear.

The scene had to smell right, so I sprayed musk oil from the small crystal atomizer into the air, onto the covers, and finally onto my fingers so I could paint the oil into my cheek hollows.

I stroked my tail to disperse the last of the scent from my hands. The kind of lubricant that I used on the plug warmed up over time, and I could almost feel musk glands burning where the tail joined the spine.

Next came the "wolf paws", modeled as realistically as possible by wrapping rabbit fur around a dowel. I had carved their claws from horse hoof clippings I found sold in a pet store as dog chews. I grasped them with my hands and laid back in the pile of cushions, imagining it a bed of pine needles and spongy moss. I rolled in it, and the dampness of the soil beneath matted my coat. The paws caressed my chest and teats, claws raising red streaks on my skin until I whimpered, dropped them, and rolled over onto all fours.

I rammed the inflatable butt plug into my cunt and pumped it with the valve closed, so it steadily expanded inside me. This simulated the "tie" when the wolf's cock balloons inside the bitch and locks them together. My lips and interior walls were still slick with a combination of condom lubricant and lingering arousal, so the imitation cock penetrated me without resistance, but it wouldn't lock in place until it distended my cunt well past the normal inch in diameter. The pressure was so strong that I could not close my legs completely.

As I reached for the hair clips that I used to imitate bites, I braced myself for the weight of the other wolf's body and rolled onto my side to snap at him.

Teeth nip my neck, my teats, my haunches, and I writhe with the pleasure of being filled. I roll and roll, to one side and the other, but I cannot shake him loose, nor do I really want to. It is simply part of the battle that is mating.

Back on all fours, I arch my back and hang my head in submission. As I raise my muzzle to his, I see a pair of grey eyes set in the unblinking stare of a mature wolf, flat and wary.

Gods! I know those eyes, even in fantasy.

The brindled wolf has me trapped and pinned; I bare my teeth and loose a howl that I cannot stop. Darrow curls around me, licking and caressing me, as I quiver, spasm and jerk into unconsciousness.

That weekend I holed up in my lair, knowing better than to go outside in my out-of-control state. Every time I woke from my fitful sleep I was possessed, physically and mentally, by Darrow in the guise of a wolf. I wore the inflatable plug all weekend, removing the tail plug only when I had to defecate. I kept a rubber sheet and paper towels in an unused corner of my bathroom for times like this, when my wolf nature consumed me. Feeling the piss trickle around my swollen cunt as I raised one leg over the absorbent material, my eyes watered and my cunt burned and even before the last drop had passed I had my legs in the air and one hand rubbing my slit raw.

I lost track of the hours I played with myself, the times I came. But I could not lose those eyes.

*   *   *

I tapped the final keystroke. "Finally. The manual for Parkland Two is done, finished, gone, out of here. Hurry up and print it, before that perfectionist comes up with another 'just one more' feature."

Word shook his head, his hands plunged into the entrails of our balky printer. "Not yet, Jo. I need ten more minutes to fix this, twenty minutes with the final diagrams, and another fifteen to produce the camera copy. At minimum."

"Forty-five minutes?" It was past midnight as it was. "Darrow might revise the whole system in forty-five minutes, Word, unless we tell him we're done with this manual and any other changes have to wait until the next version."

"Go distract him, then," sighed my exasperated partner. "Get him talking about Wilderland; he hasn't discussed it yet with me and we ought to get started on it tomorrow. You're good at getting shy people to talk."

I snorted. "The man of monosyllables? He isn't shy; he's downright closemouthed. Especially about Wilderland."

"Then take him out for Chinese food—bring me back some while you're at it. Anything. Just get me forty-five—" a loud snap issued from a newly broken gear in the printer. "Better make it at least an hour. Go!" he yelled, "before something else goes wrong."

I trotted out the door and down the hall to Darrow's office. He didn't answer my knock, so I pushed the door open slowly.

He lay curled on the floor, the VR helmet locked around his head. I rushed to him and shook his shoulder, worried that he had fainted.

He flew awake and, disoriented, clawed at me. I backed off immediately. His chest heaved for a moment, and then he unlocked the helmet and threw it off to the side as if freeing himself from a leg-trap.

His eyes were dark, dazed and wild.

My arms burned where he had touched me. I backed away farther, forcing normal breaths to calm myself.

"I'm sorry, Darrow. I thought something was wrong."

"Sometimes I sleep like that," he said, and tossed his hair back out of his eyes. It wasn't an apology, just a flat statement.

"I wanted to tell you that we're printing the manual for Parkland now." A little white lie never hurt anyone. "Word asked me to check and see if you had had dinner."

"Yes—I mean no." His smile twitched. "Not in real time."

I motioned to the helmet. "There?" He nodded. "Where were you?" I asked, curious.

His eyes flattened at my question, a sign I had seen often in the two months we'd worked together. Whatever it was, he didn't want to talk about it, and I didn't want to press him when he looked to be finally opening up a little. "Never mind, Darrow. Are you hungry? The Golden Lion up the street is open until one."

He glanced at the clock, then the window. "It's past midnight? I had no idea."

"It's easy to lose track of time in Wilderland," I said deliberately, to see if I could get a reaction. "Perhaps in the next version you should include clocks on the trees."

His instinctive response was, "Animals can't read clocks," and then he caught himself. His eyes turned to shifting, yet impenetrable, smoke. "You know that time doesn't matter in Wilderland," he challenged me in return. "Carter says you journey a lot in there."

"The sorry state of my bank account will confirm that," I replied, as I picked up the helmet and handed it to him.

He smiled ruefully as he turned it in his thick, short-fingered hands. "I put a good dent in it this time." He displayed a pyramid-shaped pockmark where it had clipped the corner of his desk in its flight. "Hope I didn't break it."

I snorted. "That's nothing compared to the gouge in the one I use at the arcade, where I crashed into a game machine cabinet. Trust me, Amaterasu helmets are indestructible."

He tilted the helmet up, checked the viewscreen, and nodded. "Good, because this is the best of the third-generation prototypes, and the engineers will have my hide if I break it before they get a working copy."

He slid open the security locker and began to place the helmet with reverence in its raggedly-cut foam cushion. Then he glanced at me. "Did you really say you've been using Wilderland from an arcade?"

"Yeah, my pusher—I mean supplier—is Dave at Dave's Sight and Sound. He has a TacBoard link to the main system, and reconditioned VR 130 helmets."

He exaggerated his wince. "Not only expensive, but clumsy like an ox to boot. Look, why don't you use the system now, while I'm not on it? If you're that familiar with Wilderland One, you can document the changes I've made already. And maybe you'll have some suggestions for Version Two. It's hard for me to be objective—I'm too close to it."

"If you're not afraid I'll break your helmet..." I kidded.

"I'll make sure to tell the engineers it was your fault," he replied, handing over the helmet. "I'll go fetch some food for Carter, and then—not that I don't trust either of you—but I want to proofread that manual. I might have some changes..."

I groaned. "Somehow I knew you were going to say that. You can do whatever you want, Darrow, but I'm going to get some sleep. I can't work all day and howl all night, like some programmers I know."

He grinned, showing his teeth. "Before he left my mother and me in Ottawa, to return to his tribe, my father taught me a basic rule of the wilderness during our outdoor trips: Nap when you can."

"At TacBoard rates, I've never been able to afford to nap."

The grin widened. "Then try it. Waking up in Wilderland is very restful, and really intensifies the experience."

As if I needed that! I decided dinner could wait as I trotted back to my office and its VR interface with the helmet clutched in my hand.

* * *

No moon yet, but starlight burns in every direction. The crickets sing in the low lands as I climb, ears pricked and aware. The grass is dry, and the storm it desires but a distant rumble beyond the high ridges.

I seek another wolf, no longer a phantom echo of my voice but a separate—therefore real—presence. The notes ring out this time on their own, scaling low to high, then dropping into a moan. I hear howls in the mountains, mournful, aching, desirous, calling me, and I go.

Up into the black sky I climb, as the moon rises past the river. I come closer to the sound, stepping along narrow ridges of sheared, weather-blunted slate, eyes watchful for a glimpse of shadowy fur or the gleam of eyes in the silver light.

My fur bristles as all my attention focuses on the guiding whine: less than a thousand strides, I judge. I creep forward.

Silence. The howl has stopped. Frustrated, I raise up and launch all my breath into one long reply, a single downward trail from high-muzzle to low-throat.

The underbrush explodes, paws crashing in a panicked flight. Once again I have noise to follow, and I begin to close on the other wolf, who will have to run through a low, narrow cut in the ridges to gain the snowline.

I make the overhang of the cut in time, but before I can gather my feet under me, a flash of fur streaks by, nose held high. Its tail, held at level, almost brushes my own nose with its fur. I spring, but miss, and sprawl on the lichenous ground as my ears hear the fade of his retreat and his smell lingers in my nose.

The system became a ghostly gray, a superimposition against the sightless black interior of my helmet, and then Darrow glared at me. I had dozed off inside the prototype he'd loaned me, so he had to be using one of the other helmets. I could see a ghostly image of a wolf surrounding his human form, braced to defend his territory.

"So it was you I've been hearing at night," he accused. "How did you get in here, anyway? You're not supposed to be here."

The sensation of lost breath, after my fall, had not yet left me, and his tone made me angry. "What do you mean, how did I get in here? I went into TUNDRA and typed TIMBER WOLF at the selection box, like I always do."

"But that's impossible!" he shouted. "I'm the only wolf in here. There aren't even many human visitors in TUNDRA. It's not 'popular' enough; they stick to the safe, familiar temperate areas."

"I didn't know it was impossible when I did it," I interjected, as the adrenalin rush of the chase lessened and my sense of humor returned. "And as far as other wolves go, why should you hog all the fun?"

He ignored me, absorbed in the wiggle of his fingers in mid-air—a pixel-mapped duplication of touch-typing hands on a keyboard only he could view.

"The point is, Joanna, you shouldn't have been able to select TIMBER WOLF in the first place, not even from my helmet. It's not on the menu list." His fingers tapped away as he glowered at me.

"Oh, that not-on-the-menu bit is easy to explain, Darrow: I can't stand them. I've seen enough systems now that I just use the selection box and type in what I want."

"You went outside the menu?" He looked horrified.

"Never even looked at it," I admitted with a cheerful grin. "Users aren't all sheep, Darrow. We don't always follow the rules you programmers set up. Besides, you know what they always say."

"What?" he snarled, intent on his typing.

I had caught him unawares, and sprung the oldest line in the computer worker's jokebook to try to make him laugh. "It's not a bug, it's an undocumented feature."

His subvocal growl made my hair bristle. His earlier friendliness to me had completely vanished. "Well, this is one feature you won't be using anymore. I've put in a password to keep you and any other hackers from trying this little trick in the future."

I couldn't imagine why he was so angry with me. "Wait! Darrow, I've been looking for this place all my life. I didn't know this was a private dream of yours. But don't you see, we share the same dream!"

His feral grin was ugly, like that of a little boy hit moments before in the mouth with a rock. "Oh, I doubt that. You're just another one of those romantics idolizing the natural state, thinking it's cute to roam through the woods. Well, it's not really very romantic being a wolf, Jo. This isn't a dream on my part: it's my real life. I've been half-frozen, and starving, and injured, and fought my way through it because that's what wolves do: survive.

"I gave up expecting you humans to understand me years ago. All I ask is that you leave this particular wolf out of your plans to shape the wilderness to your own ends, please."

He stopped for a moment, out of breath. He had just dug up for me my own gnawed bones of discomfort and discontent, the hurt of those years and years of uneasily buried feeling: I am the only one of my kind, and no one will ever understand.

If I'd been thinking, I wouldn't have said the absolute wrong thing to him then.

"And Wilderland isn't shaping the wilderness to your ends?"

Trying to show our similarities, I had flung too much indigestable truth at him. He either had to deny it, or deny the purity of his motives.

He turned tail to flee.

"Wait! You can't just shut me out like this!"

"No? Watch me." He whirled, as swiftly as the west wind of Wilderland twisted mica dust at nightfall. The grey twinkled to black, like a shake of fur rolled in the dust, and he was gone.

I logged off and swore as my copper hair caught in the helmet. The empty feeling in the pit of my stomach reminded me of my missed dinner, so I wandered down to the employee cafeteria to force down some breakfast.

But the empty feeling refused to leave politely; filling my stomach with food didn't drive it away at all.

I had lost Wilderland, or at least that part of it I knew and loved.

What had Darrow been afraid of?

When I got back to my office, I found out.

The helmet I had left was gone. For that matter, so were all the prototypes, and all the background papers and disks, and oh yes, Darrow as well.

Word, still very much present, and not so much angry as querulous, was more than ready to tell me his side of the story.

*   *   *

"Now let me get this straight, Word. You complimented him on his Grand Canyon and he got mad at you?" The morning sun made my eyes hurt.

Word sighed. "Nearly bit my head off. Said he would rather have done Canada's Nahanni. 'I'm more familiar with it, and its canyons make that overrated hole in the ground look shabby. But they wanted well-known, American parks.'

"So I tried to reason with him. 'Amaterasu has to think of what will be most popular,' I argued. 'Perhaps it's just as well you didn't do Nahanni. Maybe the average Parkland users wouldn't appreciate it the way you do.'"

Poor Word! Considering how protective Darrow was of his creations, I was surprised only that his throat was intact enough to tell the tale.

I shuddered. "Of course they wouldn't. I suspect Darrow would have a very... unique perspective on Nahanni and would hate to see it misused. You would have hit quite a nerve with that statement."

"Did I ever! Darrow gave me this spooked look, and said in a really bitter tone, 'You may be right at that, Carter. If I did Isle Royale, I bet they'd want the wolves to act like dogs and come when called.' And then he stalked out."

I felt much as if an elk had kicked me in the stomach with its powerful hindquarters. Had Darrow seen me as little better than a tamed dog? No wonder he condemned me without bothering to listen.

"I saw him later in his office, but he was in VR, so I assumed he was working and left him alone. Then I went back to his office half an hour ago and he'd cleaned out everything like he'd never been there."

Another hoof thumped soundly into my stomach, as I thought of my ill-timed attempt to show Darrow our common ground. "What about the programs?"

"Oh, they're still mounted on his system. Mr. Secretive had already put up Wilderland Two without telling us, so we can work on the documentation for some time while Amaterasu transfers it to the public system." He punched me playfully in the arm. "So don't look so worried, Jo—we're still employed."

"What about Darrow? Will Amaterasu go after him?"

Word shrugged. "Why should they? Everything they wanted him to do right now is done. Far as they're concerned, he can be as eccentric and unsociable as he wants to be and they won't bother him, because if he's unhappy he'll just take his programs back when the contract ends in a few months."

And I had delivered the very speech that made that once-remote possibility highly likely. Had I no hope of ever getting near him, or seeing Wilderland again?

I chewed that thought over during both the rest of the day at work, and the long walk back to my apartment. If I chased him, it would scare him farther off; he was not prey that would freeze in fear, after all, but a mature predator.

An elusive, skittish wild animal may be lured near humans, but Darrow was now a frightened, if not angry, wolf who trusted nothing that smelled of the human world.

On the other hand, I recalled Word once describing his pursuit of Damask—quite the mature predator herself—as "chasing her until she caught me." So I logged onto the nets and did a little research on the characteristics and habitat of the elusive Darrow Northwalker, hoping for some inspiration.

Even congenital loners leave some tracks in the electronic forest. In reading about his parents (father Red Lake Chippewa, mother English Canadian, divorced and both dead before he reached majority), his past (rootlessly misfit, almost a mirror of mine) and his present (unmarried and very much active on the Nets), I found my plan.

I uploaded "Speaking in Tongues" out of my archives and, while leaving my real name and date written on it, e-mailed it to all of Darrow's online accounts. The email's subject line contained the only words I thought might tempt him to read it rather than just hitting the delete key: Mah een gun, "timber wolf" in his father's native language.

The trap was baited with something juicy: would he bite?

Dave hurried out of the air-conditioned office as I walked into the arcade two weeks later. "Jo! Long time no see. Listen, thanks a lot for getting your friends at Amaterasu to pick my place to test those new helmets. The kids are crazy about them."

I almost said, "What new helmets?", but I was so stunned my tongue froze. What he held up to me so proudly was the third-generation VR 330, and I knew they weren't in general production yet.

I hadn't sent them, but I had a good idea who did.

"The use of my VR system has gone up ten times in the last week!" The arcade owner was ecstatic. He would gain not only increased business from the new helmets, but increased prestige—and the two elements often pursued each other into an upward spiral of success.

"So, are you so busy that there's no room for me?"

Dave sputtered. "Joanna, I owe all this to you. I got one helmet reserved solely for you, in a padded and soundproofed booth no less... so you don't crash into any more of my machines, of course."

He motioned me into a 6 x 8 plywood booth that nestled between the Network machine and his office. "You ought to put a lock on the door, so the person in VR won't be interrupted," I pointed out.

He nodded distractedly as he plugged the cables and rebreather into the jacks set into the booth wall. "I've been so busy I just haven't gotten around to it," he said, with a guilty glance at the utility closet that held his toolchest.

He handed me the helmet and gloves. "When I talked with the guy who installed everything, he said this helmet was special to you."

I didn't have to look; my finger found the distinctive pyramidal dent in the helmet he handed me. "It is," I breathed, and strapped myself in without hesitation.

It smelled like a trap, but it was a trap I had to enter. Darrow wouldn't have gone to all the trouble and expense of giving Dave the helmets without a reason. I trusted his vision—our shared vision—and my heart rose in anticipation.

The first box opened immediately.

CHOOSE DOMAIN>

and I typed in TUNDRA.X.

The next box opened in the darkness.
CHOOSE PROJECTION> TIMBER WOLF
And I ENTER Wilderland.

The rain pelts down; mingled with it are sharp cold pellets of hail that sting even through the thick winter fur I have yet to shed. It is early, very early spring on the mountainside, but the storm strikes with all the leaf-lashing fury of the rolling thunder-clouds that threaten and bluster in summer.

I fight the wind to climb the mountain and fol-low the trail. My nose sniffs each clump of dirt, desperate to hold to the scent.

I gain the ridge and find fresh spoor, barely an hour old, in the pine groves. I cover each urination with my own mark. If Darrow retraces his path, he will smell me. I will not sneak up on him and frighten him, but make my presence known as widely and vocally as possible.

I feel stronger and heavier than before, and I notice as I pee that the stain is more pungent than last fall—signs of maturity driven home by the taste of blood as I nuzzle my crotch in investigation. A sign that Wilderland is coming of age.

The rain seems endless in its vigor and intensity, but it lessens to a steady drizzle as I approach the clearing of the rabbits. The scent of Darrow is es-

pecially strong here. Various intensities of marking, and dozens of muddy prints, give me a clear image of the other wolf pacing, howling, and rolling in the grip of strong emotions.

I lift my muzzle and howl. I am prepared to do this as long as my throat holds out, but almost at once an answer comes from upwind and uphill. It rises, in a mixture of surprise and happiness, and I hear the invitation in it: "Join me!"

I bound joyfully towards the direction of the reply, and find myself on the banks of the rapids. The other wolf stands on the far bank, and we look at each other, across the chasm that separates us.

He barks in greeting, and makes for a fallen tree upstream that spans the rapids by less than his shoulderheight. He is more surefooted on the rain-drenched trunk than I would trust myself to be in this unfamiliar weight and size, and I settle on my haunches to wait for him.

A tangle of branches, mud and small rocks swells the river at a bend above the tree. Flash-flood! I bark in warning, but he cannot hear me over the crash of the rapids.

Even as the dirty water smashes the tree and engulfs him, I spring forward into the dark flood. I hear a frightened yip as he paddles to keep his head above water, then silence. I swim into the flood towards the last sound. Everything is swirling and collapsing in the green-brown froth atop the river.

A thump-splash of a wet, furry body against mine, and I sink my teeth into him to hold on while I strike out for where I think the shore is. The soil of the banks erodes under my feet as I scramble, burdened with Darrow's weight, to climb out of the raging river.

Then I feel him twitch with life and scrabble with his paws on the slick slate just underwater, finding toeholds under his own power. I unlock my jaws thankfully, and my four paws push my weary body onto safe ground.

Our skins have cuts from jagged rocks and splintered branches, but they are surface wounds. Too cold and tired even to clean ourselves, we curl together into a small hollow on the north edge of the rabbit clearing. It offers some shelter from the sleeting wind as the eye of the storm moves southward and the backlash begins.

There, we sleep, nose to tail for warmth, as the winds howl.

I awaken in the quiet night to the soft caress of a cool nose, and hot tongue, under my tail. The glands around my anus ooze an oily yellow scent that he licks eagerly.

His hind feet cuff my head as if we are cubs playing together. But we are full-grown now, and the childish gesture takes on new meaning. I slap his feet away with a lazy paw, and roll over so that I can press my muzzle to his in submission.

He whines as I butt my nose against the short fur of his snout—unsure, even with instinct full in him, whether I am his mate. He leaps out of our shelter into the moonlight, droplets of silver flying from his fur as he quivers and shakes in tension.

I follow, determined that he shall not leave me behind again. Once more I croon to his muzzle, pushing so hard that the lip bares the teeth, begging him to accept what I am—no, to accept what we are.

He moves away again, but not as swiftly as before. It is not a rejection, but rather his disbelief that our desire may run along the same trail. He is afraid to trust me.

I roll my shoulders into the matted needles of the clearing, to expose my throat and belly to him. From my upside-down view, it is as if I look at a reflection of Darrow in a still pool, outlined against the black sky and crowned with a few bright stars. The moon over his shoulder dusts his ruff with glimmers of white and silver.

He edges closer, wary and shy, expecting me at any moment to rear up and snap at him. I remain still, even when his breath is hot on my throat, his bared teeth one easy bite away from my death.

He nuzzles awkwardly along my throat and ruff, the increasingly insistent pressure a sign that I should stand.

He backs away a few steps, and mimics my former position on the ground, as he presents his vulnerable areas to me in turn. He bares himself to me, terrified and hopeful, his longing plain to eye and ear as the short pants of his breath heave his slender flanks. His eyes are round and a soft pleading whimper beckons me closer, closer, so that I smell his fear and desire together.

Nose, throat, ribs, belly, penis and anus all receive my gentle lick of the tongue, as I taste the savage flavor of my new mate.

Since I did not attack him, he grows bolder now and springs up to put his paws on my shoulders, pressing me flat against the ground. I feel his penis shove against my tail, and I twitch it aside so that he can mount more easily. His nose is wet against my ears as his hind legs press forward and he enters me. A gush of hot fluid comes immediately, along with the swelling tie that will bind us together physically for some time. (But time does not matter in Wilderland, I remember Darrow once saying.) He jets, and jets, and jets, and we whine and whimper in the joy of our union.

As I unstrap the helmet in the dimly-lit booth I feel how I am drenched with sweat, and my panties are soaked in my own overflow of musk. "But it's not real," I whisper to myself, forcing a return to reality while my whole body screamed to return to my wolf self. Never had I felt so alone; never had I longed more for my imagination to be real.

"It's as real as we are," came a voice from just behind me.

Shy wolf eyes peered into mine, glinting red in the glow from the monitors. I smelled pine, and musk, and machine oil, and semen, as a trembling paw—hand—brushed my hair away from my neck. From Darrow's other hand dropped my old helmet, its cable plugged into a second jack hidden under a lip of the padding.

Caught.

Contributors

DEB ATWOOD marks her debut into publication with "A Moment in Time," a landmark in her life which she hopes heralds many similar times to come! The past year of her life has been an eventful one, including marriage, a new house, and the start of a family. Deb masquerades during the daytime hours as a software developer in central New York State. She is still in a state of wonder that she has found a place to share the erotica she has always enjoyed creating.

GARY BOWEN has published over a hundred short stories in anthologies and magazines and is the author of *Diary of a Vampire*, which was a finalist for the Bram Stoker Award in the category of Best First Novel, and the collection *Man Hungry*. He can often be recognized at science fiction conventions on the East Coast by his white Stetson hat. He contributes regularly to Circlet Press erotic sf/f anthologies. His work can be found in *Wired Hard*, *Wired Hard 2*, *Fetish Fantastic*, *SexMagick 2*, *S/M Pasts*, *Genderflex*, *TechnoSex*, and the chapbook *Queer Destinies*.

R. BOYCZUK has published short stories in *On Spec* and *Transversions*, and in 1995 won first prize in *Prairie Fire*'s speculative fiction writing contest. He has another piece in *Northern Frights 4* and is completing work on his first novel.

LELA E. BUIS lives near Kennedy Space Center with two parakeets and a yard full of wildlife. She's recently given up engineering to teach at the local community college, and is interested in a wide variety of activities, including martial arts, theatre, and dance. She's been writing sf/f for about six years, and has had material accepted by several small press and pro magazines. Most of her recent work has appeared in *Thirteenth Moon*, *Worthy Foes*, *Cybermagic*, and *Floating Worlds*.

RENÉE M. CHARLES's work has appeared in many erotic anthologies and magazines including *Best American Erotica 1995*, *Dark Angels*, *Symphonie's Gift*, and many others. She is single, and lives with a houseful of cats in a 90+ year old Queen Anne house in the midwest.

REINA DELACROIX is the pen name of a shy, quiet librarian, living in Northern Virginia with her cats, George and Shen T'ien, and her precious Pet, Michael. She also owns a loyal wolf, Marc. She has previously contributed to the anthologies *Feline Fetishes* and *SexMagick* and will have work in several upcoming volumes.

STEVE ELLER holds a degree in computer science and worked for over a decade as a programmer and analyst before deciding to write fiction. He has stories appearing in numerous markets, including *Terminal Fright*, *Sinister*, and *Black October*. Other erotic pieces can be seen in *Wetware* and *Women Who Run with the Werewolves*.

RHOMYLLY B. FORBES lives near Washington, D.C., with two gay housemates and several small animals. Previous short stories have appeared in the anthologies *Tomboys!: Tales of Dyke Derring-Do*, *Close Calls: New Lesbian Fiction*, and *Queer View Mirror II*. She dedicates this story to Kent and Brian, who always care.

AMELIA G is a writer whose work has appeared in markets ranging from *Chic* to *White Wolf*. She has been interviewed for various print and television specials on vampires. Amelia edits *Blue Blood*, a magazine of counterculture erotica which includes lots of vampire sensuality. And to think Amelia's parents suspected she was wasting their money when she wrote her honors thesis on cross-cultural vampire legends as a paradigm for human sexuality.

SUSAN ELIZABETH GRAY is a matrimonial attorney from western New York who has a secret life as a writer. She has published her short stories in *Artvoice*, *Libido*, *Black Sheets*, and *Shoofly* magazines.

LINDA HOOPER grew up in central California and moved to Santa Cruz to meet lesbians as soon as she could. She writes stories and essays and produces gay and lesbian cultural events. Her story "PG Diary" appears in the *1994 Best American Erotica* volume, edited by Susie Bright. She has previously contributed to the anthologies *SexMagick* and *Worlds of Women*.

RAVEN KALDERA lives, loves, and writes in Massachusetts and is a vital part of the pagan, transgendered, and leather communities there. Raven's work has been featured in the anthologies *The New Worlds of Women*, *S/M Futures*, *S/M Pasts*, *SexMagick 2*, *Bitch Goddesses*, *Butch Tops*, *Make Mama Happy*, *Leather Spirit*, and in *Best Lesbian Erotica: 1997*.

ROBERT KNIPPENBERG began writing porn, smut, erotica (you choose) because it turned him on. He continues to write it almost exclusively because:
• There isn't enough good porn, smut, erotica around
• Much of what is around is depressing and/or demeaning to women and/or to men
• Our society needs new, happier mythologies to replace our insane ones about men, women, and sex
• It still turns him on

WARREN LAPINE traded in the wild life of a rock musician for the even wilder life of a science fiction writer. He has made more than thirty sales to magazines such as *Fantastic Collectibles*, *Visions*, *Pirate Warnings*, *Gaslight*, and the audiozine *Tales from the Grave*.

JIM LEE has published a wide variety of work in a bewildering assortment of markets since 1982 when an erotic sf poem was chosen for Millea Kenin's *Aliens and Lovers* anthology. Recent publications include fiction in *Aberrations*, *Hardboiled*, *Fantastic Collectibles*, *Hustler Fantasies*, *Selling Venus*, and *S/M Pasts*.

CATHERINE LUNDOFF is a femme top who lives in Minneapolis with her girlfriend. Her fiction has been included in the forthcoming anthologies *Pillowtalk*, *1001 Kisses*, *Lesbian Short Fiction*, and *Powderhorn Writers Anthology*. "El Tigre" won an award in the 1996 Writers Bloc Fiction Contest, where it was described as "disturbing."

DAVID MAY was a nice boy from a good family who fell in with the wrong crowd. He attended the University of California at Santa Cruz where he studied Dramatic Literature, specializing in medieval religious theatre. He is the author of S/M-oriented *Madrugada: A Cycle of Erotic Fictions*. His work, both fiction and nonfiction, has appeared in *Drummer*, *Mach*, *Honcho*, *Lambda Book Report*, *Frontiers*, *Inches*, *Advocate Men*, and *Cat Fancy*. His fiction also appears in the anthologies *Queer View Mirror*, *Rogues of San Francisco*, *Meltdown!*, and *Flesh and the Word 3*. He currently lives in San Francisco with his husband, a dog, and three cats.

JAY MICHAELSON, a world-weary traveler by the improbable age of 16, now lives outside of Washington, D.C. While working Ken Kesey's old job (minus the internal chemistry) he reads, writes, fences, and abuses his cat, all the while coming to the conclusion that he is maybe one of eight people in the entire solar system who still listen to bands like Van der Graaf Generator.

A. R. MORLAN has had erotica published in *Love In Vein: Stories of Erotic Vampirism* and *Deadly After Dark: The Hot Blood Series*. Both stories were reprinted in *The Year's Best Fantasy 1994*. In addition to erotica, she's had short stories published in *The Magazine of Fantasy & Science Fiction*, *Full*

Spectrum IV, and many other magazines and anthologies. She's the author of two novels, *The Amulet* and *Dark Journey*, and currently teaches short fiction for a correspondence school.

WHITT POND was born in Lubbock, Texas, shortly after a famous UFO sighting, which explains a lot. He currently lives in Somerville, Massachusetts, two blocks from a really good Chinese restaurant. Pond has had stories published in the anthology *Ladies of Winter*, and in magazines like *Tales of the Unanticipated* and *Terminal Fright*. He also has a story in *Wired Hard 2*.

CYPRESS QUINN was born in southern Indiana in 1973. She attended Ball State University and currently lives in Indianapolis. Her work has appeared in student publications and her own self-published fanzine about local musicians and writers. "A Most Nonsensical Night" is her first professional work. Cypress is currently writing her first novel.

THOMAS S. ROCHE is a San Francisco writer, editor, and performer. His short stories have appeared in such anthologies as *Best American Erotica 1996* and *Best American Erotica 1997* and *The Mammoth Book of Pulp Fiction*. Books he edited, co-edited, or wrote include *Dark Matter*, *Noirotica*, *Sons of Darkness*, *Brothers of the Night*, and *Gargoyles*.

PAT SALAH is a Montreal writer whose work has appeared in *Hence*, *The Moosehead Anthology*, and *The Lesbian and Gay Studies Newsletter*. He is currently studying Queer theory at Columbia University and working on a manuscript of linked stories and poems entitled *Snow White's Children*.

ROBERT M. SCHROECK lives with his wife Peggy in central New Jersey. He studied creative writing at Princeton University, but has made his living since 1984 as a computer programmer. Since 1989, he has written or contributed to seven role-playing gamebooks for Steve Jackson Games, including GURPS

Werewolf: The Apocalypse, either by himself or in collaboration with Peggy. In what little spare time he has, he's a member of the Society for Creative Anachronism, where he is an archer and part-time pyromaniac. At one time he also made paper by hand, a craft he hopes to take up again soon.

ALAN SMALE is rarely seen by day, because he earns his living as a professional astronomer. His other after-dark activities include singing bass in an up-and-coming a cappella group and prancing around on various community theater stages. Alan has made numerous short fiction sales over the past few years, including an appearance in *S/M Pasts*. And he hates talking to strangers on the phone.

DAVE SMEDS is the author of the novels *The Sorcery Within* and *The Schemes of Dragons* as well as many short stories that have appeared in *Asimov's*, *The Magazine of Fantasy and Science Fiction*, *Full Spectrum*, and in the anthology *TechnoSex: Cyber Age Erotica*. He has sold over three dozen works of erotic fiction to *Club International*, *Hot Talk*, *Penthouse Forum*, *Club Mayfair*, and *Lui*.

CECILIA TAN founded Circlet Press in 1992 and has since edited over two dozen anthologies of erotic fantasy and science fiction. She also teaches workshops on erotic writing, S/M relationships, and turning erotic fantasy into reality. She is the author of the collection of erotic short stories *Black Feathers: Erotic Dreams*, the erotic novel *The Velderet*, and many essays on sex and fantasy.

KYMBERLYN TOLIVER-REED is a cigar-smoking member of the thirty-something crowd who knows that "Generation X" is the name of Billy Idol's old punk band. She dedicated "The Razor's Edge" to everyone in high school who named her "most likely to be a nun."